JOHN O'B⌐⌐⌐

TIPPING POINT:
PENGHU

BOOK IV OF TIPPING POINT

Other books by John O'Brien

A New World Series

A New World: Chaos

A New World: Return

A New World: Sanctuary

A New World: Taken

A New World: Awakening

A New World: Dissension

A New World: Takedown

A New World: Conspiracy

A New World: Reckoning

A New World: Storm

Companion Books

A New World: Untold Stories

A New World: Untold Stories II

The Third Wave: Eidolon

Ares Virus

Ares Virus: Arctic Storm

Ares Virus: White Horse

Ares Virus: Phoenix Rising

Red Team

Red Team: Strigoi

Red Team: Lycan

Red Team: Cartel Part One

Red Team: Cartel Part Two

A Shrouded World

A Shrouded World: Whistlers

A Shrouded World: Atlantis

A Shrouded World: Convergence

A Shrouded World: Valhalla

A Shrouded World: Asabron

A Shrouded World: Bitfrost

A Shrouded World: Hvergelmir

A Shrouded World: Asgard

Lifting the Veil

Lifting the Veil: Fallen

Lifting the Veil: Winter

Lifting the Veil: Emergence

Lifting the Veil: Risen

Tipping Point

Tipping Point: Opening Shots

Tipping Point: Escalation

Tipping Point: OPLAN 5015

Tipping Point: Penghu

Author's Note

Four books into my supposed trilogy and there's still more story to be written. So, I'm valiantly hammering away at the fifth. I'm hoping that will be enough to wrap up events, but I've said something similar a hundred times in the past.

I'd like to address something that's come up a few times. I've received more than a few messages expressing that China would do much better than I've portrayed in this series. I admit I may have some bias regarding the capabilities of both nations, but I have tried to also keep it as realistic as I'm able to portray.

China has the same type of centralized leadership and control system as Russia, and world events have shown some of those limitations. Lower echelon unit leaders aren't trained to make tactical decisions, which makes the decision-making at the tactical levels relatively inflexible. Battles are fluid and require flexibility at all levels. There are drastic training differences between the two countries. For instance, the average hours flown annually in the United States military is approximately 200 hours, as compared to a hundred hours for Chinese military pilots.

China has made significant advancements in their technological systems, creating a slight advantage over the aging systems still in place for the United States. The key elements for modern combat are strategy, decision-making flexibility, battlefield intelligence systems, and systems integration that creates battlefield synergies between air, ground, and naval forces.

But, enough along those lines. I'm not attempting to place any one nation over another, but just trying to tell an alternate story of the tensions in the South China Sea. My desire isn't to express any personal politics into the equation. I'm just a storyteller putting down the tales that take home inside my head. I hope you enjoy this continuation of the series, and would love to hear what you think about it.

Many thanks to all of those who helped make this book into something readable. My mother, June O'Brien first and foremost. Thank you for taking my tendency to be linear and telling me when I need some human interactions within the story. Your notes are priceless. To my editors who labored over my graceless attempts at grammar and for finding the words which often elude me.

And last, but certainly not least, to you. Without readers and listeners, a storyteller cannot exist. I am constantly overwhelmed by your support and where this has taken me. So, I thank you from the bottom of my heart!

Let's get on with the story, shall we?

John

Cast of Characters

US Personnel

Presidential Cabinet

Jake Chamberlain, *Secretary of the Navy*

Tom Collier, *CIA Director*

Elizabeth Hague, *Ambassador to the United Nations*

Imraham Patel, *CDC Director*

Aaron MacCulloch, *Secretary of Defense*

Bill Reiser, *NSA Director*

Joan Richardson, *Homeland Security Director*

Fred Stevenson, *Secretary of State*

Frank Winslow, *President of the United States*

Joint Chiefs of Staff

Phil Dawson, *General, USAF—Joint Chiefs of Staff Chairman*

Kevin Loughlin, *General, US Army—Joint Chiefs of Staff Vice Chairman*

Tony Anderson, *General, US Army—Army Chief of Staff*

Duke Calloway, *General, US Marines—Commandant of the Marines*

Brian Durant, *Admiral, USN—Chief of Naval Operations*

Mike Williams, *General, USAF—Air Force Chief of Staff*

US Naval Personnel

Jerry Ackland, *Commander, USN—Captain of the USS Texas*

David Avelar, *Commander, USN—Captain of the USS* Topeka

Peter Baird, *Commander, USN—Captain of the USS* Cheyenne

Charlie Blackwell, *Vice Admiral, USN—Third Fleet Commander*

Kyle Blaine, *Lieutenant, USN—F-35C Pilot*

Shawn Brickline, *Admiral, USN—Pacific Theatre Commander (USPACCOM)*

Jeff Brown, *Commander, USN—Captain of the USS* Connecticut

Alex Buchanan, *Captain, USN—Indo-Pacific Watch Commander*

Ralph Burrows, *Captain, USN—Captain of the USS* Abraham Lincoln

Chip Calhoun, *Rear Admiral, USN—Carrier Strike Group 5/Task force 70 Commander*

Alan Cook, *Commander, USN—Captain of the USS* Springfield

Bryce Crawford, *Admiral, USN—Commander of the Pacific Fleet (COMPACFLT)*

Jeff Dunmar, *Commander, USN—Captain of the USS* Seawolf

Sam Enquist, *Lieutenant (j.g.), USN—F/A-18F Electronic Warfare Officer (EWO)*

Ed Fablis, *Rear Admiral, USN—Carrier Strike Group 9 Commander*

Scott Gambino, *Commander, USN—Captain of the USS* Ohio

John Garner, *Captain, USN—Captain of the USS Theodore Roosevelt*

Steve Gettins, *Rear Admiral, USN—Carrier Strike Group 1 Commander*

Matt Goldman, *Lieutenant, USN—F/A-18F Pilot*

Myles Ingram, *Commander, USN—Captain of the USS Howard*

Tom Jenson, *Lt. Commander, USN—Executive Officer of the USS Howard*

Zach Keene, *Lieutenant (j.g.), USN—F/A18-F Electronic Warfare Officer (EWO)*

Tyson Kelley, *Captain, USN—Captain of the USS Ronald Reagan*

Carlos Lopez, *Lieutenant, USN—P-8 Pilot*

Ryan Malone, *Lt. Commander, USN—Executive Officer of the USS Springfield*

Brent Martin, *Commander, USN—P-8 Combat Information Officer*

Ben Meyer, *Commander, USN—Captain of the USS Illinois*

James Munford, *Lt. Commander, USN—Executive Officer of the USS Texas*

Michael Prescott, *Rear Admiral, USN—Carrier Strike Group 11 Commander*

Carl Sandburg, *Rear Admiral, USN—Carrier Strike Group 3 Commander*

Kurt Schwarz, *Captain, USN—Captain of the USS Nimitz*

Nathan Simmons, *Commander, USN—Captain of the USS Preble*

Patrick Sims, *Commander, USN—Captain of the USS* Columbus

Mike Stone, *Commander, USN—VFA-137 Squadron Commander*

Chris Thompson, *Lieutenant, USN—F/A-18F Pilot*

Warren Tillson, *Vice Admiral, USN—Seventh Fleet Commander*

Chris Walkins, *Captain, USN—Captain of the USS* Carl Vinson

Tony Wallins, *Lt. Commander, USN—Executive Officer of the USS* Preble

Charles Wilcutt, *Lt. Commander, USN—Executive Officer of the USS* Cheyenne

Joe Wright, *Commander, USN—Captain of the USS* Mississippi

US Air Force Personnel

Wayne Blythe, *Major, USAF—B-52 Pilot*

James Blackwood, *Captain, USAF—B-2 Pilot*

Jeff Hoffman, *Captain, USAF—C-130 Pilot*

Mark Foley, *Captain, USAF—F-15E WSO*

William Gerber, *Lt. Colonel, USAF—F-15C Pilot*

Dave Lowry, *Captain, USAF—F-16 Pilot*

David Miller, *Captain, USAF—F-15E Pilot*

Jerry Munford, *Captain, USAF—F-22 Pilot*

Vince Rawlings, *General, USAF—Air Force Pacific Commander (COMPACAF)*

Chris Tweedale, *Major, USAF—B-1B Pilot*

Steve Victors, *Captain, USAF—F-22 Pilot*

Tom Watkins, *Colonel, USAF—Schriever AFB Watch Commander*

Amy Weber, *Colonel, USAF—NORAD Watch Commander*

US Army Personnel

Sara Hayward, *Colonel, US Army—USAMRIID Commander*

Charles Warner, *General, US Army—Special Operations Command (SOCOM) Commander*

CIA Personnel

Tony Caputo—*CIA Operator*

Andreas Cruz—*CIA Operator*

Felipe Mendoza—*CIA Operator*

John Parks—*CIA Operator*

NSA Personnel

Allison Townsend—*NSA Analyst*

* * * * * *

Philippine Personnel

President Renaldo Aquino—*Philippine President (as of 17 May, 2021)*

General Ernesto Gonzalez—*Philippine Rebel General*

President Andres Ramos—*Philippine President*

* * * * * *

Chinese Personnel

Wei Chang, *Minister of State Security*

Sun Chen, *Admiral, PLAN—Captain of the aircraft carrier,* Shandong

Hao Chenxu, *President of People's Republic of China (PRC), Paramount Leader of China*

Tan Chun, *Commander, PLAN—Captain of the* ChangZhen 17

Lei Han, *Minister of Finance*

Hou Jianzhi, *Sergeant, PLA—Special Forces sergeant*

Cao Jinglong, *Captain, PLAN—Captain of* ChangZhen 16

Jian Kang, Sergeant, *PLA—Special Forces sergeant*

Li Na, Colonel, *PLA—Penghu invasion force commander*

Tien Pengfei, Captain, PLA—WZ-10 Pilot

General Quan, *General, PLAN—Fiery Cross Commander (as of 30 May, 2021)*

General Tao, *Fiery Cross Commander (prior to 30 May, 2021)*

Hu Tengyang, *Captain, PLAN—Captain of* ChangZhen 14

Huang Tengyi, *Captain, PLAN—Captain of* Kilo 12

Liu Xiang, *Minister of Foreign Affairs*

Zhou Yang, *Minister of National Defense*

Xie Yingjun, *Captain, PLAN—Captain of* ChangZhen 15

Zheng Yunru, *Major, PLAN—H6M Pilot*

Hu Yuran, *Captain, PLAN—Captain of* Kilo 6

Lin Zhang, *Admiral, PLAN—Southern Fleet Commander*

Xhao Zhen, *Captain, PLA— WZ-10 Pilot*

*   *   *   *   *   *

Taiwanese Personnel

Cheng-han, *Captain, ROCAF—F-35 Pilot*

Chia-ming, *Commander, ROCN—Captain of the ROCS Hai Lu*

Chia-wei, *Captain, ROCAF—F-CK-1 Pilot*

Chih-hao, *Sergeant, ROCA—Penghu Defense Command*

Chin-lung, *Major, ROCAF—F-16 Pilot*

Chun-cheih, *Vice Admiral, ROCN—Flotilla Commander*

Hsin-hung, Chief of General Staff

Kuan-yu, *Captain, ROCAF—F-35 Pilot*

Kuan-lin, *Sergeant, ROCA—Penghu Defense Command*

Pai-han, *Commander, ROCN—Captain of the ROCS Hai Lung*

Shu-ching, *President of Taiwan*

Tsung-han, *ROCAF Commander*

Wei-ting, *ROCA Commander*

Wen-hsiung, *Penghu Defense Commander*

Yan-ting, *Minister of Defense*

Yu-hsuan, *ROCN Commander*

MAPS

Penghu Islands

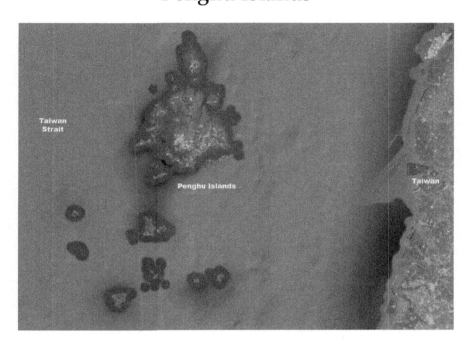

Penghu Main Islands

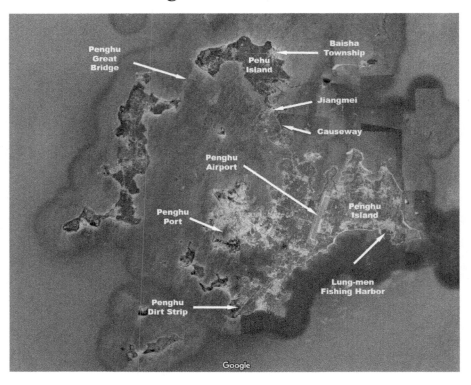

Pehu Island

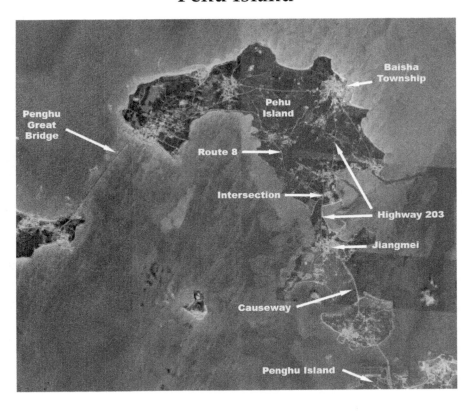

What Went On Before

China pushed to become the global economic power, engaging in a trade war with the United States. At the same time, they sought to expand their empire into the South China Sea by creating manmade islands and building military bases. The territorial waters China claimed was challenged in the World Court and ruled that they had no basis for making the claims. China ignored the ruling and continued to claim the waters surrounding the Spratly Islands. It was a claim that was continually challenged by warships of the United States, who conducted FONOPs (Freedom of Navigation Operations).

Along with their attempts to push into a world economy, China sought to establish the Yuan as world currency. Nations balked at using the Yuan as a trading currency, thus keeping China relegated as the world's second largest economy. Although many of the nations in Southeast Asia were swinging in China's direction, the Chinese government sought a quicker remedy to their sluggish economic gains. The devised a virus which would run rampant throughout the world and disrupt the various economies. China's goal was to emerge from the crisis as the number one economy. Markets fell as the highly contagious virus spread throughout the world. However, other events soon overtook China's attempts.

One general was fed up with the constant intrusion of the United States into what China viewed as territorial waters. One warship was targeted, but in a procedural lapse, the defensive systems were left in automatic mode and missiles launched. The USS *Preble* and the USS *Pinckney* fought valiantly but just didn't have enough time to fend off the sudden swarm of missiles. Hit several times, the USS *Preble* sank rapidly. Only twelve survived.

China rescued the twelve survivors and kept them hostage, claiming them as prisoners. The United States sortied their submarine fleet in case matters turned south. Fed up with China's refusal to release the twelve sailors, United States SEALs conducted a rescue. This rescue was coordinated with a follow-on attack which levelled the island of Fiery Cross, the Chinese military installation from which the USS *Preble* was fired upon. In response, China devised a response along many fronts and sortied their own submarine fleet.

*   *   *   *   *   *

As part of their response to the American attack on the Chinese base on Fiery Cross Island, China fire submarine-launched cruise missiles at Anderson Air Force Base situated on Guam. Undersea battles ensued between LA-class fast-attack subs and the Chinse vessels who fired the cruise missiles and their accompanying escorts. Backed into corners and not wanting to show signs of weaknesses, both nations reinforced their presences in the South China Sea.

After much deliberation, the United States launched attacks against the remaining Chinese military installations located in the contested Spratley Island Chain. The destruction of those two bases prompted China to strike out against the two American aircraft carriers operating in the South China Sea, resulting in the sinking of one carrier and a cruiser. This ignited a regional war between the two superpowers, expanding into the East China and Philippine Seas. Most of the preliminary battles were conducted undersea between fast-attack submarines.

In the ensuing battles, the United States sank one of China's aircraft carriers while damaging a second. China damaged a second American carrier as it was departing San Diego, thus limiting the firepower that the United States could bring to the Far East.

Nudged by China, North Korea mobilized its forces and began a march toward the demilitarized zone separating North and South Korea. There were also signs that China was gathering an invasion fleet pointed toward Taiwan. Although the United States destroyed much of China's submarine fleet, they now found themselves facing attacks on many fronts. They urgently needed to eliminate a second surge of Chinese submarines so they could bring their carriers within striking distance.

* * * * * *

The undersea war continued unabated as China prepares for its invasion of Taiwan. The threat from North Korea built as men and equipment were sent south to staging areas near the DMZ. Meanwhile, the United States was slowly building its forces with Guam, Japan, and Okinawa receiving a massive influx of reinforcing aircraft.

As tensions built in the region, Taiwan sortied its naval fleet in anticipation of China sending invasion fleets. An encounter with a Chinese nuclear fast attack submarine and Taiwan anti-submarine assets led to a rapid escalation of events. In a night filled with hostilities, fighters from both sides took to the skies. Before long, the strait separating the two nations became a warzone as cruise missiles crossed the narrow waterway.

Dawn arrived with Taiwan's navy no more than pieces of twisted metal lying at the bottom of the East China Sea, and their air force decimated. However, the island's forces were able to damage China's ability to wage war. Cruise missiles flying out from Taiwan destroyed a number of China's mobile launch platforms. In a mad dash north, under constant fire from China's land-based anti-ship batteries, Taiwan's navy managed to send volleys of missiles into the ships China was planning on using for their invasion. When morning arrived, funeral pyres dotted the countryside of both countries.

The next evening, China ramped up their invasion plans by initiating cruise missile attacks against Taiwan's defenses and communications. The island was pummeled by hundreds of low-flying missiles. Having been forced back to the defensive, Taiwan waited for the invasion ships from China to arrive.

With North Korea ignoring warnings, the United States initiated one of their contingency plans against the secretive state. OPLAN 5015 called for a preemptive strike against the north if war seemed imminent. The resulting attacks focused on North Korea's command and control structure, their artillery and anti-aircraft platforms, along with their ability to use weapons of mass destruction.

Prologue

The USS *Nimitz* shook, and almost seemed to come to a full stop from its thirty-knot dash, as the last Chinese missile crashed into the forward flight deck. The kinetic energy caused a powerful tremor to run through the entire ship as the thousand-pound warhead tore through the flight deck, crashed through the bow, and detonated right in front of the carrier.

Smoke roiled up from the strike and explosion, the blast rolling aft as the ship continued to plow forward. Pieces of razor-edged shrapnel shot out, slicing through several deckhands. With the high-pitched screech of tortured metal, a section of the front flight deck tore free, taking some of the bow with it. It hung onto the main ship for nearly thirty seconds before it ripped free and was dropped into the ocean.

Steam from ruptured lines hissed into the air along with the smoke from multiple fires that started below deck. Several F-18 attack fighters were swept clear from the impact with two more rolling off their strip and into the Pacific when the forward section of the flight deck and part of the bow fell away. Although it wasn't what was expected by either side, China had proven that their vaunted "ship killers" could indeed be devastating.

Chapter One

With a scream of distressed metal, the forward section of the flight deck and part of the bow fell away. The anchor chain on the right side had been severed by the impact, the heat of the high-speed warhead melting clean through it. That anchor dropped listlessly away, dragging along several heavy links of chain and sinking below the waves where it would slowly rust away over the next millennia.

The sheared-off bow swung away into the ocean, hitting with a monstrous splash. The anchor chain on the left side was still intact, and it tugged at the anchor on that side, pulling against the bow end of the carrier as it swept aft of the *Nimitz*. As it was drawn out, the continuous rattle of anchor chain grated against the wreckage. The increase in drag swung the carrier into an unintended left turn.

A few of the sailors in the forward section managed to find their way to an exit amid the tangled mess. Bodies leapt from twisted girders and warped decks. Most of those who jumped managed to hit the waves, but there were some who misjudged and hit twisted wreckage on their way down, bouncing once or twice before slamming into the ocean, leaving behind smears of red.

The survival situation was just beginning for those who managed to make it clear. Attached by the anchor and its trailing chain, the bow section was inexorably being pulled by the *Nimitz*. The bow and carrier were in constant danger of colliding together, and it was in this gap that many sailors found themselves. A few were killed when the fallen bow surged over frantic swimmers. Rescue crews among the airborne helicopters were busy darting close to the carrier in their efforts to pluck sailors from the moderate swells.

Inside the fallen section, others were striving to work themselves free. They searched darkened corridors for routes, often finding the way blocked by warped bulkheads or watertight doors that were wedged closed. As the survivors worked away from the front, they started running into wounded or trapped crew members. They stopped when they could to lend assistance, but most of the time, there was nothing they could do except offer a few words of comfort; a promise to visit a sister or friend.

Oftentimes, survivors negotiating the wreckage heard cries for help or whimpers in the darkness, but found themselves unable to get to those calling out. The floating wreckage was creaking and groaning as it was pulled along by the rest of the ship, slowly moving aft of the damaged carrier. Eventually, those staying behind to offer comfort to those trapped or too injured to move found themselves weighed down by tough decisions. If they were to have a chance at survival, they would have to move on to search for a way out. With a tear and parting words meant to comfort, the survivors moved aft, leaving behind their fellow sailors.

*   *   *   *   *   *

Aboard the bow section:

Standing her watch toward the bow, Seaman Sara Lyons felt anxiety clench her stomach into knots. She hadn't been in the Navy long and found herself in a warzone on her first tour. When she joined, the United States was in the midst of pulling out of Afghanistan, so she'd thought her timing was good. But, bigger than shit, here she was on the fringes of a war with China.

She was pretty sure that the fleet was under attack, and here she was, sitting on what had to be the largest target in the world. Standing in the middle of a room, surrounded by gray-painted steel bulkheads and under attack, wasn't the most comfortable of situations. Personally, she'd rather be topside in the open air where she could see what was going on. She felt that it would give her a better chance at survival, but that wasn't the lot she had drawn. Instead, she was stationed underneath the forward flight deck with the rest of her emergency crew.

Conversation among her fellow sailors sounded forced.

The jokes and banter were not terribly funny, but they elicited subdued laughter nonetheless. The fire gear she had donned felt bulky, and she wondered how in the hell she was expected to navigate the narrow passageways.

Readjusting her helmet, Sara was suddenly off the ground. It wasn't so much that she was lifted off her feet, but rather the floor just fell away. A godawful reverberating clang accompanied the abrupt drop of the deck. The room, the walls, everything around her, including the very air she was breathing, seemed to vibrate as if it were a giant tuning fork.

The entire deck rose to meet her again, forcing the wind out of her as her legs were rammed up into her gut. Screams filled the room as others were caught in the wild gyration. It was as if they were riding a fast-moving elevator that was rocketing toward the top. A monstrous roar coming from the front of the ship pounded on the bulkheads and seemed to compress the air, forcing what little Sara still had in her lungs out through her mouth and nose. Disoriented, she felt hot streamers of snot running down over her lips, and she briefly wondered if she had a bloody nose.

Slamming hard onto the deck, Sara heard a horrendous screeching of metal on metal. Accompanying the unbearable noise, were the gunshot sounds of welds breaking and sheered rivets popping. Sara had a momentary internal video of two speeding train engines colliding.

Oh fuck, we've been hit, she thought, partially regaining her senses.

The thought sent panic shooting through her mind and body. A small, measured urge told her she should be doing something. After all, she was on one of the emergency firefighting crews.

The room tilted again, this time to the side. Those in the room were slammed into one of the bulkheads, along with pieces of unsecured equipment. Sara had just started to gather her thoughts when she hit a thick support beam and was thrown off balance. Stars danced in her vision when her helmeted head bashed into a solid steel bulkhead.

A jumble of screeches penetrated her consciousness as heavy equipment shifted in the room, sliding to impact the same wall. The brackets holding a set of lockers broke with a loud pop, and the entire set careened down to slam into some of the sailors stationed with her. One other sound penetrated her mind above the cacophony; Sara gagged and nearly threw up when she realized that the snap and crunch she'd heard were bones and bodies being crushed.

The lights flickered once, twice, and then went out. Emergency lighting, operating on their own battery backups, cast dim illumination throughout the room. What had been identifiable objects became a disturbing jumble of shapes and shadow.

Spitting dust out of her dry mouth, Sara took a moment to mentally go over her body, probing to see if she felt any painful areas. Once she was certain she'd not suffered any serious injury, she rolled over and pushed to her hands and knees. The helmet fell from her head and landed in front of her. In the dim lighting, she saw a giant crack running across it. Darker splotches were gathered on top with drip patterns branching off.

In a moment of panic, she pawed at her head, waiting for the sensation of pain to shoot through her body. But nothing of the sort occurred. Frightened beyond compare, Sara shakily rose to her knees. Kneeling on the bulkhead, which was now functioning as a deck, she once again felt down the rest of her body. Satisfied she was intact and focusing on the gloomy area around her, she could hear others moving.

Retrieving her helmet, Sara removed the attached flashlight and turned it on. The orderly room in which she had been standing was now a complete mess. Panning the light near her, the beam ran across the pale and bloodied face of Warner, a sailor that had just been with her. His smashed head was pinned beneath heavy lockers. Streamers of red fanned out from his head and mouth, shooting across the gray paint. She now knew what had caused the splotches on her broken helmet. Sara remembered the man's corny jokes and levity he had always attempted to bring to an otherwise tense situation.

"Who's that with the light?" a voice choked in the shadows.

Swallowing the rising bile, Sara moved the light from the dead sailor's face.

"It's Sara…Sara Lyons," she called out, and then realized where she was.

"I mean, Seaman Lyons."

"Okay, who else is here?" the man called.

Several other voices answered.

"There's a dead man over here. It's…it's Warner," Sara stated, her voice quivering.

"Taylor's over here," another called. "He's not moving or breathing."

Metallic groans and vibrations continued to ring through their area of the ship.

Sara heard movement and flashed the light in that direction. A figure was scrambling over debris and then knelt beside another. Voices murmured for a moment. Sara saw the kneeling sailor shake his head before rising.

Outside her beam of light, Sara saw several other forms moving, all of them slowly working in her direction. Aside from the dim lights on battery power, hers was the only source of light, and was therefore a natural congregation point.

"Okay, listen up. We need to find a way out of here. Our best bet is to work our way topside on the island side," a man said.

"What about damage control?" Sara asked.

"This ship is on its side. That's why the bulkhead is now the deck. I think our portion of damage control is over and we need to get out. If we find ourselves needed once we get away, then so be it. But for now, we move as a team to escape the wreck."

A weak, watery feeling flooded through Sara when the man mentioned that the ship was on its side. And a fucking aircraft carrier at that. A ship on its side meant sinking. Sara experienced another moment of panic at the thought of seawater rushing through the passageways and flooding compartments. Would they be able to escape through the watertight doors? Were they already under water, stuck inside an air bubble that would eventually become compromised?

Looking around, Sara saw that the glows of emergency lighting were coming from the side. Everything was flipped ninety degrees. That was going to make it more difficult to escape. All the doors on a particular deck were now at her feet and head.

As if reading her mind, one of the team spoke out, "How in the hell is that going to work? The doors are above and below us. And the stairs, well, that's just going to get confusing."

"Well, we can't stay here. We'll just have to stay oriented. Now, unless anyone has a better idea, we need to get moving."

Sailors crawled over debris piles, moving lighter pieces out of the way. With Sara holding the light, they slowly moved over to the exit hatch, which was at their feet. A few other beams of light stabbed into the dimness as others found their flashlights.

"One light at a time, unless it's absolutely needed," the sailor who had taken charge called out. "We need to conserve."

At the doorway, the passageway was wider than it was tall. On the other side was another open hatch. To step through would be to fall through both doors and wind up on the far bulkhead in the other room. Sara turned onto her stomach and eased her legs through the exit, slowly lowering herself. The ship lurched and nearly bounced her through the door. As it was, her waist slammed into the edge of the hatch. She panted as a horrible screeching rang throughout, followed by a deep grinding that she couldn't locate. The sound persisted and Sara was afraid that it was bulkheads collapsing from the pressure of the deep.

She paused, expecting to hear rushing water, but there was only that persistent grinding. It sounded like a semi was being pulled through a tunnel that was too narrow.

"We have to move it," the man stated, urging Sara on.

Gripping the side of the hatch, Sara eased herself down,

swinging her legs. Timing it as best as she could, she let go so that she landed on the bulkhead beside the opposite doorway. She then moved aft to make way for the next person to come through.

Shining her light down the passageway was like looking at a warped version of what should be there, almost like looking through a carnival mirror. The passageway was wider than it was tall, forcing her to stay in a crouch. The deck, actually a bulkhead, was littered with debris. Hatches formed at intervals above and below with curtains swaying down from the overhead openings. It was disorienting, but Sara forced herself to focus. Finally recognizing where she was, and picturing the route to reach topside. That would require ascending ladders, which were now also at her feet and head.

Another sailor coming through the exit landed next to her. Sara moved farther down the corridor to make room, stopping at a hatch to wait for the others. Before long, boots rang on the bulkhead as the team left the room. Turning back aft, Sara pondered how to move across the doorway. It was narrow enough that she could have stepped across, had there been enough height to stand. But having to remain crouched made it infinitely more difficult.

Grabbing pipes running along where the ceiling had become a wall, Sara pulled herself across the opening. It was slow-going, maneuvering through the crew quarters with open hatches every few feet. At one point, a locker had come through an opening and wedged itself in the hall. She and the others couldn't move the impediment. It was a tight squeeze, but they managed to bypass the locker and continue. All the while, that horrible grinding sound accompanied them as they inched their way toward freedom.

After a tiring crawl through a section of crew quarters, the team of six gathered in a small foyer. Steps led to what used to be a higher deck, but now was just a lateral move. Behind was a sealed hatch. Shining a light through a small inset window showed the passage on the other side clear of water.

"Up or through?" one of the crew inquired.

"We can go up, but if the route is clear aft, then that's a quicker way to the flight deck," the leader stated.

Two sailors spun the wheel. The heavy hatch door, aided by gravity, swung quickly open, slamming into the bulkhead with a clang. The sound echoed eerily down both dimly lit passageways. Tension again gripped Sara's gut as if any sound they made could somehow make their situation worse. Hoisting themselves through the opening, the team moved into the next passage.

They hadn't moved far when they ran into a warped section of the ship that was piled with debris. Shining the light into the mess revealed that the route was impossible to navigate. The leader, whom Sara only occasionally glimpsed in the poor lighting, and whose name she had forgotten, turned them back. They soon found themselves climbing back through the hatch and then navigating the stairs to the next deck level.

Crawling through the wreckage of the ship, they came to another closed hatch. Shining the flashlight through the glass, Sara saw nothing but gray-painted metal on the other side. The steel was warped in places with deep scratches gleaming bright in the beam of her light. They could spin the wheel, but they couldn't push the hatch open more than a crack. However, Sara felt a draft against her cheek through the tiny opening.

Thinking they were near to escaping, Sara commented, "Do you guys feel that? There's a breeze coming through."

The leader removed a glove and held a hand to the crack.

"That doesn't make any sense. We're nowhere near the top. Unless someone screwed up and left some of the hatches open, we shouldn't be feeling that."

"But it's there," Sara iterated. "And the ship is on its side."

The leader shrugged. "Well, regardless, we can't go that way. We have to backtrack again."

Sara's heart felt heavy. They were so close to a surface opening, yet couldn't manage to get there. She wasn't sure how long they had been crawling through the broken ship; time meant nothing in these quarters, where even up and down was distorted. It could have been hours or minutes since they'd begun their journey. The passages were sometimes dimly lit and at other times, completely dark. If it wasn't for their flashlights, it would have been impossible to grope their way through the wreckage. As it was, Sara had a few gouges on her hands and face from running into jagged pieces of protruding metal. Her knees and elbows felt bruised, as if they had been beaten with hammers.

As she worked her way down one passage, Sara heard moaning coming from ahead. Moving past openings below her, she came upon another obstruction partially blocking the passageway. Crawling over the debris, she flashed her light on a sailor's face. Sara closed her eyes, thinking she had come across another dead man like the one that had been beside her. When she opened them again, she was startled to see the man's eyes blink. Below her was a young man, his lower body trapped by chunks of heavy metal that she couldn't identify.

The man's eyes were narrowed, and his forehead creased, betraying his pain. Sara eased down next to him.

"Do you have any water?" the young man croaked.

Sara clawed through her pockets, extracting a nearly empty water bottle. She opened it and dribbled water between his pasty lips. The man coughed once, blood dribbling down his cheek. He was able to swallow on the second attempt.

"Thank you," he whispered.

His body tremored as a wave of pain went through.

As the others arrived, they tried lifting the heavy objects, but were unable to shift them. Sara crouched next to the man, taking his chilled hand in hers. The man's eyes said thank you as a tear trickled down.

She looked up when a hand grabbed her shoulder. It was their leader. He bent over and whispered in her ear.

"He's done for. Leave some water if you want, but we need to move on."

"I can't just leave him," Sara whispered in return.

"We have to. I don't know how much time we have left, if any. It's a horrible situation, but we need to go."

Sara shook her head, returning her attention to the trapped man. For some reason, all fear fled and a warm calmness flooded through her. For the first time since being upended, she wasn't in fear for her life, didn't need to feel a fresh breeze caress her face. This man was going to die, that was apparent, but she would remain with him. In her mind, being alone in a sinking ship was the most horrific thing she could think of. She was going to make certain that this man had someone with him.

"I'm staying."

"Are you sure?"

"I'm sure," Sara quietly stated.

The leader then rose and began crawling away. The others briefly paused next to Sara, and then followed. The last man in the party looked back.

"Sara, please," the man beckoned. "Come with us."

She again shook her head and turned back to the man.

"You have...to..." the man coughed, "go with...them. I'm dead...save...yourself."

Sara wiped a streamer of blood from his cheek and offered the man additional water. He coughed some more down. "Thank...you."

Sara lifted the man's head into her lap and held his hand. Time seemed to stand still as the two of them remained silent. Sara comforting the dying man as best she could. She thought to ask questions to ease the time, but it was obvious that talking hurt, so she just sat quietly with him.

The glow of the group's lights had gone, leaving the two of them alone in the passage. Sara had set her light to the side so that it wasn't shining in the man's eyes. The man convulsed. His body tremored and his lips turned a deeper shade of blue. He looked up and locked gazes with Sara.

"Mommy...I want my mommy."

Sara felt the man squeeze her hand and then it went limp. The light left his eyes and they glazed over.

Sara patted his hand. "You're free of the pain, now." She reached over and closed his eyes.

Sad, but freed from her moral obligation, she rose and looked down the passage where the rest of her team had gone. There wasn't any indication of which way they went.

Working down the corridor as quickly as possible, she thought she felt a cooler brush of air across her cheek. She tracked up and across a flight of steps. The grinding that had been a continuous presence abruptly ended. Sara paused, wondering what the significance was.

Suddenly, her world tumbled. The ship rolled again, slamming back upright. It then started tipping on end. Sara grabbed at the edge of a nearby hatch and held on while the ship went through a series of gyrations. Her knee slammed into the side of a bulkhead, sending a wave of agony through her body.

In the distance, she heard screams. One of the screams grew louder by the second. With her feet dangling in open air, Sara watched as a figure fell past. The screaming sailor tried to grab the edge of the hatch, but failed. Tumbling, he fell down the upended passageway, his screams fading and then ending with a crunch.

Sara took a moment to gather her jumbled thoughts. Aft was now up and her mind again flittered at the edge of panic. The bow of the carrier was now pointed down, and there was no denying that the ship was sinking. It might have been before, but with the ship's current position, any small measure of doubt or hope was erased.

Dangling, Sara contemplated just letting go. If she was sure that the drop would end instantly in death and not an agonizingly painful and lingering one, she might have just let her fingers slip. However, the draft was still blowing against her cheek, the one she'd been following. It was not only still there, but it somehow felt stronger. That just didn't make sense. How in the hell could a sinking ship manufacture a breeze?

And then she realized that the influx of seawater could be displacing the air and forcing it through the parts of the vessel that weren't flooded. If that were true, then she was done for. However, there was a slim chance that the flow of air could still signal a way to freedom. Still hanging from the hatch frame, it felt like the ship was bobbing up and down. There was a certain lightness and then heaviness with her grip.

Deciding not to accept certain death, Sara wrapped her feet on adjacent pipes. Pulling with her aching hands and pushing with her booted feet, she raised herself closer to the hatch. She then lifted her feet through the opening and wrestled through. Standing next to the open hatch, she pulled the flashlight from her mouth and looked up.

The task of pulling herself through the portal left trickles of sweat running down her cheeks. That only amplified the fact that air was flowing down the passageway, and by down, it was truly that. The lit passage contained some larger debris, but was clear for the most part. Ironically, the cleared spaces made the matter of scaling the corridor more difficult.

Grabbing the steel conduits, Sara started climbing. With the flashlight in her mouth, she had to pause every couple of minutes to relax her tired jaw muscles. Open doorway ledges also allowed her to rest before tackling the next section. Maneuvering through and around loose equipment, she managed to make it to the end of the passageway. Once there, she had to again pull herself through.

Groans and creaks echoed throughout the tortured ship. Mixing in were dim shouts, but Sara couldn't identify where they were coming from. As she scaled upward, she hoped briefly that the shouts could be rescuers calling for survivors. While resting on the lip of a doorway, Sara wondered if she shouldn't be trying to narrow down where the voices were coming from and work her way there.

She yelled, listening to her shout fade down the passageway. No return call answered. Instead, the ship emitted a long moan that reverberated everywhere. Shaking her arms to relieve trembling muscles, Sara grabbed a pipe and resumed climbing.

She had ascended through several more hatchways and corridors when she saw a dim speck of light. Resting again on the lip of a door, she shielded her light and looked again. Sure enough, there was a bright spot, like an evening star shining through the day's fading sky. She wasn't sure if the smell of seawater that was carried on the draft was a good thing or not, but the light sparked hope in her chest.

As she climbed higher, the pipes, passageway, and doorways all started becoming more warped. She paused by a door, resting until her arms stopped shaking. Ahead, the corridor was bent. Several of the pipes she was climbing had sheared off, leaving sharp, jagged edges. Taking a long intake of breath to steel herself, she again grabbed hold of a pipe and hoisted herself up. With her feet anchoring her, she resumed the arduous climb.

It was tricky moving past the breakages without getting cut. The fire jacket she was sweating in helped. The passageway was bent and warped, the sides forced in at some points and split in others. As she ascended, the corridor became more cramped, but there was that pinprick of light, her guiding star, shining through the mess of tangled wreckage.

Sara eventually came to a point where the passageway was so pinched that she couldn't wedge herself through. The spot of light beckoned, becoming her goal, but was now beyond reach. Wires dangled from broken conduit, the ruins looking like melted plastic that had been stretched. The light and the stronger breeze were so tantalizing close, but there was just no way she could worm her way through.

Her heart sank. She could almost touch it. There was no doubt in her mind that she was looking at open air. She yelled, pounded her fist, and kicked her feet, but there was only the groan of twisted metal that supplied an answer. Tears blurred her vision. The spot of light vanished for a brief second and then reappeared. Sara was now mostly certain that the *Nimitz* wasn't sinking, or at least not yet. But she still didn't understand why the bow was pointed down and what all those gyrations were. Maybe she was dead and cursed to forever prowl the warped corridors.

Sara slowly descended back to the last hatch where she had rested. With one hand maintaining her balance, she reached out to undo the latch holding the portal closed. At first, it didn't budge. She pulled harder, aware that if the latch suddenly gave way, she'd lose her precarious perch and fall like the sailor had. With a squeal of metal, the latch moved. Taking a deep breath and bracing herself, Sara again put her strength into it.

With a sound like a fork raking across a blackboard, the latch gave way. The heavy steel door swung inward and slammed into the side with an echoing clang. A wash of light and air flooded her passageway. Warily, Sara stuck her head through and was rewarded with the sight of blue sky. Her heart was so light that it seemed as if she could float to safety. It was a beauty so magnificent that she felt like weeping. But that would have to wait for later.

Coming from somewhere out of sight, the heavy thump of distant rotor blades filtered down to her position. Sara climbed through the hatch. She was met with a breeze coming from below, or what had been the carrier's bow. It took a moment for the meaning to register. If there was sky above and a rush of air from below, that meant the ship was indeed sinking, and sinking fast. To put it simply, she had to move, and move quickly.

The room she had entered was open to the sky; debris and equipment filled the bottom end with an open hatch leading to another corridor. Eyeing the way up, Sara thought she could manage the climb. Not needing the flashlight any longer, she tucked it away in her coat pocket. Like a freestyle rock climber, she started her ascent, finding hand and foot holds along the way. Ignoring the aching in her fingers, her hands, and trembling thighs, she drew closer to the sky.

She knew she had to move fast, but avoiding the twisted pieces of metal that seemed to protrude everywhere slowed her ascent. At long last, Sara wrapped an arm around the jagged remains of the edges of the room. She hoisted herself atop the broken vestiges of a bulkhead and stood.

In the distance, she saw the flat flight deck and aft end of the *Nimitz* sailing away. That was confusing because she'd thought she was on the carrier. It took a moment for her to reconcile the two disparate truths. One of the escort cruisers was nearby and there were several helicopters orbiting what she now understood to be only part of the carrier. Somehow, the bow had fallen away and was busily sinking with her in it.

The waves below her were steadily growing closer. Sara gazed at the long fall below and then felt the heaviness of her firefighting gear. If she leapt into the waves, the water would fill her pants and boots, dragging her under. Pulling off her coat, she tossed it back into the room. Nothing was going to make her go back inside the trap she had escaped, so she wouldn't need it. It was this or nothing.

Still perched on the end of the jagged bulkhead, she managed to slide out of her boots and pants. She kicked them into the room, watching as the suspenders fluttered. She then focused on the blue waves. She would have to leap outward if she was to clear the ship, or what was left of the bow end. With a deep breath, she jumped.

The wind rushing past her as she fell was refreshing, clean. For a heart-stopping moment, she thought she might catch a protruding arm of steel, but almost as soon as the adrenaline-fueled fear took hold, she flew past the wreckage. Waves rushed up and then she hit.

The groaning sound of the sinking section of ship vanished, becoming instead a roar of water and bubbles. Light streamed into the sea, the sun wavering just a few feet overhead. Sara struggled to gain the open air, her lungs screaming for oxygen. With a rush, she broke free of the water's hold.

She was lifted up the frontside of a swell, the crest crashing over her head. Coughing up the water she'd swallowed, Sara was taken by surprise as another cresting wave crashed over her before she could take a breath. Her tired arms and legs struggled to keep her afloat and Sara went under for a second time, water invading her nose and mouth.

With another effort, she was able to surface. She caught a glimpse of the forward flight deck a few feet away, sliding below the waves before her eyes. She wasn't far away, and it was possible the bow end might suck her under as it sank. She turned to swim away but was met with another cresting swell. Struggling for air, Sara fought to again surface.

Something tugged at her and she was again in the clear. Thinking that the sinking ship was pulling her under, Sara fought against the force, trying to swim away.

"Don't fight me, I have you," a voice yelled in her ear.

It was another person...close...rescue.

"Don't fight me."

Sara now felt arms encircling her and from somewhere came a strong, rhythmic beating. She turned her head. There was a face-masked person next to her, keeping her afloat. Sara relaxed, allowing her rescuer to save her.

The rotating arms of a helicopter moved into her vision and then the dark body of the chopper. She was placed in a sling. Streams of water ran off her as she was lifted clear of the swells. As she was hoisted up, Sara could see the wreckage of the bow as it slid lower in the water. In the distance was the unmistakable silhouette of her carrier. Nearby was the patrolling cruiser that she had previously seen.

The Pacific Ocean wasn't the only salty water dripping from Sara's chin. Less than a minute later, she was pulled into the helicopter and wrapped in a blanket. The chopper started forward, the seas slowly moving underneath. Through the open door, Sara was able to see the bobbing forward section of the carrier. As she watched, the section sank into the water. With a hiss of air shooting streamers of mist from openings, the compartments slipped below the waves. It was only much later that she discovered that the others that had been in her team were missing and presumed dead.

*   *   *   *   *   *

Aboard the Nimitz:

With the radar screens showing clear, the USS *Bunker Hill*, one of the escorting cruisers, pulled in closer to the turning carrier to lend assistance with the overboard crew members.

Slowly, the floating section of the carrier continued to fall further aft. If the section were to sink entirely, it would severely hamper operations to save the rest of the *Nimitz*. The weight of the damaged bow section could conceivably pull the rest of the carrier under.

Emergency crews were sent into the bowels of the *Nimitz*. There, they sought to burn their way through the thick steel of a link. Sparks flew from torches as workers cut into the hard metal, all the while listening to the clanking of the chain slowly unraveling. Although there weren't much the crews could do to speed up the process, the distant sound inspired them to try.

It took a little while, but they managed to cut through a single link. The bow section pulled the anchor chain until it came to the cut link, and a large section of the anchor chain fell away from the ailing ship, effectively stopping the drag that was pulling on the *Nimitz*. The ship righted itself and was able to again steam in a straight line.

The portion of the ship that had fallen away trailed in the wake of the giant carrier. The anchor fell completely away, freeing the floating section of the dragging weight. With the shift in weight and the decreased drag of being pulled by the *Nimitz*, the bow and flight deck section rolled and began taking on more water. It started sinking faster and it wasn't long until it slid beneath the waves, taking the trapped sailors with it. Prayers and pleadings echoed throughout the steel tomb as it sank into the blue waters of the Pacific. Corridors and rooms filled with fear, and then desperation, as the waters rose and the depths crushed the compartments. Years later, ships plying those waters would report the sound of distant, echoing screams.

Aboard the ship, forty yards of the forward flight deck was now in the Pacific. The Chinese warhead had come down at an angle that sliced through the flight deck, emerging again into open space approximately thirty feet above the water level. The explosion from the hypersonic weapon blackened the hull, but did little in the way of additional damage.

Smoke from the damaged section rolled over the top of

the remaining flight deck. Rescue operations were underway in the surrounding waters. Below decks, emergency crews worked to stifle the few fires that burned, each member wary of the escaping steam from the ruined catapults. Parties working to shut off the steam feeding the forward catapults, finally managed to locate working valves in the wreckage and turned them off. Considering how hard the ship was hit, it was nothing short of a miracle that the damage wasn't far worse than it was.

The intake of seas through the forward section was minimal, as Captain Kurt Schwarz had ordered a reduction in speed as soon as the bow fell into the sea and started dragging the mighty ship to one side. If the sea swells remained moderate or lower, the rest of the ship wasn't in danger of sinking or taking on more water.

Once damage control parties were able to bring the few fires under control and reroute some of the ship's damaged functions, Schwarz was better able to ascertain the ship's status. It was afloat and able to maintain power and steerage. The forward catapults were out of operation, and the crews would have to double up in some cases as some of the quarters were heading toward the ocean's bottom. And, of course, the ship wouldn't be anchoring any time soon.

* * * * * *

Walking along the flight deck, the sight of the carrier's shortened front end was something that Captain Schwarz couldn't quite wrap his mind around. A fifteen-knot breeze blew across the ship as the *Nimitz* commander strode to a waiting helicopter. The wash of rotors brought the smell of burnt jet fuel, which was better than the smell of burned rubber and other materials smoldering from the damaged section of the ship. Stepping aboard, Schwarz readied himself for what he might see.

The chopper went light as it lifted off, spun in place, and headed laterally to the ship's movement. Turning to parallel the carrier, Schwarz caught his first glimpse of the damage. From approximately forty yards back, the forward section of the

Nimitz had been sliced at an angle, ending about thirty feet from the surface. From this distance, the cut looked clean, like some strange new American carrier design. However, a closer look revealed a tangled mass of wreckage.

From a dozen places, brownish-gray smoke flowed, rising and rolling over the top of the flight deck. Like a yard full of kids playing with sparklers, broken live wires created showers of sparks, the embers falling to fade in a mass of broken pipes and bent metal. Steam from the forward catapult system had sent jets of white into the mix until valves had been shut off.

Schwarz looked at the bow wave and judged that, in the current seas, the ship was safe from a massive influx of water. If the swells kicked up too much, then the ship could be in danger of becoming inundated. When the captain first ordered a helicopter to be readied, he thought he would be looking over the damage to see if the *Nimitz* would be able to make it to the nearest port in Japan. Now, he was pondering whether the ship could actually be operational.

If the waist catapults were working, along with the arresting gear, then flight operations would be limited, but possible. The initial indication from engineering was that the ship could make twenty-five knots. However, that was under ideal conditions. With the seas as they were, Schwarz felt like eighteen knots might be a more realistic number. The steering was still fully operational. Circling the damage, the captain's mind started flipping from a salvage venture to working on how to bring the *Nimitz* back into operation.

Emergency crews were busy putting out the smoldering fires while electricians sought out the best way to cut off power to the damaged sections without also shutting down essential functions. The explosion of the weapon's warhead outside of the ship was a lifesaver as far as the ship was concerned. Had the thousand-pound charge detonated inside, just a few yards closer, Schwarz would be looking at a completely different picture.

Landing, Captain Schwarz ordered an immediate test of

the waist catapults and arresting gear. The *Reagan* took over the task force's flight operations, launching several tankers for the *Nimitz's* aircraft to remain aloft. Not initially knowing the status of the *Nimitz*, a call went out to Kadena Air Force base for the use of several KC-135 tankers. The *Reagan* couldn't accept the aircraft from the *Nimitz* and still maintain its operational status, so the plan was to direct the *Nimitz's* aircraft that were currently aloft to a base in either Japan or Okinawa.

Back on the bridge, Schwarz went straight to the phone and called Admiral Prescott, the Carrier Strike Group 11 commander.

"Prescott," the admiral answered, anticipating the call.

"Schwarz here, sir, with a sitrep."

"Go ahead, Kurt. What are we looking at?"

"Well, sir. We've lost the forward catapults for sure, along with both anchors. I don't have casualty reports yet, but we've lost our forward ready rooms and a good portion of our crew quarters. Damage control states that they have the fires under control and are in the process of shutting down the electricity to the damaged sections.

"It looks like we can maintain eighteen knots in the current seas, perhaps a little more once we test it. Our steerage hasn't been affected; it's one hundred percent operational," Captain Schwarz reported, gazing down at the flight deck as the waist catapults were tested.

Other crew members in a variety of colored vests and shirts were gathered around the arresting cables. All those that were topside wore personal protection masks as thin streamers of smoke still wafted down the length of the deck.

"That's good news, Kurt. Once we've completed rescue operations, I'm tagging the *Bunker Hill* to escort you back to Pearl. I'm also going to OPCON the rest of DESRON 17 to CSG 5 and the task force," Admiral Prescott stated.

Out of the corner of his eyes, Captain Schwarz saw the bridge watch officer as she picked up a phone. She nodded a couple of times, asked a question, nodded again, and then replaced the receiver. Turning, she caught Schwarz's gaze and walked toward him.

"Sir, excuse me a moment," the captain said, covering the receiver with his hand and nodding for the watch officer to report.

"Sir, that was the flight deck," she opened and then paused.

"Go ahead, Lieutenant. Spit it out."

"Yes, sir. Both waist catapults are fully operational, or at least the tests indicate that they haven't sustained damage. Commander Wilson, the air boss, reports that the arresting cables are also intact and able to be used to recover aircraft. However, he cautioned that they will have to be load-tested before he can certify that they're fully operational."

"Thank you," Schwarz said, passing the same information along to Admiral Prescott.

The captain knew that the air boss was placing a buffer on his affirmation. He wanted to land an aircraft to fully test the gear before committing. If the cables failed, the plane would be under full power and could take off again. There was an increased risk due to the nature of what they just experienced, but it was an acceptable one. Launching an aircraft was a different matter. If the catapult failed, the aircraft would likely just be flung into the sea.

Both measures could end with an aircraft in the water, which left out using F-35s to test with. Those aircraft had secrets which would necessitate lengthy salvage operations to recover the aircraft.

"So, sir, if those systems prove to be operational, I'd like to further discuss removing the *Nimitz* from the task force. Future flight operations would be limited, with our surge capability cut in half. We will also be restricted from performing recoveries at the same time as we are launching, but we could still put aircraft into the air," Schwarz said.

There was a pause on the other end of the line.

"Okay, Kurt. Test the systems and let me know. I'm going to discuss that possibility with Admiral Calhoun and the fleet commanders. Keep me updated on any situational changes."

The line clicked dead before Schwarz could utter a "Yes, sir."

*   *   *   *   *   *

Commander Stone eased the throttles forward, the F/A-18E straining against the holdback bar as the aircraft's towbar eased over the catapult shuttle and locked into place. The VFA-137 squadron commander held his hand on top of the instrument panel as the flight deck crew ran under and around the aircraft. Gazing to the front of the carrier, Stone saw where part of the bow section had been cut from the ship. Jagged pieces of the ship's interior and hull rose above the lip of the remaining flight deck, reminders that the ship wasn't whole.

Turning his attention out in front of the Super Hornet, he wondered if the catapult would succeed in generating enough speed for the fighter to remain airborne or whether he'd soon be testing his ability to keep his head above water. He could swim, but he would never say it was a strength of his.

When the call came from the wing commander, Stone had volunteered for the mission to test the catapults and arresting system. There's no way he'd let one of his pilots conduct the test if he could help it. Of course, once he'd learned the full extent of what he was to do, he contemplated kicking his desk hard and then reporting to the sickbay with broken toes.

But here he was, sitting on top of a candle about ready to be heaved into the air by a system that no one was sure would work. On top of that, he was to bring a fifty-thousand-pound hunk of metal around to land on a short and narrow deck, hoping that the system that was designed to stop him could do its job. Could life possibly get any better?

The shooter was circling two fingers. Stone ran the throttles up, moving over the mil power detent and into afterburner for a combat takeoff. He then cycled the flight controls through their full ranges and placed his hands on the canopy bow. One at a time, the shooter checked over the other stations. Receiving a thumbs up from all, he gave Stone a thumbs up. The commander saluted the shooter to let him know he was ready, although in his stomach, he wasn't exactly sure of what he was ready for.

The shooter touched the deck and pointed forward. Stone normally loved carrier launches, but this is one he'd rather already have behind him. The jolt pressed his body tight against his seat as the F/A-18E surged forward. The vibrations and rumbling of the wheels racing over the deck seemed normal, as did the acceleration. Before he knew it, the Super Hornet passed the end of the deck and was over the water.

Commander Stone reached down for the flight stick and then retracted the gear and flaps. Pulling back, the Super Hornet climbed into the clear air. He was airborne with flying airspeed. The catapult had worked. But now came the tricky part…landing.

Turning a downwind leg, Stone ran through the pre-landing checklist. Looking back at the ship, he could see the damaged front end for the first time. The sight was something that he'd remember his entire life. He shook his head at the miracle. The *Nimitz* had been hit by one of the vaunted Chinese ship-killers and had survived. Not only that, but it was still partially operational. Or would be, if Stone managed to live through what was coming next.

Before he knew it, he was lined up behind the carrier, coming in at a slight angle. He checked the gear and flaps and then concentrated on the moving flight deck.

"Call the ball," a voice radioed.

"Pride five zero zero, Hornet ball, fourteen point five," Stone returned.

Pride was the VFA-137 callsign and he was flying aircraft number 500. He let the landing system officer know that he was flying a Hornet, could see the lighting system that was a visual representation of the glide slope, and had fourteen and a half thousand pounds of fuel on board.

There had been a minor debate about whether to conduct

the test with minimal or maximum fuel, or something in between. The lighter the aircraft was, the easier it would be on the systems. However, if the plane managed to get airborne, but couldn't land, then the minimum fuel situation could complicate matters, if all the *Nimitz's* airborne aircraft had to divert. In the end, it was decided to launch with a full load of fuel.

Stone moved the throttles in order to maintain airspeed as he tried to keep the orange ball in the middle of the side datum lights. If the highlighted ball was below the center, then he was below the optimal glide path. Consequently, if it was above the datum line, then he was coming in too high.

When the ship was gripped in the throes of rough weather, keeping the ball centered was a virtual impossibility. Then you just had to manage an average and trust that you could slam onto the deck through its rising and falling. Of course, rough weather meant that the pilot was also fighting the elements, many times popping into the clear with only a few hundred feet to go, or seeing the lights through squalls of rain.

Coming down, it was difficult not to keep looking at the damaged front end. The back lip of the deck passed underneath the nose. Stone pulled back the power, and the Super Hornet dropped toward the deck. The jolt as the plane hit rocked the squadron commander and he ran the throttles forward to the stops. The tail hook grabbed the number three cable and Stone felt the strain against his shoulder harness as the F/A-18E slowed abruptly. With a signal from the deck crew, he brought the throttles back to idle and the aircraft rolled backward from the arresting cable tension.

Under the direction of the handlers, the aircraft was guided to catapult number four, the second waist catapult. The fun was only half over.

* * * * * *

Testing of the waist catapults was successful, as was the arresting system. For all the twisted metal up front, most of the proud ship was still operational. The jolt had shaken loose many mountings which would require attention, but those would be seen to on a priority basis. The status of the *Nimitz* left Admiral Calhoun, the Task Force 70 commander, and the rest of the Indo-Pacific Command, with a difficult decision.

* * * * * *

The situation reports coming in from the western Pacific were a mixed bag. On one hand, the *Nimitz* had taken a hit from one of China's infamous hypersonic anti-ship missiles. On the other, only one of twenty-one fired weapons managed to strike its target. The other missiles were either disregarded because of their trajectories or shot down with the experimental laser systems aboard some of the escorting destroyers and the USS *Portland*.

It was comforting to know that the Chinese missiles weren't ready for prime time. It was also encouraging to find out that the test systems were able to knock down many of the maneuverable glide vehicles. The flip side of that was that another of the carriers available in the Pacific theatre was damaged and likely out of action. In the current situation, that meant a twenty-five percent reduction in the available firepower. Another attack like that and the United States would be down to just two operational carriers.

Something had to be done to guard against future attacks, but that was a discussion for a later time. Right now, Admiral Brickline had a tough decision to make. The fleet commanders and the Task Force 70 commander were on screen, holding their silence while Brickline contemplated the situation at hand.

The *Nimitz's* captain had asked for and recommended that his ship be returned to operational status. The carrier operations would be limited, but they could still put planes in the air, which meant the ability to put weapons on targets. Right now, that was paramount. However, the thought of keeping a heavily damaged flattop in danger didn't sit well. Standard protocol dictated that the carrier return to Hawaii to effect repairs.

The admiral thought about the speed limitations the carrier would be operating under. That would place it in greater danger from both submarines and China's rocket forces. But his field commanders were recommending that the *Nimitz* continue its mission and remain with Task Force 70. The added firepower would be invaluable for the upcoming defense of Taiwan.

It was a choice only he could make: to sail home with a damaged carrier, out of action, but that could be repaired in time, versus floating her back into action with the greater possibility that the *Nimitz* could be permanently lost. One carrier was already resting in Neptune's locker, and it would be a tremendous blow to add another. Not only would it represent a significant reduction in the firepower the United States could deliver, but it would give China added confidence. That was something that had to be avoided.

There was another side to that coin. If China saw that none of the carriers had been put out of action due to their attack, that could conceivably lower their morale. There was a slim chance China would believe their foray had been unproductive and therefore preempt further missile attacks, at least until their strategies could be reevaluated. Admiral Brickline doubted that scenario, but it would show the world that it wasn't as easy to sink an American carrier as the enemy had boasted.

"Okay, Chip, keep the *Nimitz* with you," Brickline instructed the task force commander. "But, if things get worse, then the *Nimitz* is to make all due haste to Pearl."

"Aye, sir. I'll inform Prescott."

"I mean it, Chip. If *anything* else happens to that ship, if someone trips over a chock, then that's it. The *Nimitz* heads home," Brickline affirmed.

"I'll personally send them on their way," Calhoun replied.

With that, the *Nimitz* retained its role within the task force.

Later determinations concluded that the carrier had been extremely lucky. Studies later showed that with its kinetic energy, coupled with the thousand-pound warhead, a single hypersonic missile could indeed provide a soft kill on a carrier. And if it impacted in the right location, it could conceivably sink it.

Chapter Two

White House, Washington D.C.
30 July, 2021

The atmosphere in the room was anything but cordial. Tension hung thickly, seeming to compress the air with angry overtones and a hint of hostility. If it was all combined into a beverage, it would surely cause heartburn that would stretch through a restless night.

Many of the department heads were upset over the ballistic launch of the Chinese hypersonic anti-ship missiles which managed to hit the USS *Nimitz*. The carrier was still in action, but the ship's operations were limited. Though, "upset" was probably not the correct terminology. Outrage might be better suited to the staff's reactions. Aaron MacCulloch, the secretary of defense, was livid.

"You know, Frank, I have over five hundred cruise missiles in the area that I can happily send up their ass," MacCulloch continued from an earlier tirade. "I'm serious. If we focus those on the bloody ships riding in their harbors, then we won't have to worry about a fucking Chinese invasion."

The other secretaries in the room looked to Winslow. Even the secretary of state, Fred Stevenson, who would normally speak up urging caution, remained silent and waited on the president's reply.

"Aaron, I know you're angry. Hell, we all are," Frank responded. "But I want you think this through. I want *all* of us to think this all the way through. How do you think it will end up if we pursue that kind of response?

"We were attacked in international waters. Considering the rules that we're both operating under in order to keep it confined to a regional conflict, to keep it from escalating into something much larger, China's attack was legitimate. I don't like it, but there it is nonetheless. If we were to respond by attacking their territory, how do you think they'd react? An attack, conventional or otherwise, on Guam? On Okinawa?

Perhaps even Japan? Hell, they could open up on our West Coast naval bases.

"If we escalate in that manner, it will open those possibilities, and more. The escalations will continue until one of us sends a single nuke. And that will end with an exchange neither of us can afford."

MacCulloch slammed his hand on the table and locked eyes with Frank. "Dammit, Frank. They already escalated matters. I say we end this shit right here, right now. Let's sink those ships, sink the rest of their Navy, and see how powerful they feel when their invasion fleet is lying on the bottom of the sea. How much will China continue to push without a navy? I mean, we can't be expected to just sit back and let them hit our carriers from space. From *space*, Frank."

"I know you're pissed off, Aaron. But we must make sure the situation remains controllable. And by that, I mean we can't afford to open a path that could lead to an uncontrolled escalation. The *Nimitz* is still operational, is it not?"

"Yes. It's limited, but it can still be used for defensive and offensive operations. But we need to figure out how we're going to prevent another attack like this. I'm sure you all know that we were lucky this time. Those bastards on the other side of the Pacific will take note of the results. We can expect this to happen again, only next time, they'll send more."

"It seems we did pretty well defending against the, what? Twenty-one missiles, and only one hit? Seems like we were able to defend the task force," Stevenson added.

Aaron turned sharply toward the secretary of state. "Fred, doing well against an attack like that means that none of our carriers were hit. Our best intel places sixty of those hypersonic weapons in China's inventory. They fired twenty-one and Taiwan managed to hit several during their attack. I think that bastard Hao believed the missiles were better than they proved to be. Hell, so did we. However, we both now know that they can get through our defenses. If they fired their remaining missiles all at once, then it's likely that they could put two carriers out of action. And if that happens, then we might as well just quit.

"Taiwan would be lost for sure, and there is a strong likelihood that South Korea would be gone as well. We should count ourselves fortunate that their accuracy was what it was. So, Fred, yes, we managed to defend the task force. But we were also lucky, and I'd rather not count on luck."

"Okay, Aaron," Frank chided. "You've made your point. Without resorting to hitting China within their boundaries, what can we do?"

"Well, in the longer run, we need to increase the integration of the HELIOS laser systems for the Arleigh-Burke destroyers, focusing on those stationed in the Pacific theatre. And we also need to move up the testing on the high energy laser weapon systems. Both of those systems needed to be operational yesterday.

"The ballistic missile defense systems we have in place have little chance of intercepting weapons traveling at Mach 10 speeds. And the time from reentry to impact with these kinds of weapons doesn't leave much time to retarget misses. The one that hit the *Nimitz* was one that we missed and didn't retarget. We've already identified the problem and fixed the software, but that won't fix the problem of hitting a maneuvering missile traveling at Mach 10.

"For the interim, if we want to avoid losing any more carriers, or reduce the risk of it, then we need to be able to destroy the weapon systems before they reach orbit," MacCulloch commented.

"Are you talking about hitting the rockets over Chinese airspace?" Frank asked.

"We can't do that," Fred stated at the same time. "That's the same thing as attacking them directly."

"Yes, sir, that's what I'm talking about. With regards to Fred's assertation, the upper limit of a nation's boundaries is a nebulous gray area. It's commonly recognized that the twelve-mile boundary also extends upwards, placing the upper limit at around sixty-thousand feet. That gives us plenty of margin for hitting the rockets before they reach a low earth orbit.

"Let me explain a little about the ballistic defenses we have in place and why they don't necessarily work in this instance. First, the nuclear and conventional reentry vehicles follow a set course, so it's easy to calculate trajectories. With these missiles, the same doesn't hold true. They're highly maneuverable, making them harder to track. With their reentry speeds, the glide time to target is measured in seconds. That's one reason why retargeting is so difficult.

"If our strike groups were fully operational with laser weapon systems, I'd feel more confident about our ability to defend against these kinds of weapons. But for now, if we're going to win this conflict, then we need to look at taking out these hypersonic weapons *before* they enter their orbit. That means hitting them during their powered ascent, in particular before the first rocket stage separation."

"Let me get this straight so I understand what you mean. You're asking me for authorization to hit China's ballistic missiles before they enter orbit, even if that's over mainland China?" Frank inquired.

"I am. Warn the bastards that any further ballistic launches will be treated as an imminent threat to the United States, for as long as the conflict lasts. That's not far from the truth. If we hadn't been closely monitoring these weapon systems, then NORAD might have arrived at the conclusion that the launches were something else entirely. Hell, there were Chinese thinktank studies done not that long ago, that concluded that the use of hypersonic weapons might invoke a nuclear response."

"Again, for clarification. You're talking about using anti-ballistic missiles and the test lasers in operation to shoot down any ballistic missiles that China fires," Winslow said.

Aaron nodded.

"Wait, wouldn't that mean shooting down satellite launches as well?" Stevenson asked.

"I'm all for preventing any rocket launches from China, but that would surely provoke China into an escalation," MacCulloch answered.

"On this point, you see an escalation," Tom Collier, the CIA Director, chuckled.

"It seems different somehow. If the order were given, I'd sink every ship China has and apologize afterward," MacCulloch stated.

Some of the tension eased as the department heads bantered back and forth. Only Fred failed to join in. Frank ignored them as he withdrew into his thoughts. Issuing an order to fire on missiles over China's mainland was a risk. Hao certainly wouldn't recognize the upper limitation to his airspace. Even though many of the weapons positioned on China's eastern coast could possibly be clear of the 12-mile horizontal limits by time they reached sixty-thousand feet, China's leadership might not view it that way.

But Aaron was right. Something had to be done about the hypersonic missile threat if the United States was to have any hope of winning the war with China. If Frank didn't give the order, then it was extremely likely America would be pushed out of the South China Sea, and quite possibly the Philippine Sea in the not-too-distant future. The United States had staked its doctrine around its carriers. If those now proved to be useless, then it was only a matter of time before America faded from its top position.

The dollar would eventually be replaced as the global currency. That would invoke a recession and rampant inflation from which the United States might not recover. NATO would lose its power as a threat, prompting Russia to become more aggressive in their maneuvering to reinstate their empire.

Frank's mind went down many alleyways, all of them painful to travel. Throughout the entire history of humankind, there have always been evolving weapons which required evolving defenses. For a while, whoever owned significant weapon advancements elevated to the top until defensive measures were developed to counter them. Luckily, China experienced problems with their hypersonic weapons, and the United States was able to develop counters. But those counters weren't fully operational or disseminated, thus creating a gap.

Frank couldn't allow China to gain the upper hand, that much was undeniable. Reaching a decision, he looked up from his thoughts.

"What I mean is, maybe we can handle it two ways? We can restrict any defensive measures we take to just rockets fired from mobile platforms. Or we can restrict our countermeasures to include a certain number of ballistic missiles fired at once," Aaron was saying.

"Aaron, are these glide vehicles only fired from mobile launchers?" Frank inquired.

MacCulloch nodded.

"Okay. I am authorizing the use of defensive measures to counter them. This means that you can only fire on rockets sent from these specific types of mobile platforms. This is in addition our standing orders regarding ballistic missile defenses."

Aaron rose from his seat. "Thank you, Mr. President. If you don't mind, I'd like to issue that order immediately. Time is of the essence. If I were China and had analyzed the data from my first attack, I'd already have missiles in the air."

Frank nodded and waved his secretary of defense out of the room.

*   *   *   *   *   *

Sea of Japan
30 July, 2021

It was tough to portray calmness and confidence when tension gripped Commander David Avelar. The USS *Topeka* had been assigned undersea escort duties for the USS *Ohio* while the cruise missile sub launched nearly its entire payload into North Korea. It was David's first full-fledged command, and the fact made itself known by the anxiety wreaking havoc in his gut. He knew he was ready, but he had envisioned having several peacetime patrols with which to break in and become used to being at the top of the chain. Having his first command amid an active conflict didn't allow for the usual mistakes a first-time commander made.

The *Ohio* had secured from firing its large contingent of cruise missiles and the two boats were heading south. The plan was to exit the Sea of Japan and sail east to reload. Remaining together, the two boats would then reenter the area off North Korea's east coast to support the South.

Commander Avelar knew that North Korea had a few older diesel-electric subs. As a matter of fact, the northern country had one of the world's largest submarine fleets. Although most of the inventory was comprised of coastal subs, they were still considered deadly in certain conditions. Intel suggested that most of the North's inventory was likely operating off the southern and western shores of the Peninsula, prowling around South Korea's naval bases. The narrow strait separating Japan from the Korean Peninsula could very well be littered with North Korean and Chinese attack boats, even though Japanese and South Korean surface and airborne anti-submarine warfare forces were heavily patrolling the strait.

The passageway provided a natural chokepoint which all sides would like to have control of. For that reason, even though speed was called for to replenish as quickly as possible, Avelar had ordered the *Topeka* to creep south. As they drew closer, David glanced toward the sonar room more often.

"Conn, Sonar. I have a transient bearing one four zero. Unable to determine speed or course. It was there for a second and then gone."

David turned at the call. The *Ohio* was behind them on a bearing of one niner zero. Could the transient sound have been a North Korean sub that had somehow located the missile boat trailing behind?

"Conn, Sonar. There it is again, same bearing. I'm labeling it as contact Alpha One."

"Roger, Sonar. XO, make your heading one four zero. Maintain speed and depth," Avelar ordered.

"Aye, sir. Right standard rudder to one four zero," the executive officer replied.

David internally winced. He should have stated the rudder setting. He'd said it a thousand times before. Why did he choose now to forget such a simple command? He nodded toward the exec, thanking him for putting in the correction.

Traveling at ten knots, David knew that the *Topeka* should be able to gain on any North Korean boat. The coastal subs in their inventory were only capable of speeds less than ten knots. That put them at a huge disadvantage when faced with any modern weapons systems. Even though David willed sonar to report updates, they were frustratingly silent for ten minutes while the *Topeka* chased down what might be just another natural noise in the depths.

"There you are," the sonarman muttered.

"Something to report, Sonar?" David inquired.

The sonarman held up a finger for quiet as he pressed the headset closer to his ear with his other hand. His eyes were squinted in concentration. They opened abruptly.

"Got you now," the sonarman again mumbled. "Sir, I have screw sounds on Alpha One. It's definitely a North Korean Shark-class submarine. The bearing to Alpha One is one four zero, now moving left to right. Screw sounds indicate seven knots, range seven thousand yards."

"Make your heading one six zero, ready tubes one and two. Update the FCS," David commanded.

"Aye, sir. Both tubes showing green. FCS has been updated with the latest data."

The three-dimensional mental map playing in the commander's mind had the North Korean sub chasing after the *Ohio*, possibly getting closer to fire one of their Russian type 53 torpedoes. The range and speed were limited with the older torps, so the North Korean commander must be racing to close the distance to the *Ohio*. David had to destroy the enemy boat before it had a chance to fire.

"Fire One," Commander Avelar ordered.

"One away," the XO reported.

"Tracking," sonar stated.

"Fire two."

Two Mark 48 torpedoes left their tubes, entering the cold waters off the South Korean coast. Quickly accelerating to sixty knots, the weapons sped toward the North Korean vessel, which was unaware of their presence. When the first torpedo entered the specified kill box, the lines were cut and the internal guidance software initiated the torpedo's sonar. Pinging continuously, the Mark 48 actively homed in on the slow-moving submarine.

"Torpedo number one has gone active. Alpha One screw count increased slightly. He's making nearly eight knots. Aspect ratio changing. He's trying to run," sonar reported.

Approximately a minute and a half after leaving the confines of its tube, the first Mark 48 ran across the back of the enemy vessel near the conning tower. A thousand pounds of explosive ripped through the older submarine. The tower was crushed by the compressed water, the forward and aft ends of the sub bending upward like a banana. Water poured into the bridge, filling it in less than two seconds. Most of the fifteen-person crew died instantly.

Five seconds later, the second torpedo arrived, completely destroying what was left of the Shark-class submarine. When the sub settled toward the bottom, very little remained to be compressed by the depths.

David thought that the kill would alleviate some of the tension riding in his gut. Although he shared in the crew's silent cheering, his anxiety increased. Before, the thought of enemy subs out there was fiction. They had suddenly become all too real and, in his mind, were everywhere. After all, North Korea operated some ninety older submarines. That's a lot to cram into small, defined areas. It felt as if he could shoot a torpedo in any direction and be assured of a hit.

A hand slapped his shoulder. Turning, he caught sight of his grinning executive officer. The man leaned over, "A kill is a kill. Nicely done, sir."

Although he wouldn't diminish his focus on every sound, he felt some of the tension dissipate. He'd been an XO in LA-class boats, had participated in several wargames, had tracked many enemy vessels. David felt the confidence he'd been lacking begin to settle in.

"Thank you," he whispered. "Left standard rudder, make your heading one niner zero."

*   *   *   *   *   *

Pentagon, Washington D.C.
30 July, 2021

On the helicopter ride back, Aaron MacCulloch contemplated the Far East situation. He hated to think that America's carriers were becoming obsolete, especially considering the fortune the United States had put into them. Unfortunately, China's latest hypersonic missiles had brought that question to the front. It seemed to be a continual argument that arose every budget time.

The carrier strike groups presented an enormous amount of firepower that could be delivered almost anywhere in the world. Shoot, China had built two of the things and were currently working on a third and fourth. India had one, was building a second, and was also considering a third. The United Kingdom, France, Spain, Italy. Heck, even Thailand had an operational carrier. Everyone in the world coveted the floating fortresses, so the stratagem had to be sound. But they were also large targets, and vulnerable, evidenced by China's latest attack.

Aaron knew that the carrier strike groups could project a tremendous amount of firepower, but was their time coming to an end? Everything ended at some point. The battleships of yore, a force to be reckoned with in their day, had all faded into the past. Was it time for the carriers to follow suit? What would be next? Unmanned vessels and vehicles? Would it eventually become a world of long-range hypersonic glide vehicles?

These questions encompassed Aaron's mind. However, he also knew that he'd be long gone before any changes came into play. At the moment, the United States had put its eggs into the carrier basket. And the platforms worried nations, thus the expenditures to come up with weapons that could sink them. No, it would be a long time coming before America would give up its precious carriers. After all, the first of a new generation had just been completed.

Lost in his thoughts about the Far Eastern conflict, Aaron barely acknowledged salutes as he made his way into the Pentagon. Several times on his way to his office, staff members tried to cut him off. MacCulloch hastily motioned them away, asking them to contact his office for an appointment.

During his brief flight, he had made the call to the Indo-Pacific command to initiate the commencement of firing on any further Chinese ballistic launches. As with every order these days, there were limitations. Any ballistic missile fire from a mobile launch platform was fair game. In addition, any ballistic launch from a Chinese silo or launch pad in groups of five or more was also allowed to be hit with America's ballistic defenses, which included the test laser platforms. It was Fred Stevenson's job to inform China of America's new stance.

"Get me the Taiwanese Minister of National Defense," he told his secretary.

"Yes, sir."

Aaron then closed his office door on the few people who were still asking for some of his time.

"You'd think they would have learned by now," he muttered.

For years now, Aaron had a reputation for being gruff and for ignoring people who seemed to gather around him the moment he left his office. At times, the growls turned to sharp barks when he grew too annoyed by the constant demands for his attention. That still didn't seem to deter some who glommed onto him from every direction in the busy corridors of the Pentagon.

His phone rang. "Sir, I have Taiwan's Minister of National Defense on the line."

"Thank you. Put him through."

"Putting him through now."

A click told him that the call to Taiwan's underground command and control bunker had been established.

"Yan-ting, thank you for taking my call in these tense moments," Aaron started.

"Of course, Mr. MacCulloch. What can I do for you?"

Aaron relayed America's decision to take out China's ballistic missiles if they were fired.

"However, if possible, we'd rather it not come to that to avoid any escalation. As you know, we need to get our carriers within striking range if we're to thwart a Chinese invasion of your island. Fact is, sir, we both know that the likelihood of Taiwan winning the war without our help is low. Although it will cost them a bundle, China will likely invade and occupy your island in a hot minute, given the chance. In order to get our assets within range, we'll need some help taking out the DF-21 mobile launchers."

"I appreciate the situation. First, I want to thank you for the continuous resupply of missiles. As you know, with China's nearly constant attacks, we have nearly depleted our supply of surface-to-air and air-to-air missiles. Is it possible that you could increase the supplies?"

"I'll certainly see what can be done. We'll have to sneak in between attacks, but I'll make a call as soon as we hang up. Come hell or high water, you'll get your missiles."

"Very well, thank you. I will see what we can do about attacking those sites. Please keep in mind that we have very few cruise missiles remaining, and we will need to keep a certain number for defense against the invasion fleets. But I will help to the extent that I can."

"Thank you. I will make sure the locations are sent to you within the hour. The United States will do everything in its power to help safeguard Taiwan," Aaron stated.

"I will await the target list."

* * * * * *

Yan-ting stared at the receiver before replacing it in its cradle. He knew that the Americans were using Taiwan as their proxy to attack China's mainland. If he and the rest of the country wanted help from the United States, then there was a price to pay. Sure, he understood their reasoning, and their reluctance to bring their carriers closer. The problem was that Taiwan didn't have an endless supply of cruise missiles. Yan-ting doubted that there were enough remaining in the inventory to hold China off for very long once their ships finally did sail. And the Minister of Defense thought that day wasn't far off.

Reports were coming in of another Chinese missile attack. The telephone exchanges were down, as were other communications centers. Major unit communications had been particularly hard hit, the antenna farms destroyed almost as soon as new ones were erected. As much as Yan-ting wanted to hold off using even one missile on targets that weren't Chinese ships, he really didn't have much choice other than to accept the American target lists.

The resupply flights sent by the United States replenished some of the weapons Taiwan was using in order to mitigate the damage from the missile launches across the strait, but the reality of it was that the inventory was being used up at a rapid rate. It was a difficult choice whether to use what they had for defending against the long-range missile attacks, or to wait until the Chinese ships came within range. There was no real definitive solution. And now the Americans were asking Taiwan to use more of its weaponry against targets that only indirectly affected the country.

The unfortunate truth was, without the United States, Taiwan would eventually come under the control of the People's Republic of China. That meant going into its precious inventory to take out some of the DF-21 mobile launch batteries. The trade-off meant more ships would be able to land troops on Taiwan's shores.

True to MacCulloch's word, the requested target list was promptly in Yan-ting's hand. With the heaviness of command weighing on his shoulders, the minister lifted the receiver and gave the order to his rocket forces.

An hour after the conversation with the American defense secretary, heavy doors opened from hidden sites across the mountainous island terrain. With roars that echoed down tight ravines, smoke shot out from within hardened bunkers.

Hsuing-Feng 3 missiles emerged from within the clouds, flames from their boosters glowing in the night.

Pushed to their supersonic speeds, the strap-on rocket boosters separated as the projectiles transitioned to their ramjet engines. A carpet of cruise missiles swept over the Taiwan Strait, crossing the passageway in five minutes. Skimming over the top of the waves and nearing China's coastline, the internal software programs recognized the probing signals from search and fire control radars. The missiles then employed internal electronic counter countermeasures to give them better chances of penetrating the layers of anti-air defenses.

Roars sprayed across the coastal towns as the weapons crossed over shorelines, the heavy growls turning to whines once the projectiles began fading as they flew further into the interior. Once over Chinese territory, the missiles began high-g random lateral maneuvers to further complicate China's use of close-in defenses. As much as the missile programming attempted to defeat being intercepted, they weren't successful in all instances.

Large caliber tracers arced into the darkened skies. Guided by radar and infrared, missiles and bullets reached out toward the invading threats. Flashes in the night sky erupted from successful intercepts. In other places, fireballs marked where HF-3s collided with the ground.

Within seven minutes from launch, the first cruise missiles began arriving over their targets. Focusing on the transporter erector launchers, the two hundred and fifty-pound warheads detonated in bright balls of flame, smoke, and sharp concussive blasts. The fuel contained in the DF-21 missiles added to the explosive nature of each hit, turning the mobile platforms into flaming pieces of twisted metal.

Following the strike on the American carriers, China had been expecting a proxy attack against their hypersonic anti-ship sites. Given how few remained in China's inventory, and their desire to use them rather than lose them, standing orders had come from Beijing that the missiles were to be launched if there were verified attacks against the launchers. Satellites had constantly provided targeting updates to the individual missiles.

Confirmation arrived with the first hit. Chinese battery commanders received orders for immediate launches. They had been prepared for the contingency and only the final step in the process remained. Across the backcountry lanes and narrow roads, large gouts of flame lit up the night. Rumbles that were felt internally roared across the countryside as the giant weapons lifted from their containments.

The launching of the hypersonic glide vehicles was a race against time, the Chinese ship-killers attempting to beat the arrival of Taiwan's attack. Rockets roared aloft, clawing for the safety of altitude. Some made it, others were destroyed before they could clear their containers. Those that cleared the launchers powered skyward, heading to escape into low-earth orbits. Satellites continued sending a stream of data as to the position of the American Task Force 70 carriers.

* * * * * *

Inside the Indo-Pacific command center, Captain Alex Buchanan was leaning back in his chair. With his fingers clasped behind his head, he was lost in thought. Foremost in his contemplations was the news his wife had shared the other night. The Navy captain had been thinking about retirement, and then came the revelation that he was going to be a father once again.

It seemed that he had just sent his other two kids out into the world. His daughter had become an attorney and had just signed on with a prestigious New York law firm. His son was working as a waiter in Los Angeles, trying to make a go of becoming an actor. He shook his head every time he thought about it and had to constantly remind himself that his son was pursuing his dream. Well, it was actually his wife who was constantly reminding him.

And now his wanting to retire in San Diego, without anything to do other than walk the beaches or lay in the sun, was in jeopardy. It's not that he was torn about having the baby, it was just going to take some thought adjustment. Although there were times when the thought of another eighteen-plus years of raising a child terrified him. If he or she even looked at a stage, Alex would—

The alert immediately brought the captain out of his personal thoughts. Sitting up, Alex looked out of the windowed office toward the large screen occupying the center of the room. He grabbed the phone as soon as it rang.

"Buchanan."

"Aye, sir. We have a ballistic launch warning coming out of China."

Alex stared at the dots that appeared on an enhanced map of China's eastern coast. "Number and type. Trajectory analysis."

"Sir, twenty-seven mobile ballistic launches coming from eastern China. Initial trajectory matches China's previous DF-21 launches."

"Very well. The number and type of launches fits within the new rules of engagement. Notify the strike groups that they are weapons free on the ballistic missiles."

Twenty-five seconds after the first Chinese missile cleared its launch tube, word was sent to the carrier strike groups sailing in the western Pacific.

*   *   *   *   *   *

The bow of the cruiser crashed into a rising swell, sending sheets of water arcing to the sides. Droplets splashed against the windows of the bridge, blurring the view of the foredeck before being swept away by wipers. A sudden blare of an airhorn resounded across the rolling waves of the Pacific, warning of an upcoming event.

One of the doors of the forward vertical launch system snapped open. A tall column of whitish smoke shot upward, looking much like steam being released from an iron. Partially hidden within the cloud, a sharp-nosed projectile rose with a roar that evoked images of sheer power. Clearing the canister, the RIM-174 Standard Extended Range Active Missile trailed a long tail of flame as it accelerated to its max speed of Mach 3.5.

Shortly after the missile cleared the top of the ship, another VLS door popped open. A second alert, barely heard above the trembling roar of the first ERAM, signaled that a second anti-air missile was about to leave the protection of its canister.

The volleys of missiles fired by the cruisers of Task Force 70 raced to catch up with the Chinese ballistic threats thundering their way to higher altitudes. Normally reserved for the terminal phase of a ballistic attack, meaning targeting the nuclear or conventional warheads as they reentered the atmosphere, the RIM-174s were fired at the climbing DF-21s in the hope they could catch and destroy the weapons before they reached orbital altitudes.

As the cruiser escorts were sending volleys toward the heavens, the USS *Kidd* and the USS *Benfold* plowed through the heavy seas. The two Arleigh-Burke destroyers carried the sixty-kilowatt test laser systems. Inside the CIC, operators were keeping track of the multiple Chinese missile launches. Once each of the DF-21s cleared sixty-five thousand feet, or flew outside of the twelve-mile horizontal limit to China's airspace, the lasers would engage the rockets carrying the glide vehicles.

The missiles fired by the cruisers wouldn't reach the Chinese threats prior to them flying past the territorial boundaries. Traveling at the speed of light, the lasers had to wait until the specific engagement parameters handed down from the Pentagon were met.

When the first DF-21 sailed through the sixty-five-thousand-foot mark, the *Kidd's* targeting system locked onto the missile. With the laser stabilization component keeping the weapon steady, the narrow beam sped skyward. The laser hit the side of the ballistic missile and stayed locked into place. The narrow beam, smaller than one millimeter, rapidly heated the metal shroud of the missile.

Burning through the thin metal protecting the interior

components, the laser then punched through the fuel casings. The solid propellant ignited under the heat, with a thin gout of flame shooting through the tiny hole. The hole quickly widened from the force of the lit fuel, the flames shooting out of the side growing larger by the second. The fire was forceful enough to provide side thrust. Within seconds, the DF-21 started to turn. The guidance system, sensing the missile deviating from its pre-planned track, provided correctional thrust from the nozzle.

The flames shooting out from the side grew larger as the hole widened. With the thrust coming from the side and the subsequent corrections, the missile started a series of abrupt maneuvers. Three seconds after the burn-through, the ballistic missile started coming apart. Four seconds after, the DF-21's entire load of solid propellant detonated. The front end was shredded from the explosion and began a long fall toward the East China Sea.

A second Chinese missile, engaged by the *Benfold's* laser, began exhibiting the same destructive progression once the beam hit. The weapon's guidance system was unable to properly correct the deviations. The tail end of the missile passed through the same horizontal plane as the front, the propulsion temporarily driving the DF-21 toward the waiting seas below. The corrective measures proved too much, and the rocket tumbled, tearing itself apart in the process.

The effects from the more powerful laser system aboard the USS *Portland* were quicker in showing themselves. The solid propellant of a third Chinese missile just exploded when the beam penetrated the casings. The flashes from the missiles exploding were visible for miles around. Once their targets were confirmed kills, the lasers from the three warships locked onto more of the Chinese threats racing for the heavens.

The southern carrier strike groups were too far away to be able to add their firepower and could do nothing but anxiously watch the engagement as it played out on the data replicated from orbiting satellites.

Struggling to keep up with China's DF-21s attempting to break free of earth's gravitational pull, the RIM-174s started intercepting China's rockets. Proximity fuses triggered warhead detonations. Heated shrapnel cut through the outer skins like a hot knife melting through butter. Guidance systems were obliterated, sending several of the Chinese missiles on wayward courses, triggering their self-destruct mechanisms.

One DF-21 had its first stage completely separate, the rocket motor driving part of the missile through random maneuvers. Without propulsion, the top stages soared aloft, slowing down as earth's gravity became the dominant factor affecting the weapon. Arcing through the thin atmosphere, the missile tumbled down harmlessly.

With several of the warheads impacting the seas without being destroyed, the race for recovery began. However, China was unable to send its ships to the seas off the southern tip of Japan, thus leaving the United States time to pull the DF-ZF maneuverable glide vehicles from the depths.

One after another, the DF-21 delivery rockets were destroyed before they were able to deploy the maneuverable reentry vehicles (MaRVs). What Taiwan had started to systematically destroy on the ground, the United States was able to finish in the air.

*   *   *   *   *   *

Winslow had a difficult time emerging from his deep sleep, but the phone was relentless with its shrill ringing. Feeling like his head was filled with cotton, Frank forced one eye open. Turning on the bedside lamp sent a dagger of pain into his eye. Lifting the receiver, Frank was able to croak out his name. He didn't catch who was on the other end of the line, but it didn't matter much; he was pretty sure it was someone from the Pentagon.

"Sir, I'm calling to inform you that, as of fifteen minutes ago, the Navy has fired on and destroyed Chinese mobile ballistic rockets."

That sentence penetrated his foggy mind, the wisps of sleep vanishing like a vampire recoiling from sunlight. He acknowledged the call and immediately began dialing his circle of advisors. China's reaction was something he wanted to observe firsthand in case critical, timely decisions needed to be made.

"Well, here we go," he muttered, hanging up. Quickly throwing on some clothes, he hastened down to the situation room.

Traversing the corridors, he wondered how China might escalate the situation. The possibility, however remote, that humanity might not witness another sunset struck fear in his heart.

Chapter Three

Beijing, China
30 July, 2021

Hao impassively listened to the briefing. It was yet another round of disappointing news coming from his military staff. He was sure that the latest Taiwanese attack was at the behest of the United States. And he couldn't raise a hue and cry, as the rockets destroyed by the Americans were outside of China's territorial boundaries when they were engaged.

The Chinese leader felt like he was being ripped apart internally. His mind and heart were at war with one another, and this news only served to strengthen that disparity. His mind begged him to come up with a face-saving move that would allow for him to pull back his plans for the invasion of Taiwan. He could claim that the attacks on Taiwan were merely a response to the island's attacks on Chinese assets. After all, there was still some debate as to the sequence of events.

Hao could go even further and state that the invasion had been a Chinese exercise. Then he could accept the cease-fire offer and end this conflict with the United States. He could clearly see the steps to that path, one that would preserve China's remaining assets. Exports would again commence, and the inflow of cash could lift China's economy out of its freefall. The country could then restart its plan to become the number one global economy. And once it had rebuilt its military with modern equipment, it could again contemplate the inevitable reunification of Taiwan.

The problem was that Hao's name would forever be associated with failure. And that was at the core of where his heart-mind battle lay. Right alongside the feeling that he should abandon the efforts against Taiwan, was the persistent notion that the timing for an invasion was right. China held the advantage, and was still able to hold off the American carrier fleets with the threat from its arsenal...even if that inventory was being drained by the hour. Perhaps his internal war was merely a result of his wanting it all to be over.

The ships would sail soon, and they would put troops ashore. Once there, the Chinese equipment was better than those Taiwan could put into the field. As his internal battles usually went, his clear thoughts of needing to pull back for China's survival became muddled. On one hand, he suspected that his armed forces were being beaten by the Americans. On the other, he saw that China held nearly every advantage...well, except for the submarine fleet that had been utterly demolished. They needed to get enough troops ashore in Taiwan and then matters would be mostly solved. With this, Hao hoped that would also end his internal struggle.

The Chinese leader couldn't help but think that the timing was horrible. China had manufactured what it thought to be an unstoppable ship-killer. The persistent kinks in the new hypersonic missile program would eventually be resolved, and their attack on the American carrier fleets had shown that they could be effective, especially if deployed en masse. The high-speed weapons could break through ship-based defenses, but the Americans had managed to complete an effective laser weapon program in time to counter China's advantage. It seemed unfair somehow.

There was another worrying aspect that concerned Hao. He felt that he didn't know the ministers sitting around the table anymore. Before, he understood their motives and could play those strings like delicate fingers plucking a harp. Now, it seemed as if everything was moving farther away from him, that he, his influence, was becoming lost during this conflict. Maybe it was a result of his internal struggle. Or perhaps it was his sense that there were subtle power plays in operation that he was not a part of.

His defense minister had always played along the edges, but the lies coming from his desk were becoming a distraction that Hao couldn't afford to tolerate much longer. But a sudden change in leadership would send the wrong signal. It would communicate to the military, to the country, to the world, that things in China weren't going well. That wasn't something he could afford to let out at present. For now, he would continue to bank on future chits which he would play at the right time. Once secure footing on the island was assured and Chinese soldiers were marching toward Taipei, then he could contemplate making changes.

One thing he was sure of is that he couldn't wait until Taiwan was subdued. By that point, Zhou would have gathered too much power. He could make the claim that it was his expertise and strategy that had finally conquered the breakaway province. Hao couldn't afford that. His timing in the matter had to be perfect.

Listening to the numbers, which he had already read through and discarded, Hao knew that the next four days would be crucial. Ships sail, troops land, Taipei taken over, and Taiwan brought under China's control.

* * * * * *

White House, Washington D.C.
30 July, 2021

The coffee went down like a hot stone. Staring tiredly at the steaming surface in his mug, Frank wondered what in the world had possessed him to drink caffeine on an empty stomach. Shapes swirled in the mixed-in creamer and the president eyed the beverage as if the drink would reveal some kind of divination. Knowing that the burning in his gut was only going to get worse, Winslow ordered some sandwiches to be brought. That was one of the presidential privileges that he liked best, the ability to order any food he wanted day or night. He could be content if the only stresses to the job were selecting which kind of sandwich to have.

Frank's anxiety lessened when he learned that all of the Chinese missiles had been hit outside of China's lateral boundaries. Flying downrange, the DF-21s had headed out over the East China Sea and had been thirty to forty miles from China's coastline when they were shot down. Intelligence hadn't shown any movement or increased readiness from

China's nuclear forces. Winslow wondered if that would have been the case had the Chinese rockets been destroyed over the mainland, even if hit above the nebulous twelve-mile vertical limit. He guessed probably not. After all, that measure wasn't anything anyone wanted.

China would most likely have screamed bloody murder. The first signs of an escalation might have come in the form of China readying its rocket forces. Still, Frank had a feeling that Hao wouldn't be pleased by having his rockets carrying the hyper glide vehicles being shot down.

Staring at the screen, Frank pondered where matters would have rested if China had agreed to the offered cease-fire and negotiations. Could the two countries have agreed on anything? Considering how previous discussions on economic matters went, it was doubtful that they could have come to a resolution that suited either party. That would mean that the two countries sitting on either side of the Pacific would end up here again before long.

It was a debate that Frank often had with himself. Even if the conflict didn't happen now, China and the United States would eventually come to blows anyway. The difference would be that Hao would certainly have had a stronger military with more modern equipment. If the conflict had taken place down the road, the results could have been much different, with more American lives lost. No, as much as he hated it, the timing was the best they could hope for.

The problem floating around in Frank's mind was that China wouldn't necessarily stay defeated. They would be set back for a few years, but their economy would recover and they would begin to rebuild. Shit, even if America won this conflict and kept the seas open, then it was conceivable that they'd be back here in a few short years. That was all this conflict would gain, a few years of relative peace.

There was also the fact that losing would give China pause before contemplating another fight against the United States. And if the recognition of Taiwan had led to a treaty, then the Chinese leadership might very well have let go of the idea of taking over the island. The president very much doubted that would happen, but he could hope. Something good had to come out of this.

Frank knew he was getting ahead of himself. The United States hadn't won this thing yet. Not by a longshot. The threat facing Taiwan was huge, and China might yet pull off their invasion. There was another lingering worry, and that was that countries seldom took losses well. In the face of defeat, who knows what China would do? And for that matter, North Korea? The latter was, in all practical ways, a greater concern.

Sitting and waiting was one of the things the president hated most. Idle time did not do well for his mind. He too often went down paths of self-doubt. He wasn't the most liked president, and his approval ratings fluctuated. There were plentiful memes of his failures, the inflation, his handling of the pandemic, and a myriad of other issues. The one meme that kept circulating was one of him when his sleeve caught in a car door. He was nearly thrown off his feet as he hurriedly walked away only to be brought up short. He had to admit that it was fairly amusing to watch. What was it about people falling down that was so damn funny?

Some on social media even blamed him for the Chinese conflict. The armchair quarterbacks felt that he hadn't been tough enough in his dealings with China and that was the reason why they had become so overtly aggressive. Who knows, maybe they were right. When nothing materialized on the Chinese side after a couple of hours, Frank wearily pushed up from his chair. Another day beckoned.

* * * * * *

South China Sea
31 July, 2021

The USS *Seawolf* drifted silently just outside of China's twelve-mile limit. Some unknown analyst in one of the intelligence agencies had concluded that China would pull back their diesel-electric subs in order to recharge. Along with a couple of other boats, the *Seawolf* was to patrol the edges of China's boundaries and listen for the normally quiet submarines to start their diesel engines and snorkel. The plan was for the American subs to then follow and engage the fast-attack subs once they departed the twelve-mile limit.

Commander Jeff Dunmar thought that was a shit-ton easier said than done. Electric motors were usually very quiet if the sub remained slow and didn't cavitate their prop. If they were able to locate one snorkeling, then following them once they finished would be a tricky proposition. When the Chinese sortied their boats previously, it had been easier, as they had been gunning it through the seas at high speed.

The geniuses back at Pearl thought that any remaining Chinese subs would be used to flank the invasion fleet...or invasion fleets. That meant they wouldn't have very far to travel, which then meant that they wouldn't have to sail at top speed. Jeff sometimes wondered if the think-tanks even knew what a sub looked like, let alone how they operated. Following a quiet nuke boat was easier in some regards. They left residual heat from the required cooling, which the sensors could track. There were other tricks sub captains used to remain glued to an enemy boat, but electric motors could be a hassle to follow.

The one thing on Jeff's side was that the *Seawolf* was arguably the quietest sub in the world. The class was designed toward the end of the Cold War to operate both in high threat areas and hunting in deep-ocean environments. However, with the collapse of the Soviet Union, the cost of each sub was deemed too prohibitive for the program to continue. The Virginia-class boats were nearly as quiet, but smaller and carried fewer weapons. The idea was that the Virginia subs were more flexible in the missions they could accomplish, whereas the Seawolf class was primarily designed as a deep ocean hunter.

"I have one," one of the sonarmen abruptly stated. "Sorry, shit, I mean, Conn, Sonar. I have a contact, bearing two niner zero, range fifteen thousand yards. Aspect ratio and range unchanging."

Inwardly chuckling, Commander Dunmar acknowledged the report. Remembering his awkward first days as an Ensign, he understood what it was like to be a tongue-tied youth. This was the young man's first posting following his graduation from training. Luckily, he was working alongside a veteran in the realm of sonars.

"I think it's a Chinese Kilo, sir. Labeling as contact Delta One."

"You *think* it's a Kilo?" Dunmar inquired. "Or you *know* it's a Kilo?"

"Sorry, sir. It is definitely a snorkeling Kilo," the veteran cut in. "Labeling Delta One."

Jeff then heard the whispers as the vet instructed the newbie, probably about positive identification versus speculation. Taking the information and the updates, Jeff knew that the Kilo, or Delta One, was on a parallel course and speed.

"Very well, thank you. XO, prepare a contact report," Jeff ordered.

Shortly afterward, a device broke through the surface. Bobbing in the swells, it waited until the preset delay passed before sending its flash message. More reports filtered into COMSUBPAC from sightings up and down China's coastline.

* * * * * *

Indo-Pacific Command Headquarters, Hawaii
31 July, 2021

With the door held by his driver, Admiral Nick Ramsey stepped out. The transition from the air-conditioned interior into the heat of the day was abrupt. Waves of heat rose from the baking sidewalk to brush past the admiral's cheeks. He placed his white cap with embroidered bill firmly atop his head, covering his salt and pepper regulation haircut.

He took a moment to look out over the vast naval harbor and surrounding complexes. Several destroyers were secured to their berths, waiting for the call that would take them to sea. The submarine pens and docking facilities were mostly empty, all but two of the assigned fast-attack boats were either in the Far East or on their way.

The heat of the day was only partially responsible for the warmth Ramsey was feeling. The folders securely shut in the briefcase he carried in one hand were the reason for the rest of his anxiety. The conflict with China appeared to be going well, from his perspective. Although there had been losses, and more than he would have thought or that wargames had demonstrated, intel had China losing as much as ninety percent of their underwater fleet. That had been another surprise, that China would lose so many of their fast-attack boats so quickly.

The papers Admiral Ramsey carried in his case had the potential to change that even more, perhaps completely erasing the Chinese underwater threat. If that was accomplished, and considering the expenditure of missiles that China was throwing at Taiwan, then that would leave only one threat facing the carrier strike groups: China's large bomber fleet and the missiles they could send at the carriers. But that aspect of operations would be someone else's responsibility. As far as Nick was concerned, his job had already been completed...or nearly so. What was contained in his briefcase could bring his phase of operations to completion.

His eyes drifted over the *Arizona* monument. The homage to the Pearl Harbor attack never really held the same feeling of nationalism for him that others felt viewing the memorial. Now, when he saw one of his vessels transiting the harbor, either returning from a patrol or heading out for a lengthy voyage, it stirred an emotional response. Submarine duty wasn't an easy task, and he was proud of all who stepped onto the gangplank to vanish inside the steel tubes.

Almost as if in a reverie, Ramsey then turned toward the headquarters building that housed some of the Indo-Pacific Command staff. He stared at the glass entryway doors, the windows reflecting the sun's rays. Inside of those walls, he was about to enter into a different kind of conflict. The subs had done well, so his career was secure, but he was about to stick his neck out and risk everything. He thought about just sliding back into the comfort of his air-conditioned sedan and forget about his plan. The lure of the comfortable back seat beckoned, as did retaining his career on a positive track.

"Sir?" his driver asked, concerned about the admiral's behavior.

"I'm fine, thanks. I'm just taking in one last look before my execution."

The driver chuckled.

"If you hear a commotion and see me hanging by a yardarm, you might want to make yourself scarce. They'll be looking for co-conspirators," Ramsey added.

"Aye, sir. If you need a distraction, I can crash right through those pretty doors of theirs," the driver stated.

"I appreciate the offer, but it wouldn't be the door's fault. However, keep the car running in case I come out in a hurry."

"Will do, sir."

A trickle of sweat ran down his cheek. Adjusting his hat and double-checking his briefcase, the admiral sighed deeply.

"Okay, I'm going in."

Navigating the air-conditioned hallways, Ramsey found himself in Admiral Brickline's office. The darkly colored double doors with the embossed brass plaque inscribed with 'Indo-Pacific Commander' was intimidating. Beyond those portals lay the top of the food chain for naval operations in the Pacific theater. Not one for being intimidated, and having graced the confines of the office many times, Nick nonetheless felt nervous on this visit.

For the hundredth time today, maybe even since leaving the car, Ramsey thought about how Admiral Brickline might take what he was about to suggest. The two had gone through the academy together, but had followed different routes upon leaving. Nick was about as far as his career path was going to take him. Special Ops and submarines were both surefire ways to cut careers short. Try as he might, Ramsey couldn't gauge the reaction he might receive. But that wasn't going to stop him from expressing his thoughts.

The phone on the desk of Admiral Brickline's adjutant

buzzed.

"Sir, he'll see you now," the adjutant stated, replacing the receiver.

"Nick, what brings you over this way? Your call sounded urgent," Admiral Brickline said upon the COMSUBPACs entry.

"Sir, I have something you might want to read," Ramsey replied.

"Of course. Have a seat. Would you like some coffee?" Brickline offered.

"No, thank you, sir. I've had my limit for the day."

"Very well. What do you have for me?"

Ramsey sat and unlocked his briefcase, extracting a folder. From within, he pulled out six sheets of paper and handed them over to the Indo-Pacific Commander. Admiral Brickline took the proffered sheets and laid them out on his desk. He quickly perused the papers and leaned back. Lost in thought for a minute, Admiral Brickline then leaned forward.

"Nick, I think I know why you're here, and what you are about to ask. So, let me run this through from beginning to end. Stop me if I get any part of it wrong.

"What I have in front of me are sighting reports of Chinese submarines. That's not something that would normally cross my desk unless it was a vital piece of intel. Considering that I'm not reading reports detailing enemy losses, I assume these Chinese subs are still afloat. Taken a step further then, I can also presume that the coordinates listed on the reports are not in a favorable position. That tells me, without having to look at a map, that these submarines are located inside of China's territorial boundaries."

Brickline paused, staring at his former classmate. "How am I doing so far?"

"Spot on, sir," Ramsey responded.

Brickline nodded. "Right. So, the fact that you're here in person means that you want to do something that may not be strictly in line with our current rules of engagement."

The INDOPAC commander held up a hand, forestalling Ramsey's comment. "Before you answer, Nick, give me the quick and dirty about these sightings."

Ramsey shook his head to clear what he had been about to say. "Well, sir. Our boats positioned up and down the Chinese coastline came across these six enemy subs snorkeling. Our intel had them retreating back to their territories prior to recharging. It also puts them in a perfect position to shield the Chinese invasion fleets when they sail. There are three to the north and three to the south. They could very well represent the last vestiges of Chinese submarine power, and we could eliminate them in one stroke. That would open the way for phase two of operations: allowing the carriers to move closer to Taiwan. Hell, sir, that might even completely scare China away from their invasion plans."

Admiral Ramsey handed over another sheet which mapped out the Chinese sub locations, along with those of the United States. Brickline studied the map and then leaned forward again.

"Nick, I'm going to stop you right here, before you say anything condemning...something that could land us both in the brig. You know that I can't okay an order that goes against the ROE.

"But for sake of conversation, let's take a walk down the path you're contemplating. Let's say, hypothetically, that those Chinese subs are sunk in their current locations. Someone, somewhere, knows where those boats are and might become suspicious if they were to suddenly lose contact. The bottom line is that they will eventually be found. I mean, think about it. What would we do if six LA-class boats suddenly went missing off the western seaboard?

"But, back to our discussion. Once the subs were found, then studies would be conducted and would conclude that they were hit inside Chinese territory. Then begins the process of tracking backward. It wouldn't just be an international mess, but a personal one for you, as you will have directly acted against the rules put in place. You could possibly be brought up on charges and court-martialed. Is that something you want to face down the road? Is that something you want for your family?

"Think, Nick. This war will end, and sooner rather than later. While sinking six Chinese subs will influence the current operations, it may not matter in the long run. You've done an outstanding job and solidified your career, and I think this is best kept between us. Now, I don't want to hear anything else on the matter. As it stands, we met to discuss the contact sightings and what they might mean for our continuing strategy. That's what I'll tell anyone who asks."

Nick sat in the comfortable leather chair, thinking over what his boss had said. It was true that sinking six Chinese subs could affect the upcoming invasion, and the conflict in general. But, in the long run, would it be worth sacrificing his career? Would it be worth putting his family through hell, should he be held responsible for giving an unlawful order?

His thoughts turned to his job. Yes, he had to uphold the rules put in place, and he had to assume they were there for a reason. In this case, it was to avoid an escalation that could ultimately lead to a nuclear exchange. However, in his view, the odds that this maneuver would lead to all-out war were balanced in favor of the immediate benefit the strike would make. It was likely that the Chinese subs in question wouldn't be found until after the hostilities had concluded; by then, any sort of retribution would be starting from political and economic scratch. Hitting the Chinese submarines now would make the current war effort easier, possibly saving lives in the now.

It stung Nick that his warriors were kept on a political leash. It was absolutely vital that the carrier strike groups be able to get within range and be allowed to conduct operations unmolested. There wouldn't come a better opportunity to whittle down the Chinese submarine fleet a little more...hell, *a lot* more. Perhaps, as he mentioned, this one strike might complete the annihilation of China's fast attack boats.

But there were two problems. One, the big one, if the six enemy subs were found destroyed before the conflict was resolved, then it would certainly escalate matters with China. In order to stave that off, he would be offered up as a sacrifice…and rightfully so. The other problem was his family. What would his wife of nearly eighteen years think? His children? Would they understand or cast him out as a traitor?

"I have a hypothetical question. If one were to issue an SCI (Sensitive Compartmented Information) order, what would be the chances that anyone would look at it?" Ramsey inquired.

"Well, I certainly wouldn't, and I seriously doubt anyone else would in the normal course of their duties. Unless, of course, six Chinese submarines were found to be attacked inside of territorial boundaries. Then, I would assume that the matter would be investigated…at the highest levels," Brickline answered.

By "highest levels," Nick knew that he meant people with appropriate clearances would be able to access anything connected with the sinkings.

Admiral Ramsey rose to the creak of leather. "Thank you for your time, sir."

Brickline handed back the sighting reports and extended his hand. "Anytime, Nick. And again, damn fine job out there."

* * * * * *

South China Sea
31 July, 2021

"Sir, a coded message has come through," communications informed Commander Dunmar.

"Copy that. XO, you have the conn."

"Aye, sir."

The *Seawolf* commander retrieved the message and headed down the narrow passageways to his small cabin. There, he decoded the message. Once he read through the order, he had to decode it again just to make sure. He sat on his bed, pondering the ramifications. For a minute or longer, he stared at the sheet of paper in his hand without really seeing it.

He had been placed in some precarious situations throughout his career, but nothing like where the few words printed on the current sheet of paper were about to send him. He had hoped to never be put in this kind of situation and came closer to understanding commanders in times past when they were asked — no — ordered, to conduct illegal operations. Now, Dunmar truly understood that there were special operation missions that bordered on some very gray areas.

There was kind of a tacit, worldwide understanding that special operations were conducted, and that many of the missions involved breaking laws; some drew ramifications, others did not. But this was different. Here he was being asked...ordered...to go against the set rules of engagement in the course of normal operations.

The commander was having a difficult time. It had been ingrained since day one that he was to obey the orders of his superiors. As a United States officer, it was also impressed upon him that he was free to disobey an *illegal* order. Not only was he free to, but it was his duty. He couldn't say in words just how much he disliked being put in the position of refusing to follow an order or be guilty of breaking a law.

He looked again at the secret order. It came directly from Admiral Nick Ramsey, the COMSUBPAC commander. It didn't get any higher in the Pacific for any submariner. It was very specific in that he was to engage and destroy the Chinese Kilo snorkeling just a few miles away...inside Chinese territory. Dunmar scrutinized the coordinates, verifying that there hadn't been a mistake. Maybe someone along the message chain had misreported his sighting. But no, there it was, clear as day. The coordinates were well inside Chinese territory.

Now, he had carried SEAL teams inside foreign territories before. He had conducted operations to tap into the cross-ocean fiber lines. So, infiltrating enemy territory wasn't something new for Jeff. But again, this was different and had the potential for sweeping him up in the morass that could occur. His heart so badly wanted to sink that, Kilo. Sinking the Chinese submarine, regardless of their positioning, would greatly enhance America's chances of winning this conflict with China. It might save American lives. How terrible would it be if he let the Kilo go and the Chinese captain went on to sink a carrier?

But his mind was screaming that he must disobey what he considered to be an illegal order. What if it was found that he had attacked a Chinese sub outside of the rules of engagement? Career aside, would he spend the rest of his life locked up?

Jeff reached up to the intercom. "XO to the captain's room."

Before long, he heard footsteps walking the corridor outside of his room.

"Enter," Jeff said upon hearing the light knock.

For the next ten minutes, the two of them studied the order and discussed the ramifications. Jeff even had his XO decode the order from scratch to make sure he hadn't made a mistake. For some reason, Dunmar wasn't surprised that his XO was in favor of executing the order. Hell, he might have recommended the same thing when he was an executive officer. The XO's response certainly didn't help to resolve Jeff's internal struggle.

If his XO had stated that it was an illegal order and should be refused, then Jeff might have jumped on that bandwagon. The internal war would be over. The *Seawolf* would have followed the Chinese boat for as long as it could, attacking it when it left the twelve-mile boundary...if they were still able to track it.

Following their discussion, the XO was silent as his captain further processed the situation. Reaching a decision, Jeff stood abruptly—not an easy maneuver in the tiny stateroom. The executive officer didn't need to ask what the commander intended; he could tell by his expression. Together, the two returned to the conn.

"Sonar, Conn. Do you still have a good sounding on Delta One?" Dunmar asked.

"Aye, sir."

"XO, make sure the fire control system has the latest information."

"Aye, sir. FCS is updated."

"Ready tubes one and two," Dunmar commanded.

With that sequence of orders, the crew looked up from their stations, especially the navigator. Everyone was aware of the Chinese boat's location, and what it would mean to commence an attack.

"I have received orders to attack the Chinese Kilo, labeled as Delta One. It's my intention to carry out those orders," Commander Dunmar stated.

"Has the ROE changed?" the navigator inquired.

Jeff locked eyes with his nav without replying.

The navigator nodded, understanding that his answer was in the non-reply. "Very well, sir."

Jeff wanted to say that he would take responsibility for any fallout that might arise, but felt that might either alienate his crew or divide them. No submariner talked about their missions as they had all been labeled as top secret, so he wasn't worried that someone would go off and run their mouth. SCI top secret orders were given that classification for a reason, and so those orders could become public knowledge wasn't one of them.

With the noise the Kilo was making, Dunmar knew he could sneak closer, enhancing his odds of achieving a kill. But, with Delta One snorkeling, it was doubtful that the Chinese sensors would be able to hear a torpedo passively homing in. They certainly wouldn't be expecting one. Whatever the case, Jeff wasn't going to make his situation worse by entering China's boundary for this mission. Plus, that would put them in shallower water, where he could be located via a MAD contact from one of China's few ASW remaining aircraft.

"Fire One," Commander Dunmar ordered.

"One away and tracking," his XO responded.

"Fire Two."

"Two away and tracking."

*   *   *   *   *   *

Inside the Chinese Kilo, Captain Huang had no idea that

two lethal American torpedoes were closing in on his boat. His eyes were focused on the charge meter, mentally willing the battery percentages to increase. Snorkeling was a dangerous time for any diesel-electric sub. Even though he and his crew were inside his country's territory, that didn't reduce the tension gripping his gut. He would be happy when the operation was successfully completed.

Since sinking the American sub nearly two weeks ago, his patrol area had been silent. That could be good or bad news, but he was still alive, his sub still afloat, and his crew confident. The next mission, that of running interference for the invasion fleet coming out of Zhanjiang, promised to be more intense. After all, the Americans weren't about to just let China waltz into Taiwan without a fight.

Within minutes after the SCI order was sent from Pearl Harbor, six Chinese submarines were on their way to the bottom of the South China Sea.

*   *   *   *   *   *

Sea of Japan
31 July, 2021

Leading the USS *Ohio* out of the Sea of Japan, the USS *Topeka* crept through the narrow straits separating Japan's west coast from South Korea. Sonarmen kept their headphones pressed tight against their ears lest they miss the faint indication that an enemy submarine was loitering in the area.

The surface was noisy with ships ferrying military supplies across the channel, docking in the South Korean ports of Ulsan and Busan. Commander Avelar was nervous as the busy shipping lanes were likely to attract North Korean and Chinese submarines. As his brief encounter with the North Korean sub had shown, the undersea theater didn't allow for mistakes or for a moment's relaxation.

The *Topeka's* proposed route was to swing wide of the island chain to the southwest of Japan and then turn east, entering the Philippine Sea. From there, it was to be a fairly straight shot to the rendezvous with the tender. The journey wasn't a cakewalk by any stretch as there were numerous reports of Chinese attack subs in the Philippine Sea. The North Korean kill had increased Avelar's confidence, but that boost was wearing thin as he contemplated just how crowded the depths were.

"Conn, sonar. I have something. It sounded like a single, active ping, bearing two seven zero. I wasn't able to get a range but...wait," the sonarman said, staring at the display.

The crew member pressed the headset to his head, his face scrunched in concentration.

"I had a very definitive screw sound from the same bearing. It was there and now it's gone. It could be coming from the second, or perhaps even the third convergence zone. But during the brief moment that I had it, it was clearly a Shang-class nuke boat."

Avelar's attention piqued, as that was China's best nuclear fast attack sub, and supposedly the equivalent of the LA-class with regards to noise. The edge the *Topeka* held was in its sensors and training.

Stepping over to the navigator's station, the commander looked at the map. The *Topeka's* current position was labeled, and the commander traced a finger along the bearing. The navigator drew a faint line along the reported bearing. He marked the approximate ends of the convergence zones based on the conditions. Avelar stared at the map. The end of the second convergence zone ended just south of Fukue Island.

The *Topeka's* captain thought it was a little strange for a sub to be there instead of further north where most of the shipping was sailing. Perhaps they were transitioning to another location, perhaps even heading in the *Topeka's* direction. That thought sent a chill up Avelar's spine.

"Sonar, Conn...anything further?" Avelar asked.

"No, sir...nothing."

"Left standard rudder, make your new heading one zero zero. Slow to five knots. Inform the *Ohio*," Avelar ordered.

"Aye, sir. Left to one zero zero, slowing to five knots,"

the XO mimicked.

If the Chinese sub was heading toward the narrow passage, and thus toward the *Topeka*, it was Avelar's intention to lie in wait for the enemy nuclear boat. If the Chinese vessel was heading elsewhere, well, it would be nigh impossible for the *Topeka* to catch up without making some noise.

In the back of the commander's mind was the single echo. What had the Chinese boat found that warranted a ping like that? Was there more that sonar couldn't pick up due to the possibility of being a convergence zone or two away? The thought just wouldn't leave. It would take something truly dire for Avelar to issue an active ping so close to enemy shores. Maybe the Chinese sub had found a quarry and couldn't get clear data for the fire control system. If that was the case, then sonar should be hearing an explosion within the next couple of minutes.

Those minutes passed, and the next minute, and the next. All ears were focused on word from sonar, but the station remained silent.

"Okay, let's send a contact message. It might be nothing, but maybe there are airborne assets that can assist."

* * * * * *

"Pilot, CIC," the intercom came alive.

"Go ahead, sir," Lieutenant Lopez responded.

"There's a contact report that might prove interesting," Commander Martin said. "Come right heading three three zero."

"Three three zero," Carlos repeated.

"There are two locations given, one a hundred miles away, the second a hundred and thirty."

Carlos rolled out of the shallow bank, the P-8 now heading to the northwest. Looking through the windscreen, he saw the shores of southwest Japan, along with the myriad of islands dotting the sea to the south.

"That's pretty close to Japan. How sound is the contact?"

Lopez inquired.

"It's just one that popped up. The *Topeka* is supposed to be in the area, a bit further to the northwest. They think they heard something," Martin answered. "The report says a single ping was heard coming from a Chinese Shang-class boat."

It was all the same for Carlos. They had been flying up and down the giant drop-off that separated the East China Sea from the Philippine Sea, hoping to catch a returning Chinese submarine. A string of islands from southern Japan arced around to Taiwan, marking the edge of the deep trench.

Carlos thought if they'd had a drone for this patrol, the commander in the back could have sent it to investigate what would probably turn out to be some anomaly. But he was paid regardless of which portion of the globe he flew over. He hoped to find another enemy sub to add to his commendations; every Chinese boat that was sunk meant another step closer to his going home. He was ready for a break in the relentless flying schedule.

Ten minutes later, the P-8 arrived over the first position. None of the sensors onboard detected anything unusual. Flying a box pattern, sonar buoys fell into the water. The pattern surrounded the contact location, expanded by the amount of time since the contact report. Nothing showed up on the screens or was heard coming from any of the buoys. A second pass, this one swinging wider, resulted in the same.

"Okay, let's head along a course of three three zero. We'll try the next possibility," Martin ordered.

Five minutes passed. Buoys were repeatedly dropped to no avail. The depths were quiet. If there was a sub in the area, it was being successfully elusive. Everyone aboard the P-8 thought that it was too bad that they didn't warrant a drone for this mission. In the shallow waters close to Japan, they might have been able to pick up a MAD contact. The hyper-perceptive sensors that were part of the sub hunter should be able to find a sub without the MAD gear. Still, it would have been nice to have it along.

"Carlos, I don't see or hear anything here. You don't

happen to see a Chinese submarine sailing along topside, by chance?" Martin asked jokingly.

Lopez stretched upward in his harness, looking over the dash; they did surface occasionally, didn't they? There was only the sun glinting off the surface and a narrow line of white where surf crashed into the rocky Japanese shores. A few thin wakes marred the sea's surface from ships and larger fishing vessels plying the waterways, but none of the wakes ended in the familiar outline of a submarine.

"I wish it were that easy," Carlos remarked.

The lieutenant made another scan of the surface. "Nope, nothing to be seen, sir."

Subsequent buoy drops didn't reveal anything that would answer the question of what had created the anomalous ping heard by the *Topeka*. The P-8 flew further east and then backtracked to the west with nothing to indicate that a Chinese nuclear fast attack sub was south of Japan.

Commander Martin worried that the presence of an enemy sub so close to Japanese shores might mean that China was about to escalate the conflict. If the submarine was one that China had upgraded with vertical launch systems, then they could very well fire cruise missiles into American bases with little-to-no warning. That thought made the commander keep the P-8 searching for far longer than they normally would have. Finally, they returned to Kadena at the end of their patrol without finding any sign of the enemy contact.

"Well, Lieutenant, next time," Commander Martin remarked upon exiting the aircraft. "I hope our luck hasn't run dry."

Carlos smiled at the commander and nodded absently. He wasn't sure what to think or feel about the missed opportunity, but that could be the result of his constant state of fatigue. Regardless, he felt a little conflicted. He was a touch disappointed they didn't find anything, but he also felt relieved. There was no way they could have a kill on every patrol, and their successes had added stress levels of their own. It was a hard to live up to that standard each and every time, and it caused anxiety, especially when that success rate became expected. Even though he'd relished locating and sinking the subs they had, he felt a lot lighter walking into the ops room. It was good to be back to normal and not elevated on some kill pedestal.

* * * * * *

A few miles south of the Japanese coast, *Changzhen 14* slid through the depths. Captain Hu Tengyang felt nervous about operating in such shallow water, but it was necessary. China had conducted detailed mapping of the seafloor in the South and East China Seas. In that endeavor, they had discovered a narrow cut in the seabed that ran nearly the width of Japan. It provided a relatively safe path for Chinese submarines transitioning from the East China Sea to the Philippine Sea and vice versa. The problem was that the entrance on both sides had to be precisely entered. Once in the ravine, echo sounding the bottom to navigate couldn't be heard from the sides. Only someone positioned directly above the cut would be able to hear the periodic active pings. As far as China knew, the West wasn't aware that the passage existed.

"Sir, we're near the entrance," *Changzhen 14's* navigator stated.

Captain Hu nodded his acknowledgement.

The Chinese nuclear fast attack boat was level at three hundred feet. The route was a descending one that emptied out near the massive drop-off that marked the boundary of the Philippine Sea. Hu had been patrolling east of Shanghai when new orders had arrived. *Changzhen 14* was to sail east, entering the Philippine Sea and then proceeding northeast to the Pacific Ocean. There they were to locate and destroy the American carriers that were sailing east of Japan.

Hu understood that the assignment was going to be difficult, and most likely fatal. But his country needed him to eliminate one of the greatest threats to China's efforts to break free of the stranglehold placed on his nation by the Americans.

He also knew that the task wasn't impossible. It wasn't that long ago that a Chinese submarine had surfaced three and a half miles from one of the vaunted American carriers, demonstrating that it could be done. Had that been a real attack, the entire strike group would likely have been sunk...at least it had that potential. From the reactions, the Americans had no clue that the Chinese vessel was even there.

"Sir...the entrance," the navigator reminded Hu.

"Yes, yes. Send a single ping," Hu commanded.

The sounding detailed the sub's precise location, verifying that the inertial navigation system was reading reliably.

"We're in the correct position," the navigator said.

"Increase speed to fifteen knots."

Chapter Four

Xiamen Port, China
31 July, 2021

The waters of the port shimmered from the brightness that lit up the long line of concrete berths. Cranes that had busily loaded the nestled ships were drawn back, the military vehicles that had flooded the docks with their throaty roars were now silently resting on interior decks. The march of boots from laden soldiers had ceased their reverberations. Even the trucks transporting containers to the few cargo ships sharing the dock space were nowhere to be seen or heard.

The momentary quiet that followed the squeal of treads from the last armored vehicle, the last tramp of boots on the gangway, seemed as if the entire line of ships was holding its breath. That tense silence was broken by voiced shouts. Workers gathered near stanchions, worn and calloused hands gripping thick ropes. Working in conjunction with sailors standing by the rails, lines were lifted over their holds and tossed into the water lapping against the docks. Dripping water, those same ropes were then lifted and secured aboard.

Numerous tugs assisted the floating tons of steel, easing the ships away from their berths. Transmissions engaged the single propellors, churning the water aft of each vessel. The bows of the ships swung around, moving past the warehouses situated on the opposite bank, their yards and buildings lit by pole-mounted lights.

Closer to the port entrance, the rattle of heavy chains drifted across the bay as loaded ships weighed anchor. Soldiers and armored vehicles were just beginning to get underway, their next stop, the Penghu Islands. They were the vanguard, the lead in a tremendous undertaking. The starting motions seemed sluggish, but it was the beginning of a giant momentum meant to swamp Taiwan under its might.

Further offshore, four Jiangkai II-class frigates patrolled. Their active sonar pings rang through the shallow waters, searching for American submarines. The RORO ships pointed east. Increasing their speed once they cleared the ports, the roll-on/roll-off ships intended to race across the intervening miles.

* * * * * *

Penghu Islands, Taiwan
1 August, 2021

Submerged, the fast attack submarine's black hull was darkly silhouetted against the waters of the Taiwan Strait. Pushing through the open hatch that separated the flooded chamber from the wilderness that was the open sea, Sergeant Hou Jianzhi was only too happy to get clear of the cramped quarters.

It seemed as if human occupancy had been a design afterthought. Space was a commodity aboard a submarine, but add six extra bodies and it became as cramped as the front rows at a rave. It wasn't just the lack of room that made Hou antsy, it was being aboard in the first place. He didn't like submarines during training maneuvers; he positively loathed being aboard in an active war zone.

In Hou's opinion, the stealth that submarines offered was offset by the fact that the steel tubes could just as easily become a tomb, and he would be helpless to affect the outcome...the feeling of being completely out of control. He was more comfortable ashore, even behind enemy lines, than he would ever be underwater as he was transported to an insertion point.

Emerging fully from the hatch, he slowly made his way to an equipment locker that had been attached to the spine of the nuclear fast attack boat. Behind, five other members of his team appeared one by one as if the submarine were giving birth. Swinging open the heavy door, made easier by being submerged, Hou released the latches holding the individual underwater delivery vehicle in place. Attaching a bag of equipment, the sergeant waited for the rest of his team to secure their gear.

Hou double-checked that the inertial navigation system

was reading correctly. With a nod from each of his team members, Hou pushed off from the sub's deck, turning to the heading that would take him and the others ashore. As the single propeller-driven open vehicle traveled away at slow speed, the dark mass that was the submarine quickly vanished from view. Below the swells rolling under the glow of a half waning moon, the six members of the Sea Dragon Commandos motored slowly toward the westernmost island of the Penghu.

Thirty minutes after shoving off from the submerged form of the sub, Hou brought his craft to a stop. His INS system showed him a mile from his primary target. The others of his team kept their positions via their personal locators. The devices had a limited range and didn't work very well in deeper waters, thus their decision to travel relatively close to the surface.

Hou angled his craft up and soon surfaced. He bobbed up and down in the swells as he attempted to gauge his precise location. Just ahead to his right, a bright beam stabbed into the night from Shomon Island. About six miles further south, another bright light flashed at intervals. On the extreme southern tip of the island, the Yuwengdao Lighthouse flashed its warnings to those sailing the seas. The rest of the silhouetted land was dark, the Taiwanese government ordering the lights off with the coming of night.

Glittering across the surface of the strait, the moon's rays highlighted the land features in the distance. Of importance, Hou saw the long span of the Kuahai Bridge, also known as the Penghu Great Bridge. That was his target. He wasn't there to destroy the thick concrete structure, but rather to prevent its destruction. No lights shone from the long bridge connecting two islands that were part of the horseshoe-shaped chain.

Other teams were responsible for the two additional bridges connecting the other islands. Hou glanced at his watch. He was on time. That mattered for a variety of reasons, one being that it was almost high tide, which was needed to make his job a little easier. The tides could be tricky in the area when the tidal forces were at their strongest. Plus, if he didn't make it before the tide started going out, then that would be just one more battle he'd have to fight.

The sergeant watched the bridge for another minute to see if there was traffic at this time of night. Satellite footage indicated that the bridge was seldom traveled by the locals; it was used mainly by tourists, but that wasn't something he had to worry about while the conflict raged. More worrisome was the fact that armed patrols randomly crossed, day or night. Diving back under the water, Hou recommenced his trek toward shore.

Fifteen minutes later, he surfaced again. This time he was under one of the short spans, where even the light of the moon couldn't reach. Most of the bridge was just a concrete abutment, built much like a dam. Only the center sections allowed passage of the sea and it was under one of those that the sergeant had surfaced.

Hou motored over to one of the concrete pillars, anchoring his vehicle. Pulling out a flashlight, he shined a red-lensed beam upward. Just as had been briefed, shaped charges could be seen nestled in between steel girders. Wires ran from the charges and around the concrete pillar, connecting with explosives on the next span.

The special forces sergeant wondered if the engineer outfit responsible for blowing up the bridge was located on the north bank, the south, or both. The team had rehearsed taking out both sides after disarming the explosives. That was deemed the most prudent choice, but it also split his six-person team in half. Six could defend a position a lot longer than three. Hopefully, they wouldn't have to hold out for very long before reinforcing units linked up.

With the tide high, Hou wasn't too far from where the charges lay. Setting up an anchor point, much like a rock climber, he tied his craft. Pulling his bag of equipment and tying it off as well, the sergeant let the single person delivery vehicle sink below the rolling swells. After withdrawing the tools he'd need, he let the bag sink to the length of its attached rope.

Finding a crack in the concrete pillar, he wedged a carabiner into it. He could quietly drill into the surface, but even quiet drills tended to echo much louder across water.

Slinging a loop of rope in the device, Hou placed a foot into the formed stirrup and stepped up. Another carabiner found its way into another crack. Slowly, the sergeant worked his way up the pillar. Three of his team were working on the southernmost sections, while the other two of his divided team were in adjacent areas.

As he was reaching for the first of the wires attached to the charges, Hou's heart froze as a flash of light caught his attention. He looked out both ends of his enclosure to see that intense beams were playing across the water. By tracing the angles back, it appeared as if the two spotlights were coming from the northern end of the bridge. And the angles were slowly changing, which meant that the source of the lights was either handheld or coming from one or two vehicles.

The sergeant released the breath he had been subconsciously holding. There was no way for the patrol to get down to his position from the bridge. Well, unless they jumped into the sea, which he supposed was within the realm of possibility, but highly unlikely. As long as he and the team didn't make any noise, the patrol should pass without discovering them.

"Northern patrol, topside, moving south," Hou whispered into his mic.

He heard five separate clicks acknowledging the call. With his feet in the stirrups, Hou waited for the patrol to pass. The beams moved back and forth, searching. The sergeant wondered if the Taiwanese soldiers had seen something. Maybe Hou and his team had been painted on radar when they surfaced a mile out. He doubted that, as he would have been met by more than a patrol. He needed to relax. He and his team were good at what they did, even if they didn't have the experience of the Americans.

A minute later, Hou heard an engine above the slap of waves against the pillar. The beams played out over the sea, never resting in one place for long. The patrol was vigilant in its pursuit of China's infiltrators, but they were too late. Hou and his team were already here. Plus, the searchlights were only good against surface craft. Not one to rebuff a gift, he was thankful.

A throatier engine rose above that of the vehicle slowly passing overhead. Hou immediately looked into the central harbor area between the ring of islands. The moon's glow caught the churned wake of a boat speeding over the surface. He could see the arc of the bow wave as the fast boat made a wide turn and started heading directly toward the bridge.

"Water patrol inbound. Into the water," Hou radioed.

Still gripping tools he'd need, he slipped out of his rope footholds. It was a short drop to the water, but with the sight of the boat carving through the swells in his vision, it seemed to take forever. Hou hit feet first, his toes pointed downward to minimize his splash. He hit like a pin, letting his momentum carry him as deep as possible.

Light stabbed overhead, and carried underwater. It dimmed slightly as each swell passed, the wavery searchlight panning over where he had just dropped. Staying underwater, Hou swam toward the far side of the pillar. Once on the ocean side, in the shadow of the support cast by the searchlight, the sergeant surfaced.

Holding on to the rough sides and bobbing in the swells, he moved to stay in the dark as the bright beam panned back and forth under the span. Glancing to the side, he saw the dark outlines of a team member holding on to an adjacent column. Hou had a sidearm strapped to his dry suit, but any real firepower was still crammed into his equipment bag, a move he was deeply regretting now.

If he was discovered, or any of the team, a firefight would erupt. Being in the water with only a handgun, he was woefully lacking in the ability to fight. The arsenal on the boat, and the weapons carried by the soldiers on the bridge, would easily wipe out him and his team. The discovery of Chinese special forces would alert the Taiwanese military on the island more than they already were. Tonight, that was to be avoided at all costs.

The light panning the water and side of the bridge made the shadows even darker by comparison. The beam had left the span he had been under and moved to the next. His ropes had remained hidden. Perhaps those aboard the patrol boat had thought them part of the bridge, or maybe connected to the laid charges somehow. Perhaps they didn't even see them. The mind sometimes only saw what it wanted to. There was a chance that a soldier would recall seeing them after they had gone, prompting another return. By then, Hou hoped, it would be too late.

The topside vehicle had moved past his position as the patrol crossed the bridge. Span by span, beams of light from the watercraft splayed out on the ocean side. Once the light moved from his span, Hou moved back under the bridge. He didn't want to chance a soldier with a flashlight leaning over and shining their light down.

Seconds passed, a minute, then two minutes. He waited for the shrill blast of an alarm, or the shout from a bullhorn, something that would indicate they'd been found. The rumble of the diesel engine powering the patrol boat rolled across the water, filling the air underneath the span as the craft motored along the length of the bridge. All at once, the light winked out. The engine revved as the throttle was applied, and the boat sped away to search a different location.

Hou peeked around the column to see the topside patrol halfway down the bridge. The other half of his team, working to remove the charges from the southern spans, was still waiting for the patrol to pass. But Hou was in the clear for the time being. He went back to his climbing gear and again worked his way up to the wires leading to the charges.

Attaching a device to the side of a steel girder, Hou sliced through the outer insulation of the wires leading to the charges in two places. Clipping a dongle of wires from the device to the bared wires, the sergeant looked for a dim green light to illuminate. It was there. A circuit was complete. In case there was a connection circuit relayed to an engineering position, the device would send a faint charge down the wires. It was to fool the end device into thinking that there was a complete circuit from the charges.

Satisfied that all was in place, that a circuit would still be complete back to the opposite shores, Hou removed the fuses that would ignite the explosives and send the span plunging into the water. China's forces would need the bridge intact in order to conduct a swift takeover of the island chain. With the Penghu in their possession, China would have a substantial airport and small port much closer to Taiwan's coastline. The plan was to install missile batteries and squadrons with which to fire in support of the landing operation.

Hou worked his way down to the water line, removing the carabiners and rope along the way. Using the final stirrup for support, he waited for the rest of his team to complete their objectives. Once finished, the team of six submerged. Taking the oceanside, three motored south, maneuvering past the rocky shores that extended for about a thousand feet on either side of the bridge's southern entrance. There they secured their vehicles and extracted their weapons, exchanging their diving masks for helmets with a special eyepiece that allowed them to shoot around corners.

Hou and two others headed north, working their way through a series of concrete breakwater jetties shielding a small marina next to the northern bridge entrance. At a dirt ramp leading to land, the sergeant and his small team stowed their gear, extracting their QTS-11 carbines. In the shadow of an adjacent breakwater, the three special forces soldiers swapped clothing, turning from creatures of the sea to ones more suited for land.

With his gear stowed among large stones, Hou crept up and peered over the top of the ramp. Next to a low line of shrub-covered hills, a dirt road ran five hundred yards to the east. There it became a concrete road that ascended a few more feet before connecting to a parking lot. Hou lifted a pair of night vision binoculars, focusing on the parking lot and entrance.

Two light armored vehicles waited silently in the lot; the thin outline of heavy caliber barrels pointed skyward. Past the tactical vehicles, a temporary building had been constructed next to the main road. Intel had strongly suggested that it housed guards. That was strengthened by the fact that concrete barricades had been placed on the main road, arranged so that vehicles had to slowly maneuver around them.

Hou stowed the binoculars and made a last visual of his surroundings before leaving cover. Looking hard into the shadows cast by several construction vehicles, the sergeant sought out any human shapes or movement.

Satisfied that the small team was alone in the night, Hou rose from his position. Using piles of dirt and machinery as cover, the three commandos worked their way closer to the parking lot. While two of his team members hunkered near a drop-off, Hou crouch-walked to the Humvees. He briefly touched the hoods, finding one still warm. He'd likely found the vehicle that been on patrol.

That was good news. Even though well-trained units randomized their patrols, they seldom went out again just minutes after their arrival. Although that didn't mean there weren't foot patrols in the area, it was likely that the parking would be free for a little while. Other than the guards that were most likely resting in the guard post, Hou's concern was the small town on the other side of the main road. A concentration of troops could be hidden in the narrow, winding streets.

Even if there weren't, then any units coming from the north could easily turn off the main road and maneuver unseen to a flanking position. Hou understood that the three of them couldn't hold off a focused attack by anything larger than a squad, and the cover provided by the town gave any attacking force a distinct advantage.

Hou had little doubt that his small team could take the outpost next to the bridge's entrance. Night, coupled with surprise, would carry Hou to take the position. The mission planning had Hou and his team holding the bridge for an hour, two at the most. But anything could happen in that time. The key was not allowing the enemy to know that the position had been taken. To do that, they'd have to move quickly and only use their suppressed weapons. The 20mm grenade launcher that was an integral part of their weapon system was only to be used for defending the position, not in an attack. Too much noise and Hou would be lucky to hold the bridge for fifteen minutes, let alone for an hour or two.

Hou moved away from the vehicles and rejoined the other two. Hidden below the crest of the embankment, Hou listened as his second team on the southern entrance called in that they were in position. The sergeant switched frequencies and made a single call, the signal to say that his team had accomplished their primary mission and were in position.

Hou was the first to call in, but only by a little bit. Over the course of ten minutes, two other calls were sent, notifying command on the other side of the strait that the three bridges had been disarmed and were waiting to be assaulted.

Rolling onto his back, Hou looked across the wide expanse of water glimmering in the moonlight. For a brief moment, he thought about his life. He wasn't married, had no children. Instead of following in the footsteps of his relatives and friends, he chose to devote his life to the military. Many had joined and left once their enlistment had been up. But Hou really enjoyed the lifestyle and had challenged himself by opting for the special forces. It hadn't been easy, but the grueling training had been worth it.

He thought about his poor mother, who was constantly asking him if he had found a girlfriend. His usual rejoinder was that he had twenty and couldn't choose between them. The first time he'd said that, she had lit into him with a verbal lashing that had lasted a full hour. Now it was more of a running joke between the two of them. The truth of it was that Hou had met many women who had interested him. The problem was that he didn't have the energy to maintain a relationship, as he spent most of what he had on his job. Perhaps that would change down the road, but for now, even though it was highly dangerous at times, this was the life he wanted.

While enjoying the serenity of the moonlit bay, Hou wondered if he would live long enough to see China's victory, much less to settle down and find a wife.

* * * * * *

China's Eastern Coast
1 August, 2021

Over a hundred miles away, three distinct radio transmissions were received by regional command. They then issued orders to waiting units.

The still of the night was broken by a single whine. Starting slowly, the rotors atop and on the tail of the Changhe Z-18 military transport helicopter began turning faster and faster. The whine changed pitch as fuel was applied to the combustion chambers of the three turbines. Overhead, the rotor speed increased until it was just a blur with jet fumes pouring from the exhaust.

In front of the numerous helicopters lining the ramp and taxiways, men with lighted wands gestured to the pilots strapped into the front. With a twirl of a red-lit wand, the single roar was amplified by a second chopper starting up. More and more were added to the night until fifty of the transports echoed throughout the air base.

In the back, a compartment filled with the faint smell of jet fumes, thirty soldiers of the 127th Airborne Regiment fiddled nervously with their equipment. After days on end of waiting for the order, they were finally able to load up. Many looked at their neighbors, trading a joke and forced laughs. Some wondered if they would return from their planned assault, while a few others couldn't wait to get into the action.

The tone of the jet engines grew, the pitch of the rotors increasing to take bigger bites out of the night air. One by one, the medium transport helicopters lifted from the pavement, their noses tipping forward as they started on their hour-plus flight across the strait.

Similar scenarios played out across two other bases as China sent four thousand, five hundred airborne soldiers for an assault against Taiwan's island chain.

* * * * * *

Some of the orders sent from regional commands arrived at the headquarters for the mobile cruise missile battalions. They had been alerted for the upcoming missions and were ready. Within minutes of receipt, the night skies blanketing the eastern countryside of China were cut through with fiery streaks as rockets lifted off.

As with the previous missile attacks, deadly projectiles sped over the top of the waves. Primarily targeting Taiwan's anti-air defenses, their eighty-mile journey to the Penghu Islands would take only eight minutes. Ashore, like each of the previous times, Taiwan's air defense batteries detected some of the low-flying darts. The fire control systems determined that the incoming bogeys were hostile. Officers within command centers quickly verified the computer findings and released the weapons under their command.

* * * * * *

Heng Shan Military Command Center, Taipei, Taiwan
31 July, 2021

Deep underground in Dazhi in the Zhongshan District part of Taiwan's capital, high level military commanders sat with Yan-ting, the minister of defense. Even though China and Taiwan forces were engaged in hostilities, and the invasion had been nearly a guarantee for years, it was still unbelievable that the time was at hand. Many thought that China's capability to invade the island nation was at least five years away, if that fearful event was ever to truly transpire at all.

But there was no refuting the story being portrayed on the screens and surveillance footage from American satellites. China was coming. Nearly two hundred helicopters were heading across the strait, aimed like an arrow toward the Penghu. Having sustained days of constant missile bombardments, no one in the room had any hope that the airborne units were mere shows of force, like had been in years past. If there was any remaining doubt about what Taiwan was facing, it was erased by the ships making ready to depart the ports of Zhoushan and Zhanjiang. Given the weapons expenditures and losses, the leadership had some difficult decisions ahead of them.

A separate situation room was utilized by Taiwan's top leadership. At the head of the table sat Shu-ting, the nation's president. As a rule, she seldom commented on tactical decisions, saving that for those she had placed in the top military positions. During top level planning meetings surrounding China's invasion, which none doubted would occur, Shu-ting only involved herself when strategic or political decisions needed to be made.

Arranged in seats along the side were the Army, Navy, and Air Force commanders, along with the overall commander. Hsin-hung, the Chief of General Staff, sat to Shu-ting's right and was directing the meeting.

"There is no doubting China's intention at this point," Hsin-hung started, looking each of the respective commanders in the eye. "We have one invasion fleet currently underway, with more making ready to depart, and all aimed directly for our nation. Once the larger ones from the north and south set sail, it is estimated that they will be here within twenty-four hours. The much smaller one coming from Xiamen could land sometime in the next six hours. However, we only have two hours until the helicopters, currently working their way across the strait, arrive on our shores. With that in mind, and considering the short time we have to finalize our plans, let us look at what we think China will do with those forces they have arrayed against us."

General Hsin-hung glanced toward the Republic of China's Army commander, General Wei-ting, and nodded for him to begin.

With a nod toward each of the others in the room, Wei-ting stood and proceeded to a map where the inbound threats had been annotated.

"First, we do not know if the larger invasion forces China

amassed in the northern and southern ports is because they have two landing sites in mind, or whether it was done to load their regiments more quickly.

"It is believed that the invasion fleets will use the protection of territorial boundaries until the last minute to prevent attacks from the Americans. I believe they will steam north and south respectively, coming together across the strait to minimize their sailing time in international waters. As we have previously discussed, but I believe it bears iteration, China's forces will likely strike somewhere along our western coast."

"And why is that, General?" Shu-ting queried.

"Madam President," General Wei-ting said, nodding once. "China will need a port, preferably a large one, and a nearby airport. The port will be required to offload their heavy equipment, while the airport will be needed for a rapid application of reinforcements and supplies. Another requirement will be adequate landing sites nearby for their amphibious forces to come ashore."

Several chuckles arose from the last statement, stemming from the fact that Taiwan had limited beaches with most of the island edged with rocky shores. In order to put large numbers of troops ashore, invaders required the use of hovercraft and landing craft. Helicopter attacks were also expected, but only to make attempts to take strategic points; bridges, airports, and other military installations.

"So that, and the fact that Taiwan is relatively small, leaves only a few viable locations. To the south, we have Kaohsiung City. It has an extensive port and the Air Force Academy Airfield, along with a long stretch of beach to the south. We have placed breakwaters offshore to funnel any attack through narrow sea lanes, therefore making it easier for our forces to repel an invasion attempt there. Although it is the farthest from Taipei, it provides China with everything they will need. The problem is that they will then have to slog all the way up the island with minimal roads and many bridges to cross.

"The next option is Tainan City. It also meets all the

requirements, and the beach front is long. In addition, the airport, landing sites, and port are in close proximity to each other. Again though, any force will have to march north. But, with its greater infrastructure, the city provides for an ideal invasion site and remains the most logical place for Chinese units to put ashore.

"After that, we have to move farther north to Taichung City," General Wei-ting said, tapping the map with a wooden pointer. "It has the airport and port needed, but the landing sites are marginal at best. Tidal flats and marshes would make for a hazardous landing and really narrow the front we would have to cover. I doubt the location is suitable for a Chinese assault.

"That leaves us with Taipei itself. It also provides for everything China needs. Long beaches, the international airport near the coast located in a relatively open area, and the port. The capital would be within a short striking distance. They could seek to overwhelm our defenses and charge hard for the capital, hoping to make short work of their invasion. The problem for them is that we have amassed a great deal of our firepower to prevent that very scenario."

"I still believe we should concentrate additional forces in Keelung City," Admiral Yu-Hsuan stated. "It has a large enough port and is in easy striking distance from the capital."

Wei-ting nodded toward the admiral in charge of a navy that was mostly lost.

"Admiral," General Wei-ting started.

"What you say is true, but the city lacks the beachfront to accommodate a large-scale invasion," General Hsin-hung interrupted. "The road infrastructure leading away from the sandy shores is minimal. Any units putting ashore at the small beaches would soon find themselves trapped and bunched together, making easy targets. Honestly, I hope they make that mistake."

A few half-hearted chuckles sprang up, their forced nature obvious.

"Gentlemen, I know you have discussed this before, but

amuse me if you will. Why are we not looking at the eastern coast for an attack? You have focused on the populated regions which would make any landing difficult. Remind me why the east coast is not feasible," President Shu-ting inquired.

"Madam President," General Hsin-hung answered. "It is believed that the eastern ports are too small for what China will require. The terrain and minimal road network will constrain any forces China might land there. The naval port at the Su'ao Township might prove large enough and the beaches there are long, but the nearest airport is far to the south at Hualien. Now, that city has an adequate port, two major airports, and landing beaches, but there are few roads out of there. They would be forced to operate along the single coastal highway."

"I would like to point out that Chiashan air base is located there. It has underground bunkers capable of housing hundreds of aircraft. I know we have discussed this at length, but I still would not rule out China wanting that airfield to preserve their aircraft, just as we do," General Tsung-han remarked. "However, I am in agreement that China will likely hit either Kaohsiung or Tainan City…or perhaps both."

Shu-ting thanked the ranking staff members.

"So, currently, we have the Sixth Corps covering the northern sections, mostly concentrated in bunkers near Taipei. Besides the specific area commands comprising mixed battalions, we have one mechanized infantry and two armor brigades, along with field artillery.

"In the central part of the western seaboard is the Eighth Corps centered around Taichung City. The single infantry and armor brigade will initially cover any attempted landing, with the artillery arranged on the ridgelines separating the main city from the coast. And finally, the Tenth Corps in in the south. Those mechanized infantry and armored brigades will be covering both southern cities.

"Of note is the American Marine brigade, which we have also placed in the south. An airborne cavalry unit is placed with them to shuttle them quickly to where they are needed. They will operate as a mobile reserve. And speaking of army reserves, our nine infantry reserve brigades have been placed in bunkers, ready to move to where they are needed. In addition, the call-up for reserve brigades was begun at the outset of hostilities and will provide a steady manpower replacement pool," General Wei-ting briefed. "That is in addition to the various regional defense commands."

"Thank you, General. Our defensive strategy will be to determine where China will land their troops then bring our forces to bear to hit them on the beaches. If we can repel the initial waves, then China will have to regroup and analyze. If we can give them a bloody nose, then perhaps they will decide that any further attempts will be too costly, especially with the Americans loitering along the fringes. The beaches are where we will prevail or succumb," General Hsin-hung stated.

"I would like to remind everyone here that our mobility, our ability to move our units around, might become difficult once the invasion begins. China is likely to achieve air superiority at the outset. We have anti-air units inside bunkers, but they will have to be careful when they stick their noses out," General Wei-ting mentioned.

"Speaking of air defenses, we have thirty-one operational Ching-kuo and fifty-seven Falcons. That is aside from the twelve F-35s still in our inventory. Although the Americans have been resupplying us as best as they can, we are still short of weapons," General Tsung-han said. "Those planes are all stationed at Chiashan. Considering the size of the underground shelters, we have moved most of our airborne assets there. China seems keen on keeping the runways out of action, so maintaining them has become difficult.

"The plan for the use of our strike fighters is to unleash a large-scale attack on China's invasion fleets when they draw within range. Like our attack on their mainland, the Ching-kuos and some of the 16s will carry air-launched cruise missiles while the rest of the F-16s and F-35Bs provide cover. The expectation is that China will provide air cover for their fleets, so this may be the last mission our aircraft will be able to fly. Considering that the F-35Bs are more survivable, we will continue to use them as we can for ground sorties. If necessary, we will utilize roads, and have established a mobile force to keep the aircraft refueled and rearmed."

"Just for the record, we will likely face an initial wave consisting of six-to-eight Chinese marine brigades and six airborne brigades," General Hsin-hung remarked.

"The analysis of our naval attacks on their shipping may have eliminated up to two of those marine brigades. I would like to add that the Americans concur with that assessment, so it could be that we will only have to face six marine brigades. If China is able to add two brigades for their attack, they will be army brigades who will not have trained for the landings. That could present some difficulties for them...at least we can hope so. I hate to think that our sacrifices were in vain," Admiral Yu-hsuan added.

"Okay, not to cut any of this short, but we are also under a timeline with a Chinese helicopter assault on the way. So, let us discuss the forces currently crossing the strait. What are their objectives and what are we prepared to do about it?" General Hsin-hung asked.

General Tsung-han replaced the navy commander, placing a different map on the easel.

"This information was sent to us via American satellites and their E-3 orbiting to the east. A group of ships departed Xiamen, heading due east at twenty knots. Ours and the American intel missed this group, but it is believed to be carrying heavier equipment and supplies for the helicopter assault currently heading across the strait. If they maintain course and speed, the airborne contingent will be over the Penghu in less than an hour."

"With the number of transport helicopters, an estimated four thousand plus airborne troops will land on the Penghu."

"Why the Penghu islands and not push on to the main island?" Shu-ting inquired.

"For one, China will need to take the island or risk having their supplies interdicted. Secondly, the number of soldiers carried by those choppers are not nearly enough to conduct a strike against the mainland. They would have to hold out for a day or more and they would not last that long against with what we could immediately throw at them. With that and the limited number of ships, an attack against the Penghu is the only thing that makes sense," General Wei-ting answered.

"With the timing involved, there is not much we can do to reinforce Penghu, even if we wanted to. At the moment, there is only the Penghu Defense Command, consisting of a mechanized and armored battalion, along with air defense and artillery units scattered among the islands. We withdrew all fighters and helicopters to preserve them for use against the main invasion fleets. It is my understanding that all tank units were also withdrawn, and the equipment replaced with light and medium armored equipment," Tsung-han reported.

"That is correct," Wei-ting added. "The command is on their own. If you will remember, we discussed pulling the command out to augment our units here, but it was decided that we must not just hand over the islands. Plus, the battalions will not make much of a difference here. The defense command is partially made up of locals, so they would not move even if we ordered them away. I spoke with Colonel Wen-hsiung, and he would not hear of retreating.

"At this point, I do not see the islands holding out for long. China will first try for the airport so they can move in supplies and equipment. They will also try to take the port early on so they can offload the inbound ships. After securing those two vital points, they will attempt to move in aircraft, radar and air defense units, and perhaps mobile missile platforms. It is imperative that we interdict those resources as much as possible.

"The aircraft on the tarmac will be vulnerable, as will be the ships berthed at the port. Colonel Wen-hsiung will delay the takeover for as long as possible and the units in the underground bunkers will hold out for as long as they can. It will become more difficult for us if the Chinese are able to take control of those hardened shelters for their own use."

"So, what I hear you saying is that we are not going to

actively defend the islands?" Shu-ting asked.

"That is true, Madam President. The islands are only strategic in the sense that we can extend our defenses into the strait, particularly the air defenses. Plus, it also extends our territorial boundaries. It would be nice to disrupt their supply lines, but frankly, we do not have the material to accomplish that," General Shin-hung replied. "With the main Chinese forces arriving soon, we will focus our assets toward that...while attempting to keep the Penghu airfield and port inoperable."

"So, to recap the situation, we are going to leave the Penghu Islands to defend themselves while attempting to deny China the use of the facilities. In addition, we are to determine the landing point for the main fleet, or landing points on the main island, and rush our units there to defeat the invasion forces before they can establish a bridgehead. Did I get that right?" the president queried.

The chief of the general staff nodded.

"And what are our chances of defeating the invasion?"

"Considering that China may have air supremacy and their abundant cruise missiles, once our main units are in the open, it could become difficult to move them around, or for them to operate effectively. If China manages to get soldiers ashore, there will be many water obstructions as China moves north. Destroying bridges will slow them, and if we...," General Hsin-hung began.

"So, what you are dancing around is that you are not very confident in our odds?" Shu-ting interrupted.

"It would be better if we could get direct support from the Americans," Hsin-hung conceded.

Without much left to be said, Tsung-han sat back down. In the confines of the room, they would watch the satellite feeds and listen to other reports in order to determine China's intentions.

* * * * * *

A lone rain shower, releasing large droplets, passed through the area. The wet pavement left behind glistened under the glow of the half-moon and from nearby base lighting. The fresh scents brought on by the rainfall were soon shoved aside by the overpowering odor of jet fuel exhaust.

Twin fire plumes stirred the standing water, forcefully blowing sheets of it to the rear. Where water met heat, the recently fallen rain turned to steam as powerful jet engines pushed tons of metal down the runway. Glimpses of the rapidly accelerating plane could be seen whenever the attack fighter crossed in front of the base lighting. Soon, the twin streaks of fire lifted into the dark, disappearing completely when the throttles were taken out of afterburner.

Before the initial fighter took to the night skies, another began rolling down the wet runway. Mimicking the first, it too was swallowed up by the night. The long line of Chinese aircraft waiting along the taxiway grew shorter by the minute as laden aircraft turned onto the active runway and throttles were run forward. Shortly after joining up in flights and then into squadrons, the Chinese attack fighters turned east. They followed in the path of the cruise missiles that were just beginning to arrive on foreign shores. The fighters' trip across the Taiwan Strait would be significantly shorter than that of their distant cousins.

Like watching migrating flocks, a Chinese KJ-2000 AWACS, orbiting high over China's eastern shoreline, saw the missile launches and the jets taking off, observing them as they flew east. As only one of the two available airborne command posts, the operators in the fuselage were responsible for the sequencing of attack aircraft and for aerial combat, should Taiwan opt to send their fighters aloft.

A short distance away, a Chinese j-16D flew up and down the strait on the Chinese side. The wingtip pylon sported a long shape bristling with antennae while the underwing attachments hosted a variety of electronic countermeasure equipment. The pilot and electronic warfare officer in the back seat were responsible for the jamming of Taiwan's fire control system radars.

Secondarily, they were to jam communication systems, but had to be wary of this use because of Chinese special forces currently on the islands. The Chinese jamming systems still only provided blanket coverage, unlike some of the new systems the Israelis and Americans were employing which could focus the jamming along narrower tracks. That also meant careful coordination so that the J-16D didn't interfere with the Chinese missile attack, which relied on radar to home in on their targets.

*   *   *   *   *   *

From his shelter below the lip of an embankment, Sergeant Hou saw his country's attack on the islands begin. He watched as yellow tails of fire rose from various points on the island. The Taiwanese air defense missiles streaked skyward; their launches mostly silent due to the distance between them and Hou's position. The defensive weapons located their targets and arched downward to where the wave-skimming threats were rapidly drawing closer.

The entire sequence was so fast; the anti-air missiles raced aloft, flashing just over the horizon as their proximity fuses determined that they were within range. Small warheads exploded, taking several of the Chinese cruise missiles down in sprays of seawater.

Hou and the two others of his team were taken aback when a nearby whoosh split the night. On the far side of the small town across the road, first one, and then a second missile streaked over the heads of the special forces team. Hou watched the two supersonic missiles as they faded into the western sky, vanishing from sight seconds later.

That there was a Taiwanese anti-air unit so close was news to Hou. Aside from the bridge guards, intel hadn't shown any force to be near the objective. That could mean there were soldiers assigned to protect the assets, but not necessarily. Hou and his men would have to be doubly quiet in order not to arouse suspicion too soon.

Turning his attention back to the building, Hou saw that the rear door to the concrete block structure was opening. Below the lip of the embankment, he brought his QTS-11 carbine and grenade launcher closer to bear. Two soldiers stepped out from the open door, glancing quickly around before focusing on the missiles leaving the ground. They knew there was only one reason for the display, having witnessed it over several nights.

Out of sight from the Taiwanese soldiers, Hou tapped the shoulders of his two teammates. Although they were to use the exploding cruise missiles as cover for their assault on the guard post, Hou recognized an opportunity when it presented itself. He had to assume that the doors to the small facility were locked during the evening hours, so being given an open one was a gift he couldn't turn down. The open door would certainly cut down on the noise he'd make, especially when there were other units in close proximity.

His two team members thought the same as they instantly nodded to his shoulder tap. Hou reached for his vest and switched on a small device. It was attached to a thick plastic antenna jutting over his right shoulder. The portable signal jammer, much like the ones used by Mexican cartels, could suppress communications from cell phones, VHF and UHF channels, and several other radio frequencies.

In order not to present movement that might draw the attention of the enemy soldiers staring at the defensive launches, Hou eased his weapon over the embankment. The fiber connection to the sights presented a picture of the targets and the building to the helmet-attached eyepiece. Lining up one of the enemy soldiers in his sights, Hou increased his pressure against the trigger.

The grass along the embankment edges lit up as a burst of fire sent three suppressed 6.8mm subsonic rounds across the lawn. Sounding like a sack of meat dropped from a height, Hou heard the solid thuds of his rounds striking. The Taiwanese soldier dropped his carbine as he was propelled backward. Hitting the concrete brick wall, the man slid down, leaving a dark smear on the cream-colored paint.

Bursts of fire from both sides sent the second soldier collapsing to the ground, falling in the doorway. The open door, no longer being held, started closing. It would have sealed before the racing figures, running across the lawn, intercepted it had the door not lodged against the dead soldier's legs.

With blood streaming past his lips, the soldier slumped against the wall was drawing in ragged breaths. Each inhalation was labored, the brain telling the respiratory system that more oxygen was needed. But the corresponding muscles weren't reacting correctly. The pain to take in each breath was evident; the soldier's eyes betrayed the agony and fear, and the confusion as to how he ended up leaning against the wall.

Switching to single fire, Hou put another round into the man, forever silencing the agonized wheezing. For good measure, one of his team added another round to the dead man blocking the door. It was all speed now as Hou couldn't imagine how the thuds of the two bodies falling wouldn't be heard inside.

Leaping over the body in the door, Hou pulled down his NVGs. An interior corridor came into vision in a green-infused light. The shape of a figure appeared at the other end of the short hall, peering down the length. Hou saw the recognition of danger cross the man's features. The soldier was bringing his weapon up when Hou sent a burst of fire down the hallway.

The sergeant saw the rounds strike as the top part of the man's skull peeled away from the impact of two bullets to the forehead. In the light of the NVGs, a thick spray of blood blossomed behind the soldier and the man vanished from view. That was followed by a rapid, repeated pounding.

At first, Hou thought an alarm had been sounded. But upon entry into the room, he saw that the man's legs were violently hammering into the floor. Another round into his head ended the man's convulsions.

A quick glance around showed that Hou had entered the front of the building. Through the armor-rated glass enclosing the room, he saw the night beyond. Hou's heart nearly stopped when there came a flash of movement from one end of the room. Knowing that he was already dead, Hou rounded on the movement, his barrel leading the way.

A soldier was against a control panel, his hand reaching out. As if in slow motion, it was descending toward a series of controls. Recognizing what was about to occur, Hou's turn toward the man was maddingly slow. He knew that he wasn't going to get there in time, even with the shot of adrenaline now coursing through his body. As if broken free from a spell, with a sudden burst of speed, the hand slammed down on the panel.

Outside, a siren quickly began ramping up, turning from a low whirring to a blare of sound that echoed through the adjacent town. Hou fired into the man, sending him to the floor in a crumple. A second burst made sure that he was permanently down, but his mission had been accomplished. A third burst slammed into the panel just as a low-flying missile screamed overhead. Pieces of plastic showered the end of the room as the alarm panel was torn apart.

Light from a nearby explosion lit up the room. One of the cruise missiles launched from China detonated over the top of the air defense unit stationed close by. The shrieking alarm wound down from Hou destroying the panel, but the sergeant wondered if it was in time. He hoped that the alarm system wasn't connected to a remote location, eliciting a response from a rapid deployment force.

Looking toward where the missile exploded, the town's buildings were silhouetted from the glow of a fire. Aside from worrying that the alarm was heard, Hou wondered how in the hell some Chinese mobile cruise missile battery knew of the Taiwanese unit and he didn't. Maybe it was because their radar systems had come online. However, he was going to have a few words with their intel section once, if, he returned.

From all directions south, east, and north, flashes lit up the night skies as the cruise missiles began arriving. That was supposed to have been their cover as the team assaulted the guard post. Instead, they had managed to set off an alarm that could bring a rapid response. Hopefully, any Taiwan soldiers nearby would think the alarm had something to do with the current missile attack and leave well enough alone.

* * * * * *

It took only minutes for the Chinese attack fighters to reach their positions over China's eastern shores. Signals were relayed to the fighter systems from the orbiting KJ-2000, sending the passive receipt of Taiwan's fire control radars. On a signal from the airborne command post, CM-102 missiles carried on wing pylons raced into the night.

The anti-radiation weapons, China's version of America's AGM-88 HARM, meant to passively home in on radar signals, were supposed to have been fired before the cruise missiles drew within range of Taiwan's air defenses. The plan was to mitigate cruise missile losses, but someone, somewhere, had screwed up the timing of the launches. The operators aboard the flying command center realized the mistake, but far too late to do anything about it. Instead, they altered the planned sequence, hoping that not too many of the slower cruise missiles would be destroyed.

Focusing on the radar systems, the CM-102s passively received their information from the KJ-2000 until they could locate the active radar systems on their own. From there, they passively homed in on the enemy radar emissions. The J-16D jamming Taiwan's systems temporarily went "offline" so that the anti-radiation weapons could "see" their targets.

Some of Taiwan's radar stations incorporated separate electronic countermeasures. These were designed to hide or mitigate the radar signal emanating from the actual radars. When some of the Chinese CM-102s lost their passive signals, they managed to pick up the emissions coming from the jamming systems. Known as home-on jam, their internal guidance programming began tracking the jammer instead of the radar. This was to ensure a kill in the event of a successful jam as the ECM and fire control radar were often co-located.

* * * * * *

Sergeant Hou directed the other two of his team to drag the enemy bodies to one of the Humvees, then drive down the access road and hide them among the piles of dirt. Upon their return, they were to park the lightly armored vehicles adjacent to the building. With the possibility of a response force arriving, he wanted to be able to use the mounted M-240s, adding to their meager firepower.

While the two were accomplishing the grisly task of removing the bodies, Hou turned off his jamming system, as there wasn't anyone alive in the structure to radio a call for help. He then made a short radio call, alerting the KJ-2000 directing the battle and the others at the south end of the bridge that they had accomplished their mission. The northern end of the Penghu Great Bridge was under China's control.

Not long after that, other calls began coming in. The rest of his team on the southern end had taken their end without raising an alarm. Hou stared at the broken control panel, hating that he hadn't been just a second or two faster. But what was done was done. There was no going back, and the only things that mattered were events going forward.

Looking out the front windows, he could see a little way down the road to the north. It wasn't far, and he would have little warning of someone coming their way. Hou involuntarily crouched as a fast-moving tail of fire roared overhead. Descending, the missile struck in nearly the same location as before. A flash briefly highlighted the outline of the town's buildings, the sound of the explosion arriving a second later. Looking elsewhere, the sergeant caught glimpses of other red streaks descending on the island chain. The anti-radiation missiles had started arriving.

Aboard the Chinese airborne command post, an operator relayed the radio calls from the special forces teams responsible for taking control of the bridges connecting the islands. The CIC officer acknowledged the report and sent his own message off to the mix of transport and attack helicopters flying over the strait at wave-top level. The message told the commanders that the assault was a go.

The other two of Hou's team came back from depositing the bodies in the chaos of the construction efforts, parking the Humvee on the opposite side of the building. From the acknowledgement of his radio call, Hou knew that they wouldn't have too long to wait until their reinforcements arrived. But that time would seem like forever. With nothing much else to do other than wait, each minute stretched toward infinity.

At first, Hou thought it was an illusion brought on by the fires glowing on the other side of town, or perhaps even his imagination. He blinked to drive the image from his mind, to reset his vision, but when he opened his eyes again, it was still there. Out along the road, not far from the building, there were thin beams of blacked-out headlights. Once he established what he was seeing, Hou could make out the darker shapes of vehicles. The NVGs showed everything in a greenish glow, giving the entire scene an eerie cast.

Carrying a dual-band radio, Hou was monitoring one of the enemy channels. Electronic intelligence had provided unit call signs and procedures. It was the plan and hope that the teams occupying all the bridge ends could reply to normal radio traffic. The special forces sergeant wondered if the approaching vehicles would check in with the procedures they had heard and practiced.

"Checkpoint Hotel, authenticate Bravo Tango," a voice called over the radio.

Nope! That certainly wasn't within the intel Hou and his team had received. Hou frantically searched through the room. There had to be a code book somewhere. The idea was that an authentication code would be matched by a specific reply. No soldier would know all the combinations, so they'd have to have it written down. He hoped to hell it wasn't on one of the bodies they'd just dumped.

"Checkpoint Hotel, authenticate Bravo Tango."

Opening drawers and flipping through any booklet he found, Hou knew that the window for his response was rapidly closing. The vehicles had come to a stop and doused their lights.

In the glow of his night vision, he could see vehicles lined up. Several soldiers had unloaded from their Humvees and were spreading to the side of the road. He had to find that damned codebook.

The team, along with the others at their respective bridges, had dressed in Taiwanese uniforms, complete with insignia. The idea was that they could pass off as Taiwanese soldiers from a passing scrutiny. But it also meant that the team members could be shot as spies if captured. With the amount of damage China had inflicted on the island nation, Hou had no doubt that he would never see his homeland again if taken into custody. There would be an interrogation, followed by a firing squad once his tormentors had extracted what information they could.

Hou found another booklet and was about to flip through the pages when the room lit up with blazing light. Everything was highlighted in a dazzling glare of pure white. The sergeant flipped up his goggles as the powerful search light whited them out.

"Inside the building! Come out one at a time with your hands up," a speaker blared.

Hou ducked below a counter running the width of the front room, more to get out of the bright light than to hide.

"This is your last warning…come out with your hands in the air."

It was fight or give up, but either way, Hou knew he was a dead man. He hoped that the reinforcements would arrive before his team on the southern end were also overrun. Knowing that he was already dead, the sergeant was ready to fight. He'd die with a weapon in his hands, not tied to some wooden post.

"Out back, now!" Hou shouted to the other two.

Their only chance was to take the fight outside. The building was a trap in which they'd be torn apart.

Keeping low, Hou and the others moved toward the short hallway. A sudden shock of noise hit the buildings. The armored glass windows in the front of the building shattered, the broken panes crashing to the ground. Holes were torn into the back wall, plaster and the remains of framed pictures falling. Above the cacophony of destruction flooding the building, Hou heard the heavy chatter of a .50 caliber machine gun.

The large caliber rounds punched through the cinder block, filling the air with plaster and concrete dust. Larger chunks of the outer walls pummeled the three Chinese special forces as their protection came apart like a crumbly biscuit. Keeping low and moving as fast as he could, Hou heard the heavy zip of rounds passing far too close. With debris violently swirling around, he felt as if he were trapped in a tornado. The front of the building was disintegrating as Hou and the other two scrambled down the hall and out the back door.

With overwhelming fire tearing through the structure, Hou half-ran, half-stumbled toward the embankment. They were hidden by the building, but the splintered remains of heavy, .50 cal rounds that managed to punch all the way through the building plunked onto the earth all around him.

Flopping over the edge, Hou peeked over the ledge. The power of the fire being directed into the building was forcing debris out through the open doorway in the back. The light focused on the building was so bright that the color of the surrounding grass looked bleached. Ricochets whined, red tracers racing into the night before fading.

Hou had never faced such violence. He glanced upward, hoping to catch a glimpse of what had to be a circling American gunship. But, deep down, he knew that the firepower was coming from only a few vehicles. He looked toward the bridge, which was technically still in Chinese hands. The violence he had been in the midst of had momentarily taken away his ability to reason logically, the chaos infiltrating his thoughts. Now, away from being in the middle of the destruction, he was able to think more clearly.

Hidden by the embankment, he sidled to the side until he could see the front end of the vehicles still pummeling the building. Lifting his QTS-11 over the edge, Hou again activated the small fire control circuitry. He selected the airburst setting on his 20mm grenade sitting in the chamber. The electronics in the grenade altered the fuse from a contact detonation to then explode after it had traveled a certain distance. The sergeant clicked the laser range finder, focusing the beam on the bumper of the lead vehicle. The data was automatically uploaded to the grenade. Adding a couple meters to that, Hou set his aim above the target and fired.

With a soft clunk, the grenade left the chamber. Arcing over the bleach-colored grass, the small explosive headed toward the line of vehicles and soldiers still pouring fire into the building. Unseen, the grenade spun over the top of the Taiwanese Humvee in the lead, and upon reaching its programmed distance, the 20mm grenade exploded.

A yellow flash highlighted the vehicle and the soldier manning the mounted machine gun as if caught in a still photo. The windshield splintered from the shrapnel showering down. Blood splattered the top of the armored vehicle as hot metal tore into the gunner. The soldier slumped down into the interior, the barrel of the heavy caliber gun angling skyward.

Day turned back to night as shrapnel from his team's explosives knocked out the bright searchlights. Hou quickly pulled his NVGs back down. The volume of heavy fire immediately slackened. Only the fire from carbines continued, but even that momentarily ceased when the soldiers turned toward the detonation and the lack of fire coming from the Humvee.

Knowing that time was of the essence, Hou motioned for the other two to run for one of the Humvees parked close to the mostly demolished structure. Without waiting for a response, Hou raised above the lip of the embankment. Using the building as cover, he ran toward the other armored vehicle. Fire still poured into the building, and he heard the zip of bullets passing close by, heard the thud of rounds hitting the ground around his running feet. The enemy had started expanding their area of fire.

Without slowing down, Hou crashed into the rear of the Humvee and entered. Listening to the pings of rounds hitting the front and sides, the sergeant worked his way to the mounted M-240. The weapon was already facing down the road, thus the metal shield kept him from being hit as he grabbed the gun. The weapon chattered as 7.62mm tracers sailed toward the enemy, passing other tracers coming at him. He raked the vehicles, poured death toward the winking lights of fire.

It was difficult not to duck with each ringing ping when bullets struck the protective shield. He heard the chatter as the second Humvee near the guard post entered the fight. The team of three were outgunned, but now not as badly as they had been. The terrain kept the responding Taiwanese forces from driving too far off the road, so if Hou could keep the front narrowed, he stood a slim chance of lasting until the helicopter assault forces arrived.

Coming from the direction of town, a hint of movement out of the corner of his eye caught Hou's attention. Glancing in that direction, he saw that one of his fears had come to pass. Forces responding to the alarm had come through the town and the special forces team was in the process of being flanked.

Letting the other Humvee attempt to keep the heads of the Taiwanese soldiers down, and more specifically keeping anyone from operating that damned .50 cal, Hou directed his fire toward the units emerging from the side streets. He saw soldiers scatter as his tracers raked among them, the streets sparking from rounds hitting and careening deeper into the community.

Another Humvee rounded the corner. The 7.62mm rounds he was sending their direction might not penetrate the armored glass, but they served to keep them off balance. At best, he might be able to keep the gunner from manning the weapon mounted on top.

A clatter of rounds from the first force impacted near the mount ring. He could almost feel the heat as the bullets zipped past. There was no way he could possibly hope to keep the two forces at bay, but he had no option: he had to try.

He heard an extended whoosh followed by an explosion.

Yellow light splashed across the lawn. This time, the team leader felt a wave of heat wash over him, heard the crackle of flames. Lifting his goggles, Hou saw that the second Humvee his team had been manning was engulfed in flames. Tendrils of fire licked high into the air.

One of his team jumped from the vehicle; the man was fully consumed in flame. Dancing in random patterns across the grass, his hands waved wildly as if trying to put out the fire. Through the flame, Hou could see the man's open mouth. He was struck by the soundless screams as the man's skin melted away like he was made of wax. It was enough to send the sergeant, a man who had spent much of his life in the special forces, to walk away from any form of violence and enter a monastery.

Hou never heard the explosion, never saw the flash of fire. All he knew was that he was suddenly flying through the air. In slow motion, he saw the Taiwanese soldiers looking in his direction, saw the glow from burning vehicles against the windshield and hood of the enemy Humvee, saw his carbine tumbling through the air nearby. He was confused by what he was witnessing, by the discordant sounds.

The sergeant hit the ground and skidded on his side. He didn't know how or why, but when he looked at the vehicle in the distance, he knew he was looking at the specter of death. The strange-looking truck might as well have been dressed in a dark robe and carrying a scythe.

How had he come to be lying on the grass? Was he at the park down the street from his mom's? And if so, why did everything look so different? It wasn't anything like he remembered. Why was he here at night? And more importantly, where was his mom? She usually accompanied him. As a matter of fact, she wouldn't let him go there alone. After all, he was only five.

Sparks rose from the vehicle of death. He saw the windshield cave in, saw large holes appear in the hood. Then the thing that brought his death suddenly erupted in a sheet of flame. Was that death transforming and coming for him? He looked up from where he was resting on the cool grass as something dark flew over him. Somewhere in the night, there came a familiar sound, even though he didn't have the faintest clue as to what it could be. It was a steady thumping coming from somewhere beyond the range of his vision.

Perhaps that's why his mother wouldn't let him come to the park after dark, or come to the park alone. She had never mentioned that demons prowled there, but she must have known about them. He needed to get away but couldn't move for some reason. The five-year old frantically searched the area as more explosions arrived. He wanted his mom.

"Momma? Where are you, momma?" he cried out as the demons again roared, casting their flames high into the night.

Chapter Five

Penghu Islands, Taiwan
1 August, 2021

Taiwanese anti-air battery commanders noted the number of cruise missiles arriving from across the strait had started tapering off. They waited until reports came in, noting the lack of impact sites. Some of the hardened bunkers had retractable radar antennae. Rising through holes drilled into stone and earth, the dishes emerged above ground level. Other sites that survived the latest deluge of explosions opened their thick steel doors. Heavy machinery quickly pushed rubble and fallen trees clear of the entrance, creating unobstructed lanes through which radar vehicles could exit and resume their operations.

Almost immediately, several radar screens lit up with return echoes. Closing in from the waters separating the two belligerents, operators noted numerous low-level inbound bogeys. The same operators checked the gains in all directions and determined that they weren't being jammed. Computers analyzed the incoming objects. Within seconds, they determined that the returns fit attack profiles and labeled the slower moving targets as hostile. Those determinations were backed up by battery commanders who authorized the release of weapons.

From some of the hardened artillery sites (HARTS) came the rumble of powerful diesel engines. Large vehicles loaded with surface to air missiles stuck their noses out from their protective enclosures. As soon as the trucks came to a stop with a hiss of airbrakes, hydraulic motors raised quad launchers sitting on trailers. Flame and smoke erupted from the bunker entrances as long-range Skybow II and Skybow III left their enclosures. Racing at Mach 4.5 and Mach 7 respectively, the anti-air missiles sped into the night.

In some locations, the weapons themselves were mounted inside the bunkers. Smoke, glowing from the fire within, burst out from the opened bunker doors. As with their vehicular counterparts, the anti-air missiles sped off from inside. As soon as the rocket mounts emptied, the radar dishes, some mounted on trucks and others raised hydraulically, withdrew. HARTS doors began closing as crews began the process of reloading.

Those sites relying on vehicles to launch their defensive weapons were a little slower in closing the bunkers. The trucks had to maneuver their trailers back into their enclosures.

Flying over the Chinese mainland, operators aboard the KJ-2000 command post noted the appearance of multiple Taiwanese targeting radars come online. Assigning targets, two flights of J-16s orbiting near China's twelve-mile limit were directed east. Within a minute, they came within range of their CM-102 anti-radiation missiles. One by one, streaks of fire flew away from the strike fighters as each aircraft closed the distance. Those missiles took a little over three minutes before they started slamming into the islands.

The residents had grown used to hearing the echoing sound of explosions, the sharp crack of nearby blasts, and the distant rumbles of weapons detonating farther away. Those were sounds which had come to dominate their lives for the past few days and nights. Familiarity didn't alleviate their fear. Many in the communities near the missile strikes spent most of their time living in underground shelters. When the missiles stopped for a while, the shelter entrances were quickly crowded with people cooking meals and finding what joy they could from being in the open air. They knew their stints of freedom wouldn't last long, and the people kept one ear peeled for the shrill sirens that signaled another attack.

In some cases, the anti-air units were able to withdraw their assets before the Chinese anti-radiation missiles arrived. Because the weapons operated passively, they gave almost no indication that they were on the way. Although small electronic presences could be detected from some of the missiles when they received updates as they were enroute. Taiwan's crews did their best to hurriedly fire and pull their vehicles back to safety before the inevitable counterattacks arrived.

Taiwanese radar operators had their systems up only for as long as it took to locate targets and fire, foregoing their ability to provide mid-course guidance to the individual missiles. Once the weapons left their containers, they activated their internal radar systems to home in on their targets. That left the projectiles more vulnerable to electronic countermeasures and defensive fire.

China's J-16D electronic warfare fighter, operating far from the island chain, saw the missiles rise from their bunkers. The back seater determined the radar frequency and started jamming. The missile's internal software started hopping frequencies, which the Chinese electronic aircraft then tried to match. It was another, almost separate, battle that was being conducted.

Some of the Chinese CM-102 missiles lost the passive radar signals as Taiwanese radars went offline. Their internal processors searched for signs of jamming, ready to switch to the jamming signal if located. They found none. Those without targets climbed and looked for infrared signatures in the area of their targets which they could then home in on. Again, they didn't find anything to lock onto. They flew for a little longer, their software packages waiting for some input while the system continued searching. With no targets or incoming data, they "safed" themselves and crashed into the rolling swells.

Others were able to home in on radar signals and slammed into vehicles rushing to fire and get back inside their bunkers. Flames and roiling smoke erupted outside of hardened entrances as the Chinese missiles destroyed several defensive units.

Out over the water, the Taiwanese ground-launched air defense missiles began arriving in the midst of the helicopter assault closing in on the Penghu.

* * * * * *

Glistening under the light of a half moon, cresting waves incessantly rolled just feet below the attack helicopter. They seemed a blur as seen through night vision gear mounted on the pilot's helmet. Captain Shao Zhen focused on the waves flashing by as he flew over their tops at two miles per minute. Underneath the chopper's chin, a 23mm chain gun swung in response to changes in the location the Chinese captain was looking at. Attached to the outer pylons of the stubby wings were two AKD-10 anti-tank missiles. The helicopter was also carrying a compliment of two pods housing 90mm unguided rockets.

Shao Zhen was part of a squadron of Z-10 medium attack helicopters in the forefront of an armada comprised of one hundred and fifty Z-18 transport choppers. The mission of the assault group was to attack and eliminate any resistance within the chain of islands belonging to Taiwan. Over four thousand troops huddled inside the medium transports, ready to push outward once they arrived at their respective landing sites.

Shao's job was to cover the landings, prowling the skies to search for incoming Taiwanese reinforcements and any accompanying armor. The latest intelligence only had the enemy utilizing small contingents of light and medium armored vehicles, so he didn't expect to see any of the enemy's outdated main battle tanks. Intel had been wrong in the past, but those thoughts were best left unsaid. Anyone voicing dissention, no matter how small soon found themselves being reeducated. No, Shao had learned to listen to intel, but plan for the worst eventualities. His squadron commander believed the same, as did most pilots, thus the inclusion of the AKD-10s designed to take out heavily armored vehicles.

Contemplating his attack on the northern end of a bridge connecting two islands would have to come later. Now, his threat warning system was alerting him to the fact that Taiwan's air defense units had picked him up. When his missile approach warning system activated, Shao had to divide his attention between remaining above the rolling waves and searching for the fiery tails of inbound threats.

A search of the night skies quickly yielded results as Taiwan's hypersonic anti-air missiles began arriving. Once a pilot saw one of the streaks, they only had a second or two before the threats came in at blinding speeds. In back, his gunner worked with the onboard electronic countermeasures, attempting to fool the systems tracking his chopper.

Shao caught sight of multiple streaks heading for the armada. One in particular caught his attention. It was just a small dot of light, battling with the overhead stars for dominance in the visual world. The fiery tail rapidly grew larger in his vision, the position remaining steady. Shao knew that any object that didn't move from its relative position and grew bigger was on a collision course.

Although a certain amount of adrenaline kept him alert throughout his hour-long flight, Shao felt a new surge enter his body upon seeing the threat. He almost froze. The sight of the incoming missile was mesmerizing. However, contained in that captivating sight was death.

Shao felt the vibration of the rotating blades through his hands on the stick and collective, felt it through his boots on the rudder pedals. Chaff bundles were ejected from the Z-10. The captain banked the attack chopper, the vibrations increasing as the blades grabbed greater chunks of air. He was compressed into his seat as the Gs increased, the whump of the rotors taking on a lower note.

Glancing at the sea below, he kept his gaze on the incoming missile, willing it to miss. The Skybow III didn't move in his windscreen, changing direction with the Z-10. More chaff was automatically expended. Shao rolled upright and lifted on the collective. The attack chopper started a hard climb, but didn't have the time to gain more than a few feet as the Mach 7 projectile homed in.

At the last moment, the threat arced downward. It shot through his line of sight, a streak passing so fast that Shao's brain couldn't process what had happened. A faint flash of light preceded an explosion which shook the climbing Z-10. The compressed waves of air grabbed the helicopter and tossed it about in the turbulence. Just as fast as it began, the chaos subsided.

Normal time abruptly resumed. The Chinese captain felt a rush of sweat being expelled under his arms. He checked his instruments and was almost confused when they showed normal. He had just lived through a near miss that should have ended his life.

Settling the attack helicopter back toward the surface of the strait, Shao spared a glance to the sides. Others weren't as lucky. He watched as a missile slammed into the side of one of his squadron mates. A flash of light lit up the side of the chopper, a faint smudge of dark smoke showing in the light of his NVGs. The Z-10 didn't explode, nor did pieces fly off. A second after it had been hit, the helicopter just nosed over and smacked into the strait. A spray of water erupted, the moon's rays highlighting the fountain in silver.

The same wasn't true of another such hit. One of the Skybow IIIs slammed into the side of another Z-10. Shao winced as fire streamed from the rear of the stricken chopper. The helicopter continued for the length of a soccer field before nosing down. It hit and exploded, sending a pillar of flame skyward before being quickly extinguished.

In the dark, other explosions suddenly erupted when the slower Skybow II missiles started arriving. And then it was over. Shao felt almost dizzy from the shocking surge of adrenaline that had been released. He wasn't sure if it was the helicopter shaking his hands or the other way around. He likened it to flying through a thunderstorm. There were the tense moments of seeing the billowing clouds and knowing what was about to occur. Then there were the terrifying moments when the helicopter flew with a mind of its own, leaving Shao wondering if the tiny gnat he was in would be shaken apart. Finally, as if ejected from the storm, there was the coming out the other side, wondering if he was still alive.

The radio frequencies were frantic with voices. The missiles were striking the following armada of transports. Unseen by the attack pilot, explosions marked hunks of flying metal plunging into the uncaring seas.

Shao steadied himself and resumed his course, knowing

that the dangers were only beginning. There were the short-range weapons he'd have to wade through. Those would be comprised of heat-seeking missiles fired from mobile platforms, and heavy caliber guns ringing strategic locations. The most worrisome for Shao were the MANPADS, Man-Portable Air-Defense Systems, he might have to face. Those could come out of nowhere with little warning. He was thankful that he had been selected to provide cover for a bridge rather than an assignment like the airport or docks.

Ten miles out, the threat warning indicator flashed again, followed shortly by the missile warning system. After the initial attack from the Penghu shores, the threat warning flashed intermittently. Someone was periodically activating a search radar, most likely pinging the mass of helicopters to determine their positions before shutting back down. Shao thought it might be a mobile radar that was moving about to avoid anti-radiation missile attacks.

Even though he was beyond visual range of the islands at his current altitude, Shao knew that wouldn't prevent some short-range IR missiles from reaching them. Some of the modern systems could locate targets post-launch. That was probably what he was facing with the missile warning system going off.

Shao's instincts were correct as to what the periodic radar pulses indicated. With help from American systems, Taiwanese mobile platforms were ranging the inbound helicopters. Once they flew within the parameters of the Antelope anti-aircraft system, the short-range incorporated radar systems took over the duties of tracking the hostile force. Parked across the islands in hidden revetments, small vehicles with quad-mounted Sky Sword I missiles came alive. Although the system could be controlled from inside the cab of the attached vehicle, most were remotely controlled by a gunner and an observer.

With targets painted by the targeting radar, and the data uploaded to the individual IR missiles, the gunner sent the weapons on their way. Streaking off the rails, the deadly projectile's dual IR seekers searched the dark skies for heat sources. Once each missile found a target, an onboard guidance system took over. Flying at speeds in excess of Mach 2, the missiles quickly closed in on the assault force that was only ten miles away.

Across the lead Chinese attack choppers, flares lit up the night, trying to fool the incoming threats. The flares descended in the slipstream, burning hot and quick. Some of the IR seekers saw the increased heat signatures and sent signals to the small guidance fins. Sky Sword I missiles veered from their courses to chase after the falling flares.

Maneuvering as before, Shao watched a missile strike a Z-10 flying slightly ahead. In the green glow, there was a bright flash that quickly dissipated. He flew through a puff of smoke and the chopper bounced as it hit turbulence created by the explosion. For a few seconds, the captain thought that the missile had missed as the attack chopper in front kept flying as if nothing happened. He was about to play out a mock conversation, teasing the other pilot about his near miss when a gout of flame erupted from the helicopter. The lead chopper suddenly slewed to the side and dropped a few feet before nosediving into the strait.

With his gunner still popping out flares, Shao pulled hard on the collective, lifting his Z-10 over the crash. The numbers of the lead attack helicopters were further reduced as other explosions signaled their demise. The greater damage was to the transports following behind. Shao and the other pilots kept punching out flares, even after the missile warning systems remained dark.

Minutes later, Shao saw a dark rise of land ahead. Thin lines of white were visible from the moon bathing the breakers in its light. Red tracers started reaching out from enemy emplacements. Far away, the red lights appeared as if they were moving in slow motion, only to abruptly speed up as they zipped past. Shao maneuvered when tracers arced in his direction. Although the armored tub he was in could supposedly withstand a hit from a .50cal, the same couldn't be said of the rest of the helicopter.

The Z-10s assigned to the airport and docks veered off as they proceeded toward their objectives. Shao and one other chopper kept their course. He could see the thin ribbon of the bridge they were after. The second Z-10 went after the southern end of the long span, while he turned toward the northern end.

Climbing slightly, Shao identified an enemy position on the northern end of the bridge from the tracers being fired. He cut to the east and then banked sharply over the bridge. From the position of the firing, so close to the bridge entrance, he wondered if the special forces team that was tasked to capture it was still alive.

Flying along the bridge, he identified several vehicles on or near the main road. Two were burning beside a demolished building, while three others were a short distance away on the road itself. They all looked like American Humvees. Other fires were coming from the eastern edges of a small town that abutted the bridge, but he couldn't see what was burning.

Shao lined up the lead Humvee, trying to ignore the red streaks that were passing close down the left side of the Z-10. The gunner selected one of the 90mm pods. As the Chinese captain was delivering 23mm fire from the chin gun, the cockpit lit up as several of the larger rockets raced ahead of the helicopter. More enemy tracers flew up from the enemy position when the two other Humvees directed their fire toward Shao. The rockets fell among the lightly armored vehicle in the lead, exploding in a series of flashes. A large secondary detonation shot into the sky, a reddish-orange ball of fire rising in the midst of dark smoke. Flying over enemy concentration, Shao put the agile chopper into a hard bank while shooting flares out from the sides.

The captain heard the report from the southern end, the pilot stating that he was in contact with the special forces team. After receiving no resistance, the attack pilot called in the transports carrying the thirty soldiers responsible for linking up and holding that end of the long span. Shao made his own report, directing the transport that was to land on the northern end to land on the southern approach and make their way across the bridge from there. After ensuring that the southern end was secure, the second attack helicopter was to make its way to the northern end and assist with clearing it out.

Banking left and taking the Z-10 back out to sea, Shao heard the distinct pings of rounds hitting his chopper. Turning in the opposite direction, tracers flew along the left side, fading as they sped across the water. With flares trailing the helicopter, the captain brought it back around for another attack, this one coming from the north. He had to be careful not to fire past the enemy or he might hit the special forces team, if they were still alive. The two burning Humvees next to the destroyed building didn't give him much hope, but he'd strive to keep his attack contained nonetheless.

Racing south down the road, Shao's gunner again had one of the 90mm pods selected. More rockets shot ahead and exploded along the road, engulfing the trailing Humvee. Shao flew through the resulting fireball, the chopper shaking violently for a brief second. Coming from the direction of the small town, movement caught his eye; tracers were reaching up from a vehicle he hadn't previously spotted. The Z-10 shook as it took multiple hits.

Shao jumped as the side of the canopy right next to his head cracked. Glancing at the deep pit, a shot of fear went through his body. If the glass were weaker, he would likely be headless right now, the Z-10 crashing onto the bridge. He quickly banked away again to the west over the water. He was thankful that he hadn't had to deal with any shoulder-fired weapons so far, but he kept the flares coming, just in case.

Coming around, he opted to make his next pass from the west. He tried to keep his attacks coming from different directions to keep the enemy gunners guessing, although his trail of flares didn't exactly hide his location. Concentrating on the vehicle in town, Shao saw several soldiers hugging the sides. Fire from the mounted weapon and those from the Taiwanese troops rose to meet him.

The hills to the west of the road blocked the third vehicle sitting on it from seeing him, and thus bringing its firepower to bear. Tracers rose to meet him, zipping down both sides. It had the appearance of a space ship entering warp speed, the dots becoming long streaks that passed far too closely. Rippling fire again leapt from the pods to meet the enemy. In his night vision, Shao saw a series of explosions around the Humvee. Several bodies that had been sheltering against the vehicle were flung away to slam against building walls.

As the Z-10 flew low over the hills, coming out over the road, Shao again felt rounds hammer into the sides. Shao had expected his companion attack helicopter to join in the fight, but it was late in coming for some reason. Checking his engine instruments, Shao came around again.

This time, the chin-mounted 23mm turret was selected. The helmet-mounted sight directed the fire of the weapon. Focusing on the last Humvee on the road, the gunner pressed the trigger. The chopper slowed slightly with the force of the large caliber rounds spitting out. Tracers streaked up the road. He saw sparks from the Humvee sitting between two other burning vehicles. There wasn't a secondary explosion, but Shao saw the gunner standing in the ring on top flail violently as he was hit.

The second chopper finally called in and Shao directed it to attack the same vehicle. Turning to the west, the captain twisted around to observe the attack. Coming from the south, the other Z-10 raced along the bridge. Rockets shot out of the pods, dropping to explode among the wreckage. He watched in horror as a trail of fire rose from the town. The small ball of flame quickly picked up speed and slammed into the side of the attack chopper.

Shao could almost hear the alarm bells, could nearly see the flashing lights. The Z-10 staggered in the air and then slewed to the side. In a long ball of flame, it crashed atop the hills adjacent the road. Another of Shao's fears had come to pass: the enemy had MANPADS.

Trailing a long line of flares, the captain banked his chopper around. Clenching his teeth, partially in anger over his partner being brought down and partially from the fear he struggled to contain, Shao pressed his attack. Rockets arced toward the ground and the chin turret added a torrent of fire on the enemy position. He watched as flame passed over the bodies of soldiers with weapons glued to their shoulders.

As the captain swept over the scene, he wasn't sure if he had killed those who had shoulder-fired anti-air missiles, but none rose to meet him. Again and again, he came over the Taiwanese contingent, sending fire into their ranks. He chased them down as they scattered into the hills, sending 23mm rounds to thud into the earth and to rip through bodies. They flung their arms wide and fell to the ground as the deadly bullets tore into them. His trepidation had faded into the adrenaline-fueled fury of the angel of death he was commanded to be.

As the staccato of his powerful weapons slowed, there came a time when no more fire was seen coming from the area. Gripped by the fight as he was, he barely heard the call that the holding force had arrived on the northern end and was setting up defensive positions. His mind cleared with the feeling of a different kind of vibration coming through the stick. His stomach tightened with realization. Glancing at the instruments, his oil pressure gage quivered and dropped.

It was time to get the bird out of the sky before the choice was taken from him. Guiding the injured Z-10 back toward the northern end of the bridge, the vibrations increased until he thought he was flying a paint shaker. What happened in the parking lot could technically be called a landing, but it was actually more of an arrival than anything else. Sparks flew as he skidded into a rough landing, the attack chopper sliding forward a few more feet before shuddering to a stop. Shutting down the smoking engine, Shao felt as if he might be two inches shorter from the impact.

The two ends of the bridge were captured, but the forces holding it were without any aerial support. The troops coming up from the south found what they at first thought was a badly injured Taiwanese soldier, but they then discovered that the man was Chinese special forces, unconscious and barely alive.

Sergeant Hou was badly burned. He was given first aid and didn't regain consciousness as he was transported back across the strait to a Chinese hospital. There he laid in a coma for three months when he suddenly awoke. The rehabilitation was long and painful, and upon completing it, the long-time special forces sergeant left the military and dedicated his life to more peaceful endeavors. Years later, it was found that he had entered a monastery and had indeed remained there for the rest of his life. Unfortunately, the serenity he found remained superficial; he never completely shook the horrors of that night on the Penghu.

*   *   *   *   *   *

Xiamen Harbor, China
1 August, 2021

An American E-3 stationed east of Taiwan picked up the movements. The cross-channel ships sailing from Xiamen toward the island chain in the Taiwan Strait caught everyone by surprise. Intel had completely missed the gathering and loading of those ships. A subsequent review of satellite footage would reveal them plain as day, but the primary focus had been on the Chinese ports of Zhoushan and Zhanjiang. The submarines had been positioned to catch the Chinese diesel-electric boats when they recharged, and thus weren't in positions where they could intercept and attack the smaller invasion force. And by the time the fleet was noticed, it was too late to scramble the bombers at Guam. The Chinese attacking force heading toward the Penghu had been essentially given a free pass by the United States.

*   *   *   *   *   *

Pehu Island, Penghu Islands, Taiwan
1 August, 2021

The colonel stood in the middle of the highway just outside of the entrance to the Zhenhai Junior High School. The lines of the road glowed white under the partial illumination provided by the half-moon hanging high overhead. In direct contrast, the dense trees and foliage to his sides hid everything in layers of darkness.

Staring down the road, the leader of the Penghu Defense Command visualized approaching columns of Chinese mechanized units. Colonel Wen-hsiung could have chosen a multitude of locations to set up his defense, but this narrow corridor just outside of Chen-Hai best suited his needs. He only had two battalions, air defense assets, and a field artillery unit at his disposal, so selecting narrow fronts were best. And with the island's terrain, most roadways were exactly that.

Up the road, he had the few medium armored units under his command positioned in breaks, their barrels pointed toward the only place Chinese forces could advance. The thick terrain throughout the islands was both a blessing and a hindrance. Movement for both sides would be constrained to the roadways, and in some cases, fields cut through the foliage.

He wanted to defend the bridge coming from the main island, but that would have placed some of his soldiers and equipment in the open where they could be easily targeted. A symbolic resistance was placed at the airport in the form of several short-range anti-air units. The decision not to defend the strategic location was a matter of firepower; he just didn't have enough of it.

It was the same with his decision to leave the port undefended. He left behind a few surprises, but without a larger force, Wen-hsiung had to fight along the narrow corridors of the roads. Beside spreading his forces too thin, another reason he didn't want to defend the port was to mitigate civilian casualties. There weren't many people on the island and Wen-hsiung knew more than a few of them. He could have moved them, but to where? There were few underground shelters on the island and the air defense and rocket crews were using them at the moment. It was a tough situation.

Most of the tanks from his armored battalion had been taken away, along with his helicopter support. The colonel understood the reasoning behind the moves, but it would have been nice to have more of the heavy guns to help stave off expected Chinese attacks. It would have been a welcome security, but unfortunately, the heavy guns just weren't useful offensively with the limited sight lines and rough terrain of the island. Perhaps the Chinese troops would be content to keep and hold the main island, though the colonel doubted they would leave the rest of the archipelago in Taiwanese hands.

Artillery batteries had been placed farther away. They were using a sports field at an elementary school. Situated on a similar field at the junior high school, short-range ground-to-air missiles were ready to use against any aircraft or helicopters China might bring to break through Wen-hsiung's defenses. The colonel had no illusions about stopping China's plans to occupy the Penghu, but he hoped to extract a price. Wen-hsiung didn't expect to see the next dawn.

He had contemplated using the equipment at his disposal and then conducting guerilla warfare against the occupiers, but that futile effort might lead to reprisals against the few citizens scattered throughout the archipelago. If his battalions should become dispersed, he had given orders for the soldiers to make it to one of the hardened shelters being used by rocket and anti-aircraft units. There, they would continue to hold out for as long as they could.

For all he knew, the invasion might have already begun. He had already sent a reinforced platoon south to the Penghu Great Bridge where an alarm had been reported. They stated that they had engaged an unknown force but had since gone silent. Scouts had been subsequently dispatched to watch the roads coming out of Tongliang, but so far, no movement was reported. A reserve company was ready to be dispatched in that direction so that he wouldn't be hit blindly from the rear.

For a brief moment, Colonel Wen-hsiung allowed himself to enjoy the mild evening. A faint breeze felt cool against his cheek, bringing a relative sensation of peace, of renewal. He might not see the dawn, but he was alive right now. In the light of the half-moon, Wen-hsiung thought about his son. The boy had become a man. He had recently been assigned to the flight school at Taitung flying F-5s.

They hadn't talked much since the accident which took the life of his mother two years ago. Considering that his son blamed him, any conversation since then had been strained and awkward, if he was lucky enough to speak to his son at all. If Wen-hsiung could take anything back, it would be that. The colonel had been cleared of any wrongdoing related to the accident, but his son didn't see it that way. It was a tragedy that he didn't care to relive. Adding to that tragedy was the loss of the bond between him and his son. The two of them had been close, maybe even each other's best friend. But those times had come and gone. As much as the colonel wanted that intimacy to return, he didn't see any way of restoring it, and now he stood and watched what could possibly be his last moonrise.

Staring at the stars twinkling across a background of black velvet, Wen-hsiung hoped for two things. One was that his son would live through what was coming, and two, that he would find happiness in his life. The colonel also hoped vainly that the two of them could reconcile, but if that wasn't in the stars, then at least he wanted his son to find joy.

As his vision blurred slightly, Wen-hsiung heard a series of distant explosions. They were coming from the direction of the great bridge. There was a chance that China had launched another missile attack, but the colonel doubted it. With the radio silence coming from his dispatched platoon, and the blasts, he knew deep down that the invasion had finally reached friendly shores. It was time to get to work. Grabbing the handset from his radio, he began to deliver a series of orders.

* * * * * *

Magong Harbor, Penghu, Taiwan
1 August, 2021

Bright pole-mounted lights lit up the concrete piers extending into the waters of the harbor. It was one of the few illuminated places across the width and breadth of the island nation. Ther responsible parties knew with a fair degree of certainty that China wouldn't target the port, if their previous patterns held. All the ports stuck out like sore thumbs by China's specific avoidance from their missile attacks. The lights were to make it harder for Chinese special forces to operate; the Taiwanese military commanders wanted to be prepared for interference in their preparations.

Hidden among the numerous fishing boats and surrounding structures, small groups of soldiers waited for the command to begin their missions. It had taken some time to put together the special measures, but it had been accomplished. The port was made up of smaller harbors wrapped around the larger one. The individual ports were mostly fishing harbors, but a few of those berths were big enough to allow China's ROROs to dock and disgorge their dreaded hardware.

Commandeering freighters, ferries, and some of the larger fishing vessels, including a coast guard cutter, teams placed ships across the entrances. Bows and sterns were tied to concrete breakwaters separating the individual harbors. Below the waterlines, shaped explosions had been attached to the hulls. Connecting these floating blockades with the shores were shielded electrical cables running to detonators. It was these measures which the Penghu Defense Command hoped to keep from the spies and saboteurs of China's special forces.

Light from the port filtered through the dirt-smeared window of a portside karaoke bar. Hidden within the recesses of the tiny bar waited members of a small team from the defense command. Outside, the quiet of the night was almost unnerving considering the previous storm of explosions that shook the island. Many of the inhabitants had been moved away from the port boundaries, making the area near the harbor even quieter.

The team whispered jokes and stories, eliciting soft anxious chuckles as they waited for the inevitable radio call. One member joked about how the atmosphere seemed like they were living in one of the apocalyptic movies coming out of South Korea. The attempt at humor fell flat as they realized that they were living close to that truth. With China's impending approach, Taiwan's cities might soon be leveled by waves of missile attacks.

One of the soldiers kept glancing at a small laptop, clicking through the various cameras placed throughout their designated port area. The screen showed a line of giant fuel and oil holding tanks lining a section of one of the piers under their jurisdiction. The soldier peered into the shadows cast by the bright pole-mounted lights, searching for movement or any sign that someone was hiding within their depths.

A story being told was cut short as all eyes turned toward a radio, perched atop the bar, when it squelched.

"Waking Dragon," a crackling voice came through the radio. "I repeat, Waking Dragon."

The radio fell back into silence. Even though they had been waiting for the call, their very purpose for being there, the men stared at the black box for several long seconds. It was as if they expected the coded order to be rescinded, but knew that it wouldn't be. Their eyes then turned toward the small detonator abutting the radio.

As if returning from a dream, the fearful reverie broke when one man rose and took three strides toward the device, scooting an old wooden chair out of the way. Gripping the detonator, the man looked outside. Dust particles drifted lazily in the light pouring through the stained windows, the name of the bar cast in stark relief. With a shrug directed toward the rest of his small team, he armed the device. A tiny green light winked on and the man moved another switch.

The bright lights shining over the harbor were dimmed by a much larger flash of orange and yellow light. The charges within the fuel tanks, especially those inside the gasoline tanks, exploded with a violence and ferocity that no one on the islands had ever witnessed. For a split second, the men, and others situated around the port, thought a nuclear device had been detonated.

For those inside the karaoke bar, their silent hideout turned from a calm waiting into a maelstrom of chaos. The windows exploded inward, the sharp shards slicing into the one standing by the bar, his hands still gripping the small device.

With a concussive boom that drowned out everything else, including screams as dirt, wood splinters, and chairs whirled around the room. One of the larger fishing boats that was in the fishing harbor landed on the road in front, crushing two cars parked along the waterfront.

Engulfed in flame, the boat heeled over, the crackling roar adding its voice to the thunderous boom coming from millions of gallons of high-octane gasoline igniting at once. A high-pitched whine was all the soldiers could hear when the initial blast passed over. Replacing the white lights was an orange glow that flickered intensely.

The soldier still stood by the bar, an unconnected cord dangling from the device. His uniform was in tatters, his face blackened from the blast. The grime covering his body was mixed with blood that streamed from a dozen or more cuts. The only part of him that was truly visible were his widened eyes reflecting the glow of the conflagration burning outside.

The others stared at the figure. Shards of glass and splinters of wood fell from them as they rose to help their comrade. The man's eyes turned to track them as they approached, allowing them to pry the device from his hand. Even though they couldn't hear themselves, the men talked to him in an attempt to keep him from going further into shock as they guided the man from the bar. Together, they made their way toward a waiting boat that would carry them to Pehu Island.

The explosion completely obliterated two fishing harbors, the burning fuel and oil spreading across the once placid waters. The storefronts along the two harbors were in tatters. Windows were shattered and doorways smashed open. Weakened by the blasts, some of the restaurants and a hotel fell in on themselves.

Flaming gouts of fuel arced across the city, landing on wooden roofs. Spot fires broke out and quickly spread across the city, the summer dry spell allowing the structures to rapidly combust. In short order, fires soon engulfed sections of the city and threatened to consume the entire regional capital. The very thing Colonel Wen-hsiung hoped to prevent by avoiding combat in urban areas was becoming a reality by his efforts to deny the port to China.

Although paling in comparison to the fuel storage tanks erupting, the radio call caused additional explosions to rock the harbor. Shaped charges punched holes in the hulls of the vessels strategically placed across the mouths of the smaller harbors. Water poured through gashes in the thin skins. Mist shot out of open topside portals as the water forced air from inside the ships. The vessels slipped lower below the surface, their keels hitting the bottom of the harbor entrances. Many of the ships tipped over, their hulls flickering from the flames. Others settled with their superstructures jutting above the waves. The Magong Harbor was effectively closed for the time being.

The one asset that was saved from the numerous explosions was the naval base on Observation Island. However, that facility wasn't lost to the military staff plans. There, Taiwan expended some of their few remaining cruise missiles to help close the harbor. The ground-launched weapons arrived shortly after the radio call went out. Streaking only a few feet above the surface, weapons designed to take out hardened shelters began arriving over the small naval base.

Following their programming, the missiles zoomed upward when close to their objective. The internal software recognized their targets and dove toward the surface. They impacted the jetties. The delayed fuses blew gigantic chunks of concrete into the air. Splashes showed where heavy objects were thrown into the interior bay then bobbed and sank like reticent sea monsters. When the smoke and debris settled, huge sections of the three harbors lay cratered. If China's intention was to utilize the port, they would have their work cut out for them.

*   *   *   *   *   *

Hiding below the lip of an embankment near the entrance to Magong Harbor, a Chinese special forces team peeked over the crest. Their faces were lit from a giant fireball that rose over the harbor, the thunderous sound of the blast reaching them a split second later. Even from this distance, the six members of the team could feel the heat emanating from the explosion.

More demolitions came from other sections of the harbor. With sickened stomachs, they watched ships sink across the various entrances throughout area. They had failed in their mission. The delay of the submarine carrying them to their objective had caused them to arrive too late, as evidenced by the rising cloud of flame and dark smoke.

The leader, Sergeant Jian Kang, sent a coded message, giving the inbound assault force the status of the port. Seeing as their primary mission hadn't been successful, and that there was nothing he could do to fix it, the team leader slipped out of sight. He thought about what his next move should be. The original plan had called for them to hold after a successful completion of the mission and to subsequently link up with the assault forces. That was no longer an option.

He could work his way over to the airport and join with the forces landing there. Or he could wait in his present position for the Chinese attack that was surely to come, only this one from inland rather than the originally planned helicopter assault. After all, the port was vital, even though it might now be some time before it became operational.

Peeking back over the crest, Jian Kang wondered just how long that would be. The supplies carried on the transport ships would be essential for the drive to take over the archipelago. The sergeant again slipped out of sight and produced a folded map. Under the light of a red-lensed flashlight, he pored over the perimeter of the main island, tracing it intently with his finger. There were several fishing harbors dotting the coastline. Some of them were obviously too small to accommodate the transport ships, even with their modified ramp systems.

His finger traced the shoreline to the south. The nice thing about the fishing harbors was that they had wide concrete piers, almost overkill for the fishing boats. But they needed to be built that way in some instances to allow for commercial trucks to enter. Some of them even looked strong enough to support armored vehicles.

As the special forces sergeant focused on the map, another feature caught his eye. On the southern tip of the main island sat a long unpaved strip free of the island's choking foliage. It looked like it might be an abandoned airfield, complete with a dirt ramp area. Some of the buildings set off from the runway looked newer. The sergeant thought it could also be an army training base, although it hadn't been on any of the briefings he had been in on. Did anyone know of its existence? Likely not, or it would have been included in the plans.

Jian Kang noted that it was conveniently located near several fishing harbors that might support one transport ship at a time.

Which is better than none, the sergeant thought grimly, looking back at the flaming debris of the blocked harbor.

Risking exposure from a lengthy radio transmission, the sergeant contacted his headquarters. As he ended his call, the six hidden members that were part of the Guangzhou Military Region Special Forces Unit slid back into the dark waters. They had a new mission on the southern tip of Magong Island.

*   *   *   *   *   *

Penghu Airport, Penghu Island, Taiwan
1 August, 2021

As with Magong Harbor, the Penghu Defense Command attempted to deny the main airport to the inbound Chinese threat. When the coded radio message arrived, crews began detonating the explosive charges set within the main facilities. A series of explosions shook the main terminal building. The tall glass windows looking onto the tarmac blew outward, sending shards scattering across the concrete and hitting the surfaces of parked commuter and other narrow-bodied aircraft.

The control tower was rocked as charges arranged near

the base detonated. With a slow, wrenching groan, the building began toppling, gaining speed as the momentum of destruction took over. It hit the ground and sprayed concrete across the ramp. Parked aircraft then went up in flames and shrapnel from explosives placed under their fuel tanks. Even though the jet fuel had fire retardants in the mix, it wasn't enough to withstand the incendiary components included in the charges.

Flaming fuel flew into the shattered remains of the terminal gates. The fire flickered within dark smoke as it poured out from smashed windows. Burning pieces of aircraft arced into the night skies, falling like meteorites onto green fields separating the taxiways from the runway. Additional blasts knocked down hangars, the result of the airplanes parked within going up.

Like the grand finale of a fireworks show, the underground fuel tanks erupted. Chaotic swaths of earth, concrete, and flame reached for the heavens. Any standing structure around the airport environment was leveled by the concussive forces rocketing outward from the gigantic blast. As with the naval base, missiles began arriving from Taiwan. The weapons plunged deep into the single runway and adjacent taxiway. Two more cratered the tarmac that was awash in flames. Although runways could be fixed with relative ease with the right equipment, for now, the airport environment was in complete ruin. China wouldn't have access to any of the normal airport services and would have to bring in their own.

*   *   *   *   *   *

The other helicopters to the left and right were only silhouettes darkened by the surrounding night. Ahead, moonlight shone on the long span of the Penghu Great Bridge, which connected two of the landmasses that made up the chain of islands. Diamonds glistened atop the waters of the Taiwan Strait, making the shadowy shapes of the isles appear as black holes. Their forms were only defined by thin rings of white as the waves crashed into rocky shorelines.

At the northern end of the bridge, streaks of fire streamed down, seeming to materialize from empty space. Two vehicles were burning next to the smoldering ruins of a building, while farther up the main road, tracers arced into the skies as gunners tried to find the dragon breathing fire on their positions. That's at least what Captain Tien Pengfei thought when he glanced toward the fight in progress.

Before he knew it, the whitish line of the span zipped beneath the nose of his Z-10 attack helicopter. When he took off, the captain had been eager to get into the fight. It was what he had trained for and he couldn't wait to experience combat firsthand.

That attitude changed about halfway across the strait. There, he survived not one, but two attacks. Tien Pengfei had never before felt like a sitting duck while Taiwan fired volleys of anti-aircraft missiles. He could only dodge and release countermeasures into the night without a chance at retaliation. The memories of exploding missiles and the subsequent fireballs were still fresh in his mind as he left the bridge behind.

Tien Pengfei knew that he would have to again face defensive fire when it came time for his unit to attack the main airfield. As much as he tried, he just couldn't shake the images — the yellowish streaks descending from the starlit skies, the sight of a chopper being hit and nosing into the sea, the tracers rising from the ground…those scenes were seared into his brain. Almost two hours ago, the captain had departed eager to show his mettle. Now, he just hoped to survive. Or, at a minimum, that his death wouldn't be painful.

As if to remind him of what he was facing, a bright flash of light preceded a giant fireball that rose from the direction of the main port. The moonlight highlighted a roiling mass of dark smoke with red and orange tongues of flame licking within the angry mass. It rapidly climbed into the night sky. Several other flashes rose from the same location.

For a moment, the captain and his gunner were confused. Since the bridge units peeled off, he was now part of the vanguard. So, who was attacking the port? The crews who had been assigned to provide support for the port were behind him. It then dawned on him that Taiwan was destroying their own port, denying the Chinese its use. Shortly after, that was confirmed by a radio call directing all units assigned to the port to divert to the airport.

Tien Pengfei was relieved to hear the change in plans. That meant there would be additional helicopters to help suppress the defensive fire that would certainly rise to greet him. In his view, the more there were, the less his chances of being targeted and shot down. He knew that didn't make a ton of sense, but it nonetheless eased some of the tension he was holding.

Appearing as if a small nuclear device had been detonated, a similar fireball rocketed upward from the direction of the airport. Billowing mushroom clouds were driven violently upward from the heat, their undersides glowing orange from the building conflagration. Secondary explosions continued to jolt the area around the airport as the assault force drew closer.

Off to the right, in the direction of the harbor, fires arose throughout the adjacent city. As he watched, they began to grow, the flames spreading quickly among the tightly packed buildings. Tien Pengfei didn't know exactly what he expected combat to be like, but what he was witnessing both agreed with what he had envisioned, but also didn't.

As he drew close to the shores, time seemed to flow faster. He felt the urge to rein it in, to give him some time to adapt and ease into the situation. Flying at a hundred twenty miles per hour, that just wasn't possible. He tried to ease back into the normal by running checklists with his gunner. The 57mm rocket pods and two HJ-10 anti-tank missiles slung under the stubby wings were waiting to enact their fury on any ground forces that rose to challenge the numerous attack choppers charging their positions.

A second radio call came over the net. For the second time, the units originally slated to assault the port were diverted. There was supposedly a dirt airfield on the southern end of the main island which the airborne forces would invest in. Tien Pengfei felt a tinge of jealousy wash over him. A dirt airfield that had been missed in the planning couldn't be very well defended.

"Are you okay up there?" his gunner spoke up over the intercom.

"Yeah. I'm doing fine," the captain replied.

"You missed our call," the gunner informed him.

Dammit! Tien Pengfei said to himself.

It wasn't like him to miss something like that. He had exemplified himself during training missions and annual exercises. What in the fuck was wrong with him? If he didn't get his act together, he would wind up just a smoldering ash pile on this godforsaken island. Shaking his head to pull himself from the fearful place in which he had been residing ever since the first enemy missile slammed into the side of another Z-10, the captain tried to reorient himself toward the upcoming fight. It didn't work entirely, but it did make him feel a little more confident.

The gunner knew that his pilot had been shaken. Normally conversive over the intercom, this flight had been conducted mostly in silence. It just wasn't like Tien. He stared at the back of the helmet in the front seat, saw it turn back and forth, and heard a subdued curse.

In front, the captain knew that the call had to be about attack sequencing and area of responsibility. From the mission briefing, he knew what he was expected to do. The call had to be an assignment verification as they were drawing close to the target area. He knew he was scheduled to be a part of the first wave going in and was responsible for defeating any defensive positions they encountered on the peninsula to the north.

"We're covering the north with Dragon Three Four," he responded to the gunner.

Tien was a little surprised that their missile warning indicator hadn't gone off. He would have expected the close-in defenses to react by now. The Z-10 hit the final approach fix. Still offshore and without slowing, he banked the attack helicopter to the left, angling for the arm of land stretching north from the fire-engulfed airport.

Going feet dry, the chopper crossed over the shoreline. It was as if that was a signal for the island defenses to come to life. From multiple positions, missiles flew aloft. Tails of fire streaked toward the inbound units, which left their own trail of hot flares descending in their wake.

With the ground sweeping past fifty feet below, Tien knew he didn't have much margin for error. Expending flares, he banked hard. The tips of the rotors nearly clipped bushes and stunted trees, the wingtip vortices leaving behind a swirl of leaves as they were shaken loose. The captain watched one missile rise from a position just north of the burning airfield. The tiny streamer of fire turned slightly and was coming directly at Tien. He punched out another series of flares and was relieved when the missile made a downward arc, chasing after the white-hot countermeasures.

The captain rolled in the opposite direction until his nose was pointed directly to the place where he saw the missile fly aloft. In the glow of his NVGs, Tien saw a major road that looped around the northern end of the runway. A truck was parked at an intersection. Focusing on that target, with the reticle centered, Tien pressed the trigger.

The chopper vibrated as 23mm tracers streaked downward. The road surrounding the vehicle sparked from striking rounds, a maelstrom of fire engulfing the anti-air vehicle. A secondary explosion marked the end of the threat, a fireball rising directly in the helicopter's path. Tien and his gunner shook along with their Z-10 as they zipped overhead, the heat momentarily catching the chopper in its grip. And then they were past.

Tien felt another release of tension. He had been able to strike back at those who filled him with fear. Bringing the Z-10 around, the captain saw a sky filled with tracer rounds, some rising to seek the flying machines that had come, others descending. Secondary explosions flashed all around the airport vicinity. Like the stars overhead, small fires started dotting the countryside. In some places, larger fires marked where the ground defenses were successful. And through it all, moonlight bathed the top of smoke columns in silver while the bottoms glowed red. It seemed to Tien to be a stark portrayal of the West's version of heaven and hell.

Still looking back toward the airfield, the captain saw one of the Z-10s take a hit. Flying through the flash of fire, the chopper slewed to the side and started autorotating. He watched in horror as the Z-10 spun into the mass of fires raging from the burning fuel depot. The ensuing explosion was barely visible.

Movement caught Tien's eye. Trailing fire, a missile leapt up from a dirt field. As if suddenly materializing, the captain saw a line of vehicles near where the field connected with a tree line. He brought the Z-10 around again, lining up with the row of military trucks. Roaring in, 57mm rockets ripple-fired from one of the pods. Balls of fire flew past the chopper that was eating up two miles of terrain per minute. Clods of dirt were thrown skyward as explosions walked up to the first vehicle. The secondary blast came right on the heels of the impacting rocket, throwing large hunks of metal outward. The remaining missiles still attached to the enemy vehicle ignited. Without any guidance, the weapons spiraled aimlessly into the night.

The volley marched through the missile battery, tearing the unarmored vehicles apart. Through the glow of night vision, Tien saw several soldiers flee, disappearing into the tree line. Sending more flares into his slipstream, his head swiveled in all directions as he searched for more targets, and for rising missiles. He noted that the overall volume of fire coming up to meet the assault had diminished.

Thirty minutes later, the Z-10 attack helicopters were having to search wide and far for any targets of opportunity. Very few tracers rose from the vicinity of the airfield, and any that did were immediately swarmed. The commander of the assault force declared the Penghu Airport subdued and called for the arrival of the transports. In short order, Z-18 medium transport helicopters began landing on concrete pads situated on the airfield's northern end.

It was the only place that wasn't demolished or on fire. As soon as the wheels touched down, airborne soldiers poured from within. Lit by flickering flames, platoons spread throughout the airport environment. There were very few Taiwanese soldiers and most of the ones encountered had been a part of the destroyed missile batteries. Setting up perimeters, the airport was quickly overrun.

However, the commanders saw the condition of what they were guarding. The airport environment was demolished. Deep craters ran the length of the runway and parallel taxiway. The terminal was in ruins. Large chunks of rebar-infused concrete were lying among the lingering fires from demolished passenger jets. The fuel farm was non-existent, the heat from the continuing conflagration blistering any who wandered too close.

Helicopters could set down, but it would take a lot of work before the first transport aircraft could land. The heavier equipment and supplies the airborne forces would need to subdue the island chain would have to land somewhere else. As for the ships, command hoped that the fishing harbors on the southern end of the island would prove sufficient.

While securing the airport boundaries and setting up a defensive perimeter, commanders sent squads in search of any construction machinery they could locate. The sooner the airfield was in operation, the easier it would become to hold it from expected counterattacks. For now, although the soldiers had the comfort of attack helicopters, they were without air defenses. And, they wouldn't have the use of the Z-10s for long as fuel was a concern. The choppers had used up most of what they had onboard on the flight over the strait and with their attacks. Many were touching down on fumes, basically becoming useless hunks of metal until their thirsty engines could again be sated.

* * * * * *

The diverted Chinese attack helicopters, originally slated to assault the port, swung around the capital city. The spot fires that had started from the exploding fuel tanks near the harbor were growing. Red lights from responding emergency vehicles flashed down several thoroughfares as crews raced to put out the growing flames before they could engulf neighborhoods. One side of the main harbor was a firestorm, the yellow and orange blazes glimmering off the inky port waters.

The pilots and gunners glanced toward the northeast, where airport defenses had begun to make themselves known against the other group. Streaks of flame rose from a darkened landscape, their infrared seekers homing in on heat signatures. The Chinese crews from the diverted flights could only briefly observe the developing fight before they had to focus on their own.

Moonlight glistened on the surrounding seas as the choppers flew south along a narrow isthmus. Through their night vision, the lead pilots saw a long stretch of dirt that marked where special forces had located an additional untouched landing strip. Several lightly armored military vehicles were parked at the southern end of a ramp. Hidden among thick outcroppings of trees lay row upon row of long, rectangular buildings.

Under the direction of the group leader, the Z-10s split into three columns. One file swung to the east, some moving farther away from the airfield to search for threats among the dense foliage. A second swept along the western side of the runway. Rockets shot out from pylon-mounted pods, arcing downward. Explosions rippled down the dirt ramp, detonating among the parked vehicles. The armored trucks became obscured in the swirling dust and debris being tossed up.

The lead pilot was surprised by the lack of secondary explosions, then surmised that the parked vehicles weren't operational. Nevertheless, the trucks were pounded by follow-on helicopters. The orders were to keep the runway environment free of damage. That meant limiting attacks on the ramp, and the runway itself wasn't to be hit at all. The reports coming from the main airport were that it was cratered and couldn't be used in the foreseeable future. That and the loss of the port meant the dirt field was all China had to bring in reinforcements and supplies. It was still to be seen whether the fishing docks that had been reported by special forces could be used, so for now, the thin strip of dirt was all China's assault forces had.

The third column was directed to the buildings lining the west side of the airfield. Streaks of fire soared down to impact among the trees, the 57mm rockets tearing into thin-skinned buildings. As with the parked vehicles, there were very few additional explosions. Chinese attack helicopters roared over the Taiwanese base, flying directly over two sports fields. To the pilots flitting over the area, it appeared as if they were striking a small military base.

The group's leader wondered just how in the hell intel could have missed the Taiwanese asset, pondering if the location was part of the enemy defense command or if it was a training facility. If it was a permanent base, the lack of secondary blasts meant that any ammunition and operational vehicles had been pulled out before China's attack. That indicated that the main Taiwanese units, those that remained behind to defend the island chain, had opted to position themselves somewhere away from the island's strategic points.

Without receiving any return fire, the group commander called off further attacks. A radio call brought the transport choppers screaming in to disgorge airborne soldiers. In groups of thirty, troops ran from the interiors to set up an ever-growing perimeter. With a thud, one platoon's chopper set down on the ramp.

Amid whirling blades, their vision partially obscured in a rising dust storm, the soldiers ran down the ramp and halted. They had their original assignment, but that had drastically changed when the port facilities had been blown. Now, they ran, ready to return fire or set up a defensive perimeter. But with the sudden diversion, no one knew what they were supposed to do.

This was one problem with a heavily centralized command structure; the soldiers weren't used to having to be flexible. They required firm instructions, but the lower ranks, including the officers, seldom had the initiative to act on their own. Thus, the unit slowed and then stopped, unsure of what they should be doing. One of the company commanders, seeking guidance from a battalion commander, attempted to bring order to the chaos surrounding the continued helicopter landings.

The captain saw the groups of milling soldiers. With explosions dotting the perimeter from Z-10s hitting anything that looked remotely hostile, and with the thundering roar of choppers in close proximity, the company commander grabbed the platoon leader's shoulder.

"Take that building there," the captain shouted, pointing to a white structure adjacent the dirt tarmac.

Units lost cohesion as orders were disseminated by equally confused junior commanders. Objectives were given at random depending on what some officer saw or felt. The platoon given the task of securing the nearest building, likely to contain a base of operations, ran among the continued flow of incoming transports. In the dark, with everything coated in a greenish glow, the scene was very chaotic. Groups of soldiers ran here and there, directed by orders given without a cohesive plan.

The platoon ran up and stacked next to an entrance. With a nod from a sergeant, one of the men opened a wooden door. A couple of men, pressed against the wall to either side of the entry, pulled grenade pins and tossed them inside. Smoke and debris shot out of the opening from two nearly simultaneous blasts. In the aftermath, one of the doors hung at a drunken angle as one of the hinges was torn free.

Almost before the explosions had settled, the soldiers rushed through the entryway. Gunfire rang out as the troops rushed into a smoke-filled room. Splinters tore away from walls, the glass from picture frames shattering from the bursts of fire. Gunfire directed toward a long desk tossed papers into the air, where they fluttered and added to the general chaos inside the building.

Pushing ahead and with their heads on swivels, the lead men cautiously worked down hallways, others coming in behind checking out additional rooms. A shattered picture sliding down a wall received a volley of fire from anxious men with trigger fingers. The building shook several times as additional grenades were thrown into unknown rooms. Sporting sweat-stained uniforms, the men cleared the building, not finding a single enemy combatant.

However, the initial grenade blasts and volleys of gunfire, even subdued against the background noise of helicopters taking off and landing, set off a chain of reactions. Other soldiers, thinking that there was now an ongoing battle for control of the airfield, saw movements in the shadows where there were none. Gunfire broke out in all quadrants, especially among those directed to search the rest of the buildings. The one-sided battle destroyed countless footlockers and bunks. And with any confused battle scene, mistakes were made. In the end, three Chinese soldiers were killed and ten others wounded without a single shot being fired by the enemy.

But the mission was dubbed a success. The dirt airfield was taken without a serious fight, even though several company commanders would write that they had run across pockets of enemy fire. In the confusion, the main Penghu Defense Command base had been taken. Slowly, order was restored and units again became cohesive. Perimeters were pushed farther out. Transport and attack helicopters were forced to land, cramming together on grass fields between the main tarmac, taxiways, and the single runway.

Special forces air traffic controllers, originally slated for the main airport, took over ramp operations. They and the group commanders gradually created order. Units assigned to the inner security were given infrared markers, and under the guidance of the air traffic specialists, laid them along the single dirt strip. The ends of the runway were similarly marked. Radio communications were set up and the call went out.

The thunderous noise of circling choppers had faded as fuel tanks emptied, the night gradually returning to the peace it had held only hours before.

*   *   *   *   *   *

The proven concept of force dispersal wasn't observed by the Chinese contingent of attack and transport helicopters at Penghu International Airport. Due to the cratered environment and fire raging at the airport's fuel farm, the commanders were limited as to where they could park their chopper battalions. Only the northern end of the field presented enough space on the airport grounds to park the fuel-starved machines. There were brief discussions about using territory outside of the airport's perimeter, but worry over saboteurs sidelined those deliberations.

Choppers occupied nearly every available piece of ground, primarily using the grass fields between the runway and taxiway, the grass edges adjacent the western side of the runway, and concrete pads that previously held Taiwan's air units assigned to the islands. Foot patrols walked the fenced perimeters, searching the surrounding environments for signs of Taiwanese counterattacks. In the distances, faint glows from burning enemy air defense units created skeletal silhouettes out of tree branches.

Near the northeastern corner of the airfield proper, two uniformed men peeked over a low wall. Across a central highway that ran through the small community sat an elementary school. Squatting on a rooftop almost thirty feet off the ground, the two men with night vision gear surveyed their surroundings. Spot fires dotted the landscape from Chinese attacks against air defense units that had stayed behind to be a nuisance for the invasion forces. Other than that illumination, not a single light showed from the town's residential buildings.

Nearby shadows rhythmically danced from the conflagration at the airport, dark shapes swaying to unheard music on walls glowing orange. The two men noted the Chinese foot patrols and emplacements being organized. They also cautiously watched groups of gathering soldiers, worried about an eventual push outside of the current perimeters. However, all the Chinese soldiers were currently inside the airport boundaries. Although the two men were close to the fence that guarded the airfield environment, the area around them was secure for the moment.

One of the men had an unfolded map set on the half wall surrounding the rooftop. Glancing through the binoculars, he would then place markings. It was something to fill time until all the helicopters had landed. Considering the Chinese method of insertion, using helicopters to lift their invasion forces across the strait, and with the airfield out of commission due to the set explosives, the Penghu Defense commander had visualized a period where the Chinese would have to regroup.

He had based this on China not being able to immediately land their heavier equipment, assuming that the battalions taking part wouldn't want to move out without heavier firepower. That meant the Chinese commanders would wait until loads of fuel and armored vehicles were flown in, leaving the ground troops and choppers a period of vulnerability. Colonel Wen-hsiung, the Penghu Defense Command leader, had quickly formed a plan upon seeing the Taiwan strait fill with low-flying helicopters.

The two Taiwanese soldiers atop the building plotted the grouping of landed helicopters. The latitude and longitude of the airfield was noted in several publications, so it was only a small matter to pinpoint the coordinates where the choppers had landed. The last of those circling to land set their wheels down on one of the concrete pads on the northern end of the airfield, and only sixteen hundred feet from where the two men were squatting.

"Penghu Defense Command, fire mission, over," one man called into a radio strapped to his back.

"Standby," came the reply.

One of the men on the roof panned the airfield with the binoculars, looking to see if their radio transmissions sparked any activity. Although the heavier transports hadn't landed, that didn't mean that the helicopter forces hadn't brought their own scanners to triangulate radio traffic. The fact that they were able to get through meant that ground-based jammers weren't currently in effect, or if they were, they were proving ineffectual. Not observing anything other than the patrols and units gathering, the man gave his partner a thumbs up.

The radio crackled again. "Ready to copy coordinates."

One man relayed where the choppers were parked, which wasn't difficult, as they seemed to encompass the entire northern section of the airfield.

"Spotting round out," the artillery radio operator intoned.

Somewhere in the darkness to the northwest, coming from an adjacent island, a single mobile artillery piece fired a 155mm round. The shell curved through the night skies, crossing over a watery expanse before reaching its zenith and starting a downward arc. The explosive arrived with a shrieking scream. The two men watched the airfield, observing Chinese soldiers cringe or dive to the ground when they heard the incoming round.

The night flashed briefly, a roiling smoke-covered fireball rising. A secondary blast shook the airfield when the artillery round broke apart one of the Chinese Z-10 fuel tanks, detonating the fumes sitting in the tank.

"On target, fire for effect," one of the rooftop soldiers radioed.

In the distance, the horizon flashed as if it were experiencing a localized lightning storm. From the sport field of another elementary school, a battery of mobile artillery guns spit 155mm shells toward the main island. A whistling sound like a speeding freight train announced each arrival. That was subsequently drowned out by a series of percussive blasts, a string of heart-thumping detonations shattering the night. Fire-filled explosions hit attack helicopters parked in the median between the runway and taxiway.

Adjusting several yards, a second volley came screaming

onto the airfield. Smoke rose from the blasts, their sides glowing orange from the burning fuel farm. The attack was short-lived, Colonel Wen-hsiung opting to preserve his scarce ammunition for the mobile artillery. If he were to stand a chance in the upcoming ground battles, the colonel knew he'd need to conserve his resources. Following the brief attack, seven of the tightly parked Z-10 Chinese attack helicopters were left in smoldering ruins.

As the two scouts were in the middle of extricating themselves, one descending a ladder attached to the side of the structure and the other with his leg swung over the low wall, they instinctively ducked when they heard faint whistling whines coming from the darkness overhead. Thinking that another artillery volley had been fired, this one overshooting the airfield, the two spotters felt helpless. The man on the ladder hopped off the rungs, falling the ten feet to the broken ground below. He felt a sharp wave of pain shoot up his leg as his ankle rolled. The planned roll to mitigate injuries turned into something that was neither planned nor graceful. Stifling a yelp, the man grabbed his ankle, his jaw tightly clenched against the pain. Slowly, the agony receded, leaving behind a throbbing ache as his ankle swelled inside his boot.

On top of the roof, the second spotter dropped to the tarred surface. With his arms wrapped around his head, two prayers ran through his mind. The first was that the incoming rounds would miss the building altogether. The second, coming on the heels of the first, was that it would end quickly; that he wouldn't experience any pain. A memory surfaced. He could distinctly hear the voice of his drill sergeant, "It isn't the artillery rounds you hear that you should be worried about. It's the ones you don't."

As the spotter hugged the roof, willing himself through it. He noticed that the whistling roars weren't coming from the right direction. They were passing east to west. Before he could come to the correct conclusion, the surrounding area started flashing brightly. With little-to-no delay, rolling thunder accompanied the concussive explosions. Peeking over the edge of the wall, the soldier saw that there was a solid chance that the gates of hell had opened on this very spot.

Huge explosions dotted the northern end of the airfield. They came so close on top of each other, that the entire portion of the airfield was lost from view. There were only roiling detonations that thrust upward. It was difficult to tell if the blasts were secondary ones or came from the low-flying missiles that came out of the east. Mesmerized, the spotter watched another set of explosions go off, adding to the chaos.

It was over nearly as fast as it started. The smoke slowly cleared. The once grassy fields were now a churned mess of dirt clumps, craters, and crackling flames that flickered across the airfield. Broken helicopters lay canted, some with their rotors resting on the ground like kickstands. Coming out of his awe-struck attention, the spotter took a quick video and then remembered that he and his partner had been in the midst of getting the fuck away from the site.

Crouching, the man made his way across the roof. Looking over the edge, he saw his team mate lying in sparse clumps of grass, dirt, and gravel. For a moment, the spotter thought his partner had been thrown from the ladder when the missiles arrived and was either unconscious or dead. Then he saw the man on the ground roll over and attempt to get to his feet. From the way he was going about it, the one on the roof knew something was wrong.

Once on the ground, he assisted his teammate to his feet. Half carrying the man, the two started making their way through the darkened town. There was a moored boat waiting for them to the north, but with the injury, they would be slowed getting there. They left behind scenes of carnage and destruction.

Unknown to the spotters limping toward safety, they had witnessed the results of a decision made far away. Current satellite footage provided by the United States had shown the Chinese helicopters grouped tightly together. The Taiwanese high command had authorized release for several of their precious few remaining cruise missiles. The idea had been that the helicopter force could theoretically ferry troops from the Penghu Islands to the mainland, possibly achieving a Chinese breakthrough if timed correctly. Like the cargo ships that were part of the invasion fleets, Taiwan hoped to whittle down the numbers available. Damage assessments would identify forty-three helicopters of varying types destroyed or damaged beyond repair. That was over half that had landed at the main Penghu airport. It wouldn't be until hours later that Taiwan would be notified that China had diverted some of their forces to the southern base.

*   *   *   *   *   *

One of the Chinese companies that had been ordered to expand the perimeter hugged the ground. A second series of ground-shaking explosions were rocking the northern end of the airport, each arriving missile or artillery round creating a roiling mass of fire and smoke. Many lying prone didn't know if they should get up and run for shelter, or if that very act might invite death from shrapnel zipping through the air.

Some of the blasts were so powerful that more than a few of the soldiers felt the air forcefully pushed from their lungs. To many, it felt like they were fighting the very ground, that it was reaching up to punch them. With the pounding detonations, none of the troops were aware of the screams around them, or that they themselves were yelling. Like water on a hot, greased skillet, bodies nearest the attack bounced uncontrollably. And then, like a switch had been thrown, it was over.

Cautiously at first, several raised their heads to look over the destruction, while some remained one with the ground, not believing that the incoming explosions had actually ceased. Still others, still lying on the ground, mentally checked their bodies, surprised to find that they were free of pain and that their bones hadn't been ground to dust. Slowly, the living rose, shaking clumps of dirt and grass from their fatigues and hair. Flames crackled from where machines capable of delivering death had been whole moments ago. Drifting smoke now obscured a clear vision of the airfield.

Stunned soldiers watched as crews raced past, some carrying extinguishers as if they had a hope in hell of putting out the fires. Out of the chaos, order was slow to materialize, but it did eventually happen. Perimeter outposts were contacted, the overall commanders hoping to decide if a counterattack was underway. They finally concluded that the attack had been conducted solely by remote forces, perhaps even coming from the Taiwanese mainland. Tallies of surviving resources were conducted and planned maneuvers restarted. Without the cargo aircraft that were to bring air defense units and armored vehicles, the soldiers at the airfield were left vulnerable.

The company that had been in the middle of briefing for a planned foray to capture one of the towns adjacent the airport gathered again. They were told of their assignment, the taking of a community to the northeast. Units patrolling the perimeter hadn't come under fire from anywhere surrounding the airfield, but everyone felt that it would only be a matter of time. The Chinese airborne soldiers had to push out. One, to expand the perimeter; and two, to recon and make contact with any defending Taiwanese force. Without a firm hold, it was imperative that the operational tempo be fast in order to keep defending units off balance.

Once past the perimeter fencing, the company became strung out on a narrow path. The dense nature of the surrounding foliage prevented movement anywhere else and limited sight lines to more than a couple of feet to either side. The lead squad marched off, setting intervals between soldiers to minimize casualties should they walk into an ambush.

The thick brush also served to cut out any sound, making those slowly traversing the path feel as if they were in a world to themselves. Tension was palpable as the lead squad searched the shadows, the slight breezes transiting through not only carried the scent of smoke, but also caused the eight-foot grasses to undulate menacingly. More than once, the point and slack troops tightened fingers on triggers, the pressures just shy of firing when a slight gust caused shadows to waver.

The Chinese soldiers passed a Buddhist temple, many uttering a prayer. Others hoped that it wasn't an omen that the first structure they'd come across would be a holy place. Superstition had a secure place firmly cemented in men and women who hovered on the fringes of death. Feeling cut off from the security that the airfield gave, the soldiers made their way toward the town.

Coming to one of the major roads that went through the urban area, the soldiers spread out on both sides. Everyone knew that a counterattack was due, and that the airfield was vulnerable, especially with the lack of firepower from the choppers. This avenue would be one of the corridors where any attacking Taiwanese troops would have to come through, so any movement, real or imagined, was thought to be the leading edge of enemy armored vehicles rolling along.

Given the order to move out, the lead squad again rose. Walking down both sides of the street, they passed an elementary school on one side, and a tall white building on the other. Passing darkened residences, as if an apocalypse had swept through the area, painted an eerie scene for the Chinese soldiers. Twice, the leading squad opened fire. One happened when a gust moved a gate, giving the appearance that it was opening. Sparks flew from concrete walls, the gate splintering under the fire of ten or more carbines delivering focused, automatic fire.

A second instance occurred when another gate appeared to move. This one was larger than the first, the shadows playing tricks on the soldiers observing the world through night vision goggles. After a bit of creeping through a still community, many of the airborne troops wished something would happen, just to alleviate the building anxiety each of them carried. In a way, the waiting for something to occur was worse than an actual firefight. Urban warfare was one of the tensest of situations, where gunfire could materialize from a hundred different places. Where each open window could be hiding anything within their depths and could bring instant death. Even when nothing happened, the urban environment created severe cases of PTSD.

It was with some relief when the lead squad arrived at the edge of the town. Built out by themselves were a series of expensive condos. Tasked by their company commander, the lead squad began clearing the apartments. After the first couple of dwellings had been found empty of occupants, it became obvious that the residents had hastily fled. Half empty suitcases lay in living rooms and on bedroom floors, their contents spilled over the sides. In some places, dinnerware with the remains of prepared food had been left on tables. The company commander set up on the rooftop, the rest of the soldiers spread out on both sides of the road. One of the avenues inbound to the airport, one which any Taiwanese counterattack would have to pass through, was secured.

Other companies pushed out from the airfield, securing roads from the capital city and other outlying towns. The issue of finding heavy machinery to clear the airfield was then undertaken, the group commander wanting the airfield opened as soon as possible. Once located, the equipment would push aside any wreckage caused by the artillery and missile attacks. They could then start filling in the craters preventing the airstrip from being used.

*   *   *   *   *   *

From the dirt strip to the south, a low droning, seeming to come from all directions at once, gradually grew in volume and intensity. One traffic controller, his face faintly lit by a small radar screen, monitored the path of a radar return. The aircraft was out over the water to the south, turning toward the island. A Chinese Y-9, looking similar to the American C-130, lined up with the runway.

A shape darker than the night abruptly appeared low to the ground, a four-engine turboprop droning on. Slamming onto the hard-packed dirt, dust was thrown forward as the pilot reversed thrust. The transport aircraft shot past the ramp, the nose lowered with the application of reversers and brakes, the Y-9 quickly slowing.

Turning around near the end of the runway, the aircraft rolled back toward the ramp and exited. The Chinese officer's radar screen already showed another transport turning to a short final. Seeing the aircraft had to turn around on the runway, the operations would be slowed. The air traffic control group would have to carefully watch their spacing of aircraft. And with the tarmac small enough to only allow a few of the transports to park at any one time, reinforcements and resupply would be limited until the main airport could be brought to an operational status.

The first of the transports weren't on the ground for very long as they only had to disembark airborne soldiers. Those troops were put to work offloading any of the smaller supplies which came along with them. Without shutting down their engines, the Y-9s offloaded the last contingent of airborne troops meant to take the island.

The transport aircraft were soon trundling back to the end of the dirt airfield to turn around. With throttles run up to mil power and legs trembling from brakes securely held, the nose gear compressed down. The deep drone of the engines reverberated off the surrounding foliage. The aircraft seemed to lurch forward when the brakes were released, the large-bladed props creating dust storms as the Y-9s bounced down the narrow runway. Pulling up into steep ascents, the planes vanished into the gloom with the droning engines fading into the distance. When the dust settled enough, more of the transports appeared out of the dark night to slam onto the runway. It was a much slower operation than had been planned, but gradually, China's presence on the island continued to grow.

When the turboprops finished their process, larger four-engine jets began dropping out of the night. The Y-20s, like their American C-17 counterparts, were capable of short and soft field landings. It wasn't long until a layer of dust coated everything at the small airfield as transport after transport arrived. Parked in rows, ZBL-08 infantry fighting vehicles slowly emerged from within the cargo compartments. The airborne soldiers were getting the firepower they needed to finish their conquest of the island chain.

Last to offload were the fuel bladders and necessary piping to install a temporary refueling station. It took some time for the heavy bladders to be offloaded and hauled to a remote location on the ramp. It would be hours before the thirsty attack helicopters could be refueled, but the process had begun. Although the initial stages hadn't gone as planned, China was slowly establishing a secure foothold on the Penghu Islands.

* * * * * *

The sergeant and the five other members of the Guangzhou Military Region Special Forces Unit eased away from the burning harbor. With the first blast, all the men knew that their planned mission was a failure. But that didn't necessarily mean that all was lost. Sergeant Jian Kang had sent word of another airport and the possibility of using some of the fishing harbors to offload shipborne cargo. Finding a harbor that could support the oversized ferries was to be the next challenge, and one where time was of the essence. If the ships were forced to anchor in the central sea the islands surrounded, then the equipment they carried would be vulnerable to enemy missiles or saboteurs.

The underwater sleds that had carried the team to shore served their stealthy intention, but they were too slow for the purposes of getting to the docks in question. Before slipping back into the water, the sergeant noted the location of the nearest fishing harbor and set course. He knew that if the team relied solely on the underwater devices, then there was a real possibility that the war would be over before he made it to the first fishing harbor.

A while later, Jian Kang peeked above the rolling swells. Ahead, a concrete breakwater gleamed in the moonlight's glow. Waves crested and rolled against large stones piled on the ocean side, the roar of their crashes faintly heard. Guiding toward the small harbor opening, the sergeant maneuvered toward the nearest fishing vessel. As he drew closer, he heard the squeaky grinding of the boat as it gently rolled against the rubber tires placed between it and the dock.

With his head above the water, the special forces sergeant looked like a seal taking a look at its surroundings. The man listened and looked for any sign of boat owners, sentries, or someone out for a midnight stroll. The piers remained empty of flashlights; only the sound of creaking boats could be heard as they tugged at their moorings.

Easing up to one boat, the sergeant slipped aboard the low stern. Upon boarding, he paused, the barrel of his QTS-11 following his eye movements. In the distance, flashes outlined the buildings and trees, the faint booms from explosions drifting on the night air. The sergeant was worried that the noise would wake nearby residents and send boat owners down to the docks. Perhaps some might take it to mind that the open water was safer.

Jian Kang wasn't afraid of shooting a civilian if they interfered with his mission, but it was something he'd rather avoid. It might attract attention, and that was the antithesis of the mission to him. Even though he was about to make some noise and possibly draw attention by stealing a boat, the idea still went against his baser instinct. It was just better to go in and get out without anyone being the wiser.

Though the sounds of battle drifted down to the waterfront, it seemed as if the six men were the only ones who were aware of it. Nothing on the boat or along the concrete pier was moving. Cautiously, the sergeant and another of his team moved forward. A quick search of the boat revealed that no one else was aboard.

It didn't take long before the ignition was pulled apart and the wires stripped. A deep rumble vibrated the boat as the diesel engine roared to life. With moves generally only associated with Olympic gymnasts, the others of the team scrambled aboard, their dark shapes materializing as they crawled over the stern railing. Cutting mooring lines, the special forces sergeant eased the vessel away from its berth and into the narrow harbor waterway.

Behind, a light flared in the darkness. Jian Kang was unsure whether it was from one of the harbor buildings or from a flashlight. Whatever it was from, it came too late. The boat edged between the ends of the breakwaters, the bow biting into the rolling swells of the deeper sea. The rumble of the nearly idling diesel turned to a roar as the sergeant opened the throttle. Turning south, the team headed toward the first of the potential harbors.

The sounds of war drew closer as the team pounded through the swells. Cliffs rose on the southern side of the main island, the waves crashing against the steep rock walls demonstrating a relentless force battling an immovable object. The darkened silhouettes of helicopters graced the night skies, the attack choppers extending over the water after delivering volleys of rockets. Although the sergeant had radioed that he and his team would be at sea aboard a fishing vessel, they each eyed the choppers that came floating over the edge of the cliff faces. It was a very real danger that the vessel might be mistaken for a threat and attacked. However, each Z-10 that came flying into view banked sharply back toward the dirt airfield, leaving the six men to race across the sea unmolested.

Nearly adjacent to the base under attack, on the other side of the rocky cliff walls, was a blacked-out town. Flashes of light were constant, the deep rolling base of explosions echoing across the Taiwan Strait. Turning toward the town's fishing harbor, the sergeant didn't have to venture very far past the breakwaters to determine that the port was inadequate for the room the larger ships required. Turning around, the team sped along the southern shores, rounding the point and heading northward.

At the next town up the coast, the six men racing against time slowed and then eased past the twin breakwaters extending across a natural bay. As the harbor came into better view, the night vision gear revealed that one of the wide concrete piers was lined up perfectly with the harbor entrance. Studying the docking facilities, the sergeant deemed that one of the Roll-on-Roll-off ships might fit, possibly even a second one.

The berths were empty. Letting the idling fishing boat drift on the waves, the sergeant made a radio call, eventually connecting with the assault commander headquarters. Sergeant Jian Kang, part of the elite South China Sword unit, informed the busy radio operator on the other end that a viable harbor had been located just a couple of minutes away from the dirt airfield. The problem was that a medium-sized town adjacent the port facilities would have to be subdued quickly, before someone in the Taiwanese command realized that the harbor should be hit.

While floating inside the breakwaters, the sergeant contemplated his next task. He could put ashore and secure the harbor until units pushing out from the dirt airfield could link up. Who knew when that might be? He wondered if he should push for sooner rather than later.

Knowing that the harbor might be viable for some offloading duties, it wouldn't suffice for it to be the only supply point for the equipment required for conquering the entire island chain. That meant that Jian Kang and his team would have to find another harbor that could take in the ships that were only hours away. But the question facing the sergeant was whether to secure one known harbor, which only marginally met the requirements, or to continue in the hope that they would run across a better one.

With a decision made, not knowing if he was making the right one or not, the sergeant eased the throttle forward and turned the wheel. Trailing a thin wake, the fishing vessel turned about and headed back into open waters. The units at the dirt strip were in the process of securing the airfield, but had promised a force would be dispatched to the harbor in short order. Everyone with any degree of responsibility knew that the ships, and by extension their berths, were the lifeline of the units tasked with securing the Penghu Islands. Therefore, with the destruction of the main port, proper berthing facilities were given a priority.

The special forces team departed Suo Gang, hoping that the radio assurances weren't just words. The harbor faded from view as the team followed the thin line of white that was the demarcation of earth and sea. The map Sergeant Jian Kang was following showed only one small port until the much larger Lung-men fishing harbor.

Without so much as giving the smaller port a look, the team cut across the large bay, passing smaller volcanic islands along the way. As they proceeded north, they again began to see an orange glow rise in the direction of the main airport. By listening to the radio traffic, the sergeant knew it was from the central fuel depot. Taiwan had denied China access to the main port and airport, forcing Chinese commanders to significantly alter their plans.

Coming from the harbor that had promise, a bright flash momentarily lit up the night. The sergeant instantly knew that someone had blown up the facilities. Perhaps the light he saw had come from someone guarding the rigged docks. He supposed the enemy wasn't too late after all and cursed himself for hurrying instead of verifying that the harbor facilities were secured from explosives. Although it would take verification from ground forces at the site, the special forces sergeant knew that the fishing harbor ahead had to work. They were down to their last option.

Jian Kang and his small team weren't the only ones scrambling to come up with something. Flexibility and adaptation weren't part of China's strengths, but they were managing to piece together an alternate strategy. China had troops on the ground and they were extending their perimeters, fanning out into the countryside. But the equipment being delivered via transport aircraft wasn't nearly the same as what could be carried across the strait on a ship.

The moment the sergeant and his team sailed through the first set of breakwater jetties, and the harbor opened up to his NVGs, he knew he had made the right decision. It was one he had wrestled with and second-guessed during the entire passage from the smaller port, especially considering it was their last option. This one at Lung-men was all he was hoping to find, and more. There were multiple berths capable of accommodating the inbound ships. It was so near perfection, at least opposed to what the main island harbor offered, that the sergeant half-expected to see explosions reducing the thick concrete piers into rubble. That would be par for the course for how their night was going so far.

Reducing the throttle, Jian Kang eased the stolen fishing vessel up to an empty spot along the main docks. There were a couple of coastal steamers moored with heavy lines that would have to be dealt with, and the smaller confines might require tug boats to assist the larger ships into and away from their berths, but that was small potatoes compared with what they could have faced.

It took a little searching to find rope to secure the fishing boat, seeing how the team had cut the mooring lines. But it was a harbor; rope wasn't that difficult of a commodity to locate. Securing the boat to the stanchions, the team shouldered their weapons and started across the expanse of concrete toward the town, checking for signs of set charges along the way. The plan was to hold the landward side of the dock until relieving forces could make their way and link up with the special forces team.

The sergeant radioed units at the main Penghu airport, informing them of the team's find. The airport had just taken a beating from a Taiwanese artillery and missile strike. Companies were in the process of expansion, securing major inbound routes. Soldiers that had been slated to assist in taking the Penghu capital were re-tasked with the taking of smaller neighboring communities.

The airport commander argued with the sergeant, telling the special forces man that all units were otherwise committed. Even though the commander knew that viable harbors were a priority, he complained that he didn't have enough troops to allocate to Lung-men at the moment. The sergeant bristled at the words coming through the headset and had to take several deep breaths to steady himself. Getting mad at the commander wouldn't make troops show up any earlier, and might even foster the opposite. Even though his voice was terse, the sergeant explained that the loss of the Lung-men fishing harbor would result in a slower allocation of supplies. The slower that process took meant that the soldiers that were on the ground would be vulnerable to more missile bombardments and possible Taiwanese counterattacks.

Jian Kang was about to explain further when headlights flared across the pier. Telling the commander that he had to go, and that the team would secure the port for as long as they could, the sergeant ended the conversation. The last thing he mentioned was that they had visitors to take care of, and that he needed to deal with the intrusive problem.

A vehicle had pulled onto the docks, perhaps drawn by the arrival of the fishing boat. All the ports had some kind of authority near the docks, so perhaps it was a port authority investigating someone trying to sneak in without paying the harbor fees. The team scattered, hiding behind dock equipment, before the lights splayed across their position.

The moonlight betrayed the presence of emergency lights atop the vehicle, supporting the sergeant's belief that a port authority had come to investigate. The car stopped, the lights playing partially down the dock. In the gloom, the glare of a spotlight flared, revealing parked equipment in stark detail. It was so bright that it nearly robbed everything of its color.

The light panned up and down the dock, focusing on the recently tied up fishing vessel. The squeak of a car door opening drifted along the pier. The sergeant pictured some wannabe policeman, wanting to assert his control and power, emerging from within a climate-controlled interior. But he or she would have a radio, and that could travel a lot faster than any vehicle. In short order, if the team was discovered, there could be innumerable vehicles descending on the location. And with the current tensions, the sergeant might find himself facing military units. Jian Kang didn't know if the harbor was wired to blow, but like the original plan, he intended to find any and defuse them.

The sergeant lifted his QTS-11 over the top of rusting I-beams. The fiber optic cable transmitted a live video stream. The searchlight had steadied since the sound of the opening door squeaked in the night. The beam dimmed slightly as the driver crossed, the uniformed person standing in front of the vehicle with hands shading his or her eyes. The sergeant had enough of the interloper. Aiming the small crosshair at center mass on the security personnel's torso, he squeezed the trigger.

A round spun out of the barrel. Illuminated under the intense glare, the bullet streaked toward the unsuspecting man. The sight of a flash coming out of the dark wasn't truly registered for what it was, the image only forming a curiosity before the round slammed into the man's chest. The figure toppled backward, falling across the hood of his car before sliding to the ground.

With the shot, two men rose from the shadows and ran toward the downed intruder. With the body highlighted under the headlight beams, one of the two special forces soldiers made sure that the man would stay down. The other dashed around to the driver's side door and turned off both the spotlight and headlamps, plunging the dock again into darkness.

Thinking that the intrusion was taken care of, the men were startled when a voice called from a radio on the dead body. It was asking for an update regarding the boat that had entered; the call repeated when no answer was made. One of the men attempted to stave off the curious caller on the other end by answering that it was nothing. He knew they had made a mistake when the voice asked, "Who is this?"

Planned Chinese Assault on the Penghu Islands

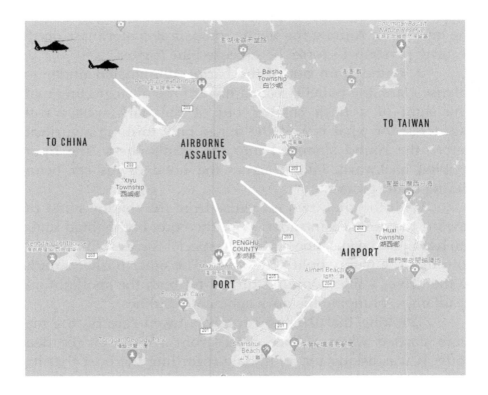

Altered Chinese Plans

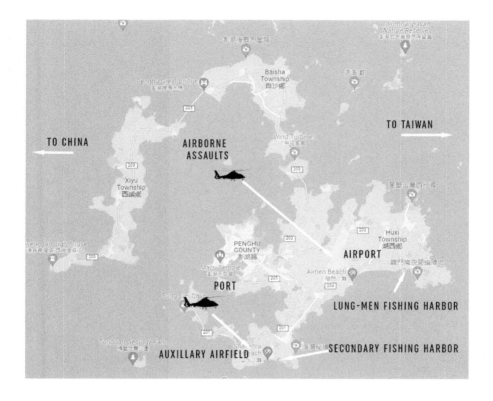

Chapter Six

Sergeant Jian Kang knew he had to move quickly. The vehicle wasn't from a port authority or some third-party security company; the marking on the side indicated that it belonged to a coast guard unit. With the prompt arrival, the station must be close, which meant that the team could soon expect more company, and in greater numbers.

Knowing that their current position wasn't tenable due to its confines, the sergeant moved his team past the idling vehicle and toward the entrance. With only six men, the entry gates made for a bottleneck with which they may be able to hold off a larger force for a longer period.

Unless they come over the water, Jian Kang thought, glancing at the waves shimmering under the moonlight. *Then we're truly fucked.*

Under the sergeant's direction, one of the men moved the coast guard sedan across the entrance to provide a semblance of cover. Others closed the entrance gates and secured them, making it more difficult for a responding force to gain entry. The sergeant wasn't out to win the war himself—he only planned on securing the docks until help arrived. He hoped that would come soon, although the airfield commander's responses hadn't been comforting.

Jian Kang again radioed the situation, asking for assistance. This time, he was promised the moon, but the timeline was vague. The sergeant knew that the commander likely had his hands full adapting to the change in plans, but the special forces leader also knew that the docks were the lifeline for the invasion. Therefore, they should hold a higher priority for the distribution of forces.

Replacing the handset, the sergeant noted lights flickering on in several buildings along the waterfront. One of them had to be the coast guard station. He didn't know how many personnel might be at the building, but it couldn't be a large garrison considering it was only a fishing harbor. On the other hand, it was one of the larger, if not the largest, fishing harbors on the main island of Magong.

The concern was the other lights coming on in other buildings. That couldn't be a coincidence and could possibly be coast guard barracks. Sergeant Jian Kang knew that the port authority had to be somewhere nearby, but doubted that they had more than two or three people who might man the office. Setting up as best as they could, the sergeant sent one man off to search the dock more closely for explosives. If the facility was wired, he didn't want to lose yet another valuable commodity. It was the same mission they had at the main port, but on a much smaller scale.

Shouts drifted across the harbor. Soon, headlights materialized on the waterfront road, all coming from the three buildings that were now lit up. Responding forces were on their way and the sergeant kept the airfield informed of the situation. It wasn't long until vehicles began showing up near the entrance. Beams of light shone through the gate, splaying along the concrete. The sound of car doors was followed by shouts, which was in turn followed by the heavy sound of boots.

Several of the vehicles parked head on, headlights and spotlights blinding the team from anything happening beyond the barrier. His team members were positioned behind equipment and other heavy debris lining the dock, peeking around or over cover through their QTS-11 optics.

The special forces sergeant kept one eye on the harbor waters, expecting to see a coast guard vessel materialize. Each second the port remained clear was a relief. To the sergeant, the lack of action by those responding indicated a level of chaos and confusion, as if the Taiwanese Coast Guard weren't sure what to do in the situation. They surely heard the explosions to the west, centered in and around the airport, and had to know that the island was under attack by ground forces. But every minute they delayed was another for responding Chinese units to arrive.

Watching through his optics, his carbine placed over the top of several I-beams, Jian Kang saw figures approach the gate, outlined in the glow of headlights. In the glare, he saw that three bodies were carrying something, but he couldn't be sure of what it was. It was long, so it could be a weapon, or perhaps a pry lever or bolt cutter. The team had locked the gates with a heavy chain, fastened with wire they had wrapped through the links. It would take some time to open them.

Whatever the figures were carrying, the sergeant knew he couldn't allow the Taiwanese free access to the dock facilities. What the responding forces didn't know was that two of his team were atop a building adjacent the entrance. His plan was to keep them hidden until absolutely needed. They were there more to ensure that the enemy couldn't use it to bypass the security gate, and to prevent them from using it as cover.

Fighting the glare of the lights, the sergeant centered his small crosshair on one of the approaching bodies. He used the team frequency to inform the others on the dock of his intentions, instructing them to follow his lead. Checking that his fire selector was on auto, the sergeant sent a burst of bullets toward the gate.

The suppressor contained much of the noise; the gunfire was barely audible to the Taiwanese unit. As the special forces were all about stealth, none of the rounds speeding from the barrel were tracers. Sparks flew from the heavy chain link gate as the bullets ricocheted, the rounds tearing past the entrance. One of the figures dropped like he had lost control of his legs, falling straight to the ground. Another flung his arms wide as he was thrown backward. He stumbled back until he slammed against the hood of a vehicle and then slowly slid down. The third was spun around, whatever he held in his hand tossed to the side to be lost in the darkness.

The team member searching for charges returned, shaking his head, meaning that he hadn't found any sign that the dock was wired. Together, the four members of the special forces team on the docks kept sending bursts of fire, the entrance gate showering sparks as if electrified. Pings of bullets hitting the vehicles rang in the night. With hisses of steam, radiators were punctured. One by one, the beams of light playing along the dock winked out, whether hit by gunfire or turned off.

Shouts rose from the enemy and tracers streamed from their positions. Sparks came from the concrete, ricochets zinging into the night skies. The Chinese sergeant ducked as bullets pinged off the protective I-beams. Readjusting his position, Jian Kang poked his QTS-11 around a corner and returned fire. It was an odd battle; one side evoked the typical firefight, tracers pouring from their weapons, the sound of gunfire echoing across the harbor. The other side was quiet and without sound, the only evidence they were even there came from the fact that bullets were slamming into vehicles and from windshields shattering.

The plunge of the docks into darkness was short-lived. Bright pole-mounted lights flickered once, twice, and then sprang into life, bathing the dock area in light. The return fire from the Taiwanese contingent became more focused as they were able to identify the Chinese positions. Not wanting to remain vulnerable, the sergeant redirected his fire. The other three on the dock noticed and added their own. It was difficult to hold fire on the lights. Sparks rang around the team, forcing the special forces members farther into cover.

Doing his best to ignore the rounds hitting so close, Jian Kang attempted to focus solely on the sight picture sent back to the tiny monitor. Holding his weapon around the corner of an I-beam, he sent fire toward one of the bright lights lining the dock area. He saw his 5.8mm rounds strike, and then bounce off the heavy glass shielding the lights. He kept firing and heard a satisfying tinkle of glass. The light flickered once before going out.

The sergeant's attention was directed toward the front gate when the sound of an engine revving rose above the cacophony of the gun battle. He saw two headlights come into view, speeding toward the entrance gate. The fight was about to take on a new phase if the enemy was able to penetrate through their barrier. The small Chinese team could then be easily overwhelmed if the Taiwanese force had the numbers to rush them.

With sparks flying from the crash, the gate bowed inward. If it wasn't for the seriousness of the situation, the sergeant might have laughed out loud when the vehicle proved to be the loser in the contest. The gate was meant to withstand such a maneuver and the car became entangled in the chain link.

With the four taking on focused fire on their revealed positions, the two on the roof couldn't hold out any longer. Rising from crouches, the two men held their carbines over the edges of a surrounding low wall. Screams rang out from within the crashed sedan when rounds slammed through the roof, the bodies of those inside riddled with bullets. Blood splashed across the inside of the windshield as figures twitched under the onslaught.

Seeing the situation under some semblance of control, Sergeant Jian Kang went back to directing his attention toward the lights that were revealing their positions like an unwelcome dawn. As with the headlights, the overhead lights went out one by one. The QTS-11 had 20mm grenades that could be launched from behind cover, but the sergeant had to avoid using them. With a flat trajectory, the explosives would only detonate against the gate, accomplishing what the vehicle couldn't.

However, that didn't apply to the two on the roof, who were now receiving their share of the incoming fire. Braving an onslaught, they held their weapons over the edge and fired grenades toward the winks of fire coming from the Taiwanese positions. Explosions were added to the battle, the shrapnel shredding the vehicles. As with many firefights, it was difficult for each side to determine exactly how the battle was progressing as they blindly returned fire in the half-lit shadows of the dock.

The sergeant heard a nearby yell. Turning toward the sound, Jian Kang saw one of his men squirming on the ground. More rounds tore into the teammate's position, sparks flying from the concrete around his writhing body. Puffs of cloth on his pants marked where rounds ripped through the fabric and shattered his legs. The man screamed once more and then went silent, his body still. Looking toward the entrance through his NVGs, he saw the figure of a second teammate draped over the edge of the building's roof. He had just lost a third of his firepower.

More headlights were quickly making their way along the waterfront. As far as the sergeant knew, vehicles hadn't landed at the airport, so the lights could only mean that Taiwanese reinforcements were on their way. Jian Kang glanced briefly at the fishing vessel tied farther down the dock, wondering if it was time to get the hell away. He could hopefully keep the enemy at bay for a while longer, but if those heading his direction brought heavier weapons, then his tenure at Lung-men would be short-lived.

Sparks were flying from atop the building as the Taiwanese force kept the lone special forces team member pinned down. Each time the man attempted to place his weapon over the edge, he was met with a hail of fire. The sergeant knew it wouldn't be long until he lost the position. In a way, he already had. And with the vehicles nearing the dock, it might not be long until the entrance was breached.

The sergeant was facing a difficult decision. Save the rest of his team and make for the fishing boat and the open water, losing the dock in the process? Although he hadn't located any wires or explosive charges, Taiwan would notice China's intention and possibly blow the harbor some other way. Or he could hold off as long as he could in the hopes that a Chinese response force would arrive. If he remained and the gate was breached, he could lose both the dock and his team. On top of that was the fact that his men were running low on ammunition. They had 20mm grenade rounds that would only become a factor if the gate was overrun, thus negating their usefulness. They could increase the number of Taiwanese casualties, but that was about it.

The Chinese special forces sergeant was watching the approaching vehicles when the lead car suddenly exploded. It didn't take long to figure out what had happened. The whomp of rotors rose above the sound of the gunfight, a dark object zooming overhead. Seeming to appear out of thin air, a stream of fire came from out of the night. The streaks all converged on the rearmost vehicle as multiple flashes appeared all around the car before it also erupted in a ball of fire. A second dark shape whipped over the head of the special forces team, vanishing into the darkness.

A third chopper came zooming in, ripples of fiery orange streaks raining down on the convoy of reinforcements. The incoming fire from the entrance abated as the forces arranged there either gave up and ran, or were obliterated as the next wave of attack helicopters came screaming in over their positions. The sergeant watched as the lone team member on the rooftop came scrambling over the side, his figure illuminated in the ghostly fires burning just beyond the gate.

The commander at the airfield had made good on his promise, but not in the manner that Jian Kang had imagined. He had thought any reinforcements would come overland in the form of soldiers. The commander, knowing the attack choppers had been low on fuel, had siphoned enough to fill the tanks of a few and sent them to help secure the fishing harbor.

Time and time again, the Z-10s came swooping in to deliver rocket and gunfire on the opposing forces. It wasn't long before the incoming fire on his position abated and then vanished altogether. A string of fires lined the waterfront from burning vehicles, those manning them either dead, wounded, or fleeing from the destruction. Thirty minutes after the arrival of the choppers, a company of Chinese reinforcements arrived.

Sergeant Jian Kang went among those whom he had fought against, finding out that he had waged a battle against Coast Guard personnel, members of a sheriff's office located at the harbor, and a mixed batch of local police officers. He lost two of his team, their bodies airlifted back to the airfield. With more soldiers arriving, the harbor and town was secured. Dispatches went out to the ships carrying the equipment needed to take the Penghu Islands. Over the horizon, RORO ships altered their courses. The problem of losing the main port had been remedied.

* * * * * *

At the dirt airfield, controllers had set up makeshift facilities. Small radar trucks panned the surrounding area, identifying the incoming transport aircraft. With the loss of the main airport, safe aerial corridors had to be quickly changed from what had been planned. On the radar scopes, long lines of inbound airplanes looked like arrivals at any major airport, the Y-20s and Y-9s adhering to strict altitudes and striving to stay within horizontal boundaries.

Chinese controllers monitored both inbound and outbound traffic, giving instructions to pilots who were in the process of veering too close to the edges of the safe airspace. No one wanted any of their precious cargo to be blown out of the sky due to overanxious air defense operators. Several short-range anti-aircraft vehicles were among the first deliveries, their weapon systems pushing out as ground forces cautiously expanded their foothold.

The act of landing was more perilous than navigating the safe corridors. Each short field landing and takeoff sent clouds of dust over the area, obscuring the vision of the descending pilots. At times, the controllers had to halt landing operations to let the dust settle. Again and again, dark objects materialized out of the night, the lumbering transport aircraft feeling their way down to the surface.

They proceeded down final and touched down without landing lights. This was partly from a security perspective, not giving the enemy a firm target to fire upon. The other aspect was because the landing lights reflected off the dust particles, creating a blinding glare, similar to driving through a snowstorm. It became so bad at times that the obscuration even blocked out night vision goggles. Pilots plotted approaches on their flight computers, flying INS instrument approaches down to the dirt runway. Sometimes, the visibility was such that the pilots were surprised when their gear collided with the ground, only catching vague glimpses of the infrared lights outlining the edges of the strip. The axiom that any landing that one can walk away from is a good one was severely put to the test.

Slowly, armored personnel carriers, ammunition, and air defenses were gathered on or near the dirt airfield and adjacent base. In addition, heavy equipment necessary to repair damaged runways was brought in, their priority increased. The 'on again, off again' system of delivering equipment due to the low visibility was hampering China's timetable. Without vehicles and the force multipliers they inherently brought, Chinese ground troops were vulnerable to a Taiwanese armored counterattack.

In the glow of the burning fuel storage facility at the main airport, commanders on the ground pushed hard for temporary fuel depots to be set up. The sooner China could refuel the attack choppers, the quicker they could provide security for the companies beginning to push outward. Until more firepower became available, a solid push by Taiwan could liberate the airfield, perhaps ultimately forcing China from the island chain. To defend against that possibility, they had to get the runway operational. Thus, when heavy equipment landed at the dirt strip, it was inventoried and rushed north, driving through unsecured terrain.

Meanwhile, the slow but steady stream of Chinese cargo planes crossed the Taiwan Strait, swinging wide to the south to avoid Taiwanese air defenses that may be present on the other islands. Flying high over the strait, keeping out of range of Taiwan's anti-aircraft units positioned on the mainland, one of the few remaining KJ-2000 AWACs searched without avail for the presence of enemy radars emitting from the Penghu Islands.

* * * * * *

A Y-9 banked over the South China Sea, moon-kissed waters passing calmly beneath. In contact with ground controllers on the small island of Magong, the Chinese pilot lined up on final. First double-checking his position with the navigation instruments keyed to the precision approach, the pilot brought the throttles of the four-engine turboprop back.

The nose dropped and he began a descent to three thousand feet.

Directly ahead were the darker-than-night masses that were the islands China was in the process of unifying. Without manmade lights emanating from the main island, the surrounding sparkling waters reflecting the moonbeams created an illusion of dark holes where landmass should be, the aircraft approaching a wormhole rather than a surface one could land on.

The pre-landing checks were complete. All that was required to complete the flight over the strait was to fly the last few miles and land. The pilot took a deep breath that was more mental than physical. Although night landings were part of the monthly requirements to maintain his flying status, it had been a while since he had practiced them. Coupled with a short field landing and an approach into enemy territory, the pilot was nervous. Some issues had arisen from his last qualification check-ride and he was determined to show his squadron commander that he had what it took to continue flying.

Lowering the NVGs over his eyes, the Chinese pilot focused on the approach. Beside him, his copilot was reading off airspeeds and altitudes. A horizontal needle glued to the top of the navigation instrument quivered, then began to drop. Passing through the instrument's midpoint, with the copilot calling that they were at the final approach fix, the pilot again brought the throttles back.

The vibration of the aircraft and the drone of the engines was soothing and added to the pilot's confidence as the Y-9 eased down through the night, descending at five hundred feet per minute. Through the windshield, the pilot could make out some of the infrared lights marking the dirt airfield that was currently the primary link from Magong to the Chinese mainland. The rest of the area was obscured by what looked like fog, but the pilot, alerted by the ground controllers, knew it was dust that had been kicked up by the many takeoffs and landings.

With an eye on the scattered lights marking the runway

threshold, and keeping the aircraft aligned in the still air, the pilot brought the large transport down through the night. As he drew closer, the forward visibility decreased. The IR beacons became sparser, but as long as he could see some of them, he could visualize the runway parameters.

Through the intercom, the copilot continued a litany of airspeeds and altitudes, switching to the radar altimeter once they descended below a thousand feet above the ground. Dust swirled in the pilot's line of sight, the visibility changing rapidly. That included which IR lights could be seen, inducing a degree of vertigo. But the pilot was still able to determine the scope of the runway and was thus mostly confident with his ability to land the aircraft. Inside his mind rang the harsh words of the check pilot and the squadron commander. The last thing the pilot wanted was to initiate a go-around, further demonstrating to his commander that he wasn't fit to fly.

The copilot continued with his readings. The pilot called that he had the runway, thereby eliminating the need for the man in the other seat to continue reading off altitudes. The communication coming from the right seat turned to constant airspeed readings, the pilot making throttle adjustments based on the speeds and their current trend.

One minute, the pilot was looking at a huge dust cloud, and the next he was immersed in it. The sensation wasn't anything unusual as he had flown in and out of a hundred clouds, flying some very tricky instrument approaches in marginal conditions. For a moment, he lost sight of the infrared lights. With rising panic, he looked to the left and right, catching a quick glimpse of one that now looked far too close for his liking.

The copilot watched the approach, his focus on the altitude and airspeed, while also keeping an eye on the navigation needles that showed the aircraft's relation to the correct descent path leading to the runway. He would call out left turn, stop turn, right turn, instructions to allow the pilot to keep the aircraft centered on the runway. The instructions would also include whether the Y-9 was on glide path, or descending above or below the desired flight path.

With only the pilot on night vision, and thereby unable to read the instruments, it was imperative that the two work together to get the large aircraft down through the marginal conditions. This type of procedure was done for every night vision approach and landing. The copilot couldn't see much of anything beyond the cockpit, the dark island growing larger in the brief glances he directed outside. His attention was focused on the instruments, comparing their readings with his occasional looks along the aircraft's flight path.

The copilot knew from previous communications that visibility around the dirt strip was marginal due to dust being stirred up, but his anxiety was eased when the pilot called that he had the runway in sight. Still, it took a little steeling of nerves to feel his way down in the dark, knowing that the ground was somewhere close.

The stars, the glimmer from the surrounding water, everything outside was suddenly lost from view. There was only a mad swirling of dust particles as the Y-9 swept down into the cloud. The copilot glanced toward the pilot, wondering if the more experienced man still had the runway in sight. From his vantage point, he wasn't sure that was possible. But still the man drove the transport down as if it was a clear night and the runway well-lit.

He continued to call out airspeed and navigational readings, his glances outside now accompanied with looks toward the man with the NVGs wrapped over his face. The pilot appeared as if he could see, looking left and right with deliberation, so the copilot forced himself into a calm. The tense feeling returned when the throttles started coming back and the nose raised.

The copilot quickly looked at the radar altimeter. They were still sixty feet in the air. This wasn't the time to be reducing power and lifting the nose. Realizing in an instant that the pilot didn't have the runway in sight, or that something was causing the man to think they were in a position to land, the copilot told the pilot to go-around. When the aircraft started to sink, the copilot hurriedly reached over and jammed the throttles forward.

The roar of the big-bladed props increased as they bit into the air, but the action came too late. The Y-9 continued dropping as if the floor had fallen away. The gut-tickling drop could now be considered a fall rather than something resembling a carefully planned and executed maneuver. The transport slammed into the ground. The wingtips drooped down like a duck landing, almost hitting the grassy medians beside the runway. Then they bounced upward, rising into the air nearly as high as they'd dropped.

For a brief moment, to anyone watching, the turboprop seemed as if it were flapping for all it was worth to get airborne. The pressures proved too much for the main spar and the outer wings tore off, separating between the two engines on each side. Gouts of fuel sprayed into the night air, the fuel vapors igniting, which in turn burned the globs of jet fuel.

As the aircraft bounced down the dirt runway, now with a shortened wingspan, a series of explosions pushed the dust particles away. Although the controllers couldn't see much of the runway, they knew one of the aircraft had crashed when the night lit up from detonations within the swirling maelstrom. Thunderous blasts rolled over the base — but it wasn't over. The two outboard engines tearing away caused the plane to start skidding. Acting as if it were a Jeep turned too sharply, the Y-9 tipped. One of the shredded wings, with flames streaming aft, dug into the dirt. The slowing transport swung violently around the other way.

When the remaining part of the opposite wing tore into the earth, it gave way and the airplane rolled and began disintegrating. Pieces were flung into the night, a rain of metal falling among those on the tarmac. The burned remains of an APC were later found nearly a half mile away. A line of flames and deep gouges in the earth marked the path of the fragmenting plane. When the Y-9 finally came to rest on its back, there was a pause, as if the world was taking in a breath before delivering a final sentence.

A momentous explosion ripped through the night, clearing the runway of dust for one of the first times since China's aircraft began landing. Chinese soldiers and airmen alike started running with no destination in mind when flaming pieces of aircraft arced through the night and began landing among them. Flames licking upward marked the temporary closure of China's sole lifeline.

* * * * * *

Colonel Wen-hsiung pored over the incoming reports from the scouts he'd placed around the main island of Magong. Put together, they told the story of China landing thousands of troops that were only now beginning to push outward from the locations at the international airport and the base farther to the south. It also appeared that the airborne firepower they brought across the strait was momentarily grounded. To the Penghu Defense commander's mind, this suggested that conditions might be ripe for a counterassault.

Staring south into the night, Wen-hsiung weighed the available choices. One option he was mulling over was his second in command's suggestion that they break up the battalions into smaller units and conduct guerilla operations against the Chinese. The dense nature of the countryside would force most of China's units to stay on the roads, enhancing Taiwan's ability to move and conduct successful ambushes. The tactic could create headaches for the invaders.

The colonel was hesitant. Aside from having to abandon his armored vehicles and mobile artillery, Wen-hsiung still felt that if they were to start a guerilla war, then China would begin reprisals against the civilian communities. Taiwanese men could be rounded up and China could order towns to be leveled. The defense commander kept the idea in the back of his mind should he lose his armor. The second in command had postured the idea, but the colonel had thought about that possibility long before and cached secret stores of weapons throughout the islands.

Another possibility was to go on the offensive. Although greatly outnumbered, he had armored force multipliers at his disposal that China didn't currently have. However, he knew that China had aircraft that could be on scene in a matter of minutes. The chief question plaguing the colonel was what to do with his force. He could go on the attack and disrupt China's timetable. He understood enough to know that he didn't have the firepower to completely eradicate the Chinese presence, but he could make them more cautious. In that scenario, he envisioned going out in a blaze of glory, riding the vanguard of his small, armored force as they tore through China's meager defenses.

Wen-hsiung chuckled at the vision. In reality, he might make some headway before Chinese missiles began arriving out of the night sky to tear apart his attack. That would leave the islands defenseless. The colonel wasn't under any illusion that he could hold off China's attack indefinitely. Like the leaders in their bunker believed, the taking of the Penghu Islands was inevitable. The forces he was given were there to delay the invasion for as long as possible, preventing China from quickly consolidating their gains and using the islands as a base for their missiles and aircraft. He was there to buy time, so there wouldn't be a grand charge that would push deep into enemy defenses.

He would do his best to delay the Chinese takeover. Other than the brief artillery attack against the massed helicopters at the airport, he would wait for Chinese forces to move beyond the main island and stage planned ambushes.

* * * * * *

The Taiwanese missile attacks had forcefully demonstrated the tactical mistake of tightly grouping assets. There were four roads leading away from the main airport, two to the east and two leading to the capital city to the west. Chinese companies worked slowly along the roads, expanding the perimeter. Slowly, the helicopters that survived the

Taiwanese attacks were moved into the countryside. The problem lay with the terrain, specifically the dense foliage covering the land. There just weren't many places to park the airborne attack choppers and transports. Placing assets around the airfield also drew away combat troops in order to protect them.

The Taiwanese commander was right; China's grip on the archipelago was tenuous at best for now. At that moment, an attack by an armored Taiwanese force might well have unseated China's hold on the island. And with the crash and subsequent shutdown of the southern airfield, this was fully brought to light. Not enough equipment had been flown in to secure China's toehold on Penghu. Whereas the priority had been to deliver armored vehicles so Chinese commanders could quickly push outward, and short-range air defense weapons, that had changed in an instant. Now one of the main priorities was to get the main airport operational. A second was to get a working temporary fuel farm. That would allow the attack choppers to get into the air in order to scout the area and to provide more firepower to the companies currently on the move.

For those reasons, the heavy equipment heading north from the dirt field was treated as if they were carrying the nation's treasury. In the dark, platoons worked along roads lined with thick bushes. In the eyes of the soldiers, each deeper shadow held the enemy, each sway of tree limbs was an ambush being sprung. There were many instances of trigger-happy Chinese soldiers emptying magazines into bushes, the one-sided firefights sometimes lasting several minutes. And with the clank of treads, bulldozers and other heavy equipment ground behind the nervous troops, the men in the convoys were nearly stretched to their mental limits.

It took the better part of two hours for the equipment to arrive at the main airport's perimeter. Under the bright beams of spotlights and the glow of the burning fuel depot, work crews put the machinery to use, repairing the damage to the airstrip. The work on filling the cratered runway went slowly, especially for the Chinese ground commanders. They needed that long, paved strip in operation so they could proceed with their invasion plans. In the first hours of the invasion, they were already acutely aware of how far behind schedule they were falling. In case they might become forgetful of their timeline, the bombardment of messages arriving from headquarters on the mainland were a constant reminder.

* * * * * *

As if a curtain were opened, a shape darker than night appeared out of nowhere. Moonlight gradually revealed details of an object that slowly crept closer to the Lung-men Fishing Harbor. At first, there was the ghost of an outline, the more defined elements still hidden in shadow. The moon's rays then highlighted a superstructure, glinting off windows up high. Then, as if suddenly taking shape, a large ferry-like ship ghosted toward the narrow opening of the channel to the harbor.

Greeting the incoming vessel was a tugboat that guided coastal cargo ships into their berths. That was an unexpected find for the Chinese troops that had been sent to secure the vital port. Like a ferret nosing into a rabbit warren, the ship's bow edged between two breakwater jetties. Under command of the ship's captain, the tugboat pushed the ocean-going vessel closer to the long concrete dock. With shouts, thick hawsers were tossed to waiting troops. When the ship was secured, hydraulic ramps were lowered, hitting the dock with echoing clangs.

The roar of an engine punctuated the interior decks. An armored personnel carrier then appeared from the aft end of the ship, slowly motoring down the modified ramp. Behind, exhaust fumes filtered across the deck as another engine was started. The heavier equipment China needed to overrun the island chain had begun offloading.

From the waters of the Taiwan Strait, a second ship appeared from out of the darkness.

* * * * * *

As the night wore on, the conflagration at the international airport diminished until it was a mere fraction of the inferno which had blazed for most of the evening. Under watchful eyes that sporadically pressured crews to work faster, the cratered runway slowly became something more useful, patched roughly back together like a shattered plate. The holes were filled and matting placed to provide for a more durable landing surface.

With the skies to the east lightening, the heavy machinery was parked to the side. Radio operators turned on their equipment, the glow of a radar screen competing with the coming dawn. Across the Taiwan Strait, transport aircraft again ponderously lifted from runways, their engines straining as they clawed for altitude.

High overhead, Chinese J-16 fighters prowled the heavens. Pilots scanned the brightening skies, searching for Taiwanese fighters that might decide to rise and give battle. Miles behind, one of the few remaining Chinese AWACs patrolled, the giant radar dome scanning thousands of miles for any sign of resistance.

When the sun announced its arrival, taming the shadows which covered the islands, the first of a long line of Y-20 Chinese transports kissed the pavement of Penghu's international airport. As with the dirt strip to the south, large fuel bladders were unloaded. Miles of pipe was connected to valves, which were in turn fastened to the bloated bladders. Shortly after the sun climbed into the sky, rotors began spinning. In small groups, attack helicopters moved to fill nearly empty tanks. As the armored vehicles arrived, China's invasion of the Penghu Islands was gaining the firepower it sorely lacked during the initial hours.

Transport helicopters were then given enough fuel to transit the strait, landing again on the mainland. This created space for the attack choppers to disperse in the event Taiwan decided to launch another missile attack.

Sunlight poured through residential windows, but families remained huddled in their rooms. They had heard the explosions throughout the night and knew that China had begun their long-dreaded invasion. When the distant sounds of war faded and they heard an endless stream of aircraft arriving at the main airport, they knew that they'd soon be hearing the tread of Chinese boots in their streets.

Chapter Seven

Colonel Wen-hsiung gazed over the tree line to the southeast. Every minute or two, another dark object would appear in the distance, climbing as the aircraft proceeded north. With the sun climbing higher above the horizon, he watched the takeoffs for the better part of an hour. When each distant airplane appeared, knowing what they had probably delivered, he willed a long-range missile from mainland Taiwan to reach out and destroy it. But each one flew on, unscathed, until it faded from view.

The colonel knew that the number of missiles Taiwan possessed was limited, but how he wished he could observe the destruction of the enemy attempting to take over his life, and those others who had lived under the shadow of invasion for all their lives. The urge to fire his remaining shorter-range surface-to-air missiles was strong, but he knew he'd need them for the protection of his meager force when China made their move to expand beyond Magong. And all the time, he was wondering exactly where the promised American support was. With a sigh, emitted partially from disgust and partially from resignation, he turned to again inspect the positions of the two reinforced battalions under his command.

* * * * * *

The sun rising higher brought a few civilians out from their abodes. As it was Sunday, some of those who would normally report to work tentatively ventured into the streets. Shop vendors, their income relying solely on that brought by shoppers, were among the first to walk through their front doors and open their shops as if the previous evening's events hadn't happened. The spot fires that threatened to engulf the city were mostly under control, a few thin smoke plumes drifting upward above a cautious people.

All eyes strayed toward the airport every few minutes, where dark columns of smoke rose from the smoldering ruins of the fuel depot. It was a constant reminder that this wasn't a normal Sunday. Some wondered why they weren't hearing the sounds of battle or seeing Chinese tanks thundering through the streets.

As many of the townspeople were fishermen and women, they wandered down to the docks to see the extent of the damage. After all, the exploding fuel tanks were heard by the entire city and there wasn't a soul that didn't know what had occurred. Most stood in shock at the destruction. Some of the waterfront shops had disintegrated under the force of the explosion, while others were so badly damaged that no one would venture inside. Owners of the shops farther from the detonation picked through the debris in attempts to retrieve something of value.

The fishermen and women openly gaped at the destroyed fishing vessels, some of which had been deposited on the waterfront streets. There was nothing remaining of fishing harbors one and two. In some of the other fishing harbors, the breakwaters had saved a few boats tied to docks, effectively stopping the mini tsunamis created by the blast. But there would be no fishing this day, or in the foreseeable future, as the larger ships had been sunk at the entrances. Without a single Chinese soldier stepping into the city, many had already lost their livelihoods.

*   *   *   *   *   *

With a steady incoming flow of supplies and armored vehicles, and with the creation of a temporary fuel farm, the Chinese commanders felt confident and decided it was time to expand more aggressively. The first order of business was to secure the main island of Magong, and that meant taking over the capital city by the same name. Urban warfare was something any commander despised, regardless of unit size. Cities could easily become meat grinders and eat up a force, but there wasn't any choice. In order to secure the populace, the government had to be subordinated.

Led by two Chinese Z-10 attack helicopters, and accompanied by light and medium armored vehicles, a battalion departed the northern end of the main airfield. At the same time, with nearly the same supporting firepower, a second battalion of Chinese elite airborne soldiers departed the southern end. The northern contingent traveled along Highway 202 while the southern force crept down Highway 204.

The attack choppers scouted ahead of the main forces. One of the Z-10s would zoom ahead while a second hung back, ready to unleash a barrage of rockets and machine gun fire into any resistance. The lead would then pull up into a hover while the second raced past. Any grouping of buildings was given special attention, the pilots and gunners surveying the windows and yards for any indication of an ambush. All they saw during the initial push were mothers gathering their children and ushering them inside when they caught sight of the approaching Chinese forces.

Behind the airborne vanguard came a variety of armor. In the lead were lightly armored scout vehicles. Helmeted figures were visible atop the scouts, heavy caliber machine guns swiveling from one possible threat to another. Following at intervals were older armored personnel carriers, their treads squeaking as they inched along the two-laned main roadway. And finally came the eight-wheeled infantry fighting vehicles, their larger muzzles ready to deliver heavier fire in support of the infantry should they come under attack. Mixed within the IFVs were short-range mobile air defenses. Lacking in the mix, or anywhere on the island, were Chinese main battle tanks. Given the terrain, those were seen as being ineffective and a possible liability, although the soldiers heading toward the capital city might argue otherwise. If they encountered armed resistance, the large-bore weapons could quickly reduce strongpoints to rubble.

The closer the battalions drew to the city, the more nervous they became. The airborne scouts were nice to have, but with the increasing number of buildings lining the sides of the road, an ambush could easily avoid detection until it was triggered. There wasn't a soul in either advancing force that didn't expect a battle for the capital. It was just a matter of where the line would form. Most expected firefights to begin outside of the city limits, but the city itself would be easier to defend.

Individual buildings turned to outskirts, which in turn became the city. Yet still nothing happened. Not a shot rang out. People looked from behind curtains or from open doors, but there was no sign of an organized Taiwanese defense. The armored vehicles rumbled along the city streets, the squeak of treads echoing off residences and shops. Overhead glimpses caught periodic sights of the preceding attack helicopters as they zipped toward the city center. Tensions within the armored interiors of the APCs grew until many wished something would happen, if only to relieve the built-up tension.

The two main roads converged in the center of the city. However, before the two battalions met, the southern contingent veered south. Their objective was the naval base at Observatory Island. The northern force continued toward the waterfront where the mayor's office was located. Upon arriving, armored vehicles took station at street corners. Dismounted infantry took positions near the vehicles while a company stormed the capital building.

With it being the weekend, they encountered few government workers. Boots reverberated down corridors as the soldiers cleared the building, rousting those they met outside where they were held. The mayor of Magong City and the governor of Penghu County met the leading units in the mayor's office. They were instructed to inform the populace that a curfew was to be affected across the entirety of the island. Police units were to lay down their arms and come under the control of a military provincial governor, as were the mayor and governor. In short order, the Taiwanese flag atop the building was replaced with a Chinese one. The capital city had fallen without a shot being fired.

The southern battalion slowly approached the gates of the naval base. It wasn't long before the battalion commander realized the base had been abandoned. The smoldering fires coming from the ruins of destroyed buildings were a huge clue, but wary of booby traps, the soldiers still proceeded with caution.

Armor was positioned to cover the main city harbor entrance while the naval port facilities were inspected. As with the main port, aside from the damage inflicted from missiles, it was discovered that ships had also been sunk at the individual harbor entrances. However, it was determined that this port could be more easily cleared than the central harbor. The news set in motion activities across the Taiwan Strait and orders were sent to salvage operations. Before long, barges with mounted cranes were being readied for the hundred-mile journey.

With the city under a semblance of control, the Chinese commander in overall charge of the Penghu operations turned an eye northward. Two spans connected the main island of Magong with the next in a long series. Platoons held the four approaches and it was time for the forces coming from the two airfields to join up with the those holding the bridge ends.

*   *   *   *   *   *

Zhoushan port, China
1 August, 2021

As if the Chinese high command was waiting for the flag to be raised, additional orders went out. While the airborne assault forces on Penghu sought to expand their perimeters, another major flotilla made ready to get underway. The grinding of metal on metal reverberated across the port waters as anchors were raised, early morning sunlight catching muddy drips as they fell from the heavy links. Orders carried softly inside the bridges of cargo vessels. Behind the laden ROROs, large propellers began to stir the dirty waters, slowly pushing the ships forward. At the docks, tugs worked to clear China's landing and transport ships.

Between the numerous islands that dotted the outer rims of the giant harbor, frigates and destroyers ventured forth into the East China Sea for the first time since being recalled in the early stages of the conflict. Once in the deeper waters, the warships spread to the north and south of the main harbor entrances. Active sonar pulses rang through the depths, the operators within the combat information centers listening intently for any hint that American submarines were in the vicinity.

Ranging farther out to sea, anti-submarine helicopters flitted across the swells. They sped swiftly from one spot to another, their systems pinging for enemy subs. Reaching predetermined grid search locations, the noses lifted as they slowed. Downwash blew spray from the tops of the crests as the choppers hovered. Through holes in the floor, dipping sonars lowered on steel cables. Sinking below the surface, the sensors within listened for the distinct sound of screws or the discharge from pump jets.

High overhead, one of the four remaining Y-8Q ASW aircraft prowled farther out. Chinese commanders knew that the Americans were likely to position their attack submarines outside of the major harbors. With the American carriers still loitering outside of cruise missile range, the sailors wouldn't have to worry about attacks from the carriers' planes. Running in pairs, the Chinese warships were creating lanes through which the cargo ships could sail. The vessels remained in near proximity to one another in order to provide for a coordinated defense in case of a missile attack. China was placing a layered anti-submarine screen that could hopefully detect the quiet hunters of the deep before they could fire on the vulnerable transport ships.

After reaching the limits of China's territorial boundaries, the escorting ships turned south. They would steam along the boundary, hopefully staving off an American attack until it became necessary to cross. However, their air defense systems were kept ready in case of a Taiwanese attack.

The channels between the multiple islands became crowded with numerous ships slowly steaming toward the East China Sea. Like the preceding escort vessels, the transports would steer south as soon as they hit the open sea. The warships maintained positions farther out while the cargo ships remained within sight of China's mainland. Once in the open, the ships began arranging themselves in orderly column formations.

In China's southern port of Zhanjiang, a similar set of actions were taking place. Due to the number of Chinese marines and their equipment involved in the main invasion, it had been necessary to utilize two ports for the embarkation process. The central idea was to use each invasion fleet in a pincer move to attack two different locations, yet be close enough so that the two forces could mutually support one another.

The plan was for the initial attack on the Penghu Islands to be conducted ahead of the assault on mainland Taiwan, but close enough together to be considered part of the same operation. That would hopefully split the resources Taiwan had at its disposal. Even though China knew there would be American involvement, it was hoped that the support would come primarily from their fleet of submarines. If China's escorting vessels could keep the undersea hunters at a distance, thus precluding the use of torpedoes, then the American sub positions could be generally located when they fired their Harpoon missiles.

Chinese commanders knew they would lose some ships to American submarines, but their plan was made to mitigate the losses. Although there was some concern about Taiwan's remaining firepower and American bombers, China would deploy some of their fighter strength over the South China Sea to patrol the limits of their range.

With the observation of the Chinese main invasion fleets setting sail, orders were disseminated from Pearl Harbor to the submarines positioned to the north and south of the Taiwan Strait. Flush with recent victories over the Chinese diesel-electric boats, the American commanders set new courses to intercept the main Chinese effort.

*   *   *   *   *   *

With the capital city and major installations under control, Colonel Li Na, the overall Chinese ground commander decided it was time to provide the long overdue linkups with the units holding the causeways to the next island. The commander wasn't sure of what to make of Taiwan's lack of resistance, but he wasn't going to complain about the seeming ease with which his portion of the invasion was proceeding.

Although his combat experience was minimal, Colonel Li Na knew that there would come a time when he met whatever forces Taiwan had left behind to defend the islands. His greatest fear was that the defensive forces would opt to run a guerilla campaign. The colonel was prepared to enact drastic measures against the populace should that happen, but he'd rather not. If Hong Kong was any indication, those kinds of warfare operations could get messy.

Two Chinese battalions were securing Magong City and the attached naval base. Other than the rocket attack on the airfield during the night, and the small firefight for the Lung-men fishing harbor, the expedition had gone well. They were behind schedule, but units were spreading out. The colonel anticipated having full control of the main island by the end of the day. It was time to see if he could quickly push across the two spans connecting this island with the next.

Crossings were always risky propositions, especially if it was a contested one. If Colonel Li Na could get more forces across and the far end better secured, then he could perhaps push quickly outward and take the next as easily as he did the main one. If Taiwan chose to fight for the passage, then he could at least draw out the enemy forces and destroy them.

Two Chinese platoons had taken over for the special forces in securing the two causeways that reached across the shallows. They spread out along the main road, digging in as best they could while they waited for the promised relief column. That was supposed to have happened during the night, but they still found themselves alone with the morning sun climbing into the sky.

It was with relief when the Chinese units at the bridges heard the news that reinforcement was finally underway. A mechanized battalion of airborne troopers was departing the main airport. The column of armored personnel carriers and infantry fighting vehicles was to proceed toward the city where they would turn to connect with Highway 203 then proceed north.

The ground vibrated as armored vehicles rumbled through small communities. People stood at windows and in doorways, their fearful and angry expressions following each tracked or wheeled war machine as it roared past. The top half of helmeted soldiers appeared above hatches, gloved hands gripping machine gun handles, the barrels swiveling on their mounts. Longer, heavier caliber barrels pointed menacingly from turrets, ready to spit out deadly rounds against the first sign of a threat.

The first linkup happened without issue. The lead armored vehicles rode past the airborne troops sitting astride defensive positions, waving as the armor rolled across the first causeway, their armored sides emitting an air of invincibility. Older six-wheeled Type 92 and newer Type 08 and 09s rumbled past, rolling over the first bridge and continuing onward as if nothing could stop the red tide of Chinese armor.

*   *   *   *   *   *

A Taiwanese sergeant crawled through the thick brush. Sturdy limbs reached out like a gaggle of reporters thrusting microphones, snagging on his clothing and weapons. It was a slog through the dense terrain, and to do it quietly was nearly impossible. It had taken hours since leaving the narrow pathway to negotiate his way through the brush one inch at a time. The agonizingly slow movement was only partially due to having to maneuver through the prickly brush; the rest was because of the presence of Chinese airborne troops positioned around the entrance to the causeway which connected Pehu

Island with Magong.

Laying on the ground, Sergeant Kuan-lin caught his first glimpse of water through the thick layers of branches. Reaching forward, he pulled himself further along, making sure to pause to remove any limb which he might become entangled with. He then grabbed the Javelin anti-tank missile he was carrying with him and pulled it even with his body. Behind the sergeant came eleven others, sweating and swearing under their breath as they snaked through the undergrowth. Each member of the squad was responsible for their own anti-tank or mobile anti-air defense weapon.

No one in the group thought they would personally beat back the Chinese invasion of their shores, but they would be the vanguard who would start whittling away at the enemy in the hopes of slowing and distracting China's attacking forces, giving their military a better chance at beating the invaders. Coming near the edge of the bushes near the tidal mark of the inland sea inside of the island chain, Kuan-lin came to a stop. Lowering a limb, he took a peek around his immediate surroundings.

He saw with some relief that he had emerged more or less where he'd anticipated. The tiny peninsula of land looked across a small bay of water toward a concrete dike that rose above the tide waters. The tops of wind turbines beyond the causeway spun lazily in the summer day. A shadow fell across the sergeant, momentarily blotting out the sun as a cloud drifted across a background of blue. Other clouds climbed into the sky, each an individual pillar striking for the heavens. The formation of the clouds and the humidity led Kuan-lin to believe that the islands might be in for late afternoon thunderstorms. He thought that a good portent, as it would hopefully ground China's airborne contingents.

The sergeant remained in place without moving for a few moments, listening for the enemy troops which were guarding the approaches to the causeway. The men had tried their best not to make noise or jostle the bushes on their way to the waterfront, but it was impossible to tell if they had been successful in hiding their approach. All Kuan-lin heard was the gentle rush of a breeze along the tops of the brush and the soft lap of waves slapping against the shore.

Satisfied that he was in the correct position, with a clear line of sight across to the concrete dike, and that the bushes weren't being actively searched, Sergeant Kuan-lin pushed back from the edge. Looking behind him, he met the eyes of the next Taiwanese soldier in line. With quick hand movements, he directed the trooper off to the side. When the next one moved up the line, he pointed to where he wanted the soldier. Slowly, as the clouds climbed higher into the summer skies, and as the breeze brought the odors of the shoreline, the twelve soldiers arrayed themselves along the edges of the brush.

Each of the soldiers carried a portable weapon. In addition, the sergeant toted a small drone. This was built for observation only, which meant that it didn't carry any weapons. The battalions had weaponized versions available, but those had been deemed too much to bring along with the anti-tank Javelin and the Stinger missiles.

After ensuring that he had a good connection with his phone, the man next to him tossed the lightweight drone into the air. The small plane climbed steadily away from the troops hiding in the bushes. Once it was high enough that it would be nearly invisible to the naked eye, the sergeant guided the drone toward the causeway. He set it into an auto-hover at a location whereby he could observe part of the 203 coming from Magong Island.

Kuan-lin froze when he picked up the faint thump of rotors. Orienting the drone's camera south, he saw black dots in the distance, growing larger with each passing second. The dots grew more detailed as they came closer, eventually resolving into the shape of two Chinese Z-10 attack helicopters. Flanking either side of the main road, the choppers flew slowly northward. The sergeant correctly guessed that the Z-10s were the vanguard edge of the force China had chosen to lead its attack.

As the attack choppers approached, the sergeant

weighed recalling the drone. It was hovering higher than the low-flying helicopters, but would be easier for the pilots or gunners to see. If he did bring the drone back, he would be blind to the details of the approaching column of Chinese troops. Not only that, but he wouldn't be able to accurately spot for the artillery units that were miles behind. But, if the drone were spotted, then it wouldn't take much of a leap for the Chinese leaders to know that an ambush was waiting.

But, Kuan-lin thought, it wouldn't take a genius to figure out the causeway was an ideal location for an ambush anyway. Any attacking force would be funneled into four exposed lanes. The sergeant hoped that crossing the first span without resistance would give the Chinese a degree of overconfidence and that they'd attempt to muscle their way across. The sergeant opted to keep the drone aloft, hoping the pilots and gunners aboard the two attack choppers would have their eyes focused on the ground and not spot the small hovering drone.

The thump of rotors increased and two Z-10s appeared over the top of the trees and hills of the adjacent island. With percussive *whumps* of rotor blades, the noses of the choppers rose and came into a hover over the opposite entrance to the causeway. On the small screen of the sergeant's phone, looking down on the choppers, he could see the barrels of the chin-turrets rotate left and right as the gunners searched the far banks. Even though China had a platoon guarding the near side, it appeared that the Chinese were advancing cautiously.

Sergeant Kuan-lin, inside the edge of the thick bushes, had to force himself not to back farther away. The density of the surrounding foliage should hide the squad from sight, and should keep their heat signatures from registering on Chinese thermal imaging. As if performing a synchronized dance, each of the two attack helicopters nosed forward. They split farther apart, picking up speed as they flew alongside the raised roadway.

On the screen, the two choppers whipped past the drone, vanishing from view. Halfway along the causeway, the two Z-10s abruptly angled away from the road. One of the choppers continued north, following the shoreline before fading away. The other turned to the northwest, heading directly for the Taiwanese squad hidden in the foliage.

The sergeant felt his heart quicken as the Z-10 headed directly toward his position. The front-on view of the attack chopper was unnerving, the slim profile with rocket pods hanging from stubby winglets, the menacing 25mm chain gun mounted underneath and pointed directly at the sergeant and his squad. The helicopter came menacingly toward them, closing the distance as if the bushes covering the Taiwanese soldiers didn't exist.

Kuan-lin lay his head down, not looking directly at the inbound threat lest his eyes somehow give away his position. The overhead branches began quivering as the downwash drew closer. For a second time, the Z-10 slowed to a hover. Leaves rained down on the team, the downwash permeating the area with the smell of jet exhaust. Limbs swayed violently. The sergeant was nearly certain they must have been observed and the chopper was marking their positions for the nearby soldiers to come pick them up. Even though he reasoned that the Chinese Z-10 would have delivered its own fire and the safest place was actually underneath the chopper, the sergeant was positive that the Chinese helicopter had spotted the squad.

When it started flying away, the flailing branches calming, Kuan-lin still didn't move, so sure was he that they had been located. With the sound of the rotors fading, the sergeant listened for the crunch of footsteps that would signal his captivity. But none came and he looked up. Across the tidal flats, he could see armored vehicles coming over a rise on the far island. Even though they were staggered at intervals, they still seemed as if they were crowded together. Blue smoke puffed into the air as the vehicles idled, waiting for the command to proceed across the dike. Sergeant Kuan-lin looked at the tiny screen, seeing a long line of armored vehicles of differing types sitting by the sides of the road.

Above the lead vehicles was another pair of attack helicopters. What felt like more than enough firepower when the sergeant departed his company, the Javelins and Stingers carried by his squad now seemed like flyswatters compared to what he was seeing through the drone's camera. The sergeant just hoped that the armored column didn't advance under the cover of artillery or firepower directed against likely ambush locations.

The two Z-10s over the head of the column started forward, slowly moving along the road toward the causeway. Exhaust from the lead vehicles showed that the armor was also on the move. The lead APCs motored down the hill while on the far bank. Chinese soldiers that had been holding their entrance clear stood from their positions and cheered the six and eight-wheeled chariots, along with their tracked cousins.

Hidden on the small peninsula, the twelve Taiwanese soldiers readied themselves. Those with Javelin anti-armor weapons hoisted the bulky devices, the soldiers wriggling forward to obtain clear lanes of fire. They had been assigned numbers so that they wouldn't end up targeting the same vehicles. The first Chinese APC, armored personnel carrier, cautiously entered the causeway, like a swimmer dipping a toe in the water to ascertain its coldness.

Emerging from behind the last of the bushes on the far side, the six-wheeled vehicle entered the raised roadway. Kuan-lin heard a faint rumble as a long line of armored vehicles motored toward the causeway. Lifting the Javelin, the sergeant looked through the thermal imaging, sticking the crosshair on the center of the Type 92 Chinese APC. When the armored personnel carrier was two-thirds of the way across the causeway, the sergeant keyed his mic and spoke a single code word.

Miles to the rear, a battery of four 155mm M-109 mobile artillery cannons opened up. Turning the drone's camera toward the near shore, the sergeant waited for the first rounds to hit so he could adjust fire for the artillery unit. Even though he and his squad were some distance from the near entrance to the span, they were still bounced when the first round came crashing in. Smoke and dirt were lifted into the air, the compressed air shoving trees and bushes laterally.

The blast from the large caliber shell rolled over their positions, the other three 155mm shells arriving on the heels of the first. Kuan-lin looked at the smoke and gouts of fire, immediately seeing that the GPS-directed shells were right on target, hitting amid the Chinese platoon positions. He radioed for the artillery to "fire for effect."

Round after round pummeled the near end of the causeway as the sergeant again picked up his Javelin. Looking through the command launch unit at the heat signature emanating from the lead vehicle, which had come to a halt before the falling artillery shells, the sergeant fired. The launch motor kicked the anti-armor missile from the tube. Sailing out over the water and away from the team in hiding, the main motor engaged once the missile was clear.

The Javelin missile quickly picked up speed, racing across the band of water. Having selected a top-down attack, the missile tracked the target on its own. Trailing a line of smoke, the Javelin arced up and then sharply down. A giant fireball boiled from the lead APC, dark smoke catapulting into the morning skies. The explosion mixed with the artillery shells still falling.

The artillery was to keep the Chinese soldiers from spotting the Taiwanese squad as they attacked the armored formation. It was also intended to give the Chinese units pause rather than trying to race past the ambush. However, the Taiwanese counterbattery radar soon picked up Chinese retaliatory fire from the infantry support vehicles at the rear of the column. As the original battery halted operations to move positions, to hopefully negate any return fire from Chinese guns, other Taiwanese artillery units began firing at coordinates provided by the counterbattery radars. The two opposing artilleries then began the game of counterbattery and counter-counterbattery fire.

Long tongues of searing flame leapt up from the lead Chinese APC. Tires melted and paint curled and melted from the intense heat. Faint screams from Chinese soldiers trapped inside the vehicle rose and then fell silent as the fire crackled and roared.

On the heels of the first Javelin, seven more sailed out from the thick bushes. Smoke trails marked the path of the speeding rockets before balls of fire and smoke announced the demise of other armored vehicles. The two Z-10 attack helicopters veered away from the armored column, racing toward the ambush site.

Lingering smoke trails marked the proximity of the Taiwanese attackers. With long whooshes, rockets left the confines of their pods, racing into the morning skies to arc toward the far shore. The initial Chinese counterattacks fell wide of the mark, the large-diameter rockets exploding meters away from where the twelve held their positions. Braving return fire, two Taiwanese soldiers rose from their positions. Carrying large tubes on their shoulders, the two tracked the incoming helicopters. Almost immediately, tones indicated that the Stinger's sensors had found heat signatures.

Almost simultaneously, the two men fired. Two missiles sped from their chambers, racing across the short distance. Inside the Z-10s, the pilots immediately saw the rising threats. Flares shot out from the sides of the encroaching attack choppers, but sensors aboard the anti-air missiles had their lock. The first missile raced alongside the cockpit, past the engine intake, detonating next to the exhaust. A puff of smoke marked where the proximity fuse exploded. Without any fanfare, the Z-10 plunged nose first into the shallow waters of the inland sea. A spray of muddy water erupted, the chopper plunging below the surface.

The second missile arced toward the other Chinese attack helicopter when the pilot tried banking out of the way. It too exploded adjacent to the exhaust. Shrapnel tore into the engine, severing fuel and hydraulic lines. A ball of flame shot out from the damaged engine, a black puff of smoke falling behind the chopper, which rapidly slowed. Fire warning lights and master caution alarms told the story. As with the first, the attack chopper nosed over. It hit the sea with a flash of flame and foam, the helicopter coming apart as it tumbled across the water's surface. Burning pieces were flung from the Z-10 before it disappeared in a mighty explosion.

The causeway was blocked from eight fires that were engulfing the remains of the leading APCs. The sergeant sent the drone a homing message, a set of GPS coordinates. They, or someone else, would collect the drone, but that was far from the sergeant's mind at the moment. Kuan-lin and the others were scrambling back the way they came, trying to remain out of sight, but not with as much caution as they used during their slow infiltration. Rounds arrived from the far shore as Chinese APCs and Infantry Fighting Vehicles began delivering their counterattack. The ground trembled beneath their boots, the area coming under intense fire.

The sergeant was thrown from his feet when a series of explosions went off nearby. Feeling the sting of shrapnel from seemingly a hundred places, he looked up from his supine position. A helicopter zoomed directly overhead, the shadow of its passage momentarily blotting out the sunlight. He looked to the side to see one of his men standing nearby, a Stinger missile aimed upward. The sergeant barely registered the subsequent whoosh of a missile leaving its tube.

Kuan-lin felt the tug of someone reaching down to grab his drag handle. He tried to shout to tell whoever it was pulling him that he was alright and to let go, but all he heard was a series of muted sounds that he didn't associate with human speech. Trying to right himself, he felt his arms flail around in a confused set of motions. He saw blasts rising from the bushes behind, their march of smoke and fire slowly drawing closer as he was pulled through the dense bushes.

Another blur of a chopper flashed overhead. This time he was able to see a white streak power after the fleeing shadow. Arcing flares flew from the chopper's sides. The sergeant thought it was a sight of beauty, the falling flares trailing thick smoke. He followed the single streak coming from the ground that chased after it, following it until he saw the flash of its explosion.

The chopper lurched sideways, looking like a motorcycle spinning cookies. The gyration didn't stop, the chopper turning circles faster and faster as it dropped from the skies. Something sharp poked him in the leg, but it was over almost before it began. The sergeant felt the sun upon his face, forgetting why he was there, only enjoying the sudden flush of warmth. He took in a deep breath, taking in the fresh scent like newly cut grass. There was also something acrid mixed in, but he ignored that in favor of the sweeter smell of the plants.

Voices came from nearby and the pulling stopped. He was put in a vehicle, the doors closing on the sunlight. Still wrapped in the warmth he had felt, Sergeant Kuan-lin closed his eyes and went to sleep.

With the loss of an M-109 mobile artillery vehicle, and two soldiers KIA and three wounded, the Penghu Defense Command had opened hostilities against the Chinese invaders. China lost eight armored personnel carriers and three Z-10 attack helicopters. With pillars of smoke rising along the 203 highway, Taiwanese artillery attacks had most likely resulted in more Chinese losses.

China's first attempt at expanding beyond the main island had been unsuccessful. The lead battalion had pulled back to the mainland as additional units were sent to join up with the main Chinese attack. The commanders, although hopeful of a quick and resolute takeover of the Penghu Islands, were almost relieved when news of the attack was radioed. At long last, they had come upon the expected resistance, and the tension of first contact was fading—only to be replaced by a different kind of worry.

*   *   *   *   *   *

Chased by artillery shells, the Chinese mechanized battalion pulled back over the hill. It wasn't until they retreated across the first causeway that the Taiwanese artillery stopped firing. The heat from fires pushed dark smoke pillars high into the morning, each column marking the demise of an armored vehicle. Eight of the vehicles were left smoldering on the second causeway, creating a blockage that prevented the remaining armor from charging across. Any subsequent attack would have to negotiate around the wrecks.

Back on the main island of Magong, the infantry fighting vehicles arranged themselves along the edges of the highway. There they set up a battery of heavier guns, registering their coordinates. With China attempting to jam the American GPS signals, and being partially successful, and with the United States blocking China's access to the GPS system in the Pacific, China had resorted to using their own BeiDou global positioning system. There were some strong indications that the Chinese system was more accurate.

The next Chinese attempt at crossing the causeway would involve artillery support. In addition, more attack helicopters began spooling up back at the international airport. Although the road network and terrain wouldn't permit attacks on a wider front, a second mechanized battalion was sent to back up the lead unit. This was so the second force could move through in case the first was chewed up during the crossing.

Distant thunder heralded China's second attempt. Like speeding freight trains, heavy caliber shells began arriving along the shore of Pehu Island. Explosions threw mud and bushes high into the air, leaving behind craters to slowly fill with water. The artillery sent by staged units raked the shoreline to either side of the causeway entrance and impacted further inland along the roadway.

For the Chinese soldiers holding onto the far end of the crossing, the sound of thunderous detonations wasn't much different than the shells sent their way by the Taiwanese forces. The only relief they had was that they knew it was friendly fire and the deadly blasts weren't landing in their midst. Still, many turned a fearful eye to the skies when the shells screeched overhead.

After fifteen minutes of the preparatory bombardment, Chinese APCs again crested the hill, driving madly down the four-laned highway toward the narrow crossing. The varying calibers of the barrels protruding from vehicles' chassis were pointed to the sides, ready to engage any resistance offered. The armor weaved past the smoldering wreckages of their previous attempt, the drivers and commanders doing their best to ignore the destruction lest they invite a similar end to their own vehicles.

Inside the troop compartments, Chinese airborne soldiers tightly gripped their weapons. Helmets were cinched down, worried and fearful expressions peering out attempting to hide their tension. More than one prayer cycled quietly inside fear-filled minds, mantras intended to see the individual through the situation.

Another Taiwanese squad peered through bushes farther down the peninsula than where the first squad had sprung their ambush. The leader stared at a tiny screen, the real-time video coming from a drone hovering near one of the wind turbines on the far shore. The ground vibrated under the twelve soldiers when each Chinese artillery shell landed a quarter mile away. China had mixed in smoke with their bombardment. At first, the squad was concerned that China had launched a chemical attack, but the drone showed no change with the enemy guarding the near end of the bridge. When the smoke drifted into the Chinese positions, the Taiwanese team came to understand that the smoke was an attempt to obscure the vehicles descending toward the causeway.

The smoke shells carried a component to create havoc with thermal imaging systems, thus preventing opposing forces from being able to look through the smoke screens. However, the drone itself was on the Chinese side of the smoke and thus had a clear line of sight to the accelerating armored vehicles. Even though the wind was light, the smoke screen didn't reach far enough to interfere with the second Taiwanese squad's ability to see the causeway.

When the lead Chinese APC crested the causeway entrance, the squad leader set down the drone's screen. Upon entering the span of concrete, the Chinese vehicles began emitting smoke from their own generators. Swerving around destroyed APCs, the Chinese armor was attempting to barrel their way past and force the crossing.

Rising onto his knees, the Taiwanese squad leader hefted a Javelin anti-armor missile launcher. He was able to get a clear thermal image of the lead APC. Once locked on, he fired. The missile streaking out from the hidden position was mostly lost to any observers by the continued artillery landing on the shoreline. With an abrupt climb, the missile then arced sharply down.

A fireball formed in the air above the lead Chinese APC. Streaming fire, the lead APC slowed as it rolled to a stop, coming to rest against a concrete abutment. More lines of smoke came streaming from the shore as additional Javelin missiles raced for their targets. Balls of fire exploded within the smoke and obscured much of the causeway, eliminating Chinese armor striving to reach the far exit.

A wave of Chinese attack helicopters appeared, racing low over distant hills. They fanned out, giving the slow-turning wind turbines a wide berth. Several squad members knelt, their nerves tight as they aimed at the approaching storm of choppers. With so many targets, the tones came quickly. In rapid succession, missiles raced from tubes and hurtled toward the incoming Z-10s.

As if in response, smoke sailed from pylon-mounted pods. The rockets fired from the lead choppers arced toward the shoreline, falling among the Taiwanese soldiers scrambling to get clear. Explosions hammered alongside the fleeing men, shrapnel cutting down four as they fought to make headway through the thick foliage.

Two of the Stingers found their targets, the Chinese helicopters nosing in after experiencing losses of power. One Z-10 hit and tumbled, spewing flaming debris across a wide area. The other merely hit the water and sank in a rather anticlimactic conclusion. With enemy targets on the run, several attack choppers closed in and released volleys of rockets at the Taiwanese soldiers slogging through the bushes.

One by one, the squad dropped as their bodies were torn

apart by white-hot shrapnel. When the last Taiwanese soldier fell, the attack helicopters began working over the area with their chain guns. Not one of the twelve made it back to their unit, all spilling their blood in a churned field filled with burning embers. However, the squad destroyed enough armor to block the roadway. Unable to proceed forward and with 155mm artillery shells landing on and around the crossing, the Chinese mechanized unit had no choice but to pull back. The Taiwanese squad lost their lives, but managed to halt the second Chinese attempt to cross from the main island.

* * * * * *

The Chinese smoke screens were slow to dissipate, but as they cleared, the destruction on the raised roadway began to show itself. The glow of burning vehicles was periodically revealed, the smoke lingering as if wanting to keep the wreckages a secret. When it did finally disperse, like a stage curtain being raised, the remains of armored personnel carriers were canted at awkward angles. The heat of some of the fires had caused some barrels to become warped. Charred remains were draped over oxidized turrets or splayed in nearly unrecognizable heaps on the roadway.

The humidity started increasing as the day progressed toward midday. Calm winds belied the destruction that the morning had brought, as if nature itself was holding its breath and waiting to see what the future held. Wisps of smoke drifted from a torn-up and cratered shoreline.

High overhead, a Taiwanese drone moved slowly across the noon skies. It revealed the blocked roadway, with glimpses of Chinese soldiers on the near side as they moved from cover to cover or ran down dug trenches. To the sides of the Yong'an Bridge, the tidal flats showed craters slowly refilling with mud and seawater as the tide crept in. In the distance, toward the main island of Magong, spirals of smoke rose above the hills, evidence that Taiwanese artillery had found targets where the Chinese had laagered.

The temporary calm of the sweltering day was suddenly broken when a low-level Chengdu J-10 attack fighter roared overhead. Spitting flares, the Chinese multirole aircraft pulled up into a tight climbing turn. In its wake, thunderous explosions rocked Pehu's northern shoreline. Roiling smoke lifted skyward from the blasts, looking much like the slowly building clouds higher up.

A second J-10 screamed over. Mimicking the leader, it too pulled up to the south, sending a series of flares into its slipstream. A series of detonations plowed through terrain already chewed up by the larger caliber guns of the Chinese Infantry Fighting Vehicles. Two more Chinese attack fighters dropped their payloads over the positions where two Taiwanese ambushes had stalled the Chinese advance. The multiple bombs created a zone of devastation which would make it difficult for any Taiwanese soldier to sneak through. It also made it next to impossible for retrieval teams to locate the bodies of the second squad.

The roar of the jets seemed to linger over the crossing, even though the jets were miles away. Just when the sound was fading from the thoughts of the Chinese soldiers tenuously holding the near bank, another fighter came roaring in from a different direction. Small dark objects dropped from underneath the wings, wobbling as they fell earthward. The objects dropped farther inland, plunging into thick foliage. Gouts of fire and smoke shot upward, unrooting smaller trees and bushes that had been growing for generations.

Another J-10 rolled in, lining up for its attack run. A line of flares marked the Chinese fighter's path. As with the lead aircraft, smaller objects dropped from where they were mounted on wing pylons. When the Chinese attack fighter pulled up, a smaller object rose from somewhere near town of Jiangmei, located just up the road from the Yong'an Bridge.

Trailing a long line of white, the launched object quickly accelerated and zoomed up toward the J-10. The Chinese aircraft pulled up and banked tightly away from the closing projectile. A series of flares shot out from the sides of the maneuvering fighter. The smoke trail veered from its path, showing that the sensors aboard the short-range ground-to-air missile saw a flare as a more enticing target. However, it corrected its course and continued streaking toward the fleeing fighter.

The missile seemed about to pass behind the J-10 when it blew up in a bright flash. A gout of flame shot from the rear of the banking attack fighter. In a steep bank, the Chinese aircraft flew on as if it wasn't streaming a long tongue of fire. The nose of the fighter wobbled once, then twice. A canopy flew from the aircraft, followed shortly afterward by an ejection seat shooting up the rails and entering the open air. In slow motion, the seat became two dark objects as the pilot separated. Below a stream of nylon that inflated into a parachute, the J-10 began violently tumbling before spinning in a nose down attitude. It vanished behind the hill that formed the small island between Magong and Pehu. A thick column of black smoke blossomed upward, marking where the J-10 crashed.

A third J-10, lining up for an attack run, climbed before its release point. The aircraft then turned south over the inland sea encircled by the Penghu chain. The fourth came streaking in, its original bombing run altered. It dropped its load next to the main road just outside of the Jiangmei township. This was followed by the Chinese fighter that had pulled up short. A long stream of flares marked the path of the aircraft as it drove toward where the anti-aircraft missile had risen from the thick terrain.

After the aircraft pulled up, long dark smears marred the green that encompassed much of the island. Flames smoldered in the blast zones, seemingly unsure if they were going to grow larger and spark wildland fires, or become smothered in the increasing humidity.

When the second group of attack fighters departed, Chinese infantry fighting vehicles began firing. The artillery fire wasn't pre-planned, but with possible Taiwanese positions identified, the battalion commander ordered the expenditure. Shells crashed around the township, flinging bushes and trees to the sides.

The fifteen-minute volley lifted when Z-10s arrived on station. A line of attack helicopters crested the hill of the middle island and came roaring in line abreast. Dozens of smoke trails shot from wing-mounted pods, the rockets arcing toward the ground. A series of explosions blasted both sides of the main road, the crump of detonations sending waves of fear among the town's remaining residents.

Flying over the area where the anti-air missile was presumed to have been fired from, the attack choppers split apart. The Chinese helicopters, staying within the bounds of the Jiangmei township, sought out targets of opportunity. Not seeing anything due to the dense shrubs, they then unleashed the rest of their rockets on likely ambush sites.

While the Z-10s were working over the crossing and beyond, Chinese recovery vehicles crested and then powered down the incline toward the causeway. Nervous drivers negotiated the wreckage of the previous crossing attempts, trying to ignore the smoldering hulks but unable to pull their eyes from the destruction. Bodies lay in the road, some with their clothes still smoldering. In places, the Chinese airborne soldiers lay in clumps too dense to avoid. With sickened feelings, the drivers rolled over the dead, the clanking treads and wheels compressing bodies far beyond anything recognizable.

Down to the causeway they drove. The first in line hooked up with the ruins of an APC and pulled it clear of the raised roadway. Another recovery vehicle took the place of the first and pulled another wreck clear. Far away, looking like tiny gnats, helicopters darted this way and that, the sound of the explosions coming like a distant thunderstorm. Slowly, and without interference, lanes across the roadway were cleared. The last of the recovery vehicles pulled away from the causeway and the attack helicopters started working farther inland. A low rumbling thunder rolled over the crossing as Chinese artillery again started firing.

Chapter Eight

Along the shores of Pehu Island, Chinese artillery shells began landing in the churned soil. Instead of the previous heart-pounding blasts sending shrapnel outward, there came soft crumps. From each shell, a thick mixture of smoke began covering the area. One batch mixed with another, forming a thick wall that obscured the far reaches of the causeway. Adjusting fire, the smoke shells started landing in the tidal flats and the water adjacent the causeway, some landing directly on the roadway where wrecked machines of war had recently blazed. Thick tendrils of white smoke blossomed, drifting on the gentle winds swirling through the area.

Looking through the lenses of hovering drones, Chinese forward observers shifted the fire of the infantry fighting vehicles once they were satisfied with the obscuration of the far crossing exit. Within minutes, the same thermal inhibiting smoke started covering the approaches. Hidden inside the smoke banks, the rumble of engines could be heard as Chinese armored vehicles rolled toward their third attempt to get across the Yong'an Bridge.

Unseen over the thickening smoke, a Taiwanese drone also hovered. The operator, working in the rear near the township of Jiangmei, tried different optics in an attempt to see through the smoke screen thrown up by the Chinese. The results were hit and miss with thermal heat signatures showing periodically.

Farther to the rear, the Taiwanese artillery batteries heard the news that fire adjustments would be sparse at best. The artillery battalion commander sighed. In his book, the Chinese commanders had made several mistakes, but had shown the capacity to adapt. On the flip side, he thought that there had been mistakes made on Taiwan's side as well. For one, he thought they should have thrown everything at the invaders before they could get a foothold on the islands, but that hadn't been his call. He understood the commander's reasoning, but he would have made a different choice. Time would tell if the stratagem they were following would pan out.

The artillery batteries weren't useless without a forward observer to adjust fire. The battery crews had the causeway azimuths. More importantly, along with the M109 mobile artillery weapons, the batteries had received 155mm American GPS-ammunition. That meant they could deliver precision strikes on any area they chose that was within range, and any of the artillerymen could damn near recite the end and mid-span coordinates from memory. The problem facing the Penghu Defense Command was that they didn't know if they were actually hitting anything without a forward observer's input. And from the news coming from the crossing, it was going to be difficult to get any unit close. They would just have to rely on reports of secondary explosions and hope that the observers were able to sift through the smoke screen being thrown up by the Chinese assault units.

The Taiwanese drone operator was able to get a definitive heat signature through the shifting smoke. There was a vehicular unit about halfway across the dike. A battery of four M109s sent 155mm shells arcing through the noon skies. The Chinese soldiers on the causeway exit involuntarily ducked when they heard the shriek of heavy rounds pass overhead.

The artillery passed down through the smoke and detonated on the roadway. Chunks of asphalt and concrete were torn asunder, momentarily clearing holes in the smoke screen. Shrapnel ripped through the thinner skins of the armored personnel carriers, tearing into vehicular systems and bone like soft butter.

The lead Chinese APC received a hit along its left side. It was a battle of armor thickness versus explosive power, one that the armored vehicle lost. Shrapnel punched through the sides, leaving behind jagged softball-sized holes. Two tensioning wheels sprung loose from their mounts, falling to become another part of the roadway debris. One of the track links failed, the forward momentum of the APC continuing until it ran clear of the track. On fire, it slewed to a stop.

Screaming soldiers engulfed in flame spilled from the

rear, their arms flailing in futile attempts to put out the fire. Unsuccessful, the Chinese soldiers fell to the ground where they continued to burn until they were smoldering husks. In some cases, the only way to determine they were once people was by the charred outlines of their bodies, almost as if chalk outlines had been filled in with charcoal. To the observer trying to pierce the veil of the smoke screen, it was if live candles had materialized from within the compartments, each dancing to an unheard beat until the flame was snuffed out.

With a limited view of their surroundings, and aware that heavy caliber enemy shells were again dropping on the crossing, the Chinese drivers gunned their heavy vehicles. One driver saw a burning APC appear through the smoke, the bodies of those it carried on fire and running crazily. One ran into the side of the racing APC, getting caught in the treads. This shortened the man's screams, sending him to whatever awaited him next a minute earlier than his comrades.

Passing the burning APC, the vehicle commander knew that he was now in the lead. A nearby explosion rocked the armored vehicle, jostling everyone inside and threatening to tip the six-wheeled vehicle on its side. The wheels on one side slammed back down once, then a second time. The commander's yells to accelerate were mostly so he felt he was doing something about the maelstrom he found himself in. The vehicle was already traveling as fast as it could under the circumstances.

Pings of shrapnel rang off the metallic sides, creating fresh gleaming scars along the APC. Then the Chinese armored vehicle was past the fully-engulfed lead, the dead commander hanging over a blown hatch, barely visible through the flames. The APC moved again into a world of its own, one with next to no visibility and rocked by momentous blasts.

The only way the driver and commander had any idea they had made it across was when they passed recently dug positions surrounded by craters. They became fully aware they were across when the smoke thinned and they shot out of the protective covering.

"Driver, stop! Back, back, back!" the commander shouted.

The APC lurched to a halt. The Chinese airborne soldiers inside were thrown again when the vehicle was put in reverse and the driver gunned the engine. The vehicle backed into a 155mm Taiwanese shell that landed almost directly beside the backing APC. Beams of light shot through the passenger compartment as shrapnel punched through the armored skin. Warm liquid sprayed in the compartment when a hot slice of metal nearly decapitated one of the troopers, the iron smell of fresh blood mixing with torn hydraulic lines and grease. The buckling earth and compressed air worked in tandem to topple the heavy vehicle, soldiers inside slamming against bulkheads and each other as the APC tipped over on its side.

The Taiwanese artillery commander just didn't have the number of guns he would have liked. Modern warfare, with its technological advancements, meant that artillery units were no longer part of the rear echelon that could safely remain in place. Counter battery radars picked up incoming shells and tracked them to their source. Thus, an artillery battery was constantly firing and moving, decreasing the volume of fire it could deliver. Already, many of the mobile units under his command were on the move to prevent their loss.

Some of those guns under his command were doing just that. The counterbattery radars had found the Chinese fire and were delivering heavy strikes on the positions determined by the radar systems. But, with some devoted to counterbattery and others on the move, that meant there were times when the crossing wasn't under fire. And in those moments, more Chinese armor was able to force their way across, offloading their troops and setting up in defensive positions.

The artillery commander, striving to deliver fire while saving his forces, knew that Taiwan and the Penghu Defense Command were fighting a losing battle. Finally, he ordered a halt to the shelling at the crossing, partly to conserve his available ammunition and partly to save his units. Slowly, the tenuous Chinese foothold on the near bank was strengthened.

With the cessation of Taiwanese artillery fire, the causeway fell securely to Chinese control. China now had a footing on the second island in their conquest to take over the entire chain.

*   *   *   *   *   *

Pacific Ocean
1 August, 2021

Under direction, the pilot ran the throttles of the V-22 Osprey forward. The tiltrotor aircraft shook as the engines ran up to full power. Six F-35B aircraft were parked along the edges of the flight deck, the helicopter contingent of the USS *America* parked in the large hangar spaces below deck. The amphibious assault ship had been attached to Task Force 70, currently positioned to the east of Japan in the western Pacific Ocean.

In the back of the Osprey, Petty Officer First Class David Hawser looked at the five others strapped to the nylon-webbed seats attached to the sides of the aircraft. The last few days, or more to the point, the last twenty-four hours, had been hectic to say the least. With SEAL Dive Team One's successes rescuing the twelve sailors that had been held by the Chinese following the sinking of the USS *Preble*, Blue Team had been selected for this latest mission.

The briefing had been, well, brief, with promises of mission updates as they progressed toward the target area. A relatively small Chinese flotilla was heading toward Taiwan, their initial presumed destination the Penghu Island chain. Petty Officer Hawser and his team had been assigned the mission of sinking the ships. With the attack submarines assigned to the area either presumed sunk or out of position, as they had been reassigned to chase down the recharging Chinese Kilos, the mission had been hastily drawn up and assigned to Hawser's team.

While waiting for takeoff, the petty officer recalled that the ideal scenario was to sink the ships in the harbor, preferably while docked, as this would further foul the berthing facilities. The higher ups wanted to do everything possible to deter China from establishing a base from which to support the main invasion of Taiwan. In particular, David knew, they wanted to prevent the islands from becoming a base from which China could launch cruise and short-range ballistic missiles toward Taiwan, as well as hosting a variety of attack aircraft.

Should China be able to position missiles on the islands, they'd be able to extend the range of their ground-based anti-ship missiles by nearly a hundred miles. That would mean the carriers would be vulnerable to a host of China's shorter-range anti-ship rocket forces — something to be prevented at all costs.

Submarines would have made short work of the few ships delivering supplies for the presumed invasion of the island chain in the Taiwan Strait, but being unavailable, that task fell to David and the others of his team.

Following the warning order and subsequent preliminary briefings, SDV 1 Blue Team had been immediately flown from Pearl Harbor out to the USS *America*. While SDV 1 had been in the opening stages of preparation, the USS *Greeneville* had been detached from its escort duties for Task Force 70, ranging far ahead of the fleet. Coming alongside the submarine tender, the USS *Frank Cable*, the LA-class fast attack submarine had been outfitted with a Dry Deck Shelter housing a SEAL Delivery Vehicle.

The detachment of the boat was a risky decision. Intelligence had determined that China still had several submarines positioned somewhere in the Philippine and South China seas, so releasing an asset that was designed to counter undersea threats placed the two carriers that were the central showcases of the task force in greater danger. However, if command wanted to slow or prevent China from building up its forces on the Penghu Islands, then there weren't many additional options. Thus, the Blue Team of SEAL Dive Team One found themselves strapped in the back of an Osprey in the western reaches of the Pacific.

With a signal from the flight deck crew, the tiltrotor aircraft lifted from the *America's* flight deck. Brief glimpses of the silhouettes from distant ships, spread over a vast expanse of blue, showed as the V-22 swung away from the LHA and picked up speed. Staying near wavetop level, the Osprey started across the rolling crests, on its way to rendezvous with the USS *Greeneville.*

* * * * * *

Causeway, Penghu Islands
1 August, 2021

Following the crossing of the causeway by Chinese forces, the lead Chinese battalion commander fumed at the lack of progress past the established beachhead. Even though the sound of transport aircraft arriving and departing was a constant background, the incoming supplies weren't reaching the front quickly enough. It was only a few miles with little to no resistance encountered, but the steady logistical support was lagging. The expenditure of ammunition, especially that associated with the support vehicles serving as artillery support for the infantry advances, was greater than the arriving supplies. Frequent calls to the regimental commander were met with the same reply, "The supplies are coming. Now, push forward."

The battalion commander wanted to respond, "Push forward with what?" But he knew that his boss was wrangling with the issue and his flippant reply wouldn't serve anything. Radio traffic gave the appearance that Chinese units were aggressively pushing outward from the airfields, which probably meant that there were few available to establish logistical convoys. The battalion commander understood that supply issues had been part of the overall design, that they had been accounted for in the planning. But he wasn't seeing any evidence of that.

The problem was that he couldn't push forward with anything but reconnaissance probes. The battle to cross the first series of bridges had proven that artillery support was going to be essential, so *pushing forward* wasn't really an option until his vehicles were rearmed.

That presented another problem. He had forces across on the other side that had formed a defensive perimeter. However, Taiwanese artillery kept hitting those grouped units and he knew it wouldn't take much for a Taiwanese counterattack to force them back to the main island. He was in a situation for which there was no right answer other than to pray that he was given enough time to resupply.

The narrow avenues through which he could approach presented difficulties. The road network only allowed attacks across a limited front. That restricted maneuverability also meant that it was hard for follow-on battalions to pass through. There just wasn't enough room. The battalion commander, facing the loss of many vehicles in the crossing, gazed to the thickening clouds that were starting to billow into the afternoon skies. To further exacerbate matters, it looked as if he'd have to fight rainstorms in addition to a slow supply train. And on top of that, there was an enemy out there somewhere, waiting to ambush his forces when he finally pushed out from the beachhead.

*   *   *   *   *   *

Distant booms rang across the landscape, the sounds seeming as if they could be coming from the darkening clouds slowly gathering into a line of storms. Seconds after the hollow booms, the edges of Jiangmei erupted into fountains of dirt and shrubs. The Taiwanese town stretched across a narrow neck of land that led away from the bunched Chinese battalion, presenting an ideal location for Taiwan's forces to defend. Urban environments favored the defender and could grind down attacking forces.

After hours of waiting for resupply, the leading Chinese battalion commander was ready to break out of the established beachhead. His prayer for time had apparently been answered. Other than harassing artillery fire from the Taiwanese forces, the counterattack he had been anticipating never arrived. Perhaps the enemy commander was too timid to engage, or there weren't many defenders to begin with. Given the nature of the battles so far and the ease with which China landed on the main island of Magong, almost unopposed, the battalion commander was leaning toward the latter. However, he wasn't going to rush his armor into the town without prepping it first. He'd learned that lesson crossing the bridges.

Peppering the city's edge, the infantry fighting vehicles parked to the rear of the leading APCs sent volleys of high explosives arcing toward the township. One shell crashed through the roof of a residence, exploding in a small kitchen. Windows blew out from the blast, sending deadly shards rocketing away from the house. Thin, shredded curtains fluttered from the newly created openings.

A second shell landed in a tiny herb garden near the corner of the same abode, tearing chunks from the weakened walls. Slowly, similar to a single footstep on a steep slope starting a slide of loose gravel, tiles began slipping from the damaged roof. The structural integrity of the residential home, undermined by the consecutive explosions, gave way. The corner that had been obliterated by the second shell collapsed, falling into what remained of the herb garden.

Additional shells started landing among other homes and small shops. One such building suddenly developed a nearly perfectly round hole in the wall next to the front door. For a brief moment, it looked like the home had been shot, a clean hole marking the bullet's entry point. Then all hell broke loose inside the house when the 105mm artillery round detonated.

The compressed air raced through the house. The windows and outer door disintegrated as the over-pressurized air sought the paths of least resistance. Smoke and flame punched out of the openings almost as if a dragon living inside had coughed. Then the walls collapsed, the roof falling in to bury a lifetime of saved valuables. Pictures of happier moments caught fire and became ash.

Along the outskirts of Jiangmei, homes were demolished. Pyres of smoke rose from fires that started within the flimsy structures. The view of the city became obscured as shells continued landing.

There were only a few ZTL-11 infantry fighting vehicles available for use, so the exploding 105mm rounds were mixed with a variety of other calibers. Satisfied with the fire being directed toward his next objective, the battalion commander lowered the hatch of his Type 08 Command Vehicle and gave the order for his unit to move out.

* * * * * *

The ground vibrated as the deafening crash of artillery shells slammed into the south side of Jiangmei. Crouching in cover near the center of the township, Sergeant Chih-hao of the Penghu Defense Command felt his heart thudding almost in rhythm to the constant barrage. His anxious breaths were dry from the adrenaline coursing through his system. Looking along the line, the rest of his squad were staring at him with fearful expressions. Their bodies cringed with each explosion impacting only a few streets away. However, there was also a measure of determination that shone deeper in their fear-filled eyes.

Aside from their usual arsenal of carbines, grenades, and pouches of ammo, many of those huddled against the homes and shops were carrying Javelins. The rest of the platoon was also humping the portable anti-tank missile systems. On the other side of town, a second platoon was waiting in cover. A third platoon, set up near the northern outskirts were acting as a reserve force and were packing a different sort of portable system. This third platoon would provide short-range anti-air cover with their contingent of Stinger missiles.

The Taiwanese company was part of Penghu's mechanized battalion sent forward to slow the Chinese when they emerged from their beachhead. Colonel Wen-hsiung knew he didn't have enough firepower to stop the Chinese, but he could pick at them in order to slow down their invasion, and in the process hopefully make it so China couldn't use the islands to assist with their main invasion efforts of Taiwan.

In this, the Taiwanese colonel had maintained the delicate balance of using his meager forces while also preserving them from China's overwhelming majority of troops and equipment. Thus, he had sent the company forward with orders to engage the approaching Chinese units but not become bogged down in an extended firefight.

"Gaining time is more important than retaining territory," Wen-hsiung had told his units.

But the colonel knew that was only part of the equation as there was only so much land he could trade. He would do the best with what he had, but outnumbered in both personnel and equipment, and without air cover, his best would likely end in defeat no matter what strategy he went with.

Sergeant Chih-hao huddled and waited for the next explosion. He was a little confused when there weren't any further ground-shaking eruptions. Instead, a hush had descended over the area. That was short-lived as the radio came alive with the company commander ordering the two leading platoons forward. The twelve soldiers of Chih-hao's squad rose from their crouched positions and inched toward the nearest corner. Ahead, the lieutenant in charge of the platoon peeked around the corner, then motioned everyone forward.

In a rapid flowing of bodies, the two platoons trotted along alleyways and through small yards. Very few of the town's residents remained, but those who chose to stay looked on from doorways and parted curtains. The cessation of artillery blasting the town's outskirts could only mean that Chinese armored units were on the move. With paced, panting breaths, the Taiwanese units furtively moved through Jiangmei to meet them.

* * * * * *

When the Chinese artillery lifted its fire, Z-10 attack helicopters zoomed forward. The leading choppers, armed with pylon-mounted rocket pods and heavy caliber guns protruding from under chins, sought out any resistance that might be holding out in the town. On the ground, deep-throated roars and whines echoed from the perimeter. Smoke belched from exhausts as armored personnel carriers rolled forward, their smaller 25mm autocannons and 12.7mm machine guns aimed toward the smoke smoldering from the ruins of houses.

Sergeant Chih-hao hugged the rear of a building when a Chinese attack helicopter zipped across the clear air between building eaves. More passed quickly in and out of sight as the deadly airborne assets moved across the township. On the move again, the sergeant and the rest of the platoon went to ground amid the debris left from destroyed homes on the edges of town.

With the third platoon in the rear, the Taiwanese company commander heard the distinct sound of approaching helicopters. There was no doubt as to the nationality of the choppers as those with a higher pay grade had made the decision not to include any air power in their defense of the Penghu Islands. In his opinion, they hadn't chosen to include much and it felt like they had left just enough to provide a token resistance. That was a quick path to an early grave or confinement. But this was his fate in life, and one he accepted.

Flying a scant hundred feet over the rooftops, a Chinese attack chopper swept over the captain's position. Hoisting a Stinger, the company commander stepped away from his cover and aimed the device as the Chinese Z-10 circled around for another pass. He heard the tone signifying the missile was locked onto the enemy chopper's heat source.

With a whoosh, the missile left the confines of the tube. Trailing a line of white, the Stinger raced across the short distance separating it from the banking Chinese helicopter. Like a story working its way toward its inevitable conclusion, the missile closed on the chopper. The pilot, seeing the threat too late, hit the countermeasures. Two flares were ejected from ports along the side when the Stinger slammed into the side of the Z-10. A belch of fire and dark smoke erupted from the exhaust. Losing power immediately, the attack chopper nosed over and smacked into thick trees, turning end over end before erupting into a flaming ball.

While more Chinese helicopters traversed Jiangmei, other missiles sped aloft as additional MANPADS were launched. Against the backdrop of brewing storm clouds, white lines arced away from the town, tearing after Chinese helicopters that were turning for additional passes.

Alerted by radio traffic and the crash of the lead Z-10, some of the pilots saw the danger rising from the town. Flares spit out from aggressively-banking choppers, the crews unaware of whether they were targeted or not, but mashing buttons nonetheless. Some of the white trails streaking away from the northern section of the township turned away from their targets, drawn by the heat generated from burning flares. Others weren't fooled and continued after the maneuvering choppers.

Bright flashes showed successful intercepts, most of the stricken choppers nosing over and slamming into the ground. The Chinese helicopters that survived maneuvered away, hugging the tops of the trees. Once secure from the immediate threats, the few remaining turned back toward the town. Rocket pods were at the ready, waiting only for a target and an electronic command to fire.

Once their missiles had been fired, the Taiwanese company commander urged his third platoon away from their positions. Secondary and Tertiary positions had been scouted and stocked with additional ammunition. As the Chinese helicopters were turning back for firing runs, the soldiers scurried toward their secondary positions.

* * * * * *

Minimizing his movements, Sergeant Chih-hao cleared smaller chunks of debris away from his position. Just as he had been trained, he wanted clear lanes of fire. But that was easier said than done. Many of the boards, lying twisted among personal possessions and clay tiles from the roof, had nails protruding from their splintered remains. Glass combined to create a hazard zone that he hadn't considered before that very moment. The smooth practice berms or fake training houses created from plywood were much different than the environment he was now laying in.

Amid the sound of the approaching Chinese, the sergeant heard the firing of missiles to the rear and a faint sound of explosions. He didn't know if those were from crashes or the choppers firing in retaliation. His hope was obviously for the former. But any thoughts extending along those lines were quickly forgotten as the first Chinese APC came into view. Behind the six-wheeled monster, other armored vehicles could be seen moving rapidly up the four-laned highway leading from the causeway through the town.

The thick foliage on the sides of the highway didn't allow for vehicular traffic, even those riding on gigantic wheels. The lead Chinese APC cleared the thick shrubs and drove off the road. As the lead armored vehicle raced across the narrow open fields close to the edges of town, Chih-hao saw the maw of the gun extending from the top turret pointing directly at him.

The sergeant hoisted his Javelin. Due to the decreased range to the targets, Chih-hao selected a direct attack mode. This would negate the missile system's rising path meant to then descend and hit the target from above. With his gunner patting him on the shoulder, letting Chih-hao know that it was clear behind, the sergeant selected a narrowed field of view to identify the target. Once the target was centered in the thermal vision, Chih-hao pressed the first of two triggers.

The view immediately switched to the lesser magnification inherent with the seeker field of view. With the target verified, the sergeant pressed the second trigger. After a moment's pause, the missile was thrown from the launch tube. Once away from its original position, the main rocket motors cut in. Acting on internal guidance using its own laser tracking, the missile accelerated away, climbing slightly to ensure that it could keep the target in sight.

The Javelin sped across the open field, closing on the

Chinese APC within seconds. The missile's two stage explosive detonated just in front of the Type 92's turret. The smaller first charge was to detonate any explosive reactive armor the enemy vehicle might have onboard. Then the larger HEAT round exploded, the shaped charge creating a narrow high velocity particle stream with the ability to penetrate thick armor.

Chih-hao watched the Javelin race away and hit, a fireball rising above the open field to his front. With tongues of flame licking upward from the Type 92 APC, the large, armored beast lurched to a stop. Smoke poured from behind when the rear crew doors were opened. Coughing and choking, Chinese soldiers who survived the initial hit scattered from the stricken vehicle. With more missiles reaching out for the follow-on armor, Chinese soldiers were ordered out of their armored carriers. Chih-hao and his gunner backed away from their position. Crouch running behind houses reduced to rubble, the two moved to another location.

From the edges of town, Javelin missiles streaked across open fields. The lead Chinese armored personnel carriers were targeted. Dark smoke belched from burning interiors as the vehicles came to lurching halts. In some, the smaller turrets were lifted from their chassis when the ammunition stored aboard was caught in the explosions, crashing to the ground next to their burning chassis. Sheets of flame rose from several whose fuel lines became severed, the metal of the armored behemoths glowing from the intense heat.

*   *   *   *   *   *

The Chinese attack helicopters, providing fire support for the advancement, circled around after being chased by a volley of heat-seeking missiles that rose from the northern part of Jiangmei. Tree branches waved from downwash as the pilots hugged the treetops.

From the corner of his eye, Captain Tien Pengfei saw drifting columns of smoke rising from downed squadron members. Having defeated one of the enemy missiles that went after the flares he discharged, the captain circled around to the east. Flying just scant feet over the tops of the trees, Tien and his gunner watched flocks of birds rising from their roosts. The pilot and gunner involuntarily flinched as the dark objects filled their windscreen and were either whisked overhead or down the sides. It was like a surfer riding the curling edge of a breaking wave, the crest not quite able to crash down to catch the intrepid boarder.

With the attack helicopter bouncing from the unstable air, the Chinese captain saw the tree line ending ahead, the break in the unrelenting green showing where Jiangmei was located. Tien had in his mind's eye the section of the town from where the white streaks rose from. With a small adjustment to his heading, he pulled back on the collective. The rooftops came into view as the chopper ascended. With a small amount of pressure to the rudder pedal, the captain brought the Z-10 into alignment with where he saw the bevy of enemy missiles appear.

Streaks of dirty brown smoke tore past the cockpit as a series of rockets left the pods mounted to the stubby wings. The weapons shot over the treetops and arced down toward several small buildings near the northern edges of the township. A chain of explosions ripped into buildings and small yards. Walls and fence boards were torn apart, the patios and lawns turning into buzzsaws of hot shrapnel.

Once his rockets were expended, Tien lowered the chopper's nose, again heading for the perceived safety of the low-level environment. He punched out flares as he sped over the top of the city, the roofs whipping past one after another. Although he glanced to the side to see the effects of his attack as he passed, he wasn't able to see through the smoke rising from the blasts.

"Oh shit! More missile launches!" his gunner exclaimed.

Without hesitation, Tien expended additional flares and banked the Z-10 sharply. The chopper shook abruptly, and the captain had his hands full for a couple of seconds, keeping it out of the trees. The shaking subsided almost as fast as its onset.

Tien concluded that one of the missiles fired from the village had almost caught him, exploding among the descending flares.

His gunner's helmet nearly slammed into the side window when Tien brought the Z-10 out of its bank only to roll into another one in the opposite direction. Looking over his shoulder as he did so, he saw a white streak sail past his tail rotor and pass from view. Sweat ran down the side of his flight suit from the continuous flow of adrenaline. The sight of the town vanished as Tien flew away.

The captain was in the process of turning back to deliver another volley of fire when new orders arrived. The remaining attack helicopters were to focus on the southern outskirts of Jiangmei, where Taiwanese defenders were holding China's advance.

* * * * * *

Some members of the two Taiwanese platoons attempting to hold up the Chinese attack had set up light machine guns among the destroyed homes. Soon the fields fronting Jiangmei were filled with the chatter of M-60s opening up.

In seemingly slow motion, red tracers crossed the open fields. The weapons initially found stunned Chinese soldiers that had emerged from APCs hit by the first Javelin missiles. The heavier slugs slammed into the troops and sent them spinning to the ground. In some places, streaks of sunlight poking through billowing storm clouds caught splashes of pink spraying from bodies.

With the first shots that streaked from the township, the Chinese battalion commander realized that he had a fight on his hands. The anti-air missiles rising from the deeper parts of the village only served to verify his initial read on the situation. Smoke and flames were erupting from the lead vehicles, some of which managed to reach the open fields in front of the town. He ordered the airborne soldiers to disembark from the back of the APCs and for the armor vehicles to provide support fire.

* * * * * *

The wall of the building behind exploded, startling Sergeant Chih-hao as he attempted to target another Chinese APC. Plaster and splinters of wood rained down on the Taiwanese sergeant and the loader with him. Brushing debris from his hair, he again set to locate a target for his reloaded Javelin.

The field and highway leading to the city was filled with a swarm of blinking lights as the Chinese soldiers and armor began returning fire. He ducked again as bullets slammed against the debris field he had set himself up in. A second string of rounds struck the top, warped boards and plaster disintegrating under the onslaught.

Hoisting the Javelin again over the mound of a shattered wall that had fallen, Chih-hao saw an armored personnel carrier tearing across the open field. He set the new target up in his thermal sight and pressed the first trigger. A second squeeze jettisoned an anti-tank missile from the launcher. A second later, the projectile's motor kicked in and the Javelin chased after the racing target.

In a steady arc as the missile's seeker kept the thermal image in sight, the white trail of its exhaust intersected the six-wheeled APC. A flash of yellow fire and black smoke erupted from the side of the armored vehicle. One of the large wheels became detached and rolled ahead of the APC. The vehicle lurched to a stop with thick, dark smoke belching from the interior.

Other streaks of white sped away from Jiangmei as more Chinese units were engaged. In the background of explosions and crackle of flames came the chatter of machine guns and carbines.

Sergeant Chih-hao ducked again as an explosion destroyed most of his cover. One of the Chinese armored vehicles had noted the location of the firing missile and had taken umbrage. Coated in dust and splinters, the Taiwanese sergeant looked up as his loader was placing another Javelin in the launcher. Chinese soldiers were moving in small groups while others provided fire. He saw an enemy squad maneuvering along a tree line as they attempted to flank his squad's position. To the front, Chinese armor was spreading out from the highway, more of them arriving up the road.

Adding to the already noisy battle, friendly artillery began arriving, blasts erupting in the field. Fire embedded in smoke lifted gouts of dirt and bushes. Chinese soldiers caught in the explosion simply vanished from sight. Charging APCs were rocked and jostled by near misses, a couple of older models losing their tracks. Those ran froward until the damaged track played out and the armored vehicle plowed into the dirt.

Chih-hao glanced again at the flanking enemy squad. Someone had also spied them. One of the machine guns sent bursts of fire in their direction, the tracers merging with the group. The Chinese squad immediately dropped from view without Chih-hao seeing whether they had been hit or not.

Something warm splashed against his cheek. Half-expecting to see that a bullet had ruptured a water bottle, he was taken aback by the image of his loader beside him. The man's face was half gone, replaced by bone splinters and meat. The man's upper teeth were clearly visible, lying in the midst of red pulp. Red bubbles formed and popped. For a moment, Chih-hao thought the man was alive and that scared him more than the gruesome sight. He was going to have to provide first aid to a man whose features were barely recognizable. Then he saw the one intact eye glazed over and knew the man was dead. He was ashamed to feel relieved, but the thought of having to perform CPR or attempt to bandage something so grisly was more than he thought he could handle now.

Chih-hao stared at the man for long moments. The loud sound of the ongoing battle was only a distant hum as he stared at the torn face. Part of Chih-hao was still present enough to wonder why the man had been beside him instead of behind. Then he realized that the loader had finished his task and had come up to let Chih-hao know.

More explosions tore around him, the sound beginning

to penetrate.

"He's gone. We're pulling out!" someone shouted beside him.

The Taiwanese sergeant startled when someone grabbed his arm. The sounds of the raging battle came back in a rush. Chih-hao looked up to see his lieutenant crouched next to him.

"What?" Chih-hao yelled back.

"I said, he's gone. Leave him, we're pulling back," the lieutenant repeated.

A string of explosions rolled along the debris where the two platoons had initially set up. While looking at the lieutenant, the officer was suddenly catapulted from his crouched position. Chih-hao saw, almost as if it were in slow motion, a piece of something dark flash into his line of sight and hit the officer. The sergeant stared for a moment at his commander, noticing a jagged hole in the man's forehead as the lieutenant's eyes crossed and clouded over.

Chih-hao ducked as a helicopter flew low over his position. Suddenly enraged at what the Chinese had done to men he had known for years, the sergeant rolled to one knee and lifted the launcher. He saw the fleeing chopper and targeted it, knowing that the Javelin could find anything with a heat source. The missile leapt from the launcher and, igniting its motor, sped after the Z-10.

Chih-hao followed the white smoking trail as it flew past a line of descending flares and detonated near the back of the chopper. The Chinese attack helicopter began spinning wildly and vanished from sight below a line of trees.

Remembering his LT's last order to pull back, and still carrying the Javelin launcher, Chih-hao turned and ran, passing across ruined streets and in between destroyed buildings.

* * * * * *

Captain Tien Pengfei felt something hard slam against his chopper, nearly throwing the cyclic from his hand. Warning lights and alarms flared inside the cockpit as the Z-10 was tossed to the side and then started spinning violently. Immediately knowing that he had lost his tail rotor and was auto-rotating in, the captain braced for impact. Being so low to the ground, the crash was short in coming.

The windscreen of the Z-10 was filled with a crazy world of spinning green. A thick line appeared across the glass, angling upward. The sharp cracks of breaking branches mixed with the blare of alarms. Disoriented slightly from the sudden spin, Tien was cognizant enough to cut off the power and turn off the electrical supply before the helicopter slammed into the ground.

For several moments, Tien hung against his straps, wondering if he was still alive. Branches crashing on top of the canopy brought him to a better state of consciousness. He looked up to see mangled rotors covered with leaves and limbs. The cockpit glass was shattered in several places, the intact portions a spiderweb of cracks.

Tien called out for his gunner, only to realize that he had shut off the power and the intercom wasn't working. Struggling against the straps holding him, he managed to release them. The Z-10 had ended up in a slight nose down attitude, causing Tien to fall against the dash. With careful negotiation, he was able to crawl through one of the larger holes in the cockpit canopy.

He was going to assist the gunner out when he noticed a thick branch protruding from the man's chest. The flight suit surrounding the massive injury was stained red. There was no doubt in Tien's mind that his gunner was dead, but he had to make sure. Reaching through a hole in the canopy, Tien sought to undo the man's mask so the gunner would have a greater ability to talk and breathe. Undoing one of the latches, a pool of blood spilled out, running down to soak more of the man's flight suit. There was no way his gunner was alive.

Standing over the cockpit, Tien looked upward. There was a circle of open air where the Z-10 had torn through the trees, the rapidly spinning rotors and chopper carving a pathway to the ground. Feeling for more injuries and finding none, the Chinese captain crawled down to the ground and began making his way through the foliage. He was unsure of which direction he should head through the dense underbrush, so he began inching his way toward the frontlines using the dim battle sounds for guidance. Battle sounds meant Chinese forces. Chinese forces meant medics and that was what he needed.

* * * * * *

The Chinese battalion commander saw the missile trails speeding out from the edges of the village, those ending with loud clanging explosions. The field was dotted with the smoking and fiery ruins of armored vehicles. The airborne companies and remaining APCs were laying down heavy fire. He couldn't fathom how anyone could be living through the hell being delivered to the town's outskirts, but the return fire from the enemy was proof that the defenders were there.

He couldn't tell exactly how many troops he was facing, but the type of return fire seemed to tell that he was facing infantry equipped with portable anti-tank weapons. Reports of anti-air missiles coming from the northern sections of the town and firing on the choppers seemed to indicate that there was infantry there as well.

Even though there wasn't any sign of bunkers or prepared defenses, it appeared that the Taiwanese were ready to defend the township. Perhaps the enemy commander thought to whittle down his forces in urban warfare, not that the village was that large. However, he had lost much of his battalion during the bridge crossings, so it wouldn't take much more until his unit wasn't combat ready.

The commander watched as a missile streaked upward. He followed the fast-moving trail as it intersected one of the fire support helicopters. A puff of dark smoke marked where the missile detonated, sending the chopper into a wild spin toward the ground. He noted the lack of an explosion and thought there might be a chance the crew survived. But that only held his attention for a moment before it was drawn back to the fight in progress.

The battalion commander made a decision. He wasn't going to grind what remained of his units in an urban brawl. Turning to one of his radio operators inside the command vehicle, he said, "'Order all units to call off the attack and pull back. Have the APCs provide smoke to cover our withdrawal."

After ordering the attack helicopters out of the area, he then sent an order to the ZBL-08 infantry fighting vehicles in the rear. The distant rumble of the 122mm and 155mm cannons firing came again. The large caliber artillery shells started landing among the standing buildings. The commander would reduce Jiangmei to toothpicks, and thus eliminate any cover for the opposing force.

*   *   *   *   *   *

Sergeant Chih-hao focused on the sound of his own panting breath as he ran northward through the township of Jiangmei. Behind him came the crash of heavy artillery, sounding as if it was coming from near his previous position. He wondered if he should stop and defend the town, but realized he didn't have any more missiles for his launcher. Besides, he spotted others of his and the second platoon on parallel tracks as he ran across the narrow streets. When in the open for short periods, his glance always went to the skies, searching for any sign of a helicopter bearing down on him. The thought of a chopper coming at him from the heavens frightened him more than the crunch of artillery behind.

"Whoa, Sergeant," a voice called.

Chih-hao turned toward the shout, dropping his launcher. He had started to pull out his carbine when he recognized the dirty face of his company commander.

"You're good," the captain said, forestalling Chih-hao from bringing his weapon to bear.

Chih-hao relaxed. Well, as much as possible given his mad flight from the ruin and destruction that was being visited to the other side of the town. Others running from the front halted when they met the rest of the company. Although the third platoon seemed to have all or most of its original members, Chih-hao saw that the same couldn't be said of his and second platoon. He counted those arriving, coming up very short of the numbers which had originally set out. Unless more showed up, first and second platoon had lost almost a third of their men.

"Your lieutenant?" the company commander asked.

Chih-hao shook his head, remembering his leader cross-eyed and staring at nothing in this world.

"I guess that makes you first platoon leader," the captain said, patting Chih-hao on the shoulder. "Now, what do you say we get our folks back to the battalion."

With eyes glancing toward the skies, and with the sound of heavy explosion coming from the town, the company began making its way across the terrain to where the main force lay in wait. Just before he dipped into the brush, Chih-hao glanced back toward Jiangmei. A wall of smoke was rising from the far end of the town. The rumble and explosions of artillery was a constant background noise. The grotesque image of his loader surfaced. Chih-hao realized that the sight would haunt him for the rest of his days, but he stuffed any emotion associated with it down as there was work to be done and he had a platoon to take care of.

* * * * * *

Captain Tien Pengfei lowered a branch and peeked beyond. He had arrived at the field in front of the village, but it looked much different than the fleeting glimpse he had of it before he was shot down. Smoldering armored vehicles lay in the field, but there were others moving along the highway that ran through the town. Soldiers moved cautiously toward the outskirts, their weapons held ready. The captain glanced at the town. There was little remaining of the homes and shops. Most of it was just piles of broken beams and roof tiles with spirals of smoke coming from smoldering fires underneath.

China had taken the village and expanded their

perimeter, but remembering a number of his squadron being hit by a bevy of missiles, he wondered at what cost. The Chinese captain guessed that the soldiers crossing the fields would be overanxious, and thus might be trigger happy. He sat at the edge of the tree line, waiting for the follow-on forces before exiting.

* * * * * *

West Philippine Sea
1 August, 2021

Three hundred miles to the east of Taiwan, an afternoon sun slowly rolled across the windscreen as the Osprey pilot rolled out of a slight bank, positioning the aircraft directly over a faint white wake cutting through the gently rolling swells of the Philippine Sea. Following the line westward, the two pilots made out the low profile of an LA-class submarine making minimal headway. Housing a SEAL delivery vehicle and other equipment, a large tubular attachment secured behind the sail marred the otherwise sleek outline of a submarine. The operation, especially this close to the Taiwanese shores, was a risky proposition.

Any American boat traveling on the surface in any region of the Philippine Sea was something to be avoided if possible. However, certain risks were necessary if the United States wanted any chance of slowing a Chinese invasion of the Penghu Islands. The cross-channel Chinese invasion had come as a surprise to western intelligence agencies. Unfortunately, that meant that any action directed toward the surprise invasion carried increasingly dangerous risk factors.

The *Greeneville* had only surfaced when the V-22 carrying the SEAL team was close, and the commander didn't plan on remaining atop the waves a moment longer than was absolutely necessary. Already, the boat's captain was wondering just who in the hell he'd pissed off to be called upon to leave his escort duties and surface in the midst of a conflict zone. If he was to be imposed with a death sentence, he'd rather it had been orchestrated in a different manner.

The Osprey slowed as it closed on the sub, the tiltrotors moving toward their upright position. Inside, Petty Officer Hawser and the other five members of Blue Team had been notified and were going through final equipment checks. The rear door of the V-22 swung open, the roar of the turboprops growing louder as the personnel inside were subjected to the open air. Exhaust fumes rolled in, mixing with the faint smell of the ocean.

Barely drifting ahead, the tiltrotor aircraft maneuvered over the *Greeneville's* dorsal section, coming into a hover over the rear deck. Several of the submarine's crew were poised near the rear airlock, ready to assist the transfer. Hawser and the others readied themselves near the rear ramp, making room for the crew chief as he prepared to kick out rope coiled near the edge.

The crew chief peeked over the ramp, signaling to the sub's crew. With a thumbs up, the chief made a last-moment check to ensure the thick rope was secured and then kicked it sharply. Uncoiling as if fell, the rope landed on the dorsal deck, metal threads woven into it discharging any static buildup when it contacted the anechoic coating of the *Greeneville's* deck.

Waves flowing down the side of the LA-class sub were whipped into a frenzy from the downwash of the Osprey's giant rotors. David grabbed the heavy rope, giving it a quick tug. He then looped the rope around a rappelling ring and wrapped a length behind him, securing it in his other gloved hand at the small of his back. He then stepped off the back of the V-22's ramp.

About halfway down, he moved his brake hand to the side and slowed his rate of descent. Although the deck wasn't moving much, it was still pitching slightly as the sub rode the waves. Timing his descent so he didn't slam onto a rising deck, David felt his boots touch and quickly unhooked from the rope and moved away. Almost on his heels, Petty Officer Second Class Bollinger landed and quickly separated. In short order, the six SEALs had transitioned from the Osprey to the

Greeneville.

The team was ushered below. It wasn't necessary to encourage haste as everyone understood the dangerous situation. Those topside hurried below and secured the hatch. With green lights showing the boat was secured, the commander, anxious to get out of sight, gave the order to dive. As David and the others were guided toward their quarters, the deck tilted under their boots. The hunter of the deep slid back into its domain, the swells of the Philippine Sea gradually erasing all signs that the submarine had graced the open waters.

Below deck, the team secured their gear and met with the boat's executive officer to receive any updates to their planned mission. It didn't take long to figure out that the initial hasty plan of penetrating the Magong City harbor was out. The Taiwanese defenders had blown part of the port and sunk ships at the entrances to the remaining harbors. Intel had shown that the Chinese ships had altered their course as a result and had docked on the southeastern coast of Magong.

David ran a finger along the shoreline, coming to rest where intel had placed the supply ships.

"Lung-men fishing harbor," he breathed.

As he stared at the map and accompanying satellite footage that had been sent, Petty Officer Hawser came to the realization that their job had just become a little easier. The approaches to the main harbor had been narrow, which would be more easily secured by China's naval forces. The open seas feeding into the fishing harbor that was now the team's target made for an easier infiltration.

"According to the latest intel," the boat's XO briefed, pointing to an area offshore from the target, "China has two frigates patrolling off the harbor entrance. That will require us to unfortunately drop you farther than originally planned."

Petty Officer Infelt leaned over the map, looking to where the executive officer was pointing. "That's a good seven miles."

"Well within the range of the SDV," Hawser mentioned.

"Not by much. And if we have to maneuver around

those frigates, well..." Infelt replied, shrugging.

"That's what we get the big bucks for," David commented.

"You and I aren't getting the same paychecks, then."

David and the others pored over the satellite photos, looking at the single narrow entrance.

"Well, sir, is there any intel as to what other defenses the Chinese might have in place around the harbor?" David asked.

The *Greeneville's* XO shook his head in response. "While it doesn't appear that Taiwan is attacking any shipping at the moment, it seems they are actively defending their airspace...meaning they've been firing at Chinese aircraft that venture in range of their long-range air defenses. So, it's doubtful if there are any Chinese airborne ASW assets in the area."

David scratched his head. "I suppose that's good news, sir."

"I'm betting they haven't had time to set up much of anything," Bollinger stated. "They had to change their plans at the last minute, so they probably haven't placed any listening devices as yet."

Hawser nodded, agreeing with the synopsis. "Sir, are the frigates operating in any definable pattern?"

"As far as we can tell, and mind you, there isn't really much data to go off, but it seems as if the two are operating in zones. One tends to stay southeast of the fishing harbor, while the other remains mostly to the southwest," the XO answered.

The commander of the *Greenville* strode into the room.

"Captain in the mess," the XO intoned, all men shooting to their feet.

The commander came to a stop inside the hatchway. Without a word, he stared at the SEAL team as if weighing who it was that had put his boat at risk. The judging went on for several moments. To David, it seemed as if birthdays had come and gone while the commander surveyed the group.

"At ease, gentlemen," the commander finally said.

The men relaxed, but remained standing. The

commander strode in, shaking the hand of each team member.

"We'll be approaching the Magong coast in twenty-six hours. I'll leave the XO at your disposal should you have any questions. Now, if you'll excuse me, I have to see about threading our way through."

*   *   *   *   *   *

Jiangmei, Penghu Islands, Taiwan
1 August, 2021

Chinese airborne soldiers dashed from one pile of debris to the next, seeking any cover they could find as they worked through the village. The fight at the outskirts had altered the Chinese strategy of assaulting Jiangmei. Instead, the ground units had pulled back after sustaining numerous casualties and let the infantry fighting vehicles pulverize the small community.

The Chinese soldiers worked their way through the township that had been small shops and homes, now reduced to smoldering ruins. They moved through a cratered landscape, looking much like the village had been pummeled by meteorites. The airborne troops found spent shell casings lying among splintered wood and the torn bodies of Taiwanese defenders who had succumbed to Chinese firepower.

Making it to the northern end of the town, the lead company halted, taking positions to cover the highway leading north out of the village. Follow-on units of the new battalion consolidated their hold on Jiangmei before pushing on. It was the first of the few villages to be captured on Pehu Island, the second island in the horseshoe-shaped chain.

The new Chinese battalion commander had seen the smoking, armored wrecks scattered in the field before the town. It was a sobering reminder that the enemy wasn't just going to roll over and hand them the Penghu Islands. There had been some setbacks taking the central island, but aside from artillery and missile strikes on the airfield, it had been easy going for the most part. The battles at the causeway and now at the first town had cost China in troops and material. More importantly, they were a sign that China might have to fight for every inch gained.

The commander pored over a map. The main road they were on ran in a nearly straight line to the main township of Baisha which lay on the island's northern coast. From there, the highway arced back to the southwest, culminating at the Penghu Great Bridge that was currently held by an understrength airborne company. His finger traced a secondary road that split from the main road and ran along the southern shore, connecting back in with the highway a little north of the bridge.

The southern road was a shorter route to the next bridge. If he could get his battalion quickly to the bridge, the commander felt like he could trap any Taiwanese units on the island for China's superior firepower to deal with. The following battalions could drive north and take the Baisha Township, therefore pinching the Taiwanese forces on the island between the two.

However, he had seen firsthand what happens when Chinese units rushed into battle, or tried to force it. The bridges and Jiangmei had reduced one battalion and part of another to become combat ineffective. As much as the Chinese commander wanted to sweep over to reinforce the vital crossing, he would advance carefully to avoid running headlong into another Taiwanese ambush.

Folding the map, he told his company commanders that they would carefully scout the area ahead, the lead units moving forward just behind the drones he planned to use. While the drones scouted the highway, he would consolidate his advanced positions.

* * * * * *

Colonel Wen-hsiung looked down the straight line of the highway for perhaps the hundredth time. He had his advance units hidden within the dense foliage lining the main road north of Jiangmei. He regretted the losses he sustained in the township, but they had inflicted considerable damage on the Chinese invasion forces. More importantly, it appeared that the ambush had slowed their advance. The lead scouts reported that China hadn't left the northern edges of the town as yet and appeared to be consolidating their positions.

The afternoon had faded into evening, the light growing dimmer as the sun lowered. The Penghu Defense Commander glanced west. The clouds that had started forming with the dawn were now considerably larger. A line of cumulonimbus was madly billowing into the evening skies. He watched as one section climbed unbelievably fast, forming a towering column that looked much like a castle turret. It was amazing just how fast they could grow, ascending miles in mere seconds. The bases of the clouds were dark, with a few showing the gray streaks of rain showers that evaporated before touching the surface. The commander shook his head. It seemed like he would have to fight the weather as well as the Chinese.

China launched several drones to scout ahead as APCs and other armored vehicles roared to life. They would advance slowly out of Jiangmei toward the secondary road. Infantry Fighting Vehicles and the lead units would concentrate their firepower on any Taiwanese force the drones located. It wasn't as fast as the commander would have liked, but it was a plan that would keep his battalion intact.

The drone operators informed command that the drones were aloft and proceeding down both sides of the highway. The Chinese commander would have preferred to have attack helicopters advance in place of the drones, but he'd seen what happened during the previous attack. When more units and equipment landed and became available to use as replacements, the Chinese airborne invasion forces could be a little more aggressive. But until then, the commander saw advancing while preserving what he had as the best strategy at the moment.

When the drones made the sharp turn to the north just outside of the village, smoke belched from exhausts as the Chinese armor began to move out.

*   *   *   *   *   *

Taiwanese scouts observed the first Chinese movements as they started out of Jiangmei. The Taiwanese commander would have used drones for his scouting purposes, but Taiwan had set wireless jammers near the highway as it led across a narrow neck of land just to the north of Jiangmei. They had been placed there to interfere with China's ability to locate the ambush before it was sprung. If that happened, then the planned trap would more than likely turn into a headlong retreat with Wen-hsiung possibly losing most of his force without any results to show for it.

Several short-range air defense systems stood ready in case China opted to scout the land with their attack choppers, but as yet, there weren't any signs of that threat. He had some scouts along the northern and southern shorelines of Pehu Island to give him warning of them approaching from different angles. So far, it seemed as if the Chinese commander was proceeding with drones instead of the Z-10s. It could be that the Antelope air defense systems had downed more helicopters than the enemy was ready to lose.

When the Chinese drones came into range of the wi-fi jamming systems, they lost contact with their operators. Some plunged into the dense growth, while others had homing systems that would return them to preset coordinates in the event that communications were lost. Either way, the Chinese operators would know there was something amiss.

Wen-hsiung picked up his handset and contacted his mobile artillery commander. "Okay, let's see if we can light a fire under them and keep them moving."

The crack of four M109A5 mobile 155mm howitzers blasted across the field where one of the batteries was set up. Moments later, the large shells landed on the northern edges of Jiangmei. As if simulating the towering cumulus clouds, smoke roiled from the explosions, further disintegrating the debris piles. Shrapnel pinged off Chinese armor that had started moving, setting off the reactive armor covering the exposed surfaces of the APCs.

As the battery started moving to another location to prevent counterbattery fire from destroying the vehicles, a second battery opened up. Four more blasts shook the northern part of the village, sending more Chinese soldiers either to discover what waited for them on the other side, or sending medics toward the screams of the injured.

Informed that his operators had lost contact with their drones, and dealing with enemy artillery pounding his positions, the Chinese commander had a choice to make. His plan of carefully negotiating the narrow corridors through the island was gone within the first minutes. He could pull back and let his IFVs pummel the road ahead, all the while sustaining damage from the enemy artillery. That would further deplete his ammunition stores. Or he could push his forces ahead in the hopes of driving the Taiwanese from their positions. To him, it was either lose troops and equipment and not gain territory, or he could lose troops and equipment while gaining ground. When he thought of it that way, the decision was an easy one to make.

He ordered his lead units to push ahead, scouting by fire if they had to. The Chinese commander hated to use too much ammunition as the resupply situation hadn't been completely sorted and he was worried about running out of ammo at a critical juncture.

Colonel Wen-hsiung heard the reports coming in from his hidden scouts. China was pushing forward with armored units in the lead. Leaving Jiangmei, the Chinese APCs and IFVs rolled along the four lanes of Highway 203. Just north of the township, they entered a narrow neck of land with dense trees on one side and ocean waters on the other. That left the Chinese forces with little room for maneuvering.

* * * * * *

When the orders came to open fire, two Taiwanese CM-11 main battle tanks surged forward from where they were hidden in amongst a thick covering of trees. The upgraded M-60s with better gun stabilizers and mated with an American M-1 fire control system poked their 105mm rifled barrels out from hidden positions. The tanks were only with the defense force because Colonel Wen-hsiung had informed his superiors that they needed maintenance, and he was therefore unable to relocate them to Taiwan.

The tank commanders saw Chinese Type 92 APC and IFV vehicles racing along the sides of Highway 203. Looking through the thermal imaging system, the commanders verified the targets and gave the gunners orders to engage. With sharp cracks that brought broken limbs and leaves to fall on the tank decks, the long barrels spit out rounds. Smoke drifted out of the recoiling barrels as the HEAT rounds rapidly spanned the distance.

Fireballs rolled up from the charging Chinese armor, engulfing the top chassis and turrets in flame and smoke. One APC emerged from the hit and rolled drunkenly toward the side of the road. Flames roared out from blown hatches. Another IFV, touting a 25mm autocannon, drove through the fireball, appearing no worse for wear other than dark smears running along the front.

"Load HEAT," both commanders ordered at nearly the same time.

"HEAT up," the loaders confirmed a second later.

The two tanks fired at nearly the same time, the sharp sounds of their firing echoing down the long stretch of highway. Two nearly simultaneous explosions pounded the IFV. The Chinese armored vehicle slowed dramatically when a secondary blast shook the vehicle. Sheets of flame shot skyward when the stored ammunition blew, the turret turning in the air twice before landing inverted on the road adjacent the burning six-wheeled infantry fighting vehicle.

Winks of fire were visible through the dissipating smoke as the follow-on armored vehicles opened fire. The two tanks were showered by sparks and flame as the cannons aboard the Chinese APCs and IFVs found their marks, detonating the explosive reactive armor surrounding the tank chassis. The crews crammed inside the CM-11s heard the enemy rounds hitting the turrets and chassis, sounding like they were inside the drums of a heavy metal band in the middle of a solo performance. The reactive armor saved the tanks from severe damage, but the 25mm cannons weren't designed as tank destroyers. The Chinese attacks were mostly to distract the tanks and hopefully destroy some of the optical systems, or at least interfere with the gunner's aim.

Two more shots from the tanks set another Chinese APC ablaze and disabled an IFV. The two CM-11s rolled onto the highway and backed toward the Chen-hai hamlet and the intersection of the southern coastal road. Taiwanese artillery alternated fire and move tactics, their shells slamming down onto the roadway behind the blazing vehicles.

Chunks of pavement lifted from the roadway as Chinese 122mm and 155mm artillery started landing just short of where the two tanks had emerged. Suddenly, like a bucket had been upended, a torrential rain squall enveloped the battlefield. The downfall was so intense that visibility was reduced to meters. Scouts directing Taiwanese fire couldn't directly observe their targets, so the artillery commander opted to advance fire by fifty meters at a time. Taiwanese fire rolled through the Chinese mechanized battalion, while at the same time, Chinese artillery started advancing through Taiwanese forces.

One Chinese 155mm round landed adjacent to a retreating Taiwanese tank, shredding its tread. The CM-11 lurched to the side as it ran out of its track, becoming stuck in the middle of the road. The crew continued firing at objects found through the thermal imaging, hitting the disabled Chinese IFV several times. Their plan was to remain with the tank for as long as possible, giving the ambush teams time to relocate. However, another 155mm Chinese round landed directly atop the stalled tank and destroyed it, taking the crew of four with it.

Most of the Taiwanese battalions departed down the secondary road. Wen-hsiung's plan was to ambush the Chinese forces as he moved toward the great bridge — he wanted to keep the fight away from residential centers as much as possible. Sometimes he thought about the hopeless position he had been placed in. His tactics would only work for a time until the Chinese figured out a counter to the ambushes. And then he would watch his units be destroyed.

He just didn't have enough firepower to throw the invaders from the islands, and it would only be a matter of time until China's greater firepower overwhelmed his brave soldiers. But he would make it as hard on them as he could. The one thing he had going for him were the narrow corridors through which China would have to navigate. He had watched his tanks maul the leading edge of China's armor and wished he had just four of America's M-1s. The colonel envisioned the indestructible tanks wading through China's invasion force, becoming an unstoppable force that left burning Chinese armor in its wake. But he was a realist and knew that those kinds of dreams and wishes were like a morning mist fading in the sunlight. Eventually, China would quit messing around and send attack aircraft streaming across the channel. When that happened, he would be in trouble.

The departure of the rain storm seemed to signal an end to the battle. The artillery fire from both sides lifted. It had been the first direct engagement between Taiwanese and Chinese main units. Six Chinese armored vehicles lay smoking across the roadway. One CM-11 Taiwanese main battle tank sat in ruins in the middle of Highway 203, its final resting place on the outskirts of a tiny hamlet that barely had a name. Two other Taiwanese CM-21 APCs were smoldering near the intersection of the two roads leading through the Pehu Island.

*   *   *   *   *   *

The Chinese battalion commander realized his mistake, one he was determined not to make again. He had attempted the safe method, moving slowly with scouts in the van, and had relied too much on those scouts to provide information. Those had become immediately disabled, and as a result, he was now in trouble.

Taiwan had shown their hand in how they were going to defend the islands. With China relegated to moving down relatively narrow corridors, Taiwan was going to set up a series of traps. Those were going to happen. What he really needed was firepower readily available to counter any ambushes he ran into. He had to admit that the tanks had come as a surprise. Prior intelligence stated that all Taiwanese main battle tanks had been transferred to the main island.

From here on out, he would have attack helicopters waiting behind the leading vehicles, ready to pounce on Taiwanese units springing their traps. His aim was to inflict more damage on the inferior enemy forces than he himself sustained. It was to become a battle of attrition, and eventually, China's superior firepower would win out and eliminate the resistance, fight by fight.

The Chinese commander took some time to reorganize his battalion. He was eager to resume the action before the retreating Taiwanese forces could recover.

* * * * * *

The light of the dying day glistened off the wet pavement of Route 8. Dark clouds reaching toward the heavens hovered a short distance away, their gray bases threatening to spill more torrential downpours onto the Penghu Islands. Within view of the intersection where the latest battle took place, Sergeant Chih-hao nestled on the fringes of the thick vegetation near the two-laned road. His fatigues were damp from the wet grass, and the water dripping from overhead limbs didn't improve the situation.

The remnants of his inherited platoon were spread along the same side of the road. On the other side was what remained of second platoon. Farther behind, hidden by two three-story concrete structures was the company commander with third platoon and two CM-34 IFVs.

Chih-hao wondered why his company had drawn the short straw again. In Jiangmei, they had been the lead company, launching the ambush against the invaders. Now, they were in the rear springing yet another trap in order to slow the Chinese advance. The sergeant understood the goal of making the enemy think twice, maybe even a third time, before moving an inch. He also knew that the overall commander wanted to exact as many casualties as possible for the ground given up. But he wondered if the task was to fall on him and his depleted company each time.

The first platoon leader parted blades of grass, looking down the road toward the intersection. Thin spirals of smoke still drifted up from the destroyed friendly armored vehicles. The sergeant wondered if the residual heat would set off the command-detonated charges placed inside the charred remains. Regardless of how the two rigged 155mm shells went off, it was sure to make a show.

In the dim lighting, the Chih-hao made out movement near the intersection. The question was whether the Chinese forces would turn onto the narrower route or proceed north toward the Baisha Township. He had placed a bet with his new loader, wagering that the enemy units would continue north as the central Pehu Island city would be the prize China was after. His loader said that they would turn as it was the shortest distance to the great bridge and would seal off the island.

"Then they can take Biasha at their leisure," the loader had added.

Chih-hao saw the logic of that, but stuck with his original idea. If the Chinese units continued north, the sergeant would happily collect his wager. If the enemy turned, there was a pretty good chance that he wouldn't have to pay off the bet.

Through the thermal imaging system of the Javelin, he saw the heat signatures of Chinese armor at the intersection. He thought the vehicles looked like APCs, but it was sometimes difficult to tell them from the infantry fighting vehicles with their larger weapons.

Chih-hao's heart skipped a beat and then started racing

when two enemy vehicles made the turn. As the Chinese armor increased their speed, he saw additional vehicles coming up behind the original two, also turning onto Route 8. The sergeant centered the rightmost target, verified that he had a flat trajectory selected, and pressed the first trigger. Across the road, he knew, or hoped, that identical actions were being taken against the enemy vehicle to the left.

When the Jevelin's targeting system indicated that it had the target, Chih-hao depressed the second trigger. A moment later, a missile was jettisoned and its motor ignited. The missile streaked down the side of the road, angling for the charging enemy armored vehicle. The fast-moving projectile slammed into the IFV. The first charge detonated the reactive armor attached to the infantry fighting vehicle, the second one burning through the armored plating. Dense smoke boiled out from the interior and the vehicle lurched to the side of the road. Another explosion stopped the second enemy armored vehicle in its tracks.

Behind the burning vehicles, two more Chinese vehicles opened up with 25mm autocannons. The chunk, chunk, chunk of the heavy caliber weapons was continuous, the tracers from the return fire seeming to move in slow motion. As they neared the Taiwanese platoons, the rounds picked up speed until they zipped overhead, exploding in the trees behind. Branches snapped and leaves fell in bushels under the onslaught.

While the Chih-hao's loader was readying the launcher for another shot, the sergeant saw tracers heading past him and down the road. The two Taiwanese CM-34 infantry fighting vehicles had driven out from their cover and were engaging the Chinese armor. Sparks flew from the fronts of the infantry fighting vehicles as the two MK44 Bushmasters found their targets. The 30mm rounds, firing at over one hundred rounds per minute, peppered the two Chinese IFVs.

With enemy fire zipping overhead, the two platoons refocused on the new threats. One of the Chinese Type 92 IFVs started smoking, its fire slacking and then falling off altogether.

Chih-hao felt a slap on his shoulder, signifying that the

launcher was loaded. He heard his loader yell into his ear, "I told you. You owe me when this is all over."

The sergeant looked through the thermal scope, pausing for a moment as the image of his previous loader's torn face flashed through his mind. Shaking his head to clear the memory, Chih-hao again sought out a target. He was waiting for one to appear when an explosion behind him caused him to glance toward the sound. One of the Taiwanese IFVs that was firing in support was a sheet of flame, the tongues of fire roaring as tall as the nearby concrete structure. Spitting flares, a Chinese helicopter zipped across the road and disappeared.

Another explosion slammed into the ground near the other Taiwanese armored vehicle. A second Chinese attack chopper flashed overhead. This time, it was followed by a streak of white as third platoon launched a Stinger missile after it. Fearing that the tables had turned on the ambush, Chih-hao looked back toward the intersection. There, he saw the sleek frontal outline of a Z-10 barreling down the road. It looked like the rocket pods and the missiles hanging on stubby wings were pointed directly at him.

Knowing that the Javelin could target airborne targets, and having fired one at a chopper at the battle of Jiangmei, the sergeant set the scope on the incoming threat. It was the only action he knew to take, really his only option to stave off death that was staring him in the face. He felt the first trigger depress, without truly realizing he had done it...and then the second. The missile leapt from the launcher and raced skyward, the white trail on an intersect course with the Z-10.

The sergeant was clenched in anticipation of seeing the rocket pods on the helicopter come alive, and the impending pain that would be inflicted on his body. Chih-hao was taken aback when the Javelin exploded right next to the looming attack chopper, which then started spinning chaotically. Trailing smoke, the enemy helicopter spun directly over the sergeant's head and vanished over a line of trees. Chih-hao never heard the crash and assumed it had either recovered and landed or crashed into the bay only a short distance away.

A line of explosions blasted the opposite side of the road as another Z-10 swung into view. Amid the sounds of the ongoing battle, he heard screams coming from second platoon. His view of the enemy vehicles was suddenly lost when a large explosion erupted in the middle of the roadway half way to the intersection. The enemy artillery was now coming into play — at least, Chih-hao thought it was Chinese rounds that were starting to land with greater frequency.

While his loader was busy reloading the launcher, Chih-hao glanced toward third platoon and his company commander. The second IFV was still firing and there were numerous fading white lines of smoke where Stingers had been fired after the Chinese helicopters. He wondered when his captain would call off the fight as it was becoming obvious to the sergeant that they were outgunned.

A giant explosion from the intersection drew the sergeant's attention back toward the Chinese attack. A huge fireball was rolling upward, the sound of the detonation momentarily overriding the other sounds of the intense fight.

"First and second platoon, pull back as briefed. Rendezvous with the main force at point Bravo," the company commander radioed.

Shouting at his men and using hand signals, the first platoon melted back into the woods. There they hustled away from their ambush positions. Using the dense covering of trees to hide their heat signatures, and being chased by the sounds of crashing artillery, Chih-hao and his men retreated toward a predetermined rendezvous point. Chinese helicopters crossed overhead a few times, but then even that halted as they trotted farther away.

Unknown to Chi-hao, the third platoon remained behind to send volleys of missiles toward the intersection to slow any Chinese response and to allow the two depleted platoons to exit the scene. Damaged, the second infantry fighting vehicle reversed and slipped from view over the brow of a hill. Chinese Z-10s attempted to chase after, but Stingers rising from the roadside made the pilots cautious. They had already lost more than a few of their number in the battles for the islands and weren't overly eager to pursue.

*   *   *   *   *   *

At the intersection, the Chinese battalion was quick to react to the Taiwanese ambush. The two leading vehicles were destroyed at the outset, but the following IFVs quickly engaged the enemy. The Z-10s, which had been loitering behind, rushed in and quickly destroyed one of Taiwan's armored vehicles, damaging a second one.

Soldiers disembarked from the rear of their APCs and were readying an assault up the secondary road the battalion commander wanted to take. Two companies were gathering in the rear of the fighting armor, ready to begin advancing through the woods toward the ambush. The helicopters were coming under fire, but their missiles and rockets had cut down the return fire coming from Taiwanese positions. Limiting the corridors through which the choppers could attack, the Chinese battalion commander brought his artillery to bear. He wanted to crush the ambush and make the enemy pay.

Standing next to his command vehicle at the intersection, studiously ignoring the occasional round that whipped past, the commander was satisfied with how his unit was responding. He would lose some equipment, but the amount of firepower he was bringing to bear would make the enemy lose more. Plus, he would receive replacements whereas the Taiwanese units wouldn't be able to replace their losses. The writing was on the wall; Taiwan's demise was at hand.

Whether the battalion commander felt the heat of the blast would never be known. If he did, then it didn't last long. The two rigged 155mm shells right next to the Chinese command vehicle exploded. The concussive blast lifted the command vehicle and sent it tumbling down the road. The thirteen-ton vehicle slammed into the commander, killing him instantly. When the tumbling vehicle came to rest, it exploded, and when it did, even the bloody smear that had been the battalion commander was erased.

* * * * * *

Taiwan Strait, south of Magong Island, Penghu Islands, Taiwan
1 August, 2021

Petty Officer First Class Hawser poked his head out from the open hatch of the rear airlock. Dappled light played against the dark hull of the USS *Greeneville*, the evening rays of the sun reaching the shallows in which the LA-class submarines drifted. Pushing clear, David swam toward the large cylindrical object mounted to the rear deck, the others of Blue Team emerging behind.

In a slow-motion dance, the masked men undid the latches holding the circular vault closed, the thick steel door swinging open. Working underwater always slowed things down, but the individuals still worked with a precision that came with years of practice. With the tie downs removed, the team slowly extricated the SEAL delivery vehicle held inside. Systems were checked, the battery levels showing full. The driver, Petty Officer Second Class Infelt, verified the GPS accuracy. He would rely heavily on the Inertial Navigation System to guide them along the planned route to deliver them inside the Lung-men Fishing Harbor.

The team worked efficiently. One, because that's how they were trained, and two, the men knew that the *Greeneville's* commander wanted to be out of there soon. The boat was barely submerged and at risk, especially if China did have airborne anti-submarine units operating topside. Even if they didn't have Y-8Qs flying in the contested airspace, the two frigates patrolling only several miles away each had a single ASW helicopter which were assumed to be aloft.

With the SDV out of its enclosure, the team pulled out the rest of their gear, stowing it in the underwater vehicle's storage compartments. When all was ready and the container resealed, David informed the *Greeneville* via the external comm port that they had completed the extrication and were moving toward shore. He then disconnected and made for the vehicle hovering above the *Greeneville's* deck.

Infelt turned the vehicle toward the initial course. The outline of the *Greeneville* faded from sight, becoming a ghostly shape, and then vanishing altogether. The captain would take his boat deeper and await the team's return, moving only to keep out of harm's way. The commander knew that he was the only American attack boat in the area that was able to engage the Chinese invasion fleet when it hove into view. However, at the moment, he was attached to the special operations currently underway and wasn't available for offensive operations. If the team was successful and returned in time, then perhaps he would get his chance to strike.

* * * * * *

As the day's light fled, the battles along Route 8 continued. Colonel Wen-hsiung set a series of ambushes that forced the Chinese to dismount each time, slowing their advance. With the death of the Chinese battalion commander and the continued loss of equipment with each sprung trap, a third mechanized battalion with airborne troops was put in the lead. A fourth battalion proceeded past the intersection and up Highway 203, cautiously probing ahead. When that fourth battalion reached the outskirts of Baisha Township, they held up for the night.

The fight in the Penghu Islands seemed archaic compared to what had previously been witnessed. The battles were more like those seen in World War II or the Korean War, without the complex long-range exchanges involving missiles with intelligent guidance systems. It was as if all sides of the conflict were holding their breath, waiting for the main show to begin.

That was precisely what was happening. China had expended much of its rocket inventory destroying the Taiwanese Navy and defending against the onslaught Taiwan had sent against its eastern shores. The Peoples Liberation

Army knew that it would be difficult getting the number of soldiers ashore that would be required to overrun Taipei. They were saving its rocket forces to cover the crossing and landings.

Likewise, Taiwan was also preserving its remaining missiles and air power, knowing that they would need everything they had to hold off the main Chinese invasion. This was especially true when hundreds more Chinese transport vessels left the ports of Zhoushan and Zhanjiang. Although both sides knew the strategic importance of the Penghu Islands, neither was committing their modern firepower to affect the outcome. Considering what was coming, the fight for the islands was relegated to a preliminary sideshow.

* * * * * *

Pehu Island, Penghu Islands, Taiwan
2 August, 2021

The Chinese commander in overall charge of the Penghu Island operations was becoming concerned. Two of his battalions had been mauled by the Taiwanese ambushes. On paper, four thousand, five hundred soldiers seemed like a lot, but considering the casualties so far, he wondered if he had enough to complete the order he had been given. The roads of Pehu Island were littered with burned out armored vehicles, the countryside dotted with crashed helicopters. Although he was being resupplied, the inflow wasn't keeping up with losses.

If he couldn't take over the island chain, he would be replaced. He wasn't about to bear that kind of shame. He was near to taking over the second island, but the third would be a difficult one. First, there was having to cross the Great Bridge. Although his troops occupied both ends of the lengthy span, his soldiers and vehicles would be exposed. If the first causeway was any indication, getting to the third island would be a difficult process. Prior to attempting it, he would reinforce the far end via transport helicopters and push the perimeter out, thereby hoping to avoid a repeat of the first time.

But he first had to get there with his units intact. If he

could destroy the enemy forces arrayed against him, that would go a long way toward his success. The commander knew that he couldn't just keep pushing the way they had. Things had to change. He would have to swallow some of his pride and ask for the needed help. With a decision made, he proceeded to his communication center and made a call.

* * * * * *

Another flash lit up the western skies, the nearby trees silhouetted in stark detail for a brief second. A crack of thunder arrived several seconds later, the sound rising to a crescendo before fading. To Wen-hsiung, the sight and sound was no different than the Chinese artillery, which continued to hound him as he traded ground for Chinese casualties. But he was running out of said room.

Already, his remaining units were approaching the far intersection with Highway 203. From there, it was only a small stretch of highway before they reached the township surrounding the entrance to the Penghu Great Bridge. Once there, he would have to break through the Chinese platoon that his scouts reported were set up in defensive positions along the road. Then, he would have to fight his way across the bridge, under fire from the far side for the entire crossing. He hoped to gain some time in order to prep those positions with what remained of his mobile artillery, and then crash through with the few pieces of armor that were still operational. He needed to gain some time.

His plan all along was to slow the Chinese forces and eventually make it to one of the hardened bunkers and cave systems that had been carved into the next island. From there, whatever he had left would fight from those fortresses. The colonel had no illusion about being able to hold out indefinitely, but he would fight for as long as he had life.

As another rumble rolled over his position, coming out of the night skies, he was proud of what his meager forces had accomplished. They had taken losses, whittling down the men and equipment who accompanied him, but they had inflicted serious losses on the Chinese. He often contemplated the "what ifs." One was that he might have been able to stall the enemy forces indefinitely if he only had two additional battalions, but the journeys down that path didn't last long. For one, China was relentless. He had to hand it to his adversary; the attacks had been near continuous, which didn't allow for him or his troops to rest. The ambushes were always too hastily set up, the ability to withdraw always hampered, the losses always too great.

Wen-hsiung ducked as a different sound rolled over his small encampment. This one was a roar that came on suddenly and faded just as fast. A string of flashes and subsequent explosions rocked one side of the roadway. The colonel knew instantly that he was under attack from the air. Another roar of jet engines flashed overhead, followed by another set of bombs exploding among his troops.

This time, he saw a single light coming from the jet's engine. A whoosh sounded from nearby, a tongue of fire racing into the night. Someone had fired a Stinger missile after the departing attack fighter. Operators hoisted their launchers, searching the skies for heat signatures. One by one, missiles soared aloft, chasing after enemy aircraft marking their path by strings of defensive flares.

The colonel knew instantly that his force was in dire straits. The enemy commander had called in the big guns. In a way, Wen-hsiung was flattered that his units had done well enough to warrant such a reception. But, as another series of bombs fell, their explosions flashing in the dark, the attention being visited upon him and his soldiers could very well spell their demise. He wished he still had the mobile air defenses that the Antelope systems had provided, but they had run out of missiles during the steady withdrawal along Route 8.

He quickly ordered his units to mount up, giving them their marching orders. The infantry fighting vehicles would lead. At this juncture, he had no choice; they were going to charge the Chinese positions at the bridge and cross while they still could. He instructed the few remaining artillery units to open up against the enemy defending the bridge, lifting it only when the IFVs neared the minimum safe distance.

More missiles were sent after the aircraft tearing into his units. The colonel couldn't see the results as the intercepts were beyond the tree tops, but the attacks were coming less frequently. Amid the crash of thunder and the explosions, armored vehicles roared onto the roadway. The careful withdrawals of the past day had now turned into a headlong retreat.

*   *   *   *   *   *

Adjusted by scouts observing the Chinese positions near the Great Bridge, the night was lit up by 155mm shells landing on the Chinese perimeter. Flashes from the explosions highlighted the sides of buildings and the faces of startled soldiers with strobe-like effects. Shrapnel tore through defensive bulwarks thrown up by the defenders, ripping into sandbags and annihilating hastily prepared barricades. Buildings near the main road collapsed under the weight of the explosions. Broken timbers were flung outward, doing their own damage.

The Chinese soldiers manning the perimeter sought cover with the first detonation. Their eyes grew wide with fright with each new blast, the ground under their bodies bouncing as if it was trying to lift them up for sacrifice. The air, previously filled with the scent of the shoreline, became pervaded with the sharp stench of gunpowder. Without any true protection from the artillery landing within the condensed perimeter, the preparations were ripped apart. The barrage was short but intense, the surviving soldiers looking around, unsure if it was over. Flames crackled from the light armored vehicles that had sustained direct hits, the acrid smoke wafting through the defensive positions. Some of the troops cautiously peeked over or around any remaining cover, their expressions changing when they saw a line of dim lights rapidly approaching their positions.

*   *   *   *   *   *

Flashes of lightning lit up the dark skies, jagged bolts arcing downward to strike both land and sea. The crash of thunder followed right on its heels as the storms, which had been building all day, closed in on the island to unleash their fury. Amid the light show all around, the lead Taiwanese CM-34 Infantry Fighting Vehicles barreled down the four-laned road.

Looking through their scopes, the vehicle commanders saw thermal signatures coming from the Chinese positions and the fires stemming from burning vehicles. As soon as the artillery lifted, smaller flashes started peppering the Chinese positions as 30mm Bushmaster chain guns opened up their own storm of fire.

Behind the vanguard, Stinger missiles occasionally soared aloft as soldiers riding atop APCs found heat signatures streaking in under the storm clouds. Some of the Chinese pilots braved the turbulent currents under the towering nimbus clouds and the lightning that had become nearly continuous. The others departed back across the strait after having expended their ordinance.

One missile missed its mark, chasing after the heat produced from a bolt of lightning. It entered the storm clouds. A lightning bolt followed the ion trail generated by the missile, striking the top of the APC with a loud clang, followed by a deafening peal of thunder. Soldiers atop the armored vehicle were thrown to the side, landing on the shoulders of the road with severe burns. There they lay unmoving, their fatigues smoking. The APC rolled drunkenly off to the side and came to rest, nosing into thick bushes lining the highway. The launches halted; the lesson was learned. That also seemed to bring a stop to the aerial attacks.

Due to the suddenness and ferocity of the Taiwanese attack, very little return fire emanated from the Chinese defenders. The IFVs crashed through the defensive line, the armored vehicles bouncing over the ruined barricades. Sandbags that were still intact were flung away as twenty plus tons of steel plowed through them. And then, the first of the Taiwanese armor entered the historic span of concrete.

At the far end of the long causeway, Taiwanese artillery started landing after the mobile units moved positions to keep up with the charging armor. The explosions were difficult to distinguish from the storm raging overhead. Gusting winds rocked the armored vehicles, the drivers having to constantly correct the sideways pushes threatening to dump the IFVs into the waves crashing against concrete underpinnings.

Following in the wake of the lead vehicles, other IFVs and APCs rolled through the Chinese perimeter and moved past the bridge entrance. Some of the Chinese defending the bridge recovered from their initial shock, as evidenced by rocket propelled grenades launching from buildings adjacent to the roadway. They struck the passing armor with the sound of ringing metal and explosions. For the most part, the reactive armor diverted the blasts. Seeming to shrug off the hits, many of the vehicles streamed past, leaving behind smoke clouds to dissipate in the night.

Some of the RPGs, however, managed to hit, the damaged armor coming to unsteady halts. The positions that fired on the vehicles were quickly pinpointed in the night by the following vehicles which delivered various calibers of fire into the enemy positions.

When the lead IFVs reached the far side, the commanders requested that the artillery fire be lifted. The exit from the Great Bridge was nearly the same as the entrance. 30mm fire was directed toward any identified thermal signatures. The Chinese soldiers manning the far end were oriented for an attack coming from the other direction, and thus were facing away from the bridge. They weren't in a position to defend against an attack coming from the across the water. The Taiwanese armor made short work of those near the highway.

A steady stream of Taiwanese armor, the remnants of the

Penghu defenses, crossed onto the bridge. The mobile artillery, among the last in line, were abruptly taken under fire from unknown Chinese armored units giving chase. The first to come under fire abruptly exploded. It was the first indication that the Chinese had opted to attack following the aerial bombardments.

When the reports came in of his armor crossing the bridge, Colonel Wen-hsiung felt positive about his chances. It was the first such good news since the Chinese warplanes appeared. However, with the new information coming from the rear, the feeling of elation vanished. If his units were caught on the long bridge in China's armored sights, then he could lose most of his remaining force.

Considering the sudden strike to the rear, he ordered one platoon to disembark with Javelin missiles to slow the Chinese attack. The colonel ordered his driver to pull to the side of the highway near the bridge entrance. He wanted to make sure his men crossed before he entered the span, feeling that he could direct the fight better. His command vehicle pulled next to a ruined check post that was flanked by two destroyed Humvees. There, he listened to reports and watched as more of his armor ran up to the bridge and began crossing.

*   *   *   *   *   *

Sergeant Chih-hao cursed his luck. At first, he was glad that he and his company had been detailed to the rear, letting someone else take the brunt for a change. The journey from Jiangmei to the Great Bridge had been an arduous one, and one filled with far too many close calls. Crouched by the side of the road, looking down the way they had come, he saw two separate flaming wrecks that had been mobile artillery vehicles only a short time ago.

The platoon leader watched the last of the remaining vehicles pass by and looked to his targeting screen. It showed the signatures coming from approaching enemy armor. The orders for his reduced unit were to fire one round for each launcher team and then load back into the APCs that were hidden behind. That would hopefully allow the entire defense force to cross the bridge.

The move was a gamble, but then that pretty much described his experience with battle to date. Shot from his launcher, the Javelin's motor igniting was a signal to another of his platoon across the road. Streaks of fire raced along the roadway, slamming into the leading Chinese vehicles. When others attempted to push through the damaged and smoking armor, more missiles sped away to meet them. With the constant flash of lightning and the crash of thunder reverberating through his position, it was hard to tell the damage his men were inflicting.

When Chinese artillery began falling near his location, Chih-hao grabbed his handset. "That's it. Everyone back to the APCs."

* * * * * *

The colonel watched as the last of his units entered the bridge. He then ordered his driver to follow. The bridge rose slightly to allow boats to cross underneath before becoming a solid concrete structure. He had just passed the last of the pylons when a loud explosion rang inside and the vehicle was lifted. It then slewed to one side and rolled over.

A bolt of lightning had hit the top of the bridge. The heat and electricity ignited the placed charges that the Chinese special ops team had cut the wires to. Exactly as was originally meant by the Taiwanese, the affected spans exploded in a series of fireballs that rose into the night. The force of the blasts tore that part of the bridge apart, leaving a wide gap. The intense flash generated by the nearby lightning strike temporarily blinded the optics of the first Chinese armored units that were approaching. The torrential downpour that followed hid the remainder of the retreating Taiwanese units.

The APC commander that was ahead of the command vehicle heard the tremendous blast and saw the vehicle upended in the middle of the bridge. Chunks of concrete started raining down, thudding into the top of the armored vehicle. Ordering the APC to a halt, he instructed the squad he was carrying to disembark and check for survivors.

With winds gusting hard against him, Chih-hao was the first to make it to the command vehicle. He and the next to arrive struggled to open the doors, which had warped with the crash. Working together, they were able to pry one of the doors open. Inside, flickering lights revealed a tumble of bodies, all bloodied and unmoving. Stepping inside, the sergeant checked for signs of life. He found a faint pulse on a few and designated some of those standing outside to help maneuver the wounded out. Grabbing arms and legs, the soldiers extracted the bloody bodies, and in the hard rain, jogged toward the idling APC.

The quarters were cramped with the additional bodies, some of the soldiers having to ride on top, braving the elements. Chih-hao squatted by the colonel, watching the man's chest rise and fall. He was startled when he looked at the Penghu Defense commander's face to see a pair of red-lined eyes staring back at him.

"Did everyone make it across?" the colonel asked weakly.

"Yes, sir," Chih-hao answered as the APC rocked across the last of the Chinese defenses.

A hand gripped Chih-hao's upper arm. "Thank you, son," Wen-hsiung replied as a medic stabbed a morphine syringe into the colonel's leg.

A short time later, freed from the Chinese chasing after them by the blown bridge, the last of the Penghu Defense Forces drove into one of the large, hardened bunkers.

The Penghu Defense Command sustained losses nearing fifty percent, but they accomplished their goal of delaying the Chinese invasion forces. It wasn't anything anyone could have planned, but Colonel Wen-hsiung and his battalions had hindered the enemy long enough for Mother Nature to intervene.

Battle at the Penghu Causeway

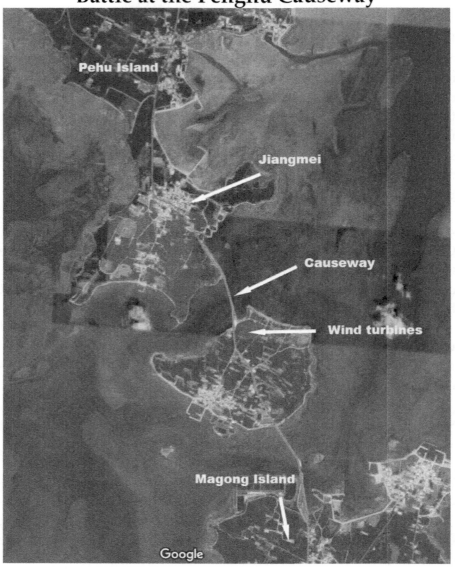

Fights Along Route 8

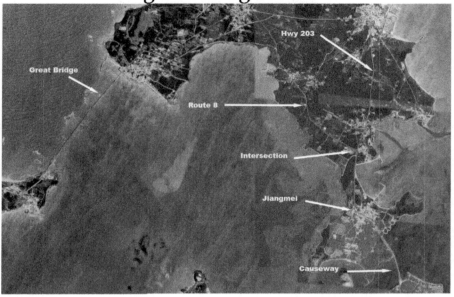

Chapter Nine

Taiwan Strait
2 August, 2021

It had taken a while to retrieve the dive vehicle. Motoring through the waters of the Taiwan Strait at four knots, the journey to the harbor was going to take the better part of two hours. The mottled light penetrating the depths weakened, the surrounding waters growing murkier as the day above ended until there was only darkness.

The long trips toward shore could be lengthy endeavors. It was difficult to stay focused through the hours as the mind tended to wander when not engaged on a particular task. David thought about his family back in Seattle. With the current conflict, and knowing what their son did, he knew that his mom and dad would spend their nights fretting about him. That's why he tried to keep in regular contact, to assuage their worries. That was about to change as he was about to be absent for an indefinite period of time.

While the Navy might risk a boat to get him and his team into position to disrupt China's invasion of the Penghu Islands, there was no way they would take the same risk to exfil them back to Hawaii. He also understood that the Navy was going to need every attack boat they could lay their hands on when the main invasion fleet finally left port. That meant he was here for the duration, or at least until the *Greeneville* needed to rearm. Considering the number of weapons each attack boat could carry, that could be a while. In the meantime, his parents' worry would increase when his regular phone calls ceased.

And he regretted not being able to spend much time with his brother before he was previously recalled. While motoring toward the port now in Chinese hands, he made a promise to rectify that when this was all over. His mind then wandered over to how simple it was for life to interfere with family bonds. He found it too easy to let time lapse between visits, the weeks and months becoming years.

For one of the first times in his career, he contemplated leaving the Navy once this enlistment period was over. However, the journey down that path was short-lived. He liked his job too much and was proud of who he had become. His gaze turned to the men riding the vehicle and knew there wasn't any way he could leave them or any of his brothers.

Something flashed far overhead, drawing David from his reveries. He internally berated himself for allowing his mind to drift. The flash came again, only truly noticed because of the utter darkness under the waves at night. The petty officer pored over the mission information, wondering if there was a lighthouse in the vicinity that he had missed. There were shoals and smaller islands away from the larger ones that made up the Penghu chain. He thought hard about what he had seen on the maps, but didn't recall seeing a lighthouse in the vicinity where they should be.

"Infelt...are you sure we're in the right location?" David inquired through the intercom.

"As sure as I can be," Infelt responded.

"What in the hell is that flash, then?" David asked, not entirely sure he wanted to know the answer.

He had an idea of what it might be, but didn't want to think about it lest it manifest itself into reality.

"Lighthouse?" Rick Dewey said.

"Not out here," Infelt replied.

"That pretty much narrows it down, then, doesn't it?" Matt Longe replied.

"Now why in the hell would you go say something like that?" Allen Crimson stated.

"All right, guys. We knew this was a possibility. Joel, shut it down. We drift until we either verify it's some anomaly or it goes away," David ordered.

"And if neither happens?" Crimson asked.

"Then archaeologists centuries down the road will have to figure out the puzzle of our bones spread across the South China Sea," Infelt answered.

"That's for sure. They'll be especially surprised to find a

Cro-Magnon driving an underwater vehicle and puzzle over how that came to be," Longe commented.

David felt the SDV shaking and turned toward the front. Petty Officer Second Class Infelt was feeling around as if searching his pockets that didn't exist.

"What in the fuck are you doing, Infelt?" David inquired.

"I'm looking for a microphone, because it's obviously open fucking mic night."

The light again flashed overhead, drifting down to the deeps through which the dive vehicle slid.

"Never mind all of that. That flash wasn't timed with the others. Shut it down," David said.

PO2 Infelt shut down the electric motor, the delivery vehicles coasting ahead in silence. All eyes turned toward the waves rolling forty feet overhead, the flashes of light growing more frequent and gaining in intensity. David thought about how they could have been located, but the *how* didn't really matter. Something was heading their way, if it wasn't already upon them.

David's mind ran through a hundred different solutions, thinking of the maneuver possibilities in case they had been located. The SDV wasn't very maneuverable, or fast, so they weren't going to escape as a submarine might. Their lives relied on stealth, and to come at the enemy in ways they couldn't imagine. If they were in fact caught, there really wasn't much they could do to escape.

Had they been caught via active sonar? David wondered with concern as the flashes increased until the light was almost a steady presence.

* * * * * *

The Chinese naval frigate *Zhoushan* cut into a rising swell, the bow wave faintly glistening in the glow of a partial moon. The clear night was calm compared to the previous night's storms that had swept through the area. The rear deck of the PLAN warship was a bustle of activity as the crew went through the motions necessary to launch the Z-9C ASW helicopter. With the rotor spinning overhead, the pilots finished their pre-launch checklist. With motions from the handler holding a lit wand in each hand, the pilot increased power.

The wheels went light, bouncing twice on the deck as the chopper became airborne. The Z-9C raised its gear and, continuing to climb, it swung its nose to the southwest. The ASW chopper began accelerating, the sound of its rotors fading as it blended with the night. The helicopter attached to the *Zhoushan* was taking over anti-submarine duties from its counterpart aboard a similar Jiangkai II-class frigate.

After a short flight, the Z-9C descended toward the cresting waves. Directed by the controller in the combat information center aboard the *Zhoushan*, the pilot flipped on the powerful search light and brought the chopper into a hover. The rotor wash whipped the tops of the waves into frothy mayhem, the beam from the searchlight catching everything in stark detail.

Hanging from a cable, a dipping sonar swung back and forth as it was slowly lowered toward the seas below. The line steadied as the device slapped the front side of a swell and vanished under the water. With headphones pressed tightly to his ears, the sonar operator began listening as the passive sensors sent information, or the lack of it.

The operator contemplated switching the dipping sonar to its active mode, a surer method for locating enemy submarines. However, Chinese protocols dictated that the passive mode be used until more precise targeting information was needed to drop one of the two lightweight torpedoes the Z-9C carried. Using passive mode wouldn't alert American attack submarines that they were being hunted.

Regardless, the sonar operator's hand hovered over the active switch. But that was as far as he went toward breaking his training and the methods handed down. To do anything different was to invite trouble, a berating by the ship's captain at the very least. He didn't want to face the possibility of ending up in prison or a reeducation facility.

With a hand pressing the headphones tight against one ear, he watched the instrumentation for any sign of a transient noise as the sensitive device lowered farther into the dark waters.

*   *   *   *   *   *

From within the delivery vehicle, six pairs of eyes gazed toward the surface forty feet above. The rolling swells created oscillating patterns of light, the diffuse lighting playing over the goggles of the masked men. The longer the light remained in place, the easier David felt. If their location had been discerned, the team would already feel the compression of the water as charges were dropped. But the fact that the light remained in its current position was disconcerting. The odds of a random encounter like this were slim, so the petty officer was thinking that someone had heard something and was investigating.

They were shallow enough that David worried they could be seen should the light pan over them. He noticed the rest of the team looking up, a mistake he had been making as well. For one, if the light was to pan directly over their position, there was a chance of it reflecting off the glass of their goggles. And two, he knew from his training and experience that looking directly at an enemy, especially at their eyes, could cause the enemy to become alerted by the feeling of being watched. Not only would they become more alert, but one could almost pinpoint from where the energy was coming from. He didn't know if that applied through forty feet of water and into whatever was topside, but he didn't want to find out here and now.

"Heads down, dammit," he breathed through the intercom.

Admonished, the others lowered their heads, each willing for the light to move on. All remained looking at the perceived threat through their periphery. The standoff between the light and the team attempting to sneak through China's outer perimeter continued for what seemed an eternity. The only sense that time was in fact moving were the oscillating light patterns and the growing chill of the water. David now wondered if they were in fact parked near a fishing vessel, but shook off that idea remembering that two Chinese frigates were on patrol during the invasion. There was no way the Chinese would allow a fishing boat in such close proximity to the only port available to the invasion forces.

The team's attention sharpened when the light began to move again. It grew brighter and then began fading in the same way it arrived, gradually dimming until the team was again surrounded by darkness.

"Well, what in the fuck was that?" Vangle asked.

"My guess would be a Chinese ASW chopper," Infelt answered.

"I wouldn't take that bet," David agreed. "How's our timing on the battery?"

"We're good for a little over seven hours yet," Infelt stated.

"Okay. We'll give it a few minutes and then move on. How far did we drift?" David inquired.

"Not far. INS shows that we're a quarter mile off course. I'll correct it on the way in," Infelt replied.

"So, I hate to be that person, but if that was an ASW chopper, is anyone else worried about where the mothership is?" Bollinger questioned.

"There you go again, man. Always with the negative," Infelt said.

"I've seen you drive. I'm just worried that you'll smack us right into the side of a Chinese warship," Bollinger responded.

"Fuck you," Infelt replied.

"You have to admit, that would make us look pretty stupid," Dewey said, turning around to look at Infelt. "Hey man, can you see up there?"

"I can see just fine, you moron. You worry about your shit, and let me worry about mine," Infelt stated.

'Well, um, at the moment, your business is my business,"

Dewey replied.

"I'm driving because I'm the diving officer. You're the comms dude, so worry about our radios or some shit like that."

"And as the comms officer, I'm communicating to you my desire for you not to ram us into the side of a fucking Chinese warship," Dewey countered.

Infelt chuckled. "Fair enough. I promise not to turn us into human torpedoes."

"Are you guys done?" David asked.

"I don't know. You guys done with your backseat driving?" Infelt questioned.

"I suppose…for now. But I'm going to hold you to that promise," Dewey said.

"Okay. Let's get this thing going again. Sooner started, sooner done," David responded.

As the vehicle was again underway, he glanced in the direction that the light went, worried that the sub wasn't far away and had no idea that an ASW helicopter was hunting in the area. However, he refocused on the mission ahead, knowing that the commander of the *Greeneville* knew his business and had to assume one was active due to the presence of the two Chinese frigates.

*   *   *   *   *   *

It took Blue Team a little over another hour to reach the dredged channel leading into the Lung-men harbor. The entire trip had kept the men on edge, each one gazing toward the surface, searching for the first glimmer of a light reappearing. Or, they looked to the sides, worried they'd see the darkened shape of a Chinese frigate cutting through the water.

The INS showed the team at the entrance, but Petty Officer Second Class Infelt had to cut the delivery vehicle back and forth a few times until he saw the dredged edges of the channel. Inwardly, the sled driver felt relief as he didn't want to have to surface in order to get their bearings. Like a sub periscope breaking through the waves being vulnerable to a surface radar, so too was the team should they surface near an active search radar. And who knows who might happen to glance in the exact spot the team was and catch a glimpse of reflected light? As with submarines, a team inbound to the beach was vulnerable on the surface and as such, avoided it to the maximum extent possible.

Infelt followed the sharper edges of the cut channel, weaving in between the narrow breakwater piers that extended into the larger bay. Maneuvering in the small channel was hazardous because the narrow defines could be shared by a few other ships, either Chinese warships or cargo vessels. The channel was deep, but any ship passing could create a myriad of problems.

Faint lights marred the darker areas of the surface. They were coming from the direction where satellite images had shown docked Chinese transports. David and the others had underwater training and experience navigating ports and understood that the lights would be from loading or unloading operations. As much as China probably wanted to keep the docks unlit to minimize intel and missile attacks, they also knew they had to unload their equipment as fast as possible to minimize those dangers. That meant having to offload at night and that couldn't be done without bright lights.

David tapped Infelt on the shoulder and pointed toward the wavering lights. Infelt nodded and guided the underwater vessel toward them. Hawser replayed the intel and satellite photos in his mind. The latest pictures had shown three berthed Chinese ships, all docked along the same concreted pier. That arrangement made it easier to accomplish their mission without having to motor across the harbor, which would have increased the chances of them being caught.

Infelt saw a silhouette a shade darker than the surrounding waters and guided the SDV toward the ship. A rudder and the still shape of a propeller slowly passed overhead as the team glided under a widening hull. Underneath the keel, Infelt brought the vessel to a halt. He remained in the driver's seat as the other five wormed themselves clear of their places.

Opening a compartment, the five each retrieved a limpet mine.

The neutral buoyancy of the devices made them easier to carry. Each of the team had been assigned locations and they swam toward their appointed places. David reached a central point along the hull near where the propeller shaft exited the ship. Hearing a faint clamor coming from the docks as Chinese soldiers unloaded heavier equipment, he reached up and placed the magnetic device near the propeller shaft seals. He double-checked the timer. Each was set to detonate at a precise time, approximately six hours later. That would allow them to return to the *Greeneville* and then for the sub to clear the area before the charges went off. Hopefully, that would be enough for them all to get away before the Chinese began to vigorously scour the surrounding waters.

Having placed a mine on the first of three Chinese transport ships, David began swimming along the bottom of the hull back toward the loitering delivery vehicle. With one hand running lightly along the rough surface, he could feel slight vibrations as equipment was offloaded. Ripples of light from the dock side of the ship cast faint glows, silhouetting the dark hull and the concrete pier in varying shades of gray.

The petty officer froze when dappling light suddenly appeared on the harbor side of the docked vessel. The new light was more intense than the stationary glows lighting the disembarkation process, and panned back and forth. David assumed the Chinese had established a harbor patrol from the movement and positioning of the brighter light. He stared intently through the darker waters, searching for darker profiles coming into view. His fear was that Chinese special forces might enter the water to search for and prevent the activities which Blue Team were currently involved in.

Quickly glancing along the long hull, David saw the outlines of two team members, their shapes only slightly darker than the surrounding water and nearly blending in with the hull. He couldn't tell, but he was left with the impression that they too were focusing on the sudden appearance of light. Amid the soft roar that was constantly in his ears from being underwater, Hawser heard the dim rumbling of an engine. The sound grew in volume and intensity, the light doing the same as a spotlight swept over the area adjacent the Chinese transport.

The light panned once more, the bright beam penetrating deeper into the harbor waters. Then, with a sudden increase in the engine sounds, the light vanished and the sound of the boat grew fainter. David looked to the bubbles coming from his rebreather, seeing his expelled air drifting upward to gather against the hull. Those same bubbles then began a slow march along the hull toward the rear of the ship. The SEAL team leader was thankful that the expelled air wasn't surfacing where it could have been seen by the patrolling boat.

With the patrol headed some other place, David resumed his swim to the underwater vessel that was hanging under the ship's keel. The rest of the team were either already there or nearby. Once they joined back up, Infelt guided the SDV to the next ship where the procedure of placing limpet mines was repeated.

Three hours later, after successfully navigating their way out of the harbor and past the Chinese seaborne patrols, Blue Team was guiding the delivery vehicle back into the sealed container sitting on the back of the USS *Greeneville*.

Once inside, the commander of the attack sub gave the news that they had received confirmation that the two Chinese invasion fleets were underway and that the *Greeneville* had been reassigned to combat the ships. David had been right; he and the rest of his team were there for the duration. Without his usual call, he became worried that his parents would become overly concerned about him as it could be a month or more before he could next make contact.

* * * * * *

Captain James Blackwood reached over to push off the crew alert warning. On a small screen, a computerized message was telling him that there was a danger of contrails forming at his current altitude of forty-three thousand feet. The computer was advising an ascent to flight level 470. James glanced to his right, to the empty mission commander's seat. The major flying with him was the designated mission commander and was currently asleep on the cot. Selecting the advised altitude on the autopilot, the throttles moved up in response as the nose tilted upward.

The captain was pleased that the alert didn't rematerialize upon reaching the new altitude. With it being nighttime, the computer wouldn't recommend changes in altitude based on lighting conditions. With nothing else to do on this long stretch toward the target, James quickly went through the weapon screen. The payload was an identical one to his last mission over North Korea. In the weapon bays were two thirty-thousand-pound GBU-57 Massive Ordinance Penetrators. All systems tested normal.

The problem with long flights was the enormous amount of dead time, when there was nothing but hours of system monitoring which allowed for the mind to wander. Although confident in his aircraft, James had to admit to himself that he had been a little nervous about flying over the heart of North Korea and dropping the massive bombs on key residences of North Korea's leader.

The aging defensive systems of the northern half of the peninsula hadn't presented much of a threat, but he had never been in a situation where his aircraft was fully tested over a hostile nation capable of launching long-range weaponry. He and the B-2 had been momentarily painted by search radars, but the record of a missile never being fired at the stealth bomber had been preserved. All of the B-2s that had been launched against the northern country had made it back without being fired upon. James seriously doubted that the North Korean leadership had even known the bombers had been there; the blips that showed up on their radar had probably been considered anomalies. At least until the bombs hit.

As the Spirit bomber glided high over the western Pacific, slicing its way under a carpet of starred heavens, James thought that the current mission could prove to be much different. The Chinese presence on the Penghu Islands, sitting to the west of Taiwan in the strait between the island nation and China, would place the expensive bomber at greater risk.

It wasn't that the captain thought the bomber would be any less effective, but China had made recent advancements in the realm of radars and their missile systems. While North Korea had relied on antique S-200 surface-to-air missile systems for their long-range air defenses, China was a much different animal with regards to its capabilities. Intel had reports that advanced Chinese frigates, and possibly destroyers, each hosting more advanced radar and missiles systems, were on station around the island chain. James felt sure the B-2's stealth capabilities would stand up to what China could field, but it was still largely an unknown. It wouldn't be the first time China had surprised the United States.

The captain glanced out of the side windows, staring into the dark skies. Somewhere out there was a second B-2. The other Spirit was also striking the island chain, but at a different target. He wondered how often he would be called upon to fly the long-distance missions from Whiteman Air Force Base. It was an exhausting trek and he wondered if they might start making temporary stops in Hawaii in the future. There were only a few hangars which could support the B-2, but it was feasible for the aircraft to be housed overnight in regular hangars without interfering with the aircraft's specialized coating.

He knew that they would be called to fly more missions in the near future. After all, there was the conflict with China which was about to expand and the Korean Peninsula was on the verge of exploding, especially with the preemptive strikes by the United States. Currently, there weren't that many pilots who were flying the stealth bomber, so he was sure to fly his share of any upcoming missions.

James was never letdown by the heavenly display flying on clear nights. The pinpoints of light from faraway stars and galaxies, with a planet thrown in here and there, were so crisp at the high altitudes the B-2 flew. There were times when he felt as if he could reach outside and pluck them from the skies, and hold the twinkling diamonds in the palm of his gloved hand. It made him feel both large and small...that he was a tiny part of something much bigger and magical.

When he really lost himself in the dazzling beauty of the universe's history, the missions and worldly matters didn't seem so important. Sometimes, it was as if the current mission, either a training sortie or a combat one, didn't seem tangible...as if he didn't seem real and was in a shared illusion. The planet just seemed so much smaller in his mind. After all, the rock hurtling through the vast reaches of space could now be circumnavigated in a single bound. On nights like this one, the darkness below, stretching from horizon to horizon, seemed like the void and the heavens above the plane upon which he trod.

The aircraft jostled slightly, the mission commander rising from his rest. The major climbed into the right seat and plugged in to the intercom with a loud click. James was only slightly annoyed at being taken from his reveries, from returning from his mind's wanderings. But it was time to return from those internal lands.

"How is everything looking?" the major asked.

The crew alert warning illuminated, the computer recommending another change in altitude.

"Just the usual," the captain remarked, reaching over to cancel the alert.

* * * * * *

The B-2s flew over the western Philippine Sea, guiding on the few lights emanating from Taiwan. Search radars painted across the aircraft without hitting any echoing returns. James saw that they were coming from Chinese warships sailing south of the Penghu Islands. As long as the fire control radars remained offline, the captain knew they hadn't been spotted. In the darkened skies nine miles above the threatened nation, James turned the B-2, rolling out on the final attack heading.

To the captain, it seemed an odd thing to say the Spirit bomber was on an attack heading. It never seemed like an attack. He was miles above any battlefield, never seen or fired at. Some of the weapons he launched traveled long distances, hitting after he had already turned on a course for home. The word "attack" just never seemed to be the right word to use. He wasn't sure what would fit, but it wasn't that one.

The autopilot was engaged, the target in the clear. From here on out, James was merely a passenger responsible for monitoring the systems. The computer would determine the correct release point for the two thirty-thousand-pound bombs. James felt the clunk of the weapon bay doors swinging open and the B-2 wanting to soar higher as it became sixty-thousand pounds lighter. For a second, the alarms went off as search radars painted the aircraft. Then, the bay doors swung closed and the Spirit bomber vanished from enemy radar screens, folding again into thin air.

Below the aircraft, turning east toward waiting tankers orbiting over the Pacific and the long flight home, the massive ordinance penetrators fell through the night. They picked up speed, the aft-mounted stabilizers keeping the giant bombs on the proper flight path. On they came, whistling as the descended. The first MOP slammed into the ground twelve feet from the edge of the Penghu main runway. Earth buckled from the impact, spreading out in a circle as the bunker buster bomb continued plunging deep into the earth.

* * * * * *

The large Chinese transport aircraft held short of the single active runway. Behind, others were lined up along a taxiway, the scene reminiscent of a busy airport during a holiday season. The pilots of the Y-20 large four-engine transport, having completed their before-takeoff checklists, watched the lights of another Chinese aircraft as it descended through the night skies. The landing plane flashed in front of the two pilots as it felt its way down to the surface. The other aircraft's wings rocked as the main gear touched down, followed by the nose lowering. A roar passed over the airfield when the reverse thrust was applied, slowing the landing plane.

As the landing aircraft taxied clear of the landing strip, the two Y-20 pilots looked back toward final, searching for the landing lights of another arrival. There were bright moving dots, but they were small and distant. Anticipating the receival of a takeoff clearance, the Chinese captain in the left seat started advancing the throttles.

Turning his gaze back toward the ramp, the pilot saw a flash of green. The signal was the clearance he had been waiting for a while now. It was tough going keeping up with the constant flow of supplies with only one airstrip handling both the takeoff and landings, but it was now his time to depart, only to repeat the process again and again. That was life at the newly acquired Penghu International Airport.

Bright beams of light shot out across the runway threshold and adjacent surroundings when the captain reached down to turn on the taxi and landing lights. Sluggishly, with the four jet engines pushing out a stream of exhaust, the aircraft crept forward. Crossing the hold line and turning, the damage inflicted on the airport was visible in stark detail.

Partially-filled craters dotted the landscape with clumps of grass growing between. The burned husks of attack helicopters lay as silent reminders that the red horse of War rode these lands. The bright landing lights washed much of the color away as the pilot lined the Y-20 up with the centerline.

The beams showed the repairs that had been conducted on the runway since the sabotage. Packed earth and steel mats covered where heavy equipment had filled in craters. On his first landing, the captain had been doubtful about running his heavily laden aircraft over the repairs. He had been unsure that the matting could withstand the weight. After he rolled over them with barely a couple of thumps, his confidence in the repairs soared and he no longer gave them a second thought. Knowing that others were descending behind him, the Chinese captain ran the throttles up to their stops.

The four engines thundered in response, propelling the huge transport lethargically forward. As the aircraft accelerated, the pilot glanced at the long line of other transports waiting along the taxiway, regretfully knowing that it wouldn't be overly long until he was again inching his way forward in that same line.

"V1," the copilot called out.

The Chinese pilot acknowledged the call. The aircraft was now past the "go/no-go" speed. If an engine failed prior to that call, then the aircraft could be safely aborted within the runway remaining. After that point, the aircraft was committed to a takeoff as there wouldn't be enough runway left to stop.

Out of the corner of his eye, the Chinese captain saw something dark flash out the sky and slam into the earth next to the runway. It happened so fast that he didn't know what to think. His brain didn't really register the movement. However, in the glow of the landing lights, he saw a wave of earth rolling toward him almost as fast as he was approaching the moving wall of dirt.

The wave hit the runway, sending ever-widening cracks spreading across the surface. Runway lighting winked out as electrical lines were severed, and chunks of pavement were tossed into the night. The Chinese captain froze, unsure of what to do. He was past the point where he was committed to the takeoff. On the other hand, the world in front of him was coming apart.

With one hand pushing hard on the throttles, he pulled back on the control wheel. In response, the front end raised slightly, but the aircraft wasn't traveling fast enough for it to do much more. He was below rotation speed and all he could do was to put his effort into willing the Y-20 to become airborne.

If willpower were how aircraft flew, then the heavy Chinese transport would have rotated and gone into a vertical climb as if it were a fighter climbing in afterburner. However, the pilot and plane were beholden to the laws of physics. The accelerating Y-20 and the rolling wave of earth collided. Still holding the control wheel nearly in his lap, the pilot felt the aircraft rise and was at first relieved that they were going to lift over the dire threat. To his dismay, it was only the nose gear wheels rolling over the rising dirt, asphalt, and concrete.

The copilot screamed when the Y-20's momentum was abruptly slowed, the nose falling when the nose gear broke under the sudden strain. The two pilots were thrown forward against their straps, the control wheel wrested from the pilot's grip, breaking his wrist. The Chinese transport slewed to the side; the mains torn from their wheel wells. Flames erupted from the engines as they too were ripped from their mounts. Pieces of aircraft were thrown great distances as the unstoppable wave of earth rolled underneath the Y-20.

The Y-20 began a fiery tumble, shedding flaming pieces. It then erupted in a fireball that rose violently into the sky, illuminating the waiting planes in a yellow glow. The Chinese captain wouldn't have to live through another agonizing wait for takeoff.

*   *   *   *   *   *

The thirty-thousand-pound GBU-57 bunker buster dove deeper into the ground, the delayed fuse timer counting down. Designed to penetrate two hundred feet, the bomb easily carved its way through the dirt, slamming with a massive amount of kinetic energy into and through the granite underlying the island. It didn't achieve its designed depth, but it came close.

The delay fuse hit its mark, closing a relay. The Massive Ordinate Penetrator detonated the five-thousand-three-hundred-pound warhead. It wasn't the largest ever, that being the previous eleven-thousand-pound monster that had nearly the explosive power of smaller tactical nuclear weapons. The GBU-57 blew up with half that power.

The runway and earth bulged upward, sending deep cracks radiating outward. Then the explosive power broke free. Like a miniature volcanic eruption, a monstrous gout of earth and rock mixed with flame rocketed skyward. A visible shockwave of compressed air rolled away from the blast, pushing against the idling aircraft on the taxiway. Some of the transports near the explosion were pushed sideways, one of them ending up with one side of its main gear in the dirt.

Carried on the expanding compressed wave of air, the sound of the blast was deafening. Some remarked later that it had sounded like the island itself was ripping apart. On the heels of the first, the second penetrator slammed into the surface a thousand feet down the runway and exploded, creating an identical twin fountain of dirt and stone. The force of the blasts triggered earthquake sensors. When the operators pinpointed the source of the disruptions and the reason, they still wondered if they should issue tsunami warnings.

The expanding wave of earth rolled outward, dissipating its energy as it went. Several Chinese transports on the taxiway had their gear shorn away, the planes collapsing to the ground. Idling engines rotating at thousands of RPMs became damaged when they hit the ground. Compressor and turbine blades cracked and came apart, shooting pieces of shrapnel through the aircraft and further ravaging adjacent engines. The wrecked engines spat gouts of flame and then exploded, showering the area with hot metal. Several of the Chinese planes became fiery infernos while others that had been damaged smoldered dangerously.

The Chinese transport that had landed and was taxiing toward the ramp was caught up in the devastation. The rolling swell of earth collapsed its gear, the engines grinding themselves into ruin. Its four engines tore themselves apart, sending white hot shards into the cargo compartment. Those burned through internally strapped crates. The ammunition it was carrying ignited, setting off additional explosions. Rockets intended for attack helicopters shot out from within the burning fuselage like a firework show gone awry. In a thundering explosion, a fireball rolled upward, spitting out ammo that had cooked off.

As if to add insult to injury, hunks of stone that had reached their zenith began falling. Great chunks slammed onto wing surfaces. Main spars collapsed under a weight they weren't designed for, segments of wings falling to the ground. As the four-engine monsters were departing, their fuel tanks were full. Jet fuel poured from ruptured tanks, spilling across the ground as fumes seeped along the low areas. When they hit the blazes emanating from other aircraft, flames rolled back toward the damaged planes. Soon, the busy taxiway became an hellscape of burning aircraft.

Even the dispersed helicopters weren't immune to the falling rocks. Tail booms separated when weighty objects slammed down onto them. China learned a second lesson against stacking aircraft in a warzone.

The masses of smoke and fire that lifted from the twin explosions at the Penghu International Airport roiled into the night skies, dissipating as they climbed, and the night robbed them of their heat. The rolling wave that spread out from the blast zones was also dispelled over a distance. When the stones stopped falling from the skies, when the roiling peals of the thunderous explosions rolled away, when the night breeze carried away the rising smoke clouds, all that was left was the crackle of flames from burning aircraft.

All of the Chinese units positioned in and around the airport were left in states of shock, unsure of what had transpired. Many panicked as they thought the Americans had dropped atomic bombs on them. When the sounds and sights of the twin explosions dissipated, there were two giant craters that covered much of where the central part of the runway had sat. The holes were deep and were beginning to fill with water seepage.

The temporary fuel facilities, which had been a Chinese priority, were severely damaged in the American bomber attack. The People's Liberation Army forces on the island were now obliged to ration fuel. That limited any helicopter support until the fuel supplies were again flowing uninterrupted. Along with other logistics, fuel would have to be included in the planning process for any subsequent attacks.

Up and down the occupied territories, soldiers began commandeering all diesel and gasoline supplies. Service stations were placed under direct Chinese control, the gas tanks of the local vehicles were emptied, the fuel trucks appropriated and filled with stolen supplies. Meanwhile, the call went out to place a priority on fuel with the airdrops that were now being planned.

The same scenes were repeated on the southern part of the island where the dirt strip associated with the Taiwanese military base was situated. The landing strips with which China could resupply their forces on the Penghu Islands were now deep craters filling with seepage. Although the weapons were designed to take out deeply buried command centers, they had proved their effectiveness at being able to destroy important points of the enemy's surface infrastructure.

The attack of the two B-2s effectively put an end to China's unending stream of supply aircraft crossing the Taiwan Strait.

*   *   *   *   *   *

Lung-men Fishing Harbor, Magong Island, Taiwan
2 August, 2021

Shouts and the metallic squeals of machinery rang through the nighttime dock area as the Chinese roll-on/roll-off ships continued offloading their cargo of heavy equipment and supplies necessary for the Chinese conquest of the Penghu Islands. Armored Personnel Carriers and Infantry Fighting Vehicles, meant to replace those damaged in battle, rolled down modified ramps. The squeak of their treads rang throughout the dock area and neighboring town, echoing across the waters of the harbor.

Makeshift cranes brought from a heavy construction site hoisted cargo nets full of materials from top decks to deposit them on a crowded dock. Trucks were beginning to arrive to cart needed provisions to temporary supply dumps, and from there to where it was required on the expanding perimeter.

Hours later, long after David and the others of Blue Team had arrived on the USS *Greeneville*, the timers on the planted magnetic mines continued their countdown.

Very few of those near the edge of the berths, focused on guiding the heavy vehicles from their internal parking, saw a flurry of bubbles rise in the dark waters alongside the various ships. Not having spent much time around ships, those that observed the strange phenomena didn't give it a second thought. There were some standing on the modified ramps that noticed stronger vibrations, but attributed them to the slowly descending armored vehicles.

The ones that had noticed things weren't right were the officers and crew that manned the bridges, and the engineers stationed below. A series of tremors ran underneath their boots as warning lights began to illuminate. Crew members working in the engine spaces were the first to sound the alert, ringing the engineer spaces and bridge that they were taking on water. Not only that, but they reported a string of resounding clangs that accompanied the growing number of alarms.

Being in a warzone, the first thought of the Chinese watch officer on the bridge of one ship was that they had been torpedoed. He was a little confused by the lack of a large explosion or cascading fall of seawater, but there was no denying that the ship was settling lower. Water began streaming from outer ports when the bilge pumps were switched to their maximum output. They still couldn't keep up with the seawater pouring in through ruptures in the hull and broken propeller shaft seals.

The Chinese watch officer hit the general alarm switch. Three long blasts from the fog horn echoed across the harbor. Most of those who were assisting with shoreside activities turned their heads toward the sound, wondering if the blasts might possibly be signaling an inbound attack. Shortly after the first vessel's alarm faded into the night, the two other ships attached to the dock sent alarms reverberating through the nearby town.

Ship crew members showed increased signs of haste. The RO/RO vessels were visibly settling lower in the water, the thick ropes attaching them to shore growing slacker by the second. Armored vehicles powered down the ramps in their haste to get clear of the ships. The semi-organized nature of the offloading process turned into a chaotic scene as the army personnel started to scatter, certain they were coming under attack.

The first ship's keel encountered the uneven harbor bottom and started to roll away from the dock. Slackened by the ship sinking, the ropes holding the large vessel creaked and quivered as they were again drawn tight. The fore and aft hawsers arrested the ship's roll. Amid the chaotic shouts, the clanks of armored vehicles, and the growl of engines, there were other shouts of warnings for people to get clear of the taut lines.

With a snap that sounded like a cannon shot, the fore line gave way. The thick rope whipped toward the dock. One Chinese soldier was too slow in moving away from the danger — the rope caught him in his midsection. With a loud crunch that seemed to override every other sound, the man's core cavity was crushed as he was nearly torn in half. Another worker shattered his upper arm and shoulder when the rope thrashed about.

A second loud crack was heard as the pressures against the aft rope became too much. With a groan and booming clangs as heavy equipment shifted internally, the ship continued its roll toward the harbor. Caught in the glow of the bright lights guiding the offloading process, crew members could be seen jumping overboard.

Many splashes as crewmembers attempted to swim away were for naught as eighteen thousand tons of steel descended. Waves moved across the harbor as the large ship rolled onto its side and settled to the bottom. When the vessel came to rest, it was easy to see what had brought the RO/RO ship to its early grave. Part of the hull became exposed, revealing giant tears that were the result of shaped charges.

Word of the sabotage went out over the radio frequencies as the other two ships nestled in their berths settled to the bottom, their superstructures visible above the concrete berth. Any equipment and supplies remaining inside the three ships were lost, at least temporarily. More important to both sides was the fact that China had lost shipping access to the Penghu Islands for the interim.

With the airfields destroyed by American B-2s dropping massive ordinance penetrators, the long, continuous train of supply aircraft across the Taiwan Strait came to an abrupt end. The thick terrain covering much of the island chain prevented the use of the countryside for emergency landing zones. The narrow nature of the roads, crowded as they were with telephone poles and trees also precluded their use for landing.

With the loss of the last port they could use, Chinese supplies would have to be temporarily air-dropped. That meant a dramatic decrease in the amount and type of supplies and equipment that could be delivered. For the time being, Chinese forces on the island would have to utilize the armor that had already arrived, without a hint of when more would become available.

When the reports came into the combat information centers aboard the two Chinese Jiangkai II frigates, they were initially spotty. It was thought at first that an American attack submarine had slipped inside the harbor. The two vessels immediately turned and made haste closer to the entrance in the hopes of catching the enemy boat when it attempted to escape. That move included the repositioning of the airborne Z-9 ASW helicopter.

The incorrect first assessment brought the Chinese seaborne protection in closer to the main island instead of searching farther out to sea with its airborne assets. This allowed the USS *Greeneville* the time to escape to the south. When the first Chinese RO/RO ship rolled over, revealing what had truly happened, the two frigates turned south to pursue the American sub it knew had to be out there…the one that had delivered the American special operations forces that had conducted the sabotage. In anger that he had been shamed, the Chinese captain in charge of the escort screen of two frigates sent both Z-9s aloft.

Unknown to the Chinese officer, the *Greeneville* hadn't

been ordered far from the Penghu Islands. With a gap in submarine forces in or near the Taiwan Strait, and with intel pointing to a likely Chinese invasion of Tainan City or Kaohsiung City, COMSUBPAC had ordered the LA-class submarine to a position just beyond of the southernmost point in the island chain.

* * * * * *

Remote Penghu Island, Taiwan
2 August, 2021

A Taiwanese battery commander hovered over the shoulder of his radar operator, staring intently at two blips traveling slowly south. Both were mentally willing the two bandits to fly closer to the tiny remote island that rose above the sea swells on the southern edges of the Penghu Islands. The radar handled the duties of the Antelope air defense system, the few quad-mounted missiles attached to truck beds served as point defense weapons guarding the tiny island.

The bandits in question had been identified as support helicopters that were part of the two Chinese frigates making their way south at top speed. The small contingent of personnel watched the enemy ships as they patrolled the waters south of the main Penghu Island of Magong. The battery commander's orders had been vague at best — defend the island by any means. He didn't know whether he was to interpret those as being aggressive and shoot at any enemy aircraft that came into range or if he was to save his meager resources and fire only if the island was directly threatened.

It was an order that he was never clear about, until the two radar blips came nearly within range of the island's defenses. The Taiwanese battery commander made up his mind that if the two Chinese helicopters came within range of the Sky Sword I missiles, then he would fire on them, thereby adding his efforts to the overall war effort.

"That's five miles, sir. They're within range," the radar operator stated.

"Very well, pass the target information to Alpha battery," the officer replied. Turning to the radio operator, he continued, "Inform the crew of Alpha to verify receipt of the targeting data. Once confirmed, notify them that they are weapons free."

*   *   *   *   *   *

In the depth of night, a motor roared to life, the sound echoing across a nearly barren landscape. A vehicle drove out from an underground shelter and parked a short distance from the entrance. A whine of hydraulics swiveled the rear mount housing four Tien Chien-I short-range heat-seeking missiles. Once locked into position, additional servos whined, lifting the deadly projectiles to point skyward.

A flare of light flashed across the darkened countryside, a tongue of fire materializing. Like a fledgling emerging from the bonds of its nest, a TC-1 heat-seeking missile raced into the night, quickly becoming a pinpoint of light before disappearing altogether. On the heels of the first, a second projectile streaked into the night. A third, and then a fourth departed, the roars of the motors igniting fading into nothing.

Silence again returned to the small island as the missile truck reversed into its hardened shelter.

The four heat-seeking missiles closed the distance quickly, the first dart arriving twenty seconds after it was fired. The Chinese pilots, focused on finding the American submarine that was reported to be in the area, never received a warning that they were being targeted. The CIC personnel within each of the Chinese frigates steaming south notified the pilots that they had picked up an enemy search radar, but there was never an order to deviate or pull away from their search.

With flashes that lit up the sea for several miles, the Taiwanese missiles slammed into the Z-9C ASW choppers. The first projectile exploded just feet from a hovering Z-9C. Shrapnel penetrated the engine compartment. Warning lights and alarms in the cockpit were the first indication the crew had that something was amiss. Tearing itself apart in a split-second, the engine seized. One Z-9C fell straight for the sea, the second missile ripping the fuel tank apart. The Chinese ASW helicopter splashed into the rolling waves, the crash setting alight an expanding pool of jet fuel.

The second chopper was hit by the third and fourth heat-seeking missiles. Fuel, oil, and hydraulic lines were severed. In a roiling ball of fire that soared aloft, the second Z-9C exploded in mid-air. Pieces of the chopper rained down into the night seas, the only evidence of its existence were seat cushions and small personal items floating in a fuel slick.

The Chinese commander in charge of the two-ship flotilla watched as the Z-9Cs attached to the frigates vanished from radar. There hadn't been any communications from the choppers alerting anyone to the presence of danger. There had been the enemy search radar that had come online a short while ago, but there hadn't been any evidence of a fire control radar. As the American subs didn't have any air defense weaponry, that meant the two helicopters had to have been targeted by passive heat-seeking defenses. Or they had collided.

The Chinese naval commander, already incensed by his failure to safeguard the Lung-men harbor, needed an outlet for his anger. He would still pursue the American submarine, made exponentially more difficult by the loss of the Z-9Cs, but he would eradicate the radar facility he felt was responsible.

As the frigates were only loaded with YJ-83 anti-ship missiles, he ordered both frigates to use their PJ26 76mm dual-purpose deck guns. They targeted the radar signal coordinates that had emanated from one of the islands a few miles to the south. The Taiwanese search radar had gone offline shortly after the downing of the Z-9Cs, a sign that they were indeed responsible.

The seas miles to the south of Magong lit up every two seconds as the two 76mm guns on the foredecks of the frigates fired. Knowing each ship only carried one hundred and fifty shells, the Chinese commander ordered the guns to fire at 30 rounds per minute. The three-inch guns sent volleys of shells to arc unseen through the night air.

On the island, dirt erupted on the ground near where the Taiwanese radar antenna elevated from its underground base. In a nearly continuous barrage, explosions rippled across the barren island, each one punching a little way into the earth. When the string of detonations ceased, the ground was pockmarked with dozens of craters, the entire area a touch darker from the churned soil.

Underground, the small contingent of Taiwanese operators stared at the roughhewn rock ceiling, wondering if the hardened aspect of the bunker would hold up to the Chinese retribution. Dust and small chips of stone fell across consoles from the drum of concussive blasts overhead. When several seconds passed without additional explosions, the Taiwanese battery commander shook dust from his uniform and smiled in relief.

*   *   *   *   *   *

Taiwan Strait, Taiwan
2 August, 2021

The commander of the USS *Greeneville* puzzled over the reports coming from his sonar operators. Their new station close to the shores of the southernmost Penghu Island made for noisy waters, but the sonarmen were certain of what they had heard. They had picked up the sound of faint explosions. Then there had come even fainter sounds that came across as breakup, but on a much smaller scale than something that might come from a sinking ship. Filtering out the noisy shoreline from the nearby island had amplified the sounds, the commander concluding that the sonar operators were correct in their initial assessments.

The boat's commander wondered if fishing vessels had braved the waters and had become victims to China's patrol ships. He was about to finally conclude that the two patrolling Chinese frigates they had previously heard had indeed sank some foolhardy fishing boats when the next sonar report came in.

"Sir, there are definitely deck guns firing from Alpha One and Two," sonar conveyed.

"XO, what do you think?" the commander asked.

"Sir, I'd say the Chinese are either shelling one of the nearby islands or they're firing at fishing vessels. We haven't heard any other ships nearby, fishing or otherwise, but these are noisy waters, so…." the XO trailed off.

The commander pondered the information for a moment. He had his orders to intercept the Chinese main assault forces steaming north from Zhanjiang, but if the two frigates had left their patrol area and were closing south, then that placed the *Greeneville* in a dangerous situation. He knew those two carried ASW airborne assets which could locate and destroy his boat. He needed more precise information on where the Chinese warships were.

"Make your heading zero niner zero, speed eight knots. Let's see if we can get a better bearing and distance on the Chinese ships," the commander ordered.

As the sound of waves crashing into the rocky shoreline faded to the rear, the *Greeneville* was able to pick up the churning propellors of the two Chinese frigates heading south at high speed.

"Alpha One, contact, bearing two six zero, twenty-one thousand yards, speed twenty-five knots, heading one seven zero," sonar conveyed. "Alpha Two, contact, same bearing, twenty-two thousand yards, speed twenty-five, heading one six five."

"Load the data into the FCS, ready tubes one through four. Passive homing, two torps per target," the commander ordered.

"Aye, sir. FCS uploaded; targets accepted. One through four showing green and set to passive," the XO intoned.

"Fire One."

A timer was set upon each Mark 48 torpedo being ejected and running true. It would take almost four minutes for the weapons to travel the distance separating the combatants. As the Mark 48s were homing in on the sound of the propellers, there weren't any outward indications that the Chinese ships were in danger. They drove through the night swells, seeking to make a few more miles before settling into their anti-submarine role. One would sit quiet and listen while the other actively searched the waters.

A towering wall of water erupted beside one of the frigates cutting through the swells. The first American torpedo struck the bow of the Chinese frigate *Zhoushan*, ripping a jagged hole. Steaming along at twenty-five knots, the bow dove into a swell, water washing over the foredeck as the sea poured into the opening. The warship's forward momentum slowed dramatically from the opposing forces, the bridge crew were thrown against their restraints. Others, untethered, were thrown toward the bow.

A second towering wall of water rose against the stricken vessel, a second Mark 48 exploding under the keel. The *Zhoushan* was lifted from the water. Settling back down, the ship was bent in two from a broken keel. The frigate sank quickly, taking many of the ship's crew with it as it sank into the cold seas.

The second frigate had scant warning before two additional torpedoes slammed into the aging hull, the two-thousand pounds of warheads proving too much for the warship to handle. The *Changzhou* remained on the surface a little longer, the waves rolling higher and higher over the ship with each passing swell. More of the Chinese sailors managed to jump into the nighttime seas before the superstructure sank from sight.

"Breakup sounds from Alpha One and Alpha Two confirmed," sonar stated.

"Copy. Make your heading one seven five, speed twelve knots," the commander ordered.

Aware that his position was likely compromised, the commander moved the *Greeneville* farther to the south. The invasion ships sailing from the Chinese ports were moving a little slower than intel had earlier suggested. All sides waited in anticipation for the morning of August 3rd, when the first of the Chinese invasion fleets would arrive off the shores of Taiwan.

# # #

About the Author

John O'Brien is a former Air Force fighter instructor pilot who transitioned to Special Operations for the latter part of his career gathering his campaign ribbon for Desert Storm. Immediately following his military service, John became a firefighter/EMT with a local department. Along with becoming a firefighter, he fell into the Information Technology industry in corporate management. Currently, John is writing full-time.

As a former marathon runner, John lives in the beautiful Pacific Northwest and can now be found kayaking out in the waters of Puget Sound, mountain biking in the Capital Forest, hiking in the Olympic Peninsula, or pedaling his road bike along the many scenic roads.

Connect with me online

Facebook:
https://Facebook.com/AuthorJohnWOBrien

Twitter:
https://Twitter.com/A_NewWorld

Web Site:
https://John-OBrien.com

Email:
John@John-OBrien.com

Printed in Great Britain
by Amazon

20939241R00185